PRETTY BOY DEAD

A Kendall Parker Mystery

JON MICHAELSEN

A Jon Michaelsen Original Publication
Published by JM Publications
On the World Wide Web at:
www.jonmichaelsen.net

Copyright©2013, 2018 Jon Michaelsen

Cover Art: Dawne Dominique
Editor: Jerry L. Wheeler
E-publishing formatting by: Marshall Thornton

ISBN: 9781792096358

❀ Created with Vellum

ACKNOWLEDGMENTS

Thank you to fellow writers David Sullivan, Kase J. Reed, Alex Morgan, and Dawne Dominique for your friendship and encouragement during the early drafts of Pretty Boy Dead. My heartfelt thanks to retired police officers; David Sullivan & former Atlanta Police LGBT Liaison, Brian King-Sharp. Also, a *special thank you* to my advisors (aka, second-eyes), Justene Adamec and author Chris Beakey.

Finally, to my husband, Rick: these thirty-plus years have been exciting, adventurous, and incredibly fulfilling. None of this would be possible without your steadfast encouragement and endless love; the best years of my life.

CHAPTER ONE

Parked in front of the gym, Jason stared at his face in the car's rearview mirror. Dark circles underscored his bloodshot eyes, and lines of stress laced the tanned skin of his forehead. It wasn't his usual day for lifting weights, but he knew pumping iron was the only way to calm his nerves. He had parked as close to the gym door as possible, hoping to minimize the time spent out in the open. After another look around the lot, he took a deep breath, opened the driver's side door and practically ran across the pavement, his head swiveling around. He reached the door with a sigh of relief and jerked open the glass frame.

For days now, he had worried that someone might be following him, *tracking* him. Worried that somebody wanted him dead. He had spent much of the last forty-eight hours looking over his shoulder, suspicious of everyone. He wore dark glasses to conceal his anguish and had changed his routine by traveling several blocks out of the way to every destination, dealing with his fear like an inept criminal on the run, with evidence stacked against him and fearing the consequences of his actions. In a few more days, he would board a small private plane for a one-way trip out of this hellhole of Atlanta, the place of his birth. Until then, he had no choice but to endure the voiceless late-night phone calls and the paranoia he felt every time he drove near or walked past a vehicle with dark tinted glass.

Once he escaped, he would move from island to island and never remain in one area long enough to attract attention, forever lengthening the distance from everyone who knew him —his family, his friends, a laundry list of adversaries all awaiting their turn to avenge.

The thought of never again seeing his remaining buddies, like Johnny, pained him. He wished like hell Johnny could come along for the ride. They'd have a blast in the tropical paradise soaking up the rays and blowing wads of cash like spoiled Hollywood starlets. They would drink Margaritas or rum-filled punch with tiny parasols under wind-swept palms on white sand and leave their troubles behind. Better yet, they'd scuba dive in the translucent waters off the coast of Cayman Brac where the brilliant colors of tropical fish resembled a child's storybook tableau.

Bringing Johnny along would prove too risky, though. Disappearing together would raise suspicion, and no doubt provoke desperate actions by those determined to see his days numbered. Ferreted out, hunted down like animals, with only a matter of time before meeting their ultimate fate. Considering all he had planned for more than a year now, alerting his enemies was simply not an option.

There was too much at stake, which was the point after all. Why else had he spent all that time planning and setting into motion such a scheme? He had created a master plan so incredible, so far-fetched; the timing of events meant the difference between sureness and failure. A scheme only he could evoke, one that he knew would work. His life depended on it.

Jason had resigned weeks earlier to disappear alone and leave behind the city he once loved as much as his mother had. A city struggling to bask in the glory days of the past, Atlanta boasted an alluring history and infectious southern charm, surrounded by waves of emerald beauty and endless tranquility. Hard to believe the town infamous for its rebel heritage and Southern pride once faced devastation as Sherman marched his men to the sea. Its young history laid bare a century before, the pinnacle of the New South had risen from the midst of the northern invasion like a phoenix from the ashes. The city's cultivated, multimillion-dollar new image boasted an attractive place to live and work, pushing a motto as arrogant as the marketing team who conceived it. A "*City Too Busy Too Hate*" campaign had paved the way for a media blitz that pumped through major outlets across the country and world, earning accolades for its creators as businesses and populaces alike flocked to the multi-cultural area.

Beyond the modern glass skyscrapers, the large homes, the dogwoods, and acres and acres of lush evergreens, Atlanta, "The City in a Forest", was still a city as mired in political scandal, organized crime, and racial tautness as any other major U.S. player in modern times.

Jason saw little choice but to abandon the town and anyone who knew him. Anthony had all but guaranteed his fate should he remain, lest he turn back now. His plan had been set in motion.

Tim, a tall, gangling bleach-blond teenager in a black T-shirt and jeans, greeted Jason as he entered the gym. The guy always chatted on his cell phone while working behind the counter, and today was no exception.

"Hey, man, what's up?" Tim finally asked, shoving his cell into the front pocket of his pants, which hung far below his thin hips to reveal an inch of plaid boxers.

"Not much," Jason said, sliding his membership card through the electronic reader on the counter.

"Nice Porsche. Boxster, right?" Tim said. "Is it yours?"

"Yeah," Jason said, disinterested and sounding aloof.

"Cool. Wish my old man would buy me something like that."

"Yeah," Jason said, with a curl of his lip. "Wish my old man would buy you something like that, too." Glancing through the front window at the sports car glistening in the morning March sun, his thoughts turned to his mother, who left him the trust that had allowed him to buy the car last year. He missed her more than ever, especially now when he needed her most. When decisions made could mean the difference between life and death.

Jason snatched the fresh towel handed him and breezed through the corridor, catching glimpses of his stride in mirrors along the way.

Like every weekday morning, the dressing room brimmed with prudish executive types donning color coordinated gym clothes and gleaming air or gel sneakers, readying themselves for a grueling forty-five-minute workout before charging off to their respective corporate offices.

At twenty-one, Jason still fit in a pair of burgundy sweats from his Catholic high school days, along with a faded muscle tank, and well-worn sneakers without the benefit of socks.

Unlike most vying for an empty locker in the stuffy room, Jason didn't hurry. In fact, he relished pushing iron so early in the morning while others had to rush off to work. The adrenaline rush helped get the day started and his blood flowing, the muscles pumped full of energy. Days of anxiety plagued his body. Why not ease the jitters by tearing down some muscle?

In the center of the room he located a locker not sporting a lock. Likely left vacant for those willing to endure silent scrutiny, he thought as he undressed, keenly aware of the eyes cutting his way. No bother. He relished the probing eyes and leering stares. He had grown accustomed to envious looks tossed his way as long as he could remember.

As a child, he'd delighted in the fuss adults made over him. Women, some men, all presenting him with small gifts of affection. He enjoyed an abundant supply of chocolate ice cream or jelly beans, his favorite. Through puberty he grew more aware of his appearance, his agile build, and the rewards of an infectious smile. He quickly learned to appreciate his Adonis-like looks, and the attention they gained him.

He faced the locker and unbuttoned his shirt, letting the starched oxford slip from his broad, muscular shoulders. He thought again of his audacious plan. Though he had rehearsed the lines over and over in his head, he agonized over the great possibility something might go wrong, and he could not afford another blunder.

He draped the shirt on the metal hook provided before straddling a bench to remove his shoes. He sat up and stared forward, focusing on a tiny crack in the far wall, mentally rehearsing his script for what must have been the thousandth time. His concentration shattered when a wave of newcomers filled the tight space.

Tugging his T-shirt over his head, Jason slipped from the fabric like a snake writhing free of skin. Tossing the undershirt into the locker, he slipped out of a snug pair of button-fly jeans. He secured them in the locker before dressing in his gym clothes and exiting the room like a rock star on his way to meet his many fans.

After thirty minutes of cardiovascular warm-up, Jason strode across the gym floor to the free weights, determined to rid his body of the nervous tension that all but consumed him. He tackled the bench press with vigor, completing four sets of twelve reps each before hitting the incline press. He pumped through another four sets, repeating the same routine on the decline, adrenaline pumping through his veins. He continued the same grueling regiment for well over two hours to the point of exhaustion, succeeding in reducing the tension plaguing his muscles. After grabbing a cold bottle of water from the cooler up front, he headed for the showers.

The regular nine-to-fivers had already left the locker room. He stripped the sweaty gym clothes from his body and walked naked to the showers, choosing the middle stall. In the white-tiled enclosure, he stood beneath the steady stream of hot water, allowing it to cascade across his aching body, soothing the joints and caressing his burning muscles. He found the warmth exhilarating, and a relaxed smile formed across his face as he lathered. Steam swirled in the enclosure, engulfing his torso as he rinsed. His body responded, the young muscles relaxing before beginning their cycle of regeneration.

Standing beneath the water several minutes longer with his eyes closed, Jason recalled the events he now regretted being party to. A whirlwind of recollection surged forth, flooding his thoughts. Sadness mingled with the anger, leaving him disheartened and irritated. Why had he become involved? Why had he let himself get suckered into such a crazy scheme?

Shutting off water, Jason stepped out to towel dry. He moved to a cubicle in the john of the third stall and latched the door. There, for a few moments, he enjoyed the stimulation of an imaginary lover as he pumped his hand into his groin, further attempting to erase the anxiety he felt creeping back into his soul.

CHAPTER TWO

Jason set out to make the call to Calvin Slade late in the evening. Slade was a multi-award-winning journalist who worked for *The Atlanta Journal-Constitution*. He was known as tenacious and maniacal, a driven reporter perfect for the cause. Jason's plan required a hungry journalist compelled by competitiveness and greed more than moral responsibility. He knew reporters had rigid reputations for protecting their sources. His search through the newspaper's online archives proved Slade demonstrated his allegiance often, a proud defender of the First Amendment. Though tossed in jail a few times by trial judges irritated with the reporter's righteous, if somewhat displaced, sense of pride, the threat of incarceration never deterred him. Slade would no doubt prove adversarial since Jason planned to impart enough information to snag the investigator's attention and set progress in motion. By the time the enemy figured out *who* had tipped the reporter, Jason would be long gone. Interest in him would fall off and be directed toward the real criminals.

The real criminals. Jason grinned at the thought as he rounded the corner off Myrtle and headed for the intersection at 10th and Piedmont, convinced when word leaked of the society of charlatans, their precious membership would be quick to retreat, putting enough distance between themselves and their deeds. Jason smiled as he stopped near the entrance to the Flying Biscuit Bistro. At least, it was the plan—that and stealing millions of dollars that never would be reported to the authorities.

Jason chose to make the call from a pay phone at the corner of Piedmont and 10th, a block south of Piedmont Park. He had selected the spot because it marked a heavily traveled intersection that guaranteed many witnesses should something bad go down. He could have purchased a disposable cell phone instead, but chose to forgo the hassle of picking one up.

He risked his captors would not grab him out in the open. Such an action would be too brazen, even for them. Still, he had to be careful with this much at stake. One wrong move could mean deadly consequences at the hands of those wishing him harm.

Swallowing hard, Jason punched in the newspaper's phone number from memory, a talent he had inherited from his mother. He possessed the rare ability to retain the tiniest of details, the most complex elements of design. He could recite a simple string of words heard weeks before, more elaborate text, a series of numbers and formulas, even computer entries viewed only once before. He had amazed people with his ability to call minutiae to mind, a flair he often used to his benefit.

A light mist permeated the air and combined with the glaring lights of the businesses, giving the area a glum atmosphere. Jason shifted his eyes all around, checking for anyone lingering in the shadows, any lurker observing him as he waited for an answer.

Jason had chosen not to contact the reporter from his cell phone since a movie he saw once showed how reporters traced and recorded their calls. He did not want to take any chances this late in the game. Going to the police was not an option either, though a much safer bet if not more practical. There would no doubt be suspicions of his involvement, accusations made even before he had a chance to speak with an attorney to proclaim his innocence. Revelations could land him in jail alongside the very scum he aimed to expose. Television crime shows called this type of involvement being an "accessory after the fact."

The switchboard operator answered on the fifth ring in a professional, southern drawl. "*Atlanta Journal-Constitution Newspapers*, how may I help you?"

"I need to speak to Calvin Slade," Jason said, bouncing on his feet. He glanced at his wristwatch. It was now a quarter shy of eleven and the mist gave way to a steady drizzle.

"One moment, please."

Jason contemplated hanging up but ignored the impulse. He had waited so long for this one chance. He was tired of debating with himself and exhausted from days of worry. It was now or never to move forward. He believed his plan was foolproof, with absolutely no chance in hell of implicating himself as long as he stayed focused.

Anxiety threatened to overtake him as he waited for the reporter to answer. His workout from earlier was shot to hell the moment the reporter's baritone exploded through the receiver.

"*Slade here!*"

Red slid his late model sedan past Jason North's Porsche, cut the corner at 8th and Myrtle and eased next to the curb. He emerged from the vehicle dressed in all black; sweatshirt, jeans, sneakers and knit cap, and a pair of leather gloves shoved in his back pocket. He backtracked to the sports car and checked his periphery for any movement.

Rounding the corner, the skulking man surveyed the vicinity as he moved along, searching for prying eyes. The fresh scent of rain from an earlier flash shower permeated the darkness. He saw no one out walking a dog along the narrow sidewalks or stepping out from a darkened driveway headed for an evening stroll. Cars raced along Piedmont Avenue one block over, their tires sloshing through rain-filled potholes.

Red, nicknamed for the shock of hair spilling out from

under his cap, slowed his pace and eyed the slick car as he passed by. Another quick glance back, and he abruptly pivoted, trotting back to the vehicle with his hands dug deep in his front pockets. Head down, chin buried, he moved alongside the parked vehicle, scrutinizing the street, and glancing at each glowing window of the homes fronting Myrtle Street.

Convinced no one had noticed his suspicious movements, he eased to the front of the low-riding vehicle, looked around one final time, then ducked beneath the bumper. On his back, Red fished a hand up through a tight crevice flanking the engine to a mass wires and hoses. The smell of oil and gasoline rising from the damp pavement roused his senses. He located the right spot to insert the elongated wire cutters held between in his fingers. Alarm disarmed, he wriggled out from beneath the vehicle.

Stepping beside the driver's door, Red slipped a slim metal instrument between the glass and rubber perimeter of the window while checking the area. *Click.* The interior light illuminated and with a quick jerk, he opened the door and slid inside. Red checked the rearview and side mirrors, searching for unwanted strangers. He marveled at his genius, confident that no one had seen him committing the crime. All in a day's work.

The criminal had been trained by the best while imprisoned in the state of Georgia penitentiary system. Red had spent his last five agonizing years at Reidsville fighting to stay alive among his fellow inmates, incarcerated for his part in a botched robbery of a convenience store in a suburb northwest of town. Fucking clerk refused to hand over the money, forced his hand, and got shot in the process. Paralyzed the fucker from the neck down. *Bum luck.*

Red needed to be swift, but precise. Somebody was bound to come along any moment now. Heart pumping with the adrenaline-laced blood known only to hardened criminals, Red pulled the release and popped the hood. He thought about pillaging the vehicle, but disregarded the idea. He was being paid a wad of cash to do the job. More than he could make in a lifetime of slinging hamburgers or mopping up after someone else's shit, and scoring an all-expenses-paid trip to the Bahamas to boot. He didn't need to take more chances than necessary.

Who the hell said crime didn't pay? Fucking jerks should be walking in his shoes right now. After getting the money, he had immediately booked himself and a voluptuous vixen on the first Delta Air Lines flight out tomorrow morning. First class passage to paradise.

Red stepped from the vehicle and waited for a slowly passing car, which eventually parked a few spaces down the street. The driver killed the lights, and the passengers exited. The foursome walked in the opposite direction toward 10th Street absorbed in spirited conversation. *Fucking faggots!*

With precious little time remaining, Red lifted the hood of the Porsche and rendered the car inoperable in seconds. It took longer to lower the hatch and press it shut without making a sound. Another quick surveillance of the area, and the criminal fled, trotting back to his car to wait.

The call rang through before deadline. Shoving a mass of paper aside in search of the telephone, Calvin Slade barked his name into the receiver.

Silence.

Glancing at the clock, Slade snapped, "Hey, I got fifteen minutes till deadline. Talk to me or bug off, I don't have time to waste." He seized a half-eaten sandwich he'd abandoned earlier sitting on the corner of the desk, and tore at the wrapper.

"Yeah well, listen up," said an arrogant voice. Male, Slade thought. Young and cocky. He knew the type all too well. "I catch your writing in the paper, online sometimes, you know? You're that investigative reporter, right? That means you want to know stuff."

Slade rolled his eyes, grumbled, and snapped a bite of salami. He chewed with his mouth open and glanced around for something to wipe his lips. Cradling the receiver against his shoulder, he fished around in the trash bin beside his desk for a napkin. "Yeah, okay, I'm listening."

Grunting, Slade glanced at the clock again. He usually ignored anyone who demanded his attention so close to deadline, and this caller spoke like a thrill-seeker. That's what he called them, "thrill-seekers." Snitches with a propensity for ratting on their bosses and neighbors, or even members of their own family, about anything to get their names printed in the newspaper. He'd heard it all a thousand times in his ten years on the beat and could peg an informant from a wise ass in two seconds flat. He'd bet his salami sandwich on the latter.

Slade contemplated hanging up, but the next words that came from the caller stopped him cold.

"That councilman you wrote about? You know, the one cops found drunk in his car a few weeks back?" the voice said. A vehicle cranking loud hip-hop thundered past in the background. The caller tried to mask the noise as he continued to speak. "Up in Buckhead, passed out on the side of the road?"

Slade knew all right. It had been none other than the notorious Mitchell Keyes, who some claimed was the most corrupt, divisive City Councilman ever elected president of the influential, mostly African-American board. "What about him?"

"There's more to the story than police let on." The caller whispered his words now. "I know some things."

"I don't buy information," Slade said, jotting down the number on the telephone's LED display.

"Check it out, then." The caller sneezed. "The man didn't leave the party alone."

Slade stopped chewing and slid to the edge of his seat. The line clicked and seconds later, he heard the static drone of a dial tone.

"Shit. *Shit!*"

CHAPTER THREE

Shortly after midnight, Red watched from within his darkened vehicle as a figure approached the sports car. The interior lights switched on at the crack of the door to illuminate its owner, a young male with tousled hair. Red couldn't judge the man's size or bulk because the guy had bundled himself tightly in a dark trench coat, but he knew without a doubt that he could take him out with one swift blow. He had the advantage of surprise and a concealed weapon on his side.

With experienced swiftness, Red extracted himself from the vehicle and slipped along the sidewalk like a cat stalking its prey. He moved within fifty feet of the intended target when a car turned onto the street and headed straight for him. He ducked behind the nearest tree, narrowly avoiding the headlights that would have exposed the baseball bat he held. Seconds later, the car disappeared. He reemerged, intent on finishing the job.

The interior of the Porsche was empty, the occupant gone. Red's eyes raced along the sidewalk and down the street in time to see his mark rounding the corner to the left. Furious, he walked back to his vehicle.

Since his target had escaped, Red spent the next couple of hours lurking in the shadows. First, he migrated across the street and moved farther down the block before finally resting a few feet away from the entrance to the only business left open after midnight. The sign overhead read Blake's. A faggot bar, he surmised, judging from the clientele trailing in and out.

Leaning against a faded brick wall near the corner, his leg hiked behind for balance, Red crushed out a cigarette. His mask and gloves were tucked safely out of sight beneath the back of his shirt, secured snugly by his belt. He waited for the mark while cruising guys coming and going to ward off suspicion. His stomach churned in disgust. Red, *the fag*, with a bat concealed behind his back fooled anyone who caught his eye, nodding when necessary. Fuck, he looked like one of *them*.

The glass and metal door swung open. A young man in a dark green trench coat fell out of the tavern. He bumped a few patrons as he swung on the door's metal frame, stepping out to the sidewalk like some college drunk.

"Hey, watch it, buddy." A tall bruiser pulled along by his wide-eyed date glared at the man.

Catching his balance, the young man trudged up the walkway in swaying stride and crossed 10th Street through intermittent traffic. He entered the south end of Piedmont Park. Red tossed his cigarette and took up pursuit.

The full moon cast its luminous glow across the night sky as broken white clouds raced across an inky backdrop. The stars danced in the heavens, showcasing constellations Red had sought out as a child. He would first spot the Little Dipper and then locate the Three Little Bears before searching mightily for the Big Dipper, which often had to be pointed out to him by his older brother.

Those were the happiest days of his troubled life, long before his father had lost his job at a local chemical plant shut down by the EPA. Long before the proud man had begun drinking to escape the rejection he faced day in and day out in a dying town. His father couldn't find work and eventually turned to beating his wife to release the fury that had all but consumed him. Not long after, the broken man had turned toward his two young sons to further pound out his rage.

Red shoved aside those memories and trailed the shadow

tracking before him. Keeping steady pace as he cut through the park, Red ducked behind a clump of trees when the target paused to extract a cigarette. The figure struck a match, expelled two quick puffs and shoved the pack into his coat pocket before filling his lungs completely and exhaling the smoke in the chilly night air.

Red ached for the crisp sting of a menthol cigarette but as a hired professional with time running out, he needed to remain focused. He slipped gloves over his large, battered hands, pulled the dark wool ski mask over his face, gripped the bat with both hands, and picked up the pace. The mark descended the embankment some twenty yards ahead.

The temperature had dropped ten degrees in the last hour. The shower had chilled the breeze skimming off the lake at the base of the slope. He stepped onto an asphalt trail and followed its winding path around the water covered in a layer of fog, deeper into the park where darkness grew dense. Adrenaline pumping through his arteries, Red calculated the precise moment of attack, that split second signaling a point of no return, that private place reserved for criminals lured by greed. He remembered the same oozy feeling as a teenager back home in northern Michigan while stalking through a neighbor's back yard in the darkness, in search of an ownerless cat. Damn stray never had a chance.

Red froze in his tracks. The figure ahead stumbled on some tree roots, staggered and turned an expressionless face skyward, peering through the spiny limbs of a giant oak tree. Though buzzed, the mark managed to keep from tumbling over before regaining balance. Red seized the moment, clenched his teeth and sprang forth from the shadows like a lion charging a zebra.

North's shadow loomed across the dark turf. Red advanced fast from behind. Startled, the smaller man attempted to turn, but a *whack* against his upper back and shoulders stopped his pivot. He screamed and lurched forward, stumbling to catch his balance. His face and chest smacked hard against the trunk of an ancient tree, scoring flesh, crushing bone, and shattering the cartilage of his nose. Blood filled his eyes and nose, spilling over into his mouth and down his neck. He gasped for air and struggled to catch his breath, managing only a light fluttering sound as the thick, coppery liquid flooded his throat and poured into his lungs. Bracing against the cold, wet bark, the victim turned to face his attacker.

Red eyed him like a nefarious hunter. North's chest heaved, wheezing as blood filled his lungs. His right cheekbone exposed, splinters of jagged bark dotted the side of his baby-smooth face, forming an arch that cut deep into the hairline. He tried to scream for help but only managed a pitiful moan. Red raised the weapon at him again before North had a chance to react.

The splintered wood clipped the dupe's right shoulder. The intense force hurled the man into an adjacent tree, the razor-sharp bark ripping at the flesh of his face, his shoulder and right arm taking the full brunt. He spun around, desperate to cover his face as Red took another blow and snapped the tiny bones of his shielding fingers, shattering his cheek and several teeth. North managed to grab one of Red's gloved hands. The leather slipped free and he fell backward, landing against the hardwood.

Terrified and in shock, the victim managed to extricate some bills and his cell phone, offering them out to Red, a pitiful pittance for his life. Red cracked the bat hard across North's jaw, then again against his thigh. Unable to sustain his balance, North pitched forward, spilling the crumpled wad of cash across the damp ground.

Before Red could aim his weapon again, North sprang forth, wiggle-waggling across the turf. He appeared dazed and confused as he limped across the rugged terrain like an injured animal. Red took up pursuit as his mark headed for the blurry lights marking the intersection of 10th and Monroe. Clumps of grass and exposed tree roots toppled him again and again.

The man scrambled to his feet and dove headlong though a thicket of shrubbery. Red followed close behind as North charged ahead toward the sounds of moving vehicles on wet pavement, toward the bright lights of a busy intersection.

In his frantic attempt to flee, the victim failed to spot the broad concrete drainage basin that cut a swath through the south side of the park. He reared back far too late when he came charging upon the drop-off into the ditch. His boots clipped the edge of the cement bastion, and he hurled forward into the abyss, arms pinwheeling as his harrowing scream sliced through the night air.

Red saw North land solidly on the angled wall of concrete, wrists and elbows snapping backward on impact. The man's ragged body crumpled like an accordion and tumbled headlong to the bottom of the basin where the head smacked hard against the surface and came to rest at a gruesome angle.

Red negotiated his way down to the wounded prey. He struck the bat against North's skull one final time.

CHAPTER FOUR

At twilight, a middle-aged man with silver-streaked hair and wire-rimmed glasses steered into the heart of Midtown. Turning off Peachtree Street, he maneuvered his long vehicle into an area of abandoned homes and vacant lots littered with beer cans and liquor bottles. He eased down a narrow side-street known to both hustlers and their tricks.

Moving along, the man saw a dozen boys heckling each other while perched on low walls and fenders of parked cars lining the street. The seeker slowed near a trio of gangly teenagers clad in low-riding baggy jeans and boat-size sneakers, with balloon jackets shielding their lithe bodies. He'd done this a few times before, but not much in this city. He'd been arrested a few years back in another state for public indecency, caught in an alleyway with his pants below the knees. A crafty lawyer, a "no contest" plea, and loads of cash buried the sordid details.

Given a newfound lease on life, he'd packed up his small family to start anew in Atlanta, joined a large Baptist church in the ritzy Buckhead community, renewed his marriage vows, and renounced his obsession in silence. Not long after, however, the urge overwhelmed him, too powerful to deny. Compulsion lured him back to the dimly lit streets and dark alleyways where young men and boys paraded themselves; yet with each indiscretion, he swore to God almighty he would never return.

Hard to explain really, that intolerable deep-seated gnawing in the gut, the undeniable allure of having sex with young male strangers, the forbidden yet exhilarating touch of a boy-hustler eager to provide but a few precious moments of sexual gratification to a middle-aged man. Whatever the urge, he fought off his denial and risked everything each time his Cadillac headed into town.

Hopper, nicknamed for the hectic pace he once kept on a day job hawking restaurant coupon booklets, spotted the shiny, dark Cadillac drifting down the lane and beckoned the driver closer, brushing the denim of his crotch to reveal the pleasure to be had. The homeless youth who spent the better part of his life in and out of juvenile detention approached the crawling vehicle with purpose. Sensing contact, he leaned into the open passenger window for conversation and, after a brief exchange, slipped into the soft leather of the empty passenger seat.

The formerly shy mama's boy hadn't finished high school before he discovered his emerging sexuality, a wonderment of confusion and angst, thrilling and frightening all the same. He confided to his mother his thoughts of being gay. She promptly told his stepfather, and the confused teenager spent the next six weeks in a lockdown for treatment of a psychological disorder. Discharged and declared sane, he returned home to parents who were stunned the doctors had failed to rid their son of his immoral thoughts and attraction for the same sex. They banished him from their house forever.

Four painfully long years ago, Hopper had learned to peddle his wares on Cypress Street, a well-known cruising area in Midtown near the Marta rail station where young men and boys traded easy sex for cash and drugs. In no time he learned to look for the nicer cars and never to get into vans or vehicles with more than one person.

"It's the rule of the trade if you wanna avoid gettin' beat up or raped by a trick," Nick had told him. He was an older, wiser unemployed construction worker walking the strip to support a wife and newborn still struggling with the effects caused him by an alcoholic and drug addicted mother. "Hustling sex for cash ain't dangerous if you learn the tricks quick, and that means puttin' yourself in a different mindset. Always scout for an exit for when you need it. Act confident and tough and you won't get hurt," he said, his emotionless eyes peering into Hopper's own. "Being scared or nervous will get you cut up and stuffed in a fuckin' bag."

Not six months later, police found Nick's body dumped in a landfill on the south side of town. He had been gagged, his arms and legs bound with duct tape before being doused with lighter fluid and set ablaze. Hopper heard the news late one night while hanging with the guys on Cypress, vowing then to get off the mean streets. If it took him knocking up johns, taking their cash and pawning off their Rolex watches, he'd damn sure do it. He intended to fucking survive and not end up like Nick in a dump somewhere.

That dream also meant enough cash to abandon the scene for good. Within weeks of his pal's death, Hopper made good on his promise. He hooked up with the owner of a new bar in Midtown that featured male dancers, overpriced drinks, and the hottest dance tunes around. Strutting his stuff during "happy hour," as required of any newcomer desperate to make the cut, he enjoyed stripping down to a tiny G-string for a more respectable, less threatening male clientele. Young, hot, and exhibiting loads of energy, he perfected an enigmatic smile the older men clamored for. The money flowed for the skinny blond kid with the southern drawl. Hell, the fuckers threw large bills at him without asking much in return, except for a peck or two or a grope here and there. He had suffered far worse being on the streets for a while. Most of the men filing into the Metro-plex that early in the afternoon came straight from the office and looked for no more than a quick fix before heading home to the suburbs. A few months of dancing, and he was well on the way to earning enough to secure a place of his own. He stashed his extra cash in a cigar box shoved between the mattresses in a cheap Cheshire Bridge Road motel room he rented by the week.

That was *before* he got fucked by that asshole Galloti, before he'd trashed the bastard's precious little office and was told to take a hike. The owner of the showplace did not want sick boys in his stable. "Bad for business," Galloti had said. A henchman, some big ox called Stewart, had noticed the dark spots on the dancer's legs and formed his own conclusions. Hopper didn't know if he had AIDS at the time since he never took the test, but he figured as much. What the hell, he'd known since the first lesion a few months back but had simply chosen to ignore it, like everything else too complicated or too *real* in his life to face. A couple of the other guys had it. Most walking Cypress did. Tricks found out, but didn't seem to care. They just kept on coming, no big deal.

Not until walking the strip again did the cruel reality of his life hit him in the gut like a sledgehammer. Though down with walking the streets, he needed the money to buy drugs and eat, the only urges pushing him along at this point. Since arriving alone in a big city, he had tired of the constant battle of wits and dumb luck needed to survive one lousy day to the next. Along the way, he countered his pain and frustrations by smoking grass and snorting crack to escape the inevitable, an endless down-ward spiral of pumping crank every now and again when enough dough flowed through his fingers to ease the pain churning deep within his bowels. The stockpile of money in the cigar box had disappeared long ago and along with it, his dreams for a better life and a place finally to call home.

For much of the night, Hopper perched himself on a low concrete wall, pushing his young body for a few dollars, passing himself from one old fart to another before he spotted the dark Cadillac moving toward him. Once he got inside the vehicle, he stared out the side window as the Caddy turned down a dead-end street well known to most johns. The driver killed the engine and turned toward him. He unzipped his pants and motioned for Hopper to do the same. Hopper held out his hand and demanded cash. The john thrust crumpled twenty-dollar bills forward and used his left hand to pump himself as his right hand dug into the hustler's jeans. Hopper faked the groans necessary, a skill he'd perfected out of need to move on to the next trick quick, increasing his pitch to coincide with the man's rising, wrinkled cock. The asshole took his sweet ass time. Forty bucks didn't go very far, and he grew bored. About the time he decided to bolt, the old man shot his load, splattering the steering wheel and concluding with a sigh. The john stuffed himself inside his pants, shot Hopper a repugnant glance, and started the car.

The big vehicle punched forward to return to the same corner to put Hopper on the street yet again. The geezer sped away from the curb, no doubt to put distance between him and his nasty deed. Hopper flipped him the finger and shouted a few choice words as the Cadillac hurled around the far corner at Crescent, its tires squealing up Peachtree Street and out of sight.

Last trick of the night. The small-town boy vowed now more than ever to make Galloti pay for fucking up his life, derailing his plans for getting off the streets, tossing away any chance at a normal subsistence as though his life meant nothing, filth discarded with the daily trash. He headed north toward the motel room with the stale carpet and peeling plastered walls he called home, tucking his chin beneath the collar of his jacket to shield the wet cold. Shoving his hands deep into his front pockets, he flinched slightly as a police car with revolving sapphire lights roared past, wishing like hell he had a joint.

CHAPTER FIVE

The call came through Sergeant Kendall Parker's cell during his regular morning coffee run to the Landmark diner on Cheshire Bridge Road. Moments later, the detective slapped a blue light on the roof of his silver-blue cruiser and sped through the Morningside neighborhood, an overpriced in-town section on the northern fringes of the city. He turned off Cheshire Bridge Road to Piedmont and punched the accelerator after maneuvering around a few startled drivers. The traffic proved thicker than he'd expected this morning, forcing him to jockey along Piedmont Avenue and zigzag through the southbound lanes. The call had directed him to Piedmont Park, a popular one hundred and sixty-eight-acre triangle of land in the heart of Midtown, originally named for its crop-producing milieu connecting downtown and the tony Buckhead community lying northeast of the city. A body found in a runoff ditch at the park's southernmost corner revealed no identification or apparent cause of death. The male victim had likely washed downstream during last night's heavy spring rain.

Turning east on Monroe, Parker spotted a pair of blue and whites angled on 10th Street across from Grady High School's new football and track field. Early rising joggers sprinkled the gravel running track that circled the perimeter of the field, several gawking at the flashing lights invading their area.

The Criminal Investigation Division dispatched at least three investigators to the scene of every death in the city: two from Homicide and another from either Sex Crimes or the Robbery unit. CID personnel received their orders from the homicide detective on call even though the homicide sergeant ultimately ran the investigation. Sgt. Kendall Parker led the charge today. Most referred to him by last name only. Parker was a major-crimes investigator for the department, CID, his rank Master Sergeant, a ten-year veteran with APD, the last six with the Homicide Squad.

Parker ran two wheels of his car over the curb and killed the motor, extricating his linebacker frame from the vehicle and striding across the grassy plane toward the dark blue uniform standing at the perimeter of a paved walking trail. He flashed his shield to a beat cop standing guard at the scene, who pointed him in the direction of the body without introduction.

Head down to protect his face from the assault of thorns, he trudged through a thicket of overgrowth and underbrush, the branches snatching at his trousers and poking through the fabric, nicking his flesh. He emerged at the crest of a wide drainage ditch. Looking out, he noticed that the storm basin sliced through the southeastern edge of the park and vanished through a giant steel cylinder set beneath 10th Street. He came upon a second cop sitting on the angled concrete about thirty yards from the body, and revealed his badge again.

"Anyone touched the body?"

"No sir," the man called, shielding his eyes from the bright sun with an upraised arm and stood to meet the sergeant. "Ain't let nobody down there, sir," he said, jutting his chin toward the corpse below. "Waitin' for the MPO." He followed along, but became alarmed when Parker did not stop. "Hey, you can't go down there."

The sergeant reached the precipice of the concrete gully. A body lay tangled in a web of branches and debris, face up in a flow of shallow water. The stiff wore a type of dark overcoat, raincoat, or canvas outerwear. A strong odor, often associated with a bloated cadaver, wafted in the breeze. Parker squatted, angled his six–foot four-inch frame to make the steep trek into the ditch, and walked the edge of water this side of the cadaver, careful not to contaminate the scene.

"Ignore me," Parker called over his shoulder. "I won't touch a thing," he said, cursing the cop under his breath. *Damn rookie.*

The officer's face glowed red. He perched himself in a spot above the basin, jotting the detective's name and badge number in his spiral notepad while, no doubt, awaiting his supervisor.

The detective pushed mirrored shades over his head of thick, dark curls, his brown eyes sweeping the area. He withdrew a pocket notepad—as much a part of him as the shield he wore clipped on his belt—and noted the time, location, and weather conditions. Surveying the area, he sketched out the scene while completing a spiral search, working his way toward the remains. A crime scene crew would trudge the same route when they arrived to videotape the scene, but Parker needed his own notes for later recall.

"Call came in at 6:42 a.m.," a voice said from behind the sergeant.

Parker scowled and glanced over his shoulder, recognizing Timothy Brooks, an overzealous rookie detective recently assigned to the squad.

Brooks clambered into the gully, slipping and sliding on his backside until the heels of his big wingtips caught hold at the bottom of the ditch but not before his right foot landed in the water.

"Watch it," Parker pointed and snapped. "You'll fuck up the scene."

"Sorry." Brooks stepped back shaking water from his shoe. "Homeless man spotted the body at first light." He continued without missing a beat and brushed the seat of his pressed khakis. "Perelli's taking his statement up near the toilet-house. Dispatch traced the call to the emergency phone up there."

Brooks sported a wide, Cheshire cat grin as he approached his new boss and stopped several feet from the body, tucking both hands in the flat-front pockets of his trousers. The beat cop resting on the embankment ventured forward.

Parker shook his head and waved his arms at both of them. "Get the hell back."

Brooks obliged, retracing his steps double-time and shuffling the objecting officer back up the embankment. The cop shouted expletives indecipherable to Parker as he turned his attention back to the cadaver. Brooks had to learn his preference for spending a few minutes alone at a fresh crime scene, so best start now. Parker viewed the precious time alone a ritual of sorts, a rite of passage earned by years of long hours spent investigating the deaths of others. He'd be chastised by his commanding officer later.

A body commanded the heart of any homicide. Parker's badge required him to confront the remains, regardless of circumstance or condition. Years of experience had taught him emotional detachment was the key to any successful investigation and although that theory may work for some, deep down inside he knew better. Soon, he'd relinquish a piece of his soul to this abandoned corpse, as with every other that followed. Truth be told, he died a little death at the beginning of every homicide investigation.

A cool breeze drifted through the basin and eased the queasiness in his gut. He popped a handful of antacids in his mouth and slipped a pair of latex gloves on before kneeling over the sunbaked cadaver. Clicking on the handheld recorder that he carried in his pocket, he described the body in detail. "Male, Caucasian, late teens-early twenties, approximately 5'10, one-hundred seventy to eighty pounds. Dark hair trimmed close, and no obvious signs of trauma. Clothes appear expensive and not threadbare, not the mark of a vagrant or a street kid," he said. He swallowed a build-up of phlegm at the back of his throat. The stale, decaying odor skimming the surface of trickling water in the gully was stifling. He continued moving his eyes in a grid pattern over the discovery.

Parker avoided looking at the blanched face, the cloudy blue eyes, and bloated skin of the body. He used a pen from his chest pocket to probe the collar of the victim's overcoat, lifting the damp fabric of the shirt beneath. A thick, gold chain surrounded the puffy neck, herringbone links wedged into the skin sparkling in the bright sunlight. In the murkiness to his left, a large dial, chrome-banded watch clung to a swollen wrist. The awkward angle of the arm displayed the crystal of the time-piece, cracked and filled with water, time frozen at a quarter past one, perhaps a clue to time of death. The right hand of the victim held a dark leather glove.

Leaning over the body for closer inspection, Parker specu-lated how the kid might have ended up like this, a technique he often used to get inside the victim's head, sifting through pieces of the scene and condition of the body to connect the dots. These days, nothing in his line of work appeared simple and straightforward. Days, perhaps weeks, would pass before he would ferret out the reason behind the young man's death, if ever.

The smell of raw sewage tickled the hairs in his nostrils as he studied the body. Despite the scripts churned out of Hollywood like a carnival music machine, cops never became used to seeing such gore, the sickly-sweet scent of rotting flesh, vicious crimes against another human being. The carnage worked to further harden their hearts from life's other assaults and question the existence of faith, forcing the soul into tolerance and accep-tance. The detective displayed impenetrable tolerance, but acceptance? *Never.* It came with the territory.

Parker stared at the corpse, seeing not the man lying before him, but the haunting image of another. The obsession was never far from his mind, clouding his thoughts and perhaps his judgment. It was an effigy of a young man taller and wider-shouldered than the one lying flat in the stream of water, an imagined reflection sinking to the depths of much deeper water no amount of scotch could erase. The urge to reach out and grasp the phantasm in his mind's eye passed as a prickly chill nipped the back of his neck and reminded him that he had a job to do.

He called out for Brooks to join him.

The rookie bounded down the slope on cue.

"Have you called the M.E.?"

Brooks nodded in bobble-head speed.

"So, where the fuck is she?"

Parker stood after finding no identification on the body. A reflection caught the corner of his eye as he turned to walk away. Shifting his feet to the outer perimeter of the corpse, careful not to disturb the zone, he reached over a mound of debris and lifted the edge of a waterlogged matchbook with the tip of his pen. He recognized the name embellished across the silvery cardboard. It belonged to a small neighborhood bar up the road and across from the park.

"Get some men to search the grounds for evidence," Parker said, leaving the matchbook where he found it. "See if you can locate the missing glove…and a cell phone."

"Cell phone, sir?" Brooks asked.

"The victim's cell. Everyone has a cell phone these days, and it ain't on the body."

Parker glanced back at the dead man, a moment of antipathy passing through his core before turning away, the lasting image taking its place among countless others extolled in his memory. "Put in another call for the ME."

The sergeant ripped off the latex gloves and stuffed them in the pocket of his coat.

Within the hour, the bustle of more officials, flashing lights, and emergency vehicles attracted a curious set of onlookers who gathered to view Atlanta's finest at work. The public's reaction was always spiked with anticipation and callous regard, perhaps a hint of the macabre. Their sordid interest caused voyeuristic impulses that led them to stare while passing car accidents or glance across the median at a mangled vehicle. Might they catch a glimpse of the victim's body beneath a sheet or witness the removal of the body bag? Whatever the case, their curiosity remained piqued, and they understood little if any of the activity surrounding them. Cops erected a three-inch wide strip of yellow Bannerguard around the perimeter of the scene to keep the curious at bay as the flashing lights attracted more of a crowd.

Sweat rolling beneath his blazer from the humidity trapped within the basin or most likely due to last night's dance with the bottle, Parker clambered up the sloped wall and through the thicket of underbrush. In the clearing, he told the GBI criminalist team where to find the body and offered a few thoughts about searching for evidence.

"Don't touch the body until the M.E. arrives," he said, before turning and walking away.

Morning joggers of all shapes trekked along the pathway that looped the edge of the park, oblivious to the goings-on, uncaring as long as the fuss didn't interfere with their workout. The trail disappeared a hundred yards beyond a patch of giant oak trees. Parker began walking in that general direction when a Channel 2 Action News van bumped against the curb with a jolt. He scowled at the scum before picking up his pace toward where his partner of three years awaited.

Brooks caught up with him on the asphalt track that circled the murky lake. "It's gonna be a while for the body snatchers, sergeant," he said as frustration pinched his forehead. "Popular morning for the morgue with the full moon last night," he said, matter-of-fact.

Parker waved him off, in no mood for the rookie's joviality today, especially with all the overtime he'd been pulling of late to make up for his time away. *It takes a certain kind of man willing to work long, grueling hours in a career offering few rewards.*

Parker pondered this thought as he scrutinized his career as a cop while traversing the perimeter of the lake. He'd been thinking a lot lately about the choices he'd made over the years, good and bad: four years in the military, his motive for joining the force, his rush to marriage, and his subsequent divorce. A flash of this latest discovery teamed with multiple others swamped his mind as he made his way to interview the bum who found the victim.

CHAPTER SIX

Anthony Galloti stepped from the penthouse onto the wide balcony forty floors up, sipping imported coffee in the morning sun. He wore a Sergio Tecchini warm-up suit and Armani slippers with a folded *Wall Street Journal* tucked under his arm. Sucking in fresh air, he shuffled to the wrought-iron table and chairs tucked in the corner between clusters of terra cotta planters brimming with greenery. The early March breeze skirting the high-rise seemed a bit nippy for native Georgians, but not to him. He hailed from the windy city of Chicago, spending most of his life in the bitter climate before escaping to Atlanta eight years before on the guise of lucrative business opportunities. He found the weather more desirable. *Southerners were such wimps.*

The business man had been awake for the last hour. Usually he'd be sleeping since business kept him from home until four or five in the morning. The call that woke him came from Stewart Callahan, the thug he charged with managing operations of the Metroplex nightclub on Spring Street, the largest, most successful of his business ventures to date. Stewart sounded harried and insisted on meeting with his boss alone. He'd arrive within the hour.

Anthony gazed up as a sleek, gym-toned young man with

blond hair and blue eyes joined him on the balcony. He ran a hand through the youth's tousled mane as he stifled a yawn, knowing that he had gotten up just to wait on him. The kid didn't know the nature of the call but must have sensed Anthony's foul mood as he kept his distance. Matt had learned the benefits of silence early on in their association. There were other hot young studs awaiting their chance to enjoy such lavish quarters, poised for him to make that first mistake.

Anthony actually enjoyed having him around. The boy learned quickly and seemed eager to please, an attribute he valued more than the kid could know. It took Matt less than a week to memorize the morning routine of ground coffee, two bagels toasted and served with a hefty portion of garlic cream cheese, finished with a glass of fresh squeezed orange juice. *Perfect.*

The doorbell rang, and Matt swooped in to welcome the guest, directing the man to his boss. Stewart passed through the home and rushed onto the balcony, taking a seat opposite the table. Matt disappeared and returned with another cup of coffee.

"Matt, run along to the gym," Anthony said, sipping his brew without glancing at his pet. "Stewart and I have business to discuss."

Matt disappeared in a flash.

"Have the police identified the body?" He took a bagel from the basket in the center of the table and gazed out across the blue horizon. The city proved breathtaking in the spring.

"Not according to the latest news reports. I've monitored the local television and radio channels. Nothing's hit the *Journal* online either."

"It's Jason, right?" Stewart's blank expression confirmed as much, as did his bloodshot eyes. "Where's Red?"

"In the Bahamas by now, I'd suspect."

Anthony smeared his bagel with cream cheese. "Have you eaten yet?" He noticed the man's grimace. Stewart probably hadn't eaten much since learning of the killing and certainly not since the discovery of the body.

"No, I'm not hungry."

"You should eat. You look dreadful." Anthony nibbled at the bagel's edge, glancing over the top of the front page to the newspaper. "Make sure Red stays in the tropics for a while out of sight. Wire the money he needs."

Stewart chewed his lip. "You promised Jason was going to be roughed up, that's all. Teach him a lesson you said." He licked his lips, lifting the cup of Jamaica's finest. "Fuck, I *knew* this would happen. Didn't I warn you?"

"The boy knew too much," Anthony hissed. "Besides, it's better this way," he said. "Who could imagine a kid with a body like that had brains? I'm not an easy one to fool." He sipped his coffee and savored the taste. "Not to worry. His murder was made to look like he was bashed by some fag hater." He locked eyes on Stewart, and a hint of mistrust nagged him. "He made a mistake trying to outsmart me, Stewart." His eyes narrowed. "Don't make the same one."

Anthony drew a deep breath, a practice he learned from years of yoga classes to calm his nerves. "Nobody screws with me, Stewart. *Nobody.*"

The man wiped his forehead. "What do we do now?"

"Nothing." Anthony sensed Stewart wanted to tear at his throat.

"*Nothing?* Are you insane? It's only a matter of time before police identify the body, and what'll we do then, huh? The kid worked for you, Anthony. Have you forgotten that fact? By tonight a dozen cops will be crawling over the club like maggots, flashing their badges and asking around. Business will suffer."

"Business will be fine." Anthony cooed, unflinching. He grew bored with the conversation. "Jason was a dancer in my club. He suffered a terrible tragedy, nothing more. I don't understand what the big deal is."

"The big deal?" Stewart perched on his seat "Someone is bound to say you two were…"

Anthony aimed a butter knife at his guest, halting Stewart's words. "Anyone talks to the fucking cops about my private affairs, they're fucked. You got that?" He turned back to the bagel. "See to it."

Stewart asked, "What about Keyes?"

"What about him?" Anthony took a bite of his bagel and chewed with his mouth open. "No harm done as far as I can tell. We'll proceed as planned. The Commissioners are forging ahead, so why the hell shouldn't we?"

"But if Jason told someone…"

"Who would he tell? You recall his partner in crime is also dead. There are no more loose ends, Stewart, so relax. I think you worry too much. It's not good for the heart and gives you wrinkles." Anthony returned to perusing the newspaper. "I assure you everything's under control. Now please, join me and have a bagel."

Stewart dropped his head and stared at his feet. "There's one other thing," he said. Hesitating, he cleared his throat and finally spoke. "There's this dancer…he hasn't shown up the past few days. Not since the night Jason was attacked in fact."

Anthony lost his appetite and tossed the bagel aside. The paper slipped to his lap. "Why haven't you mentioned this before?" Stewart chewed his lip. "Who is it this time?" Anthony demanded.

"Johnny."

Anthony knew well the young tease—medium height, big brown eyes, chestnut-brown hair, body similar to Jason's, but much too cocky for his own good. "Those two were tight, close friends." He glanced out to the tops of some trees and watched a flurry of black birds dive in and out the canopy while pondering the connection. "Jason wouldn't confide in anyone," he said, turning back to Stewart, "especially not to a fellow dancer. The boy may have been aloof at times, but he was far too self-absorbed to take such a chance. Doing so would have meant committing suicide."

"Or murder," Stewart said. Anthony scowled.

Stewart offered reassurance. "It's probably nothing. Coincidence at best," he said. "You know how these punks are,

Anthony. They show up when it's convenient, need cash or kicked out by a boyfriend. He'll be back soon, you'll see."

"Find him," Anthony said, not buying Stewart's assessment. "See what he knows, who he's been talking to." The boss leaned forward, lending strength to his words. "You know what to do."

Stewart nodded. He slapped his knees, stood and stared out across the balcony at the evergreen expanse. How the hell had he gotten mixed up in such a mess, he wondered?

Anthony rose and walked to the rail lining the perimeter, scanning the breadth of the horizon. A nephew by marriage to one of Chicago's notorious organized crime families, he'd enjoyed the richness such life provided, including money to take up residence in such a lavish penthouse in Midtown. He savored the view from the platform, a mosaic of natural colors blending to create a masterpiece. Glancing to his right, he scrutinized the jagged downtown skyline awash in a haze of morning sunshine. On the left, teeming suburbs of the north and northeast of the city lay buried in the terrain. Stone Mountain loomed in the far distance, a giant bolder of granite out of place on a flat plain. Piedmont Park lay before him roughly six blocks from the highrise. He peered, but did not see the area demanding all the attention this morning. No doubt police were hard at work collecting evidence, sifting through the muck, bagging samples, taking photos, searching for clues that might lead them to a killer.

They won't find anything. Anthony had made sure of it.

Sergeant Parker headed in the direction of three small buildings located on the east side of Piedmont Park. Constructed of granite, the structures flanked the point where the modern path angled through the north end of the park. Piedmont Road lay beyond, abutted with high and low-rise condominiums, apartments, and converted older homes.

He navigated the narrow walkway of concrete that sliced through the water to the other side and past the semi-circular European gazebo that jutted out into the lake. As a teenager, he

used to hang out under the dome smoking cigarettes and
drinking cheap apple wine in paper cups. The stone buildings
contained public restrooms. The center portico held a plaza and
entranceway to a public pool, which closed last summer for
remodeling and repair. Outside the wrought iron gates, a lone
emergency callbox impaled atop a pole was stark against the
aged gothic architecture. Sitting on the curb below, the bum
who had discovered the body smoked a cigarette.

Parker joined his partner and the witness, who drank from a
Styrofoam cup. Vincent Perelli handed Parker a cup of hot
coffee.

"What'dya got, Perelli?"

Perelli stood five-foot ten and weighed just over two
hundred pounds. He sported a granite face with thick salt and
pepper hair and a bulbous nose. Built like a lineman. A cop for
half his fifty-two years, a veteran of Homicide for the last eighteen, Perelli stared down the fast track toward retirement. A
couple more years left going through the motions before perma-
nently residing on Lake Altoona snagging prize-winning bass.
Parker prayed he'd not resemble Perelli when he retired.

"Not much." Perelli worked the muscles in his aging face.
"Old man claims he was looking for a place to sleep and came
upon the body. Says he didn't touch anything, but I kinda
doubt that. Made his way up here and called police, even asked
for a reward."

Parker smirked. "Checked his pockets?"

"Yeah, nothing but scraps of paper, a few coins, a tooth-
brush, a comb, and a few cigarette butts."

The bum's face and arms were smeared with dirt. He smelled
of urine and soiled clothes. When asked, he agreed with Perelli's
synopsis. "Have a uniform take him to the mission over on
Ellis," Parker said, lighting a cigarette. "Get him a shower, a
good meal, and some decent clothes."

Perelli motioned to a uniformed cop stationed in the
distance and gave him instruction to take the witness away. He
pulled a twenty from his pocket and held it out to the bum.
"Thanks for your help, old man."

Perelli caught up with Parker, and the two of them headed to the crime scene. "What'd you see?"

"A body with a face of mush." Parker tossed the cigarette away. It hit the ground in an array of sparks before smoldering in the damp grass. "Clean cut, average height, white kid. Nice clothes, jewelry. Definitely not a street bum, no wallet, no cash, not a damn thing to identify him."

"Could have been a mugging gone awry," Perelli said. "How d'ya figure he ended up in the ditch? It's nowhere near the walking trail or lake. Not like he was cutting through the park."

"Search me. Killer could've just tossed him there. My gut says the kid's been dead at least a few days, maybe a week. The body is swollen, large blisters on the skin showing early signs of decay. I'd guess the stiff drifted downstream because of all the rain we've had lately."

Perelli agreed. "Yeah, my arthritis has been a son-of-a-bitch." He slowed his stride. "The victim cruised the park for sex, yeah? Pissed off a dick, got knocked around a bit, wallet lifted, then tossed in the ditch like a sack of garbage."

Perelli's abhorrence for homosexuals hadn't eased over the years they had been partners. Parker sneered. "Sex, Perelli? The dude's overcoat's buttoned almost to the *knees*."

Perelli wrinkled his nose, pursed his chapped lips. "Yeah, and what's that supposed to prove?"

"It proves he wasn't having sex at the time of his death."

Rolling his eyes, Perelli glanced at Parker. "So, what are you now, fucking Sherlock Holmes?"

They laughed then walked in silence until they reached the clearing, not far from the thicket concealing the ditch where the body lay.

Parker spoke up first. "There hasn't been a homicide in this park in more than five years. So why the fuck does it have to be now? I was just making headway on a stack of old cases since coming back…and, now *this*. The media's gonna go nuts."

"Say it's not murder," Perelli challenged in an uncharacteristic tone. He caught sight of two men trudging their way. He disliked reporters, but not nearly as much as Parker. "Figure the guy was drunk, stumbled through the park, got lost in the bushes, and fell to his death. Happens all the time," he said, with a hint of sarcasm.

"It'd take more than a drunken fall to end up looking the way the kid did, Perelli." He searched for a way to escape the approaching hounds. "At any rate, it's a suspicious death until we prove otherwise." Slipping on his dark shades, he added, "Shuffle your caseload, old buddy. This one's bound to bring on lots of unwanted publicity. I'll clear everything with the lieutenant."

By the time Parker finished the initial investigation, the sun had climbed high in the clear blue sky. A break from the weekend rains came despite forecasts to the contrary. The breeze had evaporated, and the temperature soared to an unseasonably humid eighty degrees. Spring was only a couple of weeks off, but the dogwoods and pear trees were bursting to life. He glanced at his watch and noted that four hours had passed since he arrived. Brooks would stay on to finish the details. Their work done, he and Perelli headed to the office to begin a stream of paperwork.

CHAPTER SEVEN

"Do you have a physician?"

Hopper glanced up at the social worker who introduced herself as Amanda.

The large black woman with big brown eyes stared at him, unblinking. She wore tight fitting jeans and an oversized flower print blouse. Hundreds of bright-colored daisies filled every square inch of the cotton fabric. Hopper remembered a time when his mother picked daisies from the backyard and set them on the dinner table in a Mason jar. He thought it such a silly gesture since the flowers didn't smell nice. In fact, they didn't smell at all. His heart ached for her and the comforts of home as he stared at the woman. He hadn't seen his parents for more than a year.

Hopper had not followed through with the threat to his former boss. The morning after swearing revenge, he'd awakened with a nasty cough and fever, his body swimming in sweat. He'd attempted to get out of bed, but fell back on the pillow in pain. His body too weak to try again, his head had pounded like a drum and kept him flat on his back. A cleaning lady checking rooms found him and called the ambulance. EMT's connected IVs into his arms and pumped a bag of clear liquid into him, giving him new life. As with anyone without health insurance in the city, he was taken to Grady Memorial's emergency room and treated for pneumonia and dehydration. Once stabilized, staff diverted the kid to the Infectious Diseases Unit since he had AIDS.

Hopper slept through the weekend in a wonderful narcotic state, his emaciated limbs gaining rejuvenation and strength from slow-dripping medicine. Heavy doses of antibiotics cleared his lungs of infection and gave him a new lease on life until the next infection set in. He sat up in bed eating breakfast that tasted like burnt paste and listened to Amanda go on and on about treatment. The odor of disinfectant permeated the room and stung his nose.

"Seen a doctor yet today?" Amanda sounded irritated.

The question came across direct and frightening, carrying the truth that chilled him to the bone. "No," he said, glancing past daisies as a nurse entered the semi-private room and began removing the IV tubes from his arm.

"They're backed up as usual," Amanda said. "You're bein' released this morning. I have some pamphlets to take with you. You read them, hear? I put them in this package along with some condoms. You do use them, don't you?"

The warmth hitting Hopper's cheeks caused him to turn away from her. He jutted out his chin and wished she'd stop talking and let him alone.

Amanda held out a stuffed manila envelope. He saw scorn behind her fake smile. Just another unfamiliar face among many, he thought.

"You should find a steady doctor, get you some steady treatment. Disease ain't no killer like it was twenty years ago. You can live a good life with medicine. There's a list of clinics in there, too. All can be reached by bus or train." She leveled her eyes on him. "Are you listening?"

"I don't need your charity." Hopper grew irritated. He threw back the thin blanket and attempted to muster some dignity but seemed foolish lying in bed. He scooted to the side of the bed and let his legs hang over the edge, none too thrilled to touch the cold floor with bare feet.

"It ain't charity, honey. Your T-cells are below three hundred. It's up to you if you wanna live to see another year. Get some treatment, or you'll be back here in a few weeks, and you'll cost the state even more money."

The lady's tone irked him.

The nurse finished stowing away the IV lines and removing her latex gloves without a word before slipping out of the room. Hopper examined his arms and legs. Veins crisscrossed his limbs like a road map. He glanced around a moment before realizing that he didn't have any clothes to wear.

"I didn't see you had any clothes. You ain't had no visitors I could ask to bring you some," the social worker said. She adopted a more soothing tone and smiled like a grandmother about to feed him ice cream. "I rustled up things from the stuff that goes unclaimed around here." She pointed to the chair against the wall. "I think they'll fit you all right."

Who the hell are you to get gushy all of a sudden? Hopper marched over and jerked the jeans on beneath his hospital gown. He tugged the one-piece garment over his head, tossed it on the floor and pulled at the long sleeves of the shirt. The pants sagged in the seat as he liked them. The sleeves of the shirt hung way past his wrists, so he folded them over twice and glanced back at the caseworker.

"What now?"

"You have papers to sign before ya leave." The look on Amanda's face reminded Hopper of his mother's anguish the time he had insisted on walking alone to school the first time. "Is there someone I can call for ya, honey?"

"There's nobody." He furrowed his eyebrows, steeled his eyes, and straightened his shoulders. "I can take care of myself."

Hopper left the hospital through the side entrance as an ambulance pulled past. The sun blazed across his shoulders as he hugged his chest tight and walked out onto the sidewalk.

. . .

The caffeine buzz gave way to a headache as Sgt. Kendall Parker entered Police Headquarters. After leaving the homicide scene at the park, he'd grabbed a giant cup of coffee at a diner on an empty stomach, and now regretted the impulse. He nodded to other officers and staff who acknowledged him and waded through the bodies milling in the corridors. He took the stairs to the basement in twos and moved toward the back of the room past a bevy of cubicles. A trio of scarred wood desks in the far corner with creaky swivel chairs and government-gray filing cabinets suited him fine.

Parker tossed his blazer on the rack against the wall and switched on the fan behind his desk. It sputtered to life after its heavy metal fins struggled against the electric current and build-up of dust.

None of the detectives assigned to the unit were at their desks. At almost noon most were either eating lunch or out in the field investigating last night's carnage. Parker dropped into the chair behind the metal desk, its defiant squeal shooting bolts of pain through his head.

"Afternoon, Sergeant." Brooks said with an irritating cheer-fulness. He collapsed in the chair beside Parker's desk and stretched his long, lean legs across the scuffed tiled floor. "You should ask for a new desk. Is it held over from the 50s or some-thing? It's seen better days."

"In this economy? City can't give us the equipment needed to combat those assholes out there, much less, newer furniture. Union spends more time in front of the cameras threatening politicians than fighting furloughs and layoffs. No thanks, I like my little corner back here. I have a desk to myself, which is more than most in the squad."

Parker rummaged around the desk. "Did you canvass the neighborhood around the park for witnesses?"

"Sir? Perelli thought you'd need me here."

Just like Perelli to pawn him off on me. Parker lacked patience training rookies in homicide. "I need help churning up witnesses, detective. Not filling in reports," he said. "Get back out there."

"Yes, sir," Brooks said, rushing off.

Brooks never complained about the hectic, frustrating schedule required of a rookie homicide investigator. Parker admired the young man's eagerness, reveled in the memories of his own rookie days when he'd had plans to make his mark in the world. He recalled a time when justice drove his need to prove that crime didn't pay and a steady job and hard work were all anyone needed to keep straight. He'd believed in the decency and good nature of all human beings and that everyone, even criminals, deserved their break once in a while.

Parker's first month as a patrol officer on the streets was burned into his memory even today. He'd witnessed more violence in thirty days than one man should know in a lifetime. An exceptional Police Academy cadet, Brooks accomplished while others met defeat. He excelled technically, yielded excellent marksmanship, and could sprint a hundred yards in thirty seconds flat. He accepted tasks without question and relied more on textbook know-how and common sense than muscle and brawn. Detective Timothy Brooks came across as a big dork, a mama's boy, a man who needed to fit in. Through misplaced enthusiasm, he somehow did.

Not thirty minutes later, Perelli lowered himself in the chair behind the desk opposite Parker. "Still haven't ID'd John Doe yet?" he asked.

Looking up from a pile of reports on his desk, Parker shook his head. "No. You have anything to go on?"

The detective rubbed his eyes, making them red and bloodshot. Perelli's shoulders slumped forward and his chest caved. "Nada. Autopsy won't be till later in the week. That's if we're lucky. Fingerprints are blown, hands and feet too wrinkled and decomposed to get good lifts. M.E. figures the stiff's been dead four, maybe five days. The vic's description is being fed into the state's computer and faxed to the FBI. The glove found at the scene has been sent to the state crime lab for analysis, too big to belong with the body. With luck, GBI can lift prints from the lining."

"Suppose John Doe has no priors." Parker grunted. "What

then, fucking dental records?" He fumbled for a cigarette. Perelli opened his mouth to speak, but Parker held up a hand. "Missing Persons?"

"Nothing's matched so far. Sketches will be ready for the media in an hour. Not sure what good that'll do. The victim's face was a mess. Artist had a tough time looking at the dude. Can't blame him none." Perelli withdrew a cigarette and pinched it in the corner of his mouth where a permanent nicotine stain resided. "Want to go for a smoke?"

Parker followed his partner up the stairs and out a side door to the parking garage. "The victim may not be missed yet," he said, more to himself than Perelli as he flicked his lighter.

Perelli nodded. "Streets around the park are known cruising areas."

Parker sensed his partner's unease. Things between them had been subdued since he had returned to work from the accident, not the typical banter back and forth, the constant jabbing each other.

"Squad cars case the place by the hour," Perelli said. "I could check traffic records for citations going back a few days. Maybe the perp or a witness was cited."

"It's a long shot." Parker nodded to a group of patrolmen returning with takeout. He turned to Perelli. "The only thing we have to go on is a pack of matches recovered at the scene. May not be connected to the body, but I thought I'd check the bar out early this evening." He flicked away his cigarette butt. "You want to come along?"

"I'll pass. The wife's been complaining I'm not home enough," Perelli sneered. "Hell, before that she was complaining because I was home too much. We've been married over thirty years, and I still can't figure her out. I doubt I ever will."

Parker laughed and held the door open for his partner. "At this point, I wouldn't even try, old buddy," he said, trailing behind him. "By the way, I sent Brooks back into the field. He's canvassing the neighborhoods around the park for witnesses. You wanna grab some lunch at Colonnade?"

"Nah, the wife's got me eating veggies and leaves again this week." Perelli said. "I'm off to the break room. I've lost five pounds on this diet doc's put me to lower my blood pressure. You go on ahead. I'll catch you later."

CHAPTER EIGHT

Maybe I returned to work too soon, Parker thought sadly.

Witnesses and suspects moved in and out, escorted by officers and staff. The phones buzzed like a cacophony of cicadas.
Shuffling paper and keyboards clicking merged with the chorus
of chatter, and by midday Police Headquarters sounded like a
crowded bus station.

Parker glanced out across the floor and scanned the perimeter. The layout appeared different since his absence, yet the only
real change appeared to be his view of everything.

Nothing will ever be the same again.

The basement of the mid-rise building housed the Criminal
Investigations Unit, the space open and expansive but devoid of
any real design. Classic industrial, every inch was crammed with
gray metal desks and cubicles, putty-colored file cabinets and
Pend-A-Flex boxes stacked high around the room. Parker stared
at the large, square-paned windows which faced north. Though
painted over years before, some sunlight seeped through the
chipped paint.

The stairwell at the opposite end provided the lone access to
the room, save for two emergency exits that led to the garage.
Upon his return, Parker had chosen the back wall for his desk,
confounding most of his comrades. He'd also picked the spot

farthest from the stairwell as suspects descending the stairs often times proved uncooperative, handcuffs or not. Maintenance workers had long refused to repaint the walls lining the stair-case, arguing that a fresh coat never had a chance to dry before more soles had made their mark, announcing yet another disruptive detainee.

Detective Jorge Torrez of Sex Crimes plopped down at his desk not far from the sergeant and devoured a sausage and egg biscuit. "Hey Parker, heard in the morning's briefing you copped the park case."

Parker nodded and watched the detective's breakfast disap-pear in three bites. Torrez's partner shuffled up a minute later and grabbed the seat across from Torrez.

"'S'up?" Detective Derek Smith nodded. "You need help, just let us know."

"You bet." Parker nodded and watched the black man pour no fewer than five sugar packets into a steaming cup of black coffee.

"Where's Perelli?" Torrez wiped the grease and crumbs from his face with the back of his hand.

"Running a lead. I'll be sure to tell him you're trying to bust in on our case," he said, winking at the officer.

The investigator laughed off the banter and snatched up his phone.

Parker returned to the paperwork on his desk.

Monday afternoon proved as challenging as the narrow stairwell itself. Witnesses, suspects, family members, friends, bail bonds-men, attorneys, and just about anyone else connected with the weekend's crimes scurried in and out of the muggy quarters, most with complaints. He found concentrating on the forms before him difficult and after attempts to ignore the rising roar, he gave up.

Unlocking the desk drawer, he retrieved his weapon, a Glock 22 .40 caliber, fourth generation revolver. Slipping the gun in his shoulder holster, he snatched his blazer from the rack and trudged through the crowd toward escape.

After ten years, the pride of donning a crisp new uniform had faded. Parker shuffled past a battered woman huddled around her frightened children on his way out to grab lunch. People could be so cruel to the ones they loved the most. Cynicism turned into a daily battle for most of the detectives in the "hole," the nickname bestowed on the basement's humble quarters.

Nobody knew this more than Parker. He reached the stairs as a shriek from within the squash of people pierced the chatter. He ignored the pleas for help until the cries coincided with voices of the department staff. Scanning the room, he pinpointed the source of the disturbance as two officers struggled to restrain a towering, purple-sequined transvestite. Efforts to handcuff the honey-skinned Madonna failed as she landed a succession of low body blows, their howls more earnest than her cries for mercy.

The furor continued as those nearest the commotion stepped back and the drag queen used her long legs, bright pink pumps and matching handbag to beat the shit out of the two officers. A couple of seasoned cops watched from the side. When the melee threatened to disrupt other units, Parker shoved his way through the congestion and grabbed the woman by the back of her dress. The abruptness confused the giant and halted her assault. She turned and kneed him in his groin. Parker cried out as the pain burned through his stomach and into his throat like a rush of acid reflux. He lamented a second about growing lazy and not protecting himself. He brushed aside self- castigation, regained his balance and swung his fist hard. He caught the diva's jaw, and she hit the floor like a rag doll, her arms and legs splayed across the white tile. Over hoots and a few howls, Parker straightened his jacket, gave the room a quick once over and left without saying a word.

The Varsity on North Avenue in Midtown stood the test of

time, as close to a landmark as anything in the city. Parker knew its history, having lived in the city for years. He had an affinity for all things nostalgic, preferring The Varsity's greasy fast-food over the more modern drive-thru restaurants closer to the squad.

At its peak, the seventy-five-year old restaurant had employed close to a hundred carhops, each with their own number. In the fifties, the "hops" worked for tips only, which led them to sing, tell jokes, rhyme, and dance, all in the quest for bigger tips. Whenever some national crisis occurred, reporters in town flocked to The Varsity for man-in-the-street quotes. Visiting politicians from Richard Nixon to Bill Clinton had their pictures taken at the famous landmark.

Inside the packed restaurant, Parker moved with the crowd along the 150-foot stainless steel counter. At six-four, he could put away some food for a man of his thirty-five years, but he managed to stay fit by jogging and working out regularly at the local "Y". Good genes didn't hurt either. The Varsity didn't serve the popular healthy diet of late, but the food was standard fare for most cops, especially single ones.

He stepped forward to order his meal: two plain hot dogs, two burgers, onion rings, and a large diet soda. The harried counter waitress spouted out, "Walk me two naked dogs, two glorified, O-rings and an unleaded. Seven-ninety-six...*next!*"

Parker collected his tray of food and moved to the condiment counter to load up with supplies before moving to a corner table in the dining room. The Varsity was chock full of various sized dining areas, each separated by walls of glass. Large square rooms vied for space with tight cozy areas, sports memorabilia rooms and so forth, all trendy expansion efforts at the time.

A boy peddled copies of the afternoon edition of the *Journal* inside the restaurant, the ink fresh and smudged slightly to the touch. The discovery in Piedmont Park commanded a two-inch column on the first page of the *Metro* news section, the byline written by veteran staff writer, Calvin Slade. Parker handed the kid a dollar, shoved half a hot dog in his mouth, and began to read the article.

The story focused on the sketchy details of the body found by a homeless man searching out a place to sleep. According to sources close to the investigation, the identity of the victim still eluded police. The article indicated police had to await autopsy results as they have no obvious cause of death, no motive, and no identifiable suspects.

Parker noted the author filled in gaps of the report by chronicling the recent renaissance of the one hundred sixty-eight-acre triangle-shaped park, the city's largest remaining sprawl of virgin land in town, bordered by Piedmont Road. The article elaborated on its well-funded conservation plan, the nearly complete five-year, twenty-million-dollar revitalization project of planted hardwood trees, poured pathways, and the proposal to enclose the large exposed sewage basin along the southeastern edge of the park. Slade attributed the facelift to the enterprising efforts of popular Atlanta City Council President Mitchell Keyes, who police discovered weeks earlier asleep at the wheel of his car in the pre-dawn hours. An officer spotted the councilman's car straddling the left shoulder of the Lenox Road exit ramp off Interstate 400 in the affluent Buckhead community. The car keys were in the ignition and the engine running, the councilman's foot stuck on the brake.

The rest of the article circled back to the victim and called the death suspicious. Parker finished his lunch, hit the john and headed back to the station.

CHAPTER NINE

"We may have lucked out." Perelli waved pieces of paper in Parker's face. "I have copies of all citations written in and around the park last week. One seems real promising. Some john was cited for loitering in the park after closing last week, not far from where the body was found," he said. "The pervert had parked in the lot off Park Drive at 1:45 a.m. Thursday. It's a long shot, but it could prove worth our time. You up for a ride?"

The hands of Parker's watch showed 3:30 p.m. *Killers have been caught with a lot less,* he mused. If they got lucky and wrapped this one up quick, it would suit him just fine considering they had ten active cases. "Okay, where are we headed?"

"A suburb thirty-five miles north near Lawrenceville."

Parker grabbed his blazer. "Let's go."

Twenty minutes into the trip, Perelli veered the unmarked sedan off the interstate at Indian Trail Boulevard and headed east. They located the Shady Grove subdivision after traveling a series of surface streets. The neighborhood teemed with two story houses of varying shades, every fourth home the same façade. Parker could tell contractors had planned the small community priced for the masses by the lack of green space and numerous bicycles and toys scattered in driveways and near the curbs.

They located the address, displayed in black numerals against a white mailbox painted with cardinals. Perelli steered into the curving driveway, careful not to overshoot the pavement and damage the pristine lawn. A small boy stood on the cut grass, mussing his curly red hair. A taller child trotted protectively to his side. The men smiled and bypassed the wide-eyed children, stepping up to the front porch of the contemporary home.

"Mr. Martin Churchill?" Perelli asked.

The fortyish man peering through the clear glass storm-door stared at the two men and nodded.

"I'm Detective Perelli and this here's my partner, Detective Parker. We're with the Atlanta Police Department, Homicide Unit." They offered up their official identification. "May we have a few words with you?"

Churchill's slack jowls flushed pink. He turned to check the foyer was clear of prying eyes and stepped out onto the large porch. Hair as fiery and tousled as the little tyke's out front, he wore rumpled chino shorts and a powder-blue polo shirt over a thick belly. Sweat lined the ridge of his freckled forehead, and he had garlic on his breath.

"What's the problem, officers?"

"Detective," Parker said. "No problem, sir. We just want to ask a few questions about your whereabouts early Thursday morning."

"Last Thursday? I was having breakfast with my family."

Perelli sneered. The man disgusted him with his blatant lie.

"Earlier in the morning, shortly after midnight Wednesday," Parker said.

Churchill's face turned heart-attack white.

"We have proof you were in Piedmont Park on the morning in question, sir," Perelli said, not beating around the bush. "This is your signature?" He showed him the citation. The man appeared faint.

Parker asked, "What do you know about the body found in the park this morning?"

Churchill nearly convulsed. He steadied himself on the railing of the porch. "I don't know anything about that man." He swiped sweat from his brow with a handkerchief yanked from his pocket. "I'm sorry gentleman, but I can't help you." He turned to escape the inquisition.

Parker caught the man by the shoulder and squeezed hard enough to get a yelp. "We could move inside to discuss this further if you'd like. Perhaps your wife can join us."

Churchill's eyes shot past the men to the frightened faces of his children. "Run along," he said. "Daddy's fine." He snapped his fingers and the kids scattered like flies.

Churchill motioned for them to follow him out into the front yard. His hands fumbled with the hanky. "Look, I don't want trouble. I have a wife and two beautiful children, as you can see. The last thing I want is to hurt them, you know?"

The man's glance flickered between Parker and Perelli. "My life will be ruined if you remain here. Please, you must go. I'll meet you later if you want, at the station or somewhere." He turned to check the front door again. "If my wife comes out..." He caught his breath, on the verge of a stroke. "How am I supposed to explain this?"

Parker leaned in closer, enjoying the tap dance more than he was willing to admit. "We're not leaving."

"Shouldn't you be at work?" Perelli asked.

Churchill chanced another glance back at the door. "I took a wellness day."

"A wha-?"

"I had a doctor's appointment this morning."

The detectives glanced at each other and shrugged.

"Okay, okay," Churchill said, his arms twitching. "It was just a matter of time before you guys showed up anyway. But please, keep your voices down."

Perelli withdrew a pen and pad from his shirt pocket. "We're listening."

Churchill scratched at this throat as if forcing his words.

"Okay, I was parked in the park for about forty-five minutes, an hour tops, no more. I'd met this young woman at the Kaya Lounge. You know the place over on Peachtree Street? Great food, good drinks. I'd joined some of the guys from the office for drinks. We'd been working late on this big proposal…" He cut himself off when Parker raised his hand in protest.

"Anyway," he said, "I took a ride with the woman and we ended up at the park. No harm in that, right?"

Debatable, Parker mused

Churchill snorted loud, cleared his throat, and spat into the hedges. "*She* suggested we take a ride to the park," he challenged.

"Did you get her name? Where can we find her?" Perelli scribbled in his notebook. "We'll need to check your story."

"I'm a suspect?" The color drained from Churchill's cheeks.

Parker monitored the man's expressions, watching for signs of lying. The dumb fuck told the truth as far as he could tell. "Everyone's a suspect," Parker said, "until we prove otherwise. Answer Detective Perelli's question."

"I, ugh…hey, funny thing is, I don't actually recall. *Honest.* Why would I lie about a thing like that?" Churchill fretted. "We didn't talk that much about…" He broke off, embarrassed. "Look, I didn't ask questions if you know what I mean."

"How much did she cost?" Parker wiped his forehead and noted his partner growing more irritated with the man.

"She demanded a hundred bucks later when we were in my car." Churchill tapped his head with the stub of his forefinger. "I wouldn't have given her a ride if I'd known she was a hooker. Now, what was her name…Mindy, Wendy, something like that, I can't be sure."

"What did she look like?" asked Perelli, frowning. "Was she wearing a wig? What about jewelry?"

"Asian, with smooth dark skin and long black hair down to her firm little…"

"Did you see anything suspicious while you were making it with this chick?" Parker snapped.

"*No.*" The man flushed. "I mean…*wait*. Perhaps I did." He

closed his eyes as if conjuring the memory of that night from the recesses of his tiny brain. "I saw a man—I think it was a man—running through the park, over by the lake. He cut across the bridge heading in our direction in a full-outsprint, but he turned and disappeared in the shadows."

"Can you describe the man?" Parker asked.

Churchill opened his eyes. "I didn't see him all that well. It was dark, you know? I remember thinking it odd to be out jogging that late in street clothes." He eased back toward the door. "He looked tall, but then everyone looks tall to me." He chuckled at his own joke.

Perelli frowned and folded his arms.

"Anyway, I was about to crank the car when this cop started banging on the goddamn windshield ordering me to get out of the car."

"Can you come downtown and sit with a sketch artist, maybe take a look at some mug shots?" Parker asked.

Churchill nodded like a bobblehead doll, agreeing as his overweight wife peered out the glass door, a pink dishtowel clutched in her hands.

"You can reach either of us at this number." Perelli handed the man a business card. "We need you to come in within the next twenty-four hours."

Parker walked in step with his partner to their car, leaving the rest of the interrogation to Mrs. Churchill. He heard a sharp, high pitched voice followed by a deeper rough reply. He couldn't hear anything after that. Whatever the scumbag said, the words rendered the woman silent.

CHAPTER TEN

Calvin Slade cleared a spot on his desk for his laptop and booted it up. He was amazed he ever located anything atop his desk as its surface was covered with file folders, books, faxes, and stacks of paper. Slade opened a file on his desktop and added some new details to the piece about the body found in Piedmont Park for the *Journal's* online site.

Slade had spent most of the day dogging the story, contacting sources inside the police department developed over the years, the Medical Examiner's Office, and the Georgia Bureau of Investigation's Crime Lab. He chatted up anyone willing to provide insight into his investigation. It was early afternoon when he finally spoke to the police officer first on the crime scene of the discovery in Piedmont Park. The man claimed the manner in which the victim died was the worst he'd ever seen in all his ten years on the force.

Cradling the phone between shoulder and chin, Slade typed while the cop relayed what he knew. "You say the victim can't be identified?"

"That's right," the cop whispered over the line. "Victim didn't have much of a face left. Dude was mutilated beyond recognition. Since there was no ID on the body, he's a John Doe for now."

Killer's intention, thought Slade. He stopped typing. "Thanks, man. I won't forget this."

Slade made several more calls before he discovered the victim was a white male in his early twenties and well outfitted.

The condition of the body was such that investigators at the scene could not immediately determine the cause of death, he typed, quoting a duty officer who offered comment on the condition that he remain anonymous.

Slade also managed to pull a quote from APD spokesperson, Wanda Booze.

"We're not calling it a homicide, or a suicide, or anything else at this time. We treat every case as a death investigation until we know something different."

For the next hour, Slade worked on the article, flipping through his spiral notebook of scribbled facts, quotes, and sources, all dated and time-stamped in codes only he could decipher.

Police, the GBI, and medical examiners plan to work at the scene well into the night, he added. *Officials will preserve the scene and continue to look for clues into the death of the unidentified man. Authorities hope further evidence retrieved at the scene may provide more clues into the victim's death.*

Slade flipped through the pages, reviewing notes he'd written that morning after speaking to the homeless man who'd found the body. He had tracked the old bum down less than thirty minutes after the shuttle officer provided some important information. A quick visit to the Ellis Street Shelter downtown and twenty dollars later, he had his eyewitness accounts for the follow-up piece.

The homeless man, who asked to remain anonymous fearing for his safety, claimed that finding the body was horrific. "The (victim's) face didn't look like a face at all, eyes open and gorged, and all. I ain't never gonna forget that sight as long as I live on this earth, so help me God."

Satisfied, Slade added what would happen next. *An autopsy scheduled sometime later in the week should help investigators determine the cause of death. Medical examiners studying the remains will use the most up-to-date forensic techniques available to identify the body.*

Slade concluded the article by urging anyone with information about the case to contact the police department. He provided the Crime Stoppers Tip Line phone number and mentioned tipsters didn't have to give their name to be eligible for an award.

He titled the article "ATLANTA POLICE SUSPECT FOUL PLAY IN PARK DEATH" and sent the copy to editing.

The officer's report contained the name of Churchill's companion the night of the citation. Parker pulled a copy of the woman's citation and checked with his buddies in vice. He soon learned Wendy Jones, aka Woo Vu, was a prostitute who worked fancy hotels and high-end nightclubs in Midtown and Buckhead. When hounded by vice, bouncers or hotel security, she moonlighted as a dancer at the Cheetah Lounge on West Peachtree. Ms. Jones, had been arrested five times in the last year for solicitation, disorderly conduct, and possession of narcotics. When not working, the hooker was known to hang out at a bar on Cheshire Bridge Road.

The 24K Club offered everything but what the name implied. The parking lot held an array of oversized SUV's with custom chrome wheels that cost more than Parker's monthly salary. The lounge appeared rustic and cheap, a real dive judging from the peeling exterior and a crooked neon sign. The hole-in-the-wall tavern occupied a section in the rear of a strip mall. The joint catered to criminals and those who hung with them. The dark interior boasted sanctuary from reality looming beyond its cinder block walls.

Sergeant Parker removed his sunglasses and held the door for his partner. They passed through the narrow opening with ease before being assaulted with a mixture of stale beer, cigarettes, and body odor; all trapped within the humid space. The men stepped off to the side and positioned their backs against the wall while let their eyes adjust to the darkness. Parker sensed a few pair of eyes glancing their way.

Conversations continued non-stop. A hand scooped up cash the laying on the edge of the pool table as they stepped forward. Glass shattered in the distance, and a waitress in high heels bent to the floor. The smoke concentrated in such a tiny place was enough to choke a small city. James Brown blared from speakers of a jukebox in the far corner.

"You boys lost?"

Parker flashed his shield to the muscular black man with silver studs in his left ear. "Wendy Jones hangs in this dump," he said. "She here now?" He followed the bouncer's eyes in the direction he glanced. "We'd like to speak with her."

"Chill." The man grunted and narrowed his eyes. "See 'bout 'dat. You wait here."

The big lug moved away. Perelli lit two cigarettes and held one out midair. Parker fingered the filter between thumb and forefinger.

"Never did like this dump," Perelli said, scowling. "Too goddamn dark in here."

Parker remained hesitant, his senses heightened. He scanned the room, checking the corners and alcoves where criminals usually lurk.

The bouncer returned, his stride jaunty and confident. "You got five," he huffed, leading them to a tall cocktail table in the back where Wendy sat alone. "Don't fuck wit 'er," he warned. He backed away and positioned himself within pouncing distance.

"Cute," the beautiful, honey-skinned babe said, ogling the detectives. She rested her catlike eyes on Parker's crotch. He ignored the slight stir and matched her intense stare. "You buyin'?" she asked, pursing her plump, ruby red lips.

"Just need to ask a few questions," Parker said, feeling warm beneath his collar.

"Another time, perhaps," she cooed in sultry tones.

Perelli chuckled and took a seat opposite the vixen, his back to the wall for safety. Parker chose to stand instead.

Wendy stroked her long raven hair and tossed her mane over bare shoulders. A sweet scent of jasmine floated across the table, and she narrowed her eyes.

"Wendy?"

She frowned. "My real name is Woo Vu. Wendy is easier in my line of work, if you know what I mean." She arched a penciled brow and focused her attention on Parker. "What took you boys so long?" she asked.

"You don't miss much." Parker kept eye contact with her and ignored the extra cleavage she showed as she shifted in her seat.

Perelli squirmed like a dog in heat and said, "Tell us what you know."

"Not so fast, fellas." Wendy produced a long, slender cigarette holder and attached a slim filter to its tip. She leaned toward Parker. He obliged with a light but held the flame longer to get a better look at her. "If I help you, what's in it for me?" She batted her long lashes. "I've got a hearing coming up soon."

"We can't offer you anything." Perelli said.

Woo's raucous laughter drew stares. "Spare me, cop," She spat, losing her seductive charm and sliding off the stool. "We're done here."

Parker grabbed the woman's arm, her skin soft like creamy butter. Muscle Man appeared at her side.

"We'll put in a good word with the judge hearing your case if you saw something we can use," Parker said. "Tell us about that night in the park."

"Who said I saw *anything*?" Her voice sounded strong but calm. "My people hear you been hassling me, you'll be fucked."

Parker stared down the bouncer. "You wanna mess with APD? Go for it, dude. I'll have cops swarming this place in five, and they'll do it every day this shit hole remains open."

Wendy dismissed the beefy bouncer with a flick of her hand as Parker released his grip. "Get to the point," she said as she flipped her hair and sat back down.

"We've spoken to the john you were with last week, so we

know you were in the park after midnight last Wednesday, early Thursday morning," Perelli said.

"The same night as our victim," Parker added. Wendy ogled him again, her eyes flicking from his face to his crotch. "The john claimed to have seen a man cutting through the park that night. What can you tell us?"

"Who, the fat salesman?" She giggled and sucked on the end of the cigarette holder. A roar erupted around the pool table as a winning ball clipped a corner pocket. "So yeah, I saw this dude chucking through the park, if that's what you call it. Looked like he came right toward us from the direction of the lake," she said. Smoke exited her delicate nostrils and engulfed the table. "Didn't think much about it at the time, but yeah, he appeared to be trippin', you know?"

"Care to elaborate?" Parker asked.

"He staggered like hell, busted his ass a few times, but kept on going. Hobbled like a motherfucker and seemed freaked out about something." She tapped ashes on the floor, threw her head back and shook her hair out of her eyes. "I figured the guy was a base-head, you know?"

"Was anyone following him?" Perelli leaned forward. "Did you see anyone else?"

Wendy pressed her supple body against the wall. Her perky breasts strained against the ivory silk blouse. "I wouldn't know, man. It was dark and my catch was all over me." She closed her almond-shaped eyes, pinching the middle of her forehead. "All I remember is the guy in the coat. I didn't pay much attention, you know?" She leveled her eyes at Parker. "Like I said, I was busy," she said with a wink.

"Are you sure you didn't see anyone else?"

Wendy rolled her eyes. "I saw this other dude hauling ass. I remember thinkin' he looked like one of those ninjas, you know, 'cause he was dressed all in black." She shook her head and twirled the end of the cigarette holder. "He carried something long and slender in his hands, but I couldn't tell what it was. Coulda been a shotgun for all I know. He was going away from where we parked. Look like he was headed for some kind of shack on the other side of the lake."

"Can you remember anything else?" Parker asked.

"Ain't that enough?" She smiled wide, fluttered her lashes. "That's it, man. Cop showed up and started hasslin' us, made us get out of the car." Wendy's tone grew flat and indignant. "Didn't give it another thought till I heard about that body. Man, that's some bitchin' shit." She called out to the bartender to bring her a shot of whiskey before turning back to them. "You boys thirsty?"

"No thanks," Parker said, growing impatient. "Can you come down to the station and sit with a sketch artist?" Parker held out his business card. Wendy rolled her eyes, snatched it from his hand and grunted.

"You've been a great help, Wendy," Perelli said. "We'll be in touch." They turned to leave.

Wendy called out to the men. "Hey, don't forget 'bout puttin' in a good word for me," she said, tossing her hair over her shoulder.

Parker offered his best smile. "I'll pull your record, get the docket number, and call the judge. I keep my promises."

Wendy tipped a shot of amber liquid in his direction and turned the glass on end across her full lips.

CHAPTER ELEVEN

The shack the hooker referred to was actually a cement block storage unit at the far corner on the park's east side and located inside a fenced in area around a community pool. The deep end of the pool held several feet of rainwater, rotting leaves, and debris that reeked of putrefaction in the scorching afternoon heat. The outbuilding had lost its pitched roof as the wood and shingles had collapsed within its walls.

Parker located an opening in the fence and scoured the grounds outside the structure. Plywood covered the chest-high window on one side of the unit, and a rusted padlock secured the front door. Parker turned and found Perelli searching the perimeter.

"Perelli, grab a claw hammer from the trunk." His partner returned with the tool and a flashlight. Parker tried to pry the weathered plywood, but it split in two and exposed broken panes of the sectioned window. He jimmied the rusty nails holding the remaining cover, and the timber broke free, snapping back to catch his knuckles.

"*Fuck.*"

"You all right?" Perelli asked.

"It's nothing." Parker tapped away the shards of glass and directed the flashlight beam inside. "I'm going in," he said. After scraping the window free of jagged edges, he lifted himself through the small opening, straddled the wedge and winced at the pain to his crotch.

"Careful," Perelli said. "You've not had children yet."

Parker sneered. He peered inside the blackness. Except for a few rays of sunlight that sneaked through the window and rotted sections of the roof, visibility was poor. The beam from the flashlight bounced off metal objects. Stale air coursed through his nose and tickled the nape of his neck, surrounding him like a damp blanket. Similar settings in the past had resulted in the discovery of a decomposing corpse.

"I'll be back in a minute," Parker said. He swung his left leg over the edge and dropped inside. The floor buckled from his muscle. He waited for his eyes to adjust before venturing to stand. Cool dampness girdled him, the musty air thick and hard to breathe. Parker edged forward, clearing away cobwebs as his shoes crunched on broken glass. He searched for what he hoped was a weapon discarded by a killer.

"Anything?" Perelli called out.

"Nothing." Parker flashed the beam over empty wooden crates, decaying barrels of chlorine, tattered aluminum chairs, push brooms and rotting hoses. Inch-thick dust and rat droppings layered everything. He kept searching as rodents scampered for safety. In the back of the shed atop some tattered boxes, Parker noticed an object that clashed with its surroundings.

Bingo.

Parker pulled himself to the ledge and peered at Perelli's balding crown. "Grab some evidence bags. I think we have something here."

Parker dropped to the floor again with brown bags in hand. He slid one end of the paper over the base and gripped the sack around the wooden handle of the object. The fresh wood was cracked and splintered, smeared with dried blood. He slipped another bag over the opposite end of the device, wrapping the paper tight around its base to contain the evidence.

Lifting himself back through the window, Parker handed down the bag to his partner. "Batter up," he said.

Perelli listened to voicemails on the drive to the station. Parker used the time to reflect on his return, wondering if he had come back too soon after the accident. He didn't know. One thing for sure, he wasn't the same person as before.

He glanced over at his partner while stopped at a light waiting for the green arrow allowing them to turn onto Ponce de Leon. Perelli's face appeared pallid, emotionless, and withdrawn. *What's changed?* he wondered. *What is Perelli holding back?* Six weeks apart from each other didn't seem all that much time, and yet Parker felt it may as well have been a lifetime. He had tired of walking on eggshells around his partner, the tension growing by the hour. Perelli had said few words since recovering the possible evidence in the park murder. Parker stared ahead when driving and off to the left when stopped, right hand in a death grip on the steering wheel.

Perelli lit a cigarette and opened the window an inch. Parker did the same without saying a word, lowering his window also.

"You and Jane doing anything this weekend?" Parker ventured.

"Nope, grandkids are with us while Bess and Kyle are stomping around Blood Mountain up in Union County."

Parker remembered Perelli's daughter and son-in-law were adventure racers, often training weeks at a time in rugged terrain before heading off to some extreme sports competition somewhere in the world. Apparently, they chose the highest peak on the Georgia side of the Appalachian Trail to prepare for an upcoming race.

"Where're they headed this time?" Parker sensed he was forcing the conversation, but his partner's lack of chatter rubbed him the wrong way.

"Hawaii, sometime next month, they say. Kids'll stay with us for a couple weeks then. I've put in for some time off."

Silence fell again. Frustrated, Parker's thoughts drifted back to the case. Not one credible witness came forth since the discovery, though the hooker had led him to the murder weapon, she had not come forth on her own, and her credibility was questionable at best. The special "tip line" the department established to further tempt those wanting to remain anonymous produced nothing thus far. Parker knew from hearing radio news that residents of the eclectic neighborhood near the scene were demanding a meeting with city officials to discuss safety measures.

Typical, Parker thought. Threats to hire off-duty policemen to protect their community would follow. Parker switched on the radio and turned it off a few minutes later. Talk radio went nuts crying foul and claiming recent public safety cutbacks endangered everyone. Just like the public to think they could do better. *Try walking in a cop's shoes for a while,* he thought.

The weight of the investigation on his shoulders, Parker felt the stress at the base of his neck, tight muscles pinching the nerves that ran to his skull. The case had drawn a lot of attention fast and not the good kind. The Gay & Lesbian Task Force to the Public Safety Committee of the Atlanta City Council had issued a statement that it was a hate crime. The group clung to the fact the park played host to men looking for anonymous sex after dark. *Nothing good can come of this*, he thought as Perelli whipped the car into the ground floor parking garage of police headquarters.

A group of local television personalities, cameramen, and newspaper reporters waited on the sidewalk outside the station. Spotting their sedan, a few charged forward. Perelli wheeled into an emergency spot near the employee's entrance.

"Grab the evidence from the trunk," Parker said. "I'll keep the leeches occupied while you get inside." Perelli nodded, popped the trunk from the button beneath the dash and lumbered out to circle around the rear of the squad car. Parker exited the vehicle and took a few steps toward the advancing reporters.

"Detective...Detective Parker!" a voice shouted from the group. "Do you have any suspects in the park slaying?"

"The matter is still under investigation." Parker spoke in his best professional voice as he raised his arms, and reared back from the microphones thrust in his face. "We're not yet ready to call this a homicide, but you'll be the first to know when we have something to report." He glanced over his shoulder to see Perelli slip inside the station, and then he turned back to the group.

A reporter from the rear lobbed the question, "Have you identified the victim?" Another cried out, "Is this murder connected in any way with other attacks in the gay community over recent months?"

"This appears to be an isolated incident, nothing more than a routine death investigation at this point," Parker said, stepping back toward the door. "Please, let us do our jobs and you'll get your information, I promise."

The handle of the door inches away, Parker turned and gripped it with enough force to crush a skull.

"Unconfirmed reports suggest the victim was mutilated beyond recognition, as though the killer didn't want the victim identified."

Parker hesitated before opening the door. He recognized the voice of investigative reporter Calvin Slade, and took a deep breath.

"Will you confirm or deny these accusations, detective?" Slade asked.

"No comment." Parker yanked the door open and stepped inside, but not before catching the eyes of the angry reporter who knew more about him than he cared to admit.

CHAPTER TWELVE

Sergeant Parker stormed through the station and entered the hole. He needed a target for his anger. Some asshole in the department had alerted the media that crucial evidence was recovered in the park case. God help the culprit if he discovered who it was. Dropping in the seat behind his desk, he rubbed his temples, easing the pain shooting from behind his eyes. He ignored the pangs in his gut, popped a few amber pills, and swallowed the pain relievers without water. He closed the desk drawer and looked up as his partner approached like a hound returning from a victorious hunt.

"Evidence is logged," Perelli said. "Thanks for covering for me. I'll kill the fucker who leaked to the press."

Parker nodded and frowned. Detective Brooks descended the stairs and headed toward them. The pain in Parker's temples increased twofold.

"Sounds like somebody squealed," Brooks said. He turned the witness chair around and straddled the seat. A sheen of sweat glistened across his forehead beneath the fluorescent lights.

The strain etched across Brooks' face showed the rigors of being a rookie, though he probably wouldn't admit to it. Few ever complained for fear of failing and suffering a label of incompetence. Hell, Parker never did, no matter how tired he felt or what shit he took from the more senior staff.

"I'll bet my left nut that asshole Slade has a snitch in the department and set us up," Perelli said.

"The guy's a fucking menace," Parker said, noticing the manila envelope marked **Crime Scene Photos - Piedmont Park** in the wire basket atop his desk. The package contained graphic 8 x 10 black and white glossies depicting every detail, right down to the shattered bones and cartilage protruding through torn skin. The photos were taken from all angles by the crime scene technicians summoned to the scene. *Nobody deserved such torture, such pain.*

His chest tightening in anger, Parker flipped through the photos, handing off each one to Perelli. *The killer knew what he was doing.* Parker was willing to bet *his* left nut on that fact.

Brooks took the photos Perelli handed him, glanced at each one and spread them across the conjoined desks like a child searching for hidden objects in an *I Spy* illustration booklet. "I struck out on witnesses in the neighborhood near where the body was found," he said. "Nobody saw anything suspicious or they're not saying if they did. I'll try again in the morning to see if I can catch more folks at home. Oh, I stopped to see Connie on my way in. She'll cross-reference details of the case with neighboring county agencies. I asked her to look for comparisons to recent crimes, too."

"Good work, Brooks." Parker said, offering a thumbs-up. "I see you've been paying attention."

Perelli spoke up. "The Lieutenant will have to hold a press conference soon." He leaned back in his chair and rubbed his chest, the buttons of his shirt fighting to contain his gut beneath the white cotton fabric. He loosened the knot in his tie. "We should probably be prepared for that to happen."

Parker sneered. He knew his partner spoke the truth, but the idea made him nauseous. In the age of the internet, cable, and instant news, media in large cities like Atlanta thrived on such investigations for sensationalism. The more gruesome, the higher the ratings. He had no desire to be thrust into the spotlight again so soon. A matter of hours stood between him and the public pleading for answers, demanding to know police were doing to keep them safe.

"What can we say?" Parker asked. He collected the stills from the desk and stuffed them into the case file. "We don't have much to go on yet." He leaned back and stared up at the ceiling tiles, counted the water stains that seemed to multiply with each heavy rain. "Fucking amazing, you know?"

"How's that?" Perelli glanced at Brooks, who shrugged his wide shoulders and stared back at him with a blank look on his face.

Parker pinched the bridge of his nose. "I'm saying the body was discovered only this morning, and the public expects a suspect, any suspect, in custody already. They want assurances the victim died of his own vices, that the choices he made are to blame for what happened to him. Bad things happen to the perverse, right? We hear it all the time." Parker held his arms out wide. "And they assume this from clues found at the scene that may connect the guy to the gay bar up the road. Facts someone from this squad is leaking to the press." He dropped his arms in disgust. "Give me a fucking break."

His colleagues gaped at him with questioning looks. Parker continued. "Look, all I'm saying is what the people making all the noise want to hear is that something so brutal, this sinister could never happen to them or anyone they know." He locked eyes with Perelli. His partner stared at him with hooded eyes, unblinking. "They know nothing about the poor guy, Perelli. *Nothing.* Not about his life, his family…nothing." Parker sucked in a deep breath, balled his hands into fists, and tried to contain the eruption threatening within. "Where do these folks get off passing judgment so quick? They don't know if the victim was even gay. Fucking hypocrites. All of them."

"Easy there, buddy," Perelli said, lowering his voice. "It's just another case."

The sour expression etched in Perelli's face confirmed he wasn't buying Parker's ramble. Brooks, on the other hand, sat befuddled, looking afraid to speak. He'd not seen one of Parker's outbursts before. The rookie's shocked expression screamed for someone to please explain what was happening.

Parker dropped his shoulders and leaned back in his chair. "The point I'm trying to make is that it seems easier for the public to pass judgment on someone they don't know, a body without an identity, than it is to accept the reality of the situation. What happened to the victim could just as easily happen to them."

Perelli sat ramrod straight in his chair, agitated. "It's just another case," he said. "No different from the two dozen or so needing our attention right now." His voice cracked. "I know you've been under a lot of stress with the accident and all, but…"

"But what?" Parker cut him off like a parent admonishing a child. "*That* was over six weeks ago. It has nothing to do with this case." He held his temper and searched for some compassion in his partner's eyes. He found none. "All I'm saying is I just can't write the guy off as another deserving dupe, all right? In spite of what it may or may not look like, okay? The guy deserves better. It's up to us to give him that."

"Us?" Perelli's said in a sour tone. "Lighten up, will ya? You're getting too close to this case. Why? Beats the hell out of me, but you'd better get it together and quick. We need to just focus on solving the case. Leave all the bullshit for the others. It's not on us to sway the public opinion, even if I do happen to agree with them."

A zombie staring from across the desk couldn't have goaded Parker more. "He was a fucking human being, Perelli!" Parker glanced at Brooks for assistance. The rookie opened his mouth to speak but remained silent, shrugging his shoulders. Parker looked back to his partner. "The guy had a life, okay? Homosexual or not, he didn't deserve to have his face bashed in. Nobody deserves to die like that."

"When did you become so fucking liberal?" Perelli taunted.

"I know you better than this, Ken." He scrunched his forehead and glared at Parker. "What's with you anyway? You're not the same guy who walked out of here six weeks ago."

Parker grimaced. "Fuck you."

Perelli shot up from his seat, knocking back the chair. "I can't stand fucking liberals, never have. You know that, Ken." He snatched his jacket from the back of the overturned chair and jabbed a finger at Parker. "What's changed in you, huh? You should've listened to the lieutenant and taken more time off. It's the only sane reason I can think to explain this bullshit." He confirmed his gun was snug in its holster and shoved his arm through his jacket sleeve. "It's been a long-ass day and I'm tired. I've had enough." He turned and walked away.

Parker sat transfixed. His body tingled from the rush of blood flowing through his arteries. Never before had their feelings been so exposed, dipping beneath that barrier reserved for wives and lovers. Cops were pros at shielding their emotions, and Parker was no exception. Those personal, innermost feelings of self-worth and doubt he knew all too well. He turned his attention to the computer screen before him, reached for the keyboard and grabbed a pad of paper.

Brooks coughed and Parker realized he still sat next to him. Brooks looked confused, waiting to be told what to do next. "You should go on home, too," Parker said. Brooks nodded without protest and bolted from his seat.

Parker leaned back in his chair and watched the young man stride off. His emotions were a mix of angst and confusion. Were he and his partner already tiring of each other after only a few short years? Could it be that Perelli's narrow-mindedness was driving a wedge in their friendship? His partner had never masked his opinions before, so why did it bother Parker so much now? He shook his head, trying to gain some clarity. What was so different between them now than two months ago, last year even? Had he changed as much since the accident as some had suggested? He wasn't sure, and the more he thought about it, the more confounded he became.

Perelli was right about one thing. It wasn't cool for Parker to get too involved in a case, emotional or otherwise. Detective 101. Doing so would only veil his better judgment and potentially complicate things down the road. No, he could not allow his personal views or perceptions interfere.

He contemplated what about the case had sparked his anger in the first place and got under his skin. Was it the injustice of the man's death that outraged him, or Perelli's bigotry? Maybe it was the senselessness of the crime itself. He accepted death as part of life. It happened, so what? We're born, we live, and we die. Whoever said death was fair? It's as much a part of life as skinned knees or losing your virginity. No one gets to choose their time to go, except for suicides.

Besides, he thought, *bad things happen to people every day, undeserving or not, regardless of demographic. It all depends on which side of the fence you're on.*

The young man was dead and Parker could do nothing to reverse that fact. So why was he beating his head against the wall? Why did he even care what others thought? The victim was likely a member of the silent minority, an immolation of his own self-righteousness, an outcast in the eyes of most. Parker refused to get bogged down in the particulars.

Still, his thoughts drifted to those closest to the victim. The ones who loved the man, who would agonize over his passing and forever question the motivation of such violence. They would never understand, never forgive and would suffer for years to come. He knew those sentiments intimately, experienced firsthand those feelings of guilt and doubt, of complete hopelessness. He knew the anguish associated with the loss of a loved one all too well.

The emptiness that death leaves behind never goes away.

A ruckus across the room pulled Parker from his reverie. One officer held a wristlock on the handcuffed suspect as another yanked his hair.

There was a small pad he'd been scribbling on while distracted. His heart skipped a beat. Large letters written on the paper glared at him. *Michael.* That name carried a burden only he could know, one that symbolized love, adoration, death, and despair for him.

He ripped the sheet from the pad and shoved his fist deep into the wastebasket as though discarding the crumbled paper in the trash would abash the feelings that went along.

CHAPTER THIRTEEN

Sargent Kendall Parker entered Blake's. The sparse crowd filtered throughout the tavern seemed less inviting than the men clad in tight jeans and clingy T-shirts sitting at or leaning against the rectangular bar in the center of the room. Couples huddled around tall cocktail tables the size of pizzas. A few more adventurous men groped their dates in the darker recesses of the interior while still others leaned against the dark walls among framed pictures of muscled men in shirts several sizes too small. A mixture of musk, beer, and cigarette smoke permeated the atmosphere. Music billowed from ceiling speakers, a mixture of old-time classics interspersed with popular tunes and the latest dance tracks.

Standing just inside the entrance, he gave the place a good once-over and headed to an unoccupied stool near the corner of the bar. Though on official business, he felt uncomfortable and out of his element, preferring a neighborhood pub smelling of beer and fried food with a hundred television screens turned to sports. He reached into his back pocket for a pack of cigarettes and noticed a collection of matchbooks in a basket atop the counter. A quick glance around the room revealed the same silver packet displayed upright in ashtrays for anyone to take, though not actual proof the victim had visited the bar.

A bartender slapped a cocktail napkin before him. "What'll you have?" He held out a flame to light Parker's cigarette.

"Bud Light."

"Three bucks." The bartender set a mug of beer in front of him as a sliver of froth slid down the side of the frosty glass. "Popcorn?"

Parker shook his head and inhaled cool menthol. He spotted the bartender's mangled nails. "What'd you do to your fingers?"

"Popping beer cans. Its murder pulling tabs all night when your hands stay wet most of the time. I gave up manicures a long time ago." He inspected his hand and offered a smile. "Blanche would not approve."

Parker remained silent, unsure if a response was expected. He slugged half his beer one gulp, then a drag on his cigarette. "So, you work most nights?"

The bartender glanced around the bar for waiting customers before answering. "During the week mostly, sometimes on weekends if someone calls in sick." He pulled the handle on another draft and set it on the bar in front of Parker. "You from out of town? Can't say I've seen you in here before."

"Not a regular." He pulled out his ID. "Detective Sgt. Kendall Parker, Homicide Unit."

"Put that away." The bartender waved him off. "You want to freak out the customers?" A man dressed in a black turtleneck called from across the bar. "Hang on," he said before dashing off.

Several new customers came in before the bartender got back to him. "I'm investigating the body found this morning," Parker said when he returned. He jutted his chin over his shoulder in the general direction of the park. "A matchbook from this place was found near the victim." The bartender's eyes popped. "It's possible the victim was here before his death."

Parker allowed the bartender to chew on the news. "What's your name?" he asked.'

"T-Ted." Color returned to the man's face. "You really think the guy was in here before he died?"

Parker slugged the rest of his beer. Ted grabbed the mug and filled it in a flash.

Damn, that's cold, Parker thought, with satisfaction. "Yes, it's possible, but a matchbook doesn't prove anything."

"Man, that was some shit that went down." Ted offered up wide, curious eyes. "Everybody coming in here's talking about it. They say the guy was bashed, attacked for being gay. Is that what happened?"

Parker ignored the question. "Is that what they're saying?"

"Yeah, man. Most guys say it was bound to happen. Cops around here don't give a shit about us faggots. We get picked on, taunted, our asses kicked all the time with no help from the police." He stopped himself. "No offense, of course."

"None taken."

"Whatever." Ted frowned and excused himself to make the rounds yet again.

"Did you work nights last week?" Parker asked when Ted got back. "You might remember the victim."

"I worked every night but Tuesday, my day off. Pretty slow as I recall. It rained a lot and that keeps most regulars away. Girls don't like to get their hair wet, if you know what I mean."

Parker thought to ask what he meant as Ted wiped the bar around him. Before he could, the bartender said, "I doubt I'd remember the dude, so many come in here, you know? But try me."

"What about a young man wearing a dark trench coat, perhaps green? White skin, early twenties or so, with short hair and five-ten or so?"

Ted shot him a scornful glance. "You're kidding, right?" He flashed the kind of wide grin that caused a stir in Parker's crotch. "You described half the guys that come in this place. Hell, all twinks look the same to me, except for the trench coat. I'd remember it for sure. Dudes don't dress like that in the evenings. Early afternoons, happy-hour crowds, guys coming straight from the office perhaps, but not the late guys. As you can see, it's pretty much a jeans and T-shirt kind of joint after dark."

Parker crushed out another cigarette. "You noticed me," he said. Ted flushed. "In my experience, bartenders identify their customers more by what they drink," Parker pressed. "Wanna try again?"

Ted stared down the bridge of his curved nose and his lips tightened. "I remember customers more by what they tip," he said, sounding perturbed. "Or don't." His features relaxed into a wide grin. "Besides, who wouldn't notice you? Big, muscular, linebacker shoulders." Parker ignored his warm ears. "Look, I can't say I remember seeing the guy, sorry. Excuse me, but I have customers needing drinks."

The barman slipped around the counter to refresh drinks. Parker turned to see new arrivals entering the bar. The men milled about, flitting from one small group to another, most with taut stomachs beneath skin-tight shirts riding the tops of jeans. A few eyes peeled his way, many offering up a smile and a nod of the head. He turned back to his beer and stared at the bottles of liquor displayed in the center of the bar.

"Wait." Ted said, almost sliding into the counter. "There was this one guy who stood out. Thursday night, I think. Yeah, I'm sure of it," he said, shaking his head and tapping his fingers on his left cheekbone. "Strange dude. A real looker too, with a hot bod." Parker shifted on his stool and must have appeared uncomfortable. "Sorry, man."

Ted blushed and busied himself dipping cocktail glasses in a sink filled with hot water before dunking them a few times in another. He stacked the clean glasses off to the side. "The point I'm trying to make is that everyone noticed this guy. Not a regular either. I'd never seen him before that night."

A muscled barback charged through to refill the ice bins. He handled the task with one arm, winked at Parker and spun away without a word. "Never saw the trench though," Ted said. "I would've remembered that. He could have taken it off at the table, I guess."

"You mentioned strange, how so?" Parker asked and stamped out his cigarette.

Ted lowered his tone. "The guy didn't fit in with the normal crowd, you know? I mean, he ordered *White Russians.*" Ted chuckled and paused long enough to pour a few drinks for a buzz cut waiter in a lime-green tank-top. "All doubles. Drank four in a row. I remember because we don't usually get asked for high cost cocktails in this place, except from the fag hags and drag queens that come in with their boy toys," he said with a sly grin.

"The guy paid his tab with an American Express Card, gold as I recall." Ted cleaned some ashtrays, flushed more glasses in the sinks and set them up to dry. "Tipped my ass twenty bucks that night. Wish all my customers were as generous. I might be able to retire by the time I'm forty."

"What else can you remember?" Parker asked, growing intrigued, not yet convinced there was a connection to the body in the park.

"Not much. The guy sat alone most of the time over by the door." Ted nodded toward the tables near the plate glass windows up front. "He was here at least a couple hours. Some guys worked up the courage and went over to offer him drinks, but he dismissed them all. Guy seemed nervous and kept glancing out the window every few minutes or so. He watched everyone who came through the front door. Talked on his phone a lot, too."

Parker knew GBI hadn't recovered a cell phone on or near the body, so the likelihood the victim had dropped it at the point of attack seemed plausible. He made a mental note to ask crime scene techs to expand their search farther out in the morning. Considering the vegetation and brush bordering the drainage ditch where the body was found, he figured the victim had been attacked somewhere else, and the body had been dumped at another location in the park.

"He paid his tab and left before I took my break. When I returned, he was back in the same spot, staring out the window and watching the door. Though this time around, he appeared more agitated than before."

"You recall a lot for someone who minutes ago claimed you didn't remember the guy."

Ted grinned with leering eyes. "Like I said, the guy was hot." He turned when someone called his name. "Excuse me a minute."

Watching the bartender greet some apparent regulars, swapping kisses and hugs across the bar made the detective more uncomfortable than he'd expected. The casual affection shared by the men was a new concept for Parker and not one he found easy to accept.

Ted returned and Parker asked, "So, what time did you take a break?"

"It was just after midnight. I remember because I always take my dinner break the same time each night. We're not allowed to smoke behind the bar, so it's the only time I can grab a good toke, you know?" Ted swished glasses in the sinks of water. "I think the guy's phone must have lost power because he came to the bar and asked if we had a pay phone in the place." Parker glanced toward the back of the room. "It's upstairs near the bathrooms," Ted said.

Ted rushed off again to fill drinks and clean ashtrays. A group of giggling men clamored up to the bar next to Parker as Ted returned without missing a beat. Mixing their drinks, he turned back to Parker. "The cutie came back downstairs, ordered another Russian and took the same spot near the window." Ted dashed off again.

Parker was growing irritated from the repeated interruptions as the pub filled up, some customers heading upstairs. The bartender seemed at ease carrying on broken conversations with many, unfazed by the interruptions. Years of pouring drinks necessitated such behavior, he supposed. Doubtful the guy could carry on a regular conversation outside the bar.

"Wait," Ted blurted, almost toppling the martini glass he strained into. "The coat, I remember it now. The guy was wearing a dark trench coat when I got back behind the counter. Hang on a sec, will ya? It's getting busy."

Ted shot off to make his rounds again, skipping along the backside of the bar like a professional in competition. The noise in the tavern had grown louder, numerous conversations coming from all angles. More and more patrons wandered off upstairs. Ted returned in a flash. "Not long after, the guy's date showed up."

"His date?" Parker snapped to attention and lit another cigarette.

"That's what I figured. Anyhow, this hot guy showed up at his table. They looked about the same age, height, could have passed for brothers. That's really all I remember, except the new guy seemed drunk already. I got busy with customers and last time I looked up, they headed upstairs. I never saw them again."

"Do you think you could describe them to a sketch artist?" Parker asked.

"The one with the coat, sure?" Ted frowned. "I'm not sure about the other dude. Didn't get a good look at him, but they were both hot guys. Model types, you know, the kinds that don't come in here often."

"What's upstairs?" Parker asked, glancing beyond the bar and reaching for his wallet.

"Pool tables, an excuse for a dance floor, bathrooms. That's about it. Oh, and there's access to a patio bar too, but it's only open in the summer."

Having obtained everything that he could from the bartender, Parker dropped a twenty on the counter and headed upstairs. "Thanks for your help, buddy. I'll have someone from the department contact you about getting with a sketcher. You've been a big help."

The room upstairs was the opposite of the floor below except for the flashing strobe lights spinning over a parquet dance floor set off to the side. The music cranked much louder here, the bass absorbed by the murky gold carpet lining walls floor to ceiling. The odor of gyrating bodies and burning table candles roused Parker's senses as he entered the room and walked its perimeter. A semi-circular bar tucked in the back played host to twin pool tables and a scattering of cocktail tables. Adjacent to the bar, a retro-looking pay phone hung on the wall next to a cigarette machine. He'd have Brooks petition the phone records tomorrow.

After ordering a beer from the dark-skinned man tucked in the back, Parker asked him some of the same questions he'd quizzed Ted on earlier. "Name's Winston," the bartender offered with a leering smile, not bothering to hide his come-on. "Yeah, so? I worked the last eight nights straight. Too damn busy or distracted by fine looking studs like yourself to notice bros not standing buck naked in front of me."

Parker swallowed hard and reached for his badge which seemed to encourage the bartender. "Hey, I'm cool." Winston parted his pink lips wide and flashed a set of perfect teeth. "You think 'bout walking on our side, you come see your boy Winston, here."

Parker tapped out a cigarette, ordered another draft and finished his questions. Winston hadn't served any White Russians last week, and he would have remembered, he pointed out with a flair that caused a couple catcalls from his patrons. He couldn't recall two above average looking guys either and seemed to care less. Parker thanked him for his time and drifted away from the bar.

Parker took up space near the wall overlooking the pool tables to finish off his beer and go over what little he'd learned for the night. This John Doe had been very attractive, anxious, and had seemed to be out of his element. Who was he looking out for? What caused him to leave only to return to the bar a few minutes later asking for change to use the pay phone? Did the victim call a friend or his killer? The questions gnawed at Parker like a tongue flicking across a mouth sore.

He nursed his beer and watched a tall blond with nice thighs in tight jeans drape the pool table to take an impossible shot. The white cue ball banked the side, hit its target and knocked the winning ball in the corner pocket. Parker cracked a smile, nodded as the blond turned and glanced in his direction. The beers had relaxed him, though he chastised himself for feeling attraction so soon after Michael.

Parker breathed in and tried to clear his thoughts. Based on the bar's proximity to the park and the book of matches located at the scene, he was convinced that John Doe had stopped by the tavern the night of his death. Bartender Ted said the man with the trench coat was downing double shots, one right after the other. Had the victim drunk too much and decided to walk home when attacked? Why hadn't he called a cab instead? More important, who was the mystery man seen with him that night? His killer?

A roar erupted at the pool table, and the guys racked up for another game. Parker decided to stick around to watch the dazzling blond and his pals play before calling it a night.

CHAPTER FOURTEEN

"Before dawn yesterday, the body of a white male was discovered in the run-off ditch on the south end of Piedmont Park."

Spokeswoman Wanda Booze stood ramrod straight as she addressed members of the press gathered on the sidewalk. City officials had insisted police have a press conference at the urging of uptown residents who'd besieged their offices with calls and emails demanding protection in and around the city's most popular park. In attendance this morning were dozens of television news and print reporters, cameramen, and a sprinkling of advocacy group representatives. From the Atlanta Police Department were Chief Jose N. Turner, Deputy Chief of CID, William L. Hornsby, and homicide detectives Kendall Parker, Vincent Perelli, and Timothy Brooks.

Confusion rumbled throughout the assemblage gathered near the steps of APD Headquarters as Ms. Booze, fighting the sun's glare, gripped both sides of a freestanding podium like a preacher about to give a sermon. Pigeons looming overhead drew closer with each swoop. She dropped her thick shoulders and swept her eyes across the group. The air was muggy and thick, the temperature rising by the minute on this cloudless day. The humidity added to the frustration of those vying to get closer. The spokeswoman waited for everyone to settle before continuing the press conference.

"Preliminary investigation indicates the victim died some-time after midnight, approximately four days ago," she bellowed over those gathered, admitting no witnesses had yet come forward. "Due to the absence of identification, the victim's name has not been established."

A few wide-eyed responses followed her statements, some scribbling on note pads, others holding recorders. Parker and Perelli focused their attention on the woman speaking and avoided glancing at each other, as well the crowd below them. The Police Chief stared high above the mass and seemed bored, his mind far from the duties required of him.

Ms. Booze continued. "At the present time, the exact cause of death is unknown, though preliminary evidence suggests the victim may have suffered from some kind of blunt force head trauma."

The spokeswoman flinched as she caught sight of Calvin Slade rushing forward in the crowd. "There is no apparent motive for this crime," she said, her words wavering when he took his position in front of her. "Personal items of value found at the scene dismiss robbery as a motive, though detectives assigned to the case haven't discounted any possibilities." She acknowledged the two men standing to the left of her with a nod and a thin-lipped smile. Concluding her statement, she asked for the public's help in identifying the man and encour-aged witnesses to come forward. She bowed her head, scooped up the paper she was reading from, and drew in a shallow breath. "Foul play is suspected." Her final words were inaudible to all but those in the front row.

Questions began flying at her from all angles. "Can you tell us if the victim was fully clothed? Are you questioning the neighbors surrounding the park? Have you determined *why* the victim was in the park in the first place?"

"What was the condition of the body?"

Calvin Slade's baritone voice rose high above the chatter, commanding the attention of everyone on the steps above.

Wanda Booze glared at the reporter as he pressed forward. "Sources tell me the attack was particularly vicious, beyond brutal even. I've learned that members of your own department couldn't even lay eyes upon the corpse." Slade paused to allow her to swallow the lump in her throat and shot a glance to the detectives assigned to the case. "My sources say the victim's skull was crushed by a baseball bat, the same one retrieved by those two detectives from a storage shed in the park," Slade said, pointing at Parker and his partner. A gasp encircled the steps. Parker couldn't conceal his consternation. "Why haven't you shared anything about the murder weapon? Clearly, your department can see the crime was motivated by hatred."

Though short and portly, Slade commanded the audience's attention, a mess of dark curls spilling about his cherubic face. He looked like an Indiana Jones field reporter who'd flown in from a remote jungle in the Congo, yet he lacked the charisma to carry off the persona. He wore laced boots, dungarees, and a dark flannel shirt. His clothes were rumpled and faded, and he sported a three-day-old beard. He awaited the woman's reply, defiance in his eyes.

Ms. Booze wiped a bead of sweat from her brow and licked her lips. She locked eyes with the reporter. "Your theory, Mr. Slade, is without merit." She stepped back from the podium, her eyes downcast at the reporter.

Chief Turner stepped up to the podium to address the reporter's accusations. "It's too early in the investigation to draw such conclusions," he said with a soothing voice and warm smile. "Crime Scene Investigators collected very little evidence at the scene. An article of interest was located, but the tests are incomplete. Our department doesn't have much to go on at this point. As you know, cases like this take time. Now, if you'll excuse us…"

"You haven't told us *shit*," a pudgy woman with large, round cheeks yelled above the bustle, ambling her way forward and stepping on those not quick enough to avoid her advance. A well-worn Act Up T-shirt covered her large, braless bosom. "How 'bout calling it what it was, huh? A gay bashing, pure and simple. Hate motivated that man's killer. Why can't you assholes just admit it?" She rolled her shoulders back as a flash of mock surprise contorted her face. "You do know the victim was gay, don't you? Or haven't you jerks figured that out yet? You heard the reporter. The guy's skull was bashed in and his face disfigured." She pressed her chest forward. "Are you even looking for fag-bashers?"

The spokeswoman fought to control her trembling body as she edged back. A flash of anger flickered across Chief Turner's face. "We have no way of knowing the sexual orientation of the victim," she said, "but I can assure you, every effort is being made to ensure the safety of the citizens." She glanced across the heads of the crowd. "We'll update you with more as information becomes available."

The crowd roared at once, all demanding answers, each trying to elicit a response. "What are you going to do about the safety of the gay community?" a woman's voice shouted above the explosion. "What about other unsolved gay attacks that have occurred lately?" The panel retreated. "What about the future safety of gay men and women of this city?"

The news conference ended as Wanda Booze, Chief Turner, and his entourage moved inside the precinct. The crowd had grown too loud and insistent to regain order. Spectators shouted, reporters jumped off to the side with their cameramen to film live broadcasts, and a few journalists loitered a moment or two to ensure no one from the department returned before dashing off to their respective offices.

Parker didn't have much time to ponder the asshole who had leaked information about a murder weapon in the park case because his phone buzzed the moment he reached his desk. He snatched up the receiver and punched a flashing button on its base.

"Detective Parker." The caller's voice drifted through the receiver, drawing Perelli's attention. "Where?" He scribbled across a pad of paper on the desk. "What lot was that? You're sure? No, no thanks, that's all. Don't let anyone touch it," he said. "We're on our way."

Parker hung up the phone. "Patrol impounded a car this morning about a block from Blake's Tavern. Might belong to our John Doe. It's been towed to Brown & Brown's lot on Cortland." He unlocked the desk drawer to retrieve his badge and gun. "Brooks, you're with me." To Perelli, he said, "Get an order to obtain the call logs of the pay phone at Blake's." Perelli nodded. "I'll check in with you later."

Parker spent the ride to the impound lot explaining the department's relationship with Brown & Brown wrecker service to Brooks. "The city contracts with them to perform various towing services, including impounding cars. They have several lots in the metropolitan area, but the main one is located on the south end of town. It's surrounded by a twelve-foot high electrified fence." He further explained that visitors must pass through a maze of security, including a steel barricade and a metal door before reaching the main office of the towing yard. "Drug dealers go fuckin' ballistic when their chrome-plated SUVs and Mercedes' with thousand-dollar wheels are hauled in."

A heavy black woman dressed in a pink jumpsuit greeted the detectives. She spoke through holes behind bullet-proof glass.

"Hep ya?"

"Detectives Parker and Brooks with APD, Homicide Unit." Parker showed his credentials and ignored Brooks as he fumbled with his wallet. She shrugged, unimpressed. "I'm here to inspect a car picked up from Myrtle Street this morning."

"You tha own'a?"

"No," he said. "The car could be evidence in a homicide." He didn't explain further. "Where is it?"

The double-chinned woman spat into the trash bin beside the waist-high counter and read from a yellow piece of paper. "Back lot, rite, numba fo'three. Black Poorchee." She glanced up, pursed her fat lips. "City gone pay?"

Parker shook his head. The clerk snarled, pointed to a metal door to their right, and buzzed them through.

They located the Porsche near the back of the pen. A patrolman leaned against an adjacent vehicle, tossing pebbles to the ground.

Brooks offered his two cents. "Busy weekend, the lot's full."

Approaching the young officer, Parker said, "Thanks for the call." He glanced at the man's nameplate and noted the deep blue eyes staring back at him. "Anyone been inside, ah, Officer Bennett?"

"Just the guy who towed it." Bennett moved aside. Parker withdrew a pair of latex gloves from his back pocket, opened the driver's door, and slipped inside.

"Some blue-hair called it in, and I was dispatched to check it out," the officer said, peering into the vehicle. "She claimed the vehicle's been parked across the street from her house for days. Says she saw a man tampering with it last Thursday night. She heard about the body in the park, became suspicious, and called it in."

Parker rummaged through the console, searching for the registration. "It took her five days to call the cops?"

"Said she didn't want to get involved," Bennett said.

Parker cringed, knowing all too well the reluctance to speak out witnesses wrestled with. *Thank you, Hollywood.* Depictions of what could happen to those stepping forward for the sake of justice exacerbated the public's reluctance. He spent more than half his time trying to convince witnesses to come forward and give their statements.

"Brooks will get the name of the tow truck driver and the old woman who called it in from you," Parker said, dismissing the patrolman with a nod and a smile. "Good work, Bennett. And thanks for calling me."

Parker returned his attention to the sports car. The owner could be his John Doe, but had no firm evidence. The interior had already been contaminated, so he took little caution as he plundered through its contents. The idea of searching through the victim's things caused him to shiver, an unusual reaction considering all the homicide cases he'd investigated over the years.

What's different this time? he wondered. He didn't know, but something had unsettled him as he continued his search. *Get a grip, Parker.*

The console of the vehicle held crumpled bank withdrawal receipts, a ring of keys, assorted matchbooks—most from the Metroplex, a ritzy, gay nude dancing club in town—lip balm, CDs of bands he'd never heard of, credit card receipts, a collection of business cards, and some small change. Digging around, he found a stash of condoms concealed within the side panel. He scanned the floorboard beneath the seats with his flashlight but came up empty.

"Appears the owner's name is Jason North," Parker said to Brooks as he extricated himself and handed over a copy of a charge receipt. "It's time to find out if anyone's seen or heard from our pal North lately."

Brooks charged through the parking lot toward their vehicle to search the DMV's database. Parker leaned back and stretched out in the comfortable seat, sucking in the crisp scent of the leather interior. He gripped the steering wheel like a racecar driver and he let his thoughts wander. This case seemed like a race to identify the victim and identify a motive, a battle against time to catch the killer or killers responsible. *Whose race?* he wondered.

Parker relaxed in the seat and imagined cruising I-10 in the Florida Panhandle with the top open and music blasting, foot pressed to the floorboard. The vehicle's sleek design and turbocharged engine said something about its owner and perhaps about Parker himself. *Power.*

"Sergeant?" Brooks peered into the vehicle. "Did you find anything else?"

"Just some bank receipts and a set of keys," Parker said, bagging the potential evidence he'd located in the console.

They made the necessary arrangements to have the vehicle towed to the GBI Crime Lab for further inspection before leaving the yard.

CHAPTER FIFTEEN

Atlanta City Council President Mitchell Keyes thumbed through the morning's mail in a windowless office on the sixth floor of City Hall. His schedule had kept him from addressing the stack sitting on his wide desk until now. After spending the morning fielding calls from city attorneys, lobbyists, reporters—people who could influence his campaign--he began sifting through the mail.

He was angry at the reporter responsible for breathing new life into those ridiculous charges from weeks back. His efforts to fund further revitalization of Piedmont Park had nothing to do with the poor sap found in the park. The fundraiser he'd attended at the Fox Theater on the night in question had been important to his reelection bid for the City Council. He'd not eaten that day and was bone tired by the time he buckled himself into his Cadillac and headed home. Not wanting to endanger other drivers, he'd pulled to the side of the road to rest a bit but passed out from exhaustion instead. Police said his blood alcohol level had registered twice the legal limit, a charge he vehemently denied. He'd pled no contest before a night court judge and posted bail. He'd implored the public not to condemn him on hearsay and to judge him based on his conservative record.

Voters are worse than a pack of wolves in heat, he thought while sifting through the mail. They turn on a dime the minute your ass is in a sling, listening to the ugly rumors and slanderous accusations lobbed by the opposition. He knew that if the voters relied on their feeble imaginations, his chances for re-election could be dashed before the upcoming primary. He feared his opponents would seize this latest opportunity and rush to churn the scandal, but he refused to let a hard-earned political career go down without a fight. This morning was all about damage control, more so than performing the job the good citizens had elected him to do five times in a row.

The days following the misunderstanding by the police had been spent assuring his constituents, offering promises and apologies too numerous to recall, tossing harmless fibs to shore up support like confetti at a ticker tape parade. *Anything* aimed at convincing the people of his district of the truth, his truth. The distress had robbed him of sleep and plagued him with nightmares of losing the seat that represented a culmination of his life's work.

But nothing could have prepared him for the eight-by-ten manila envelope awaiting his attention. Someone had typed the councilman's name in bold letters on a plain white label, no return address in the upper left corner. What caught the man's eyes and caused his heart to skip, however, was the bold, red word stamped across the front. *Confidential.*

Keyes walked to his office door, locked it, and returned to the desk. A feeling of dread overcame him as he stared at the envelope as if it contained a poison. Unmarked mail was nothing new for him, usually containing ridiculous ramblings by disgruntled citizens. He got his share of mail from crazies now and again, but never had he received a package such as this, *sans* a return address and marked confidential. The envelope sat untouched on the desk.

Protocol called for him to refer suspicious packages to security personnel who would proceed through a series of safety checks before alerting federal authorities. Mail bombs had shown up in political offices recently in Georgia, Illinois, and

Mississippi. Not long ago, anthrax-laden parcels had targeted politicians, judges, and clergymen as well. Right wing conservatism often produced many forms of expression, the more dangerous including home-grown terrorism.

Keyes thought about his fair share of threats over the years. *Another act of intimidation,* he thought and against his better judgment, he decided to open the envelope. *Confidential* carried different meanings to everyone, and for him the word carried a special meaning of its own. He was a man of many secrets, a virtual Pandora's Box of deception and a gold mine for opponents seeking the upper hand in a campaign rife with mudslinging. No, he saw little choice than to open the package.

The envelope felt light. He flipped it over in his hands, retrieved a silver-plated letter opener given him last year by the mayor and sliced through the sealed edge, exhaling when he had completed the task without incident. He dumped the contents onto the desk while holding his breath. His heart jumped into his throat. *Oh, God!*

His blood pressure soared as a pain shot through his chest and down his right arm. He snatched open the top drawer of the desk and grabbed a bottle. A gulp of cold coffee washed the antacid tablets down his dry throat. He slumped back in his chair and took slow, steady breaths. An enlarged, color photograph sat on the surface of the desk featuring Keyes lounging naked with a young man he could not recall ever having met.

Calvin Slade didn't head straight to the office after the news conference. In his car, he dialed the local morgue and asked an acquaintance to inquire about the autopsy of John Doe. His source, a middle-aged Hispanic attendant who took cash under the table for notifying funeral homes of recent deaths, had been skillfully cultivated over the years and proved guileless. Management ignored Jose, a dedicated twenty-five-year employee who enjoyed a degree of autonomy over his peers, an important characteristic that led Slade to choose him.

Jose had little more to offer than to inform him the autopsy would take place Wednesday afternoon. Yes, he would be assisting and no, the identity of the victim had not been determined. "Prints no get 'cause decomp, agua too long," the attendant said.

Calvin thanked the man and ended the call. The autopsy's priority confirmed his hunch the case had made city leaders uncomfortable. The city morgue often ran a backlog of a week to ten days easy, so moving John Doe ahead of other cases proved the powers that be wanted this case solved yesterday.

Kirk Davenport, a Georgia State University senior interning at the *Journal* as copy clerk, filing clerk, and all-around gofer answered his call on the first ring. Slade had asked him to track down an address for the phone number he'd tagged during the suspicious call that mentioned Councilman Mitchell Keyes. He planned to head over to the man's office in hopes of questioning the alderman. Slade often juggled multiple stories at one time, the harsh pace print reporters faced in the age of CNN, Fox News and the internet. The competition these days for breaking hot stories was fierce.

"This is Kirk."

"Kirk? It's Slade. Did you get the information I requested?"

"Piece of cake," Kirk shot back. "Hang on, I have it here." The rustle of paper drifted through the receiver. "Here it is. Okay, the address for the phone number is 2263 Piedmont Road."

"Thanks." Slade disconnected the call and tapped the address into the portable GPS stuck to his windshield.

Heading up Peachtree Street, he turned right onto North Avenue and caught the light at Piedmont. He steered his coupe left and traveled several blocks before coming to the junction of Tenth and Piedmont.

The address belonged to a red brick building that housed a sandwich shop at one end and a trendy restaurant embedded opposite. Slade parked in the rear of the building and walked around to the intersection, looking over the area as if deciphering hidden clues only he could see.

Five days had passed since Slade answered the anonymous

phone call, yet the caller's words still rang fresh in his mind. He glanced west a couple blocks and up at the towering, green glass buildings lining Peachtree Street, before returning his attention back to the intersection. He considered the time the call came through, and the businesses on this corner opened at night indicated someone looking for a busy cityscape to shield himself somewhat while using the pay phone. *Why?* he wondered. What had the caller afraid for his safety? More nagging than anything however, was why Slade had received the tip in the first place.

These questions flooded his thoughts as he glanced about like a tourist, attracting a few stares but no offers of assistance. The caller had claimed the Councilman didn't leave the party alone. Slade knew the party was a political fundraiser Keyes had attended at the Fox Theater. A married man running for re-election in a hotly contested race, seen leaving the festivities with a woman not his wife meant disaster for a sixth term. *Had Keyes met someone during the event?* Slade recalled that a colleague at an AM radio news station owed him big time. He planned to cash in the favor and gain access to newsreel footage taken of the fundraiser that might capture the councilman ducking out of the party early.

The mystery voice had gnawed at Slade through the weekend, nibbling at his conscience. The caller's tone had been contemptuousness laced with fear. *Was the call a cry for help?*

Slade glanced over his shoulder and watched as a woman with a large breed dog jogged across the street and headed in the direction of the park a tenth of the mile up the road. *Piedmont Park.*

Movement across the street snagged the reporter's attention. A pair of business types deep in conversation descended the sidewalk and entered a tavern called Blake's. The pub's name fired a familiar chord as Slade recalled a conversation he'd had with a trusted source at police headquarters.

Evidence near the body found in the park had linked the neighborhood bar...

Slade turned back to the corner with a discerning eye, recalling details from this morning's police news conference about the victim's estimated time of death. His eyes darted across the street, staring at the neighborhood pub while calculating time in his head.

It can't be. Slade took a sharp breath. The cause of events seemed too impossible, improbable even, but far too coincidental for a seasoned reporter to ignore.

Slade caught the light at the corner and walked across the street with a renewed spring in his step.

CHAPTER SIXTEEN

"You wanna get some lunch?" Parker asked. He steered through traffic along Spring Street, avoiding the potholes that seemed to outnumber the patched spots.

Brooks grinned like a toothy band geek sitting next to a cheerleader. "You bet."

Parker eased the sedan into the parking lot of Jock's Sports Bar in Midtown. The restaurant had converted an old warehouse at the corner of Tenth and Peachtree into its latest bistro, a blot on the ramshackle landscape of old stores. Across the street stood the imposing white marble façade of the United States Federal Reserve, like a giant eagle puffing out its chest.

A perky hostess with hair dyed the color of an eggplant led them to a table on the outdoor deck. Brooks said, "I read that Portman had acquired most of the real estate in this area of Peachtree in the 80s." He opened his menu. "Hard to believe this was once a 70s mecca of rundown warehouses, head shops, adult bookstores, and gay bars."

A waiter set their glasses of water on the table and scooted off. Brooks continued rambling. "Portman Brothers won the admiration of conservative city council members aimed at clearing out the filth of the area. The voices of opposing minority organizations, historical preservationists and business owners were unable to fight the armies of corporate attorneys thrown at them. A shame, too, because Atlanta lost most of the in-town culture the city was known for."

Is this guy serious? Parker looked at Brooks as though he'd beamed in from another planet. A waiter put a basket of chips and salsa on the table and disappeared. "You picked all that up from reading books?"

Brooks beamed. "Plus, the Internet. I love researching local history, can't get enough of the stuff. Atlanta's mostly known for its place in the Civil War, but I believe the city's urban, black history is far more intriguing."

I'm sitting with a total nerd. Parker spooned away the wedge of lemon from his water and swallowed half the glass in one gulp. He looked up at the buildings towering over them, skyscrapers at every turn, several giant cranes atop concrete and steel under construction. A postmodern tower off in the distance resembled something straight out of the *Jetsons,* capped with twin, curved arches of twisted metal beams and light green glass, top opened to the sky. He had spent too much time wallowing in the filth of humankind to have noticed the changing skyline the last few years. Brooks continued to ramble on as he glanced back, more staring through the man than at him.

"With the exception of a few gutted buildings," Brooks said, pointing across to the adjacent corner, "only that historic apartment house once occupied by Margaret Mitchell has survived the bulldozers."

Parker recalled a time when the Mitchell House stood in decay for years, known as "the dump," an eyesore on the southwest corner of 10th & Peachtree Street. A German investor, no doubt a fan of *Gone with the Wind*, gave money to save the site from bulldozers.

Brooks blabbed like a grade-schooler as a waiter came up to take their orders and rushed off to other customers.

"Heat getting you?" Parker asked Brooks, noting sweat above his brow. Some of the women near them picked at the stockings beneath their skirts. One girl had kicked off her shoes under the table and rubbed her feet on its metal base.

Brooks wiped his forehead. "A little. Temps in Dallas reached a hundred during the summer, but I gotta say the humidity here is enough to kill a man."

"Welcome to the city," Parker chuckled. "It gets worse midsummer." His glance traveled from the rush of cars traveling Peachtree street to the blue sky overhead and over to the dogwoods in bloom on the front lawn of the Federal Reserve. "I like it, though."

Brooks agreed, chugged the rest of his water and signaled for another. "Be even nicer if I had a lady to share it with."

Parker toyed with the image of cowboy boots on the rookie's large feet and a Stetson set atop his head.

"You have anyone special, Sarge?"

Brooks' curiosity made Parker's stomach constrict. "No," he said, louder than he he'd intended. He leaned back as the waiter brought their food.

"I didn't mean to pry, just always trying to get to know people." Brooks scooped up his meal and took a large bite out of his turkey hoagie. He wiped his mouth with a paper napkin, shreds of tissue clinging to the cleft of his chin. "Hey, I heard what happened a couple months back. I can't imagine what you've been through."

"Thanks, but I'm fine." Parker picked up his sandwich, eager to change the subject. "After lunch, let's drop by Mr. North's residence to see if anyone's home."

Brooks nodded and attacked the rest of his meal as Parker finished his meal in silence.

Jason North lived in a complex of new luxury condominiums located on Lenox Road in Buckhead, a few blocks south of Lenox Square. Near the wrought iron entrance stood a large wooden sign lettered in gold and black advertising homes for sale starting in the mid-six hundreds. Parker knew the area catered to mostly young, educated professionals with fat salaries, a galaxy away from his own terrain and income.

After clearing the guard station, Parker maneuvered their vehicle through a series of winding curves leading to the rear of the compound. A small pond with grazing geese flanked several stucco buildings and the parking lot. Locating the address, they took the stairs to the upper floor of the tri-level building and stood on either side of the door marked C-12. Parker rapped on it hard, but the only door that opened was the one across the breezeway.

"He's not home."

Both men turned toward the neighbor, a portly man of forty or so wearing green Bermuda shorts, a floral smock, and leather sandals too small for his feet. Skin tanned brown, hair the color of wheat. Gold earrings bounced from both ears, and the aroma of jasmine permeated the air.

"He ain't been home for several days now," the man said, leering at Parker. "I'm surprised he didn't tell you." He batted mascara-coated lashes and glanced over at Brooks. "I see his tastes haven't changed, preferring his men older."

"You sound bitter," Parker said, ignoring the comment as he studied the man's expression.

Patting flushed cheeks, the neighbor warmed and relaxed his shoulders. "Nah, jealous is more like it, honey," he crooned and batted his lashes. "Never been invited upstairs, if you catch my drift." Mounds of flesh jiggled forward. "Boris Winecof." He extended a chubby hand.

"Detectives Sgt. Parker and Brooks, APD Homicide Unit," Parker said, shaking the man's hand.

The color drained from Boris's cherubic face. "Oh, has something happened to Jason?" He grabbed his chest and fanned himself.

"We don't know that to be a fact," Brooks offered. "Patrol Squad impounded his car this morning about a block away from Piedmont Park."

Parker chimed in. "We're trying to establish Mr. North's whereabouts."

"Did you say Piedmont Park?" Boris faltered, appearing on the verge of collapse. "Oh, dear..."

They reached out to steady the man as he staggered, and they shuffled him back inside the unit across the hall. Boris made for the sofa.

"Sorry to shock you. Take a few deep breaths. Can we get you some water?" Parker asked as he dodged a multicolored cat that sailed through the air and landed beside its owner with a dull thump. The feline hunched and dug its claws into the fabric.

"No...no, I'm fine." Boris coughed and cleared his throat. "Please, have a seat." Parker and Brooks sat in the twin chairs opposite. "I'm stunned, I guess." Tears slipped from the corners of his eyes. "Piedmont Park, you say?"

Brooks nodded. The man's face wrinkled like a bulldog. After a moment, Boris said, "I heard on the news that a body was found in the park yesterday morning."

"We haven't ID'd the victim yet," Parker added quickly, wanting to avoid rumors to the contrary.

Boris leered at him. "You needn't worry about that any longer, honey. It's him all right. He's not been seen in days. I know because I've called around. It's not like Jason to disappear like this." He rambled further without urging. "He's never done this sort of thing before, you see. I've been worried sick since friends from work called looking for him. I got that job for him, you know. He's been dancing at the Metroplex for about a year now."

Parker scribbled the information in his notebook. Boris sprang to his feet and sailed across the room like a diva crossing the stage before her audience. "Would you two care for a drink?" His voice quivered. "I need a cocktail to calm the jitters."

"No, thank you." Brooks declined for both of them. "Are you two close friends?"

"Not in the true sense of the word," Boris called out in a shrill voice that echoed off the high-vaulted ceiling. "Our acquaintance is more convenience than friendship," he said.

"Unfortunately for me, he's a child of aspiration and heartache, like most of the bunnies his age, especially when it comes to that tyrant father of his." Parker glanced at Brooks, then back at the man. Boris narrowed his eyes. "I've lost count the number of times that boy's come to me for a shoulder to cry on. The father is a vile man. You should be looking at him for this."

"Looking at his father for what?" Brooks asked, glancing at Parker.

Boris padded back across the hardwood floor and collapsed on the sofa again. A wave of fragrance assaulted Parker's nose. "Jason's death, what else?" The man took a large sip of his drink. "Beyond consoling him occasionally, Jason pretty much ignored me most of the time."

Parker spoke up. "And did that bother you?"

The question appeared to baffle Boris for a second before he rolled his eyes and offered a smile. "Don't misunderstand, detective," he said, jiggling the ice in his glass. "Jason was an absolute jewel when he wanted to be." He threw back his head. "It's so hard to believe," he whimpered. "I just saw him a few evenings ago."

"When was that?" Brooks asked.

"Uh, let's see, last Thursday evening about…" Boris glanced at the clock atop the mantle over the dormant fireplace. "Ten-ish, I suppose. Jason was on his way out as usual. I had stepped out to bring in some plants from sunning all day."

Parker shifted his butt in the unforgiving chair. *Damn thing is uncomfortable as hell.* "Did Mr. North indicate where he was headed that night?"

"No, and he never did. It wasn't his style." Boris slugged the remnants of his cocktail and pushed himself up from the sofa. "Are you sure you boys don't want one?" he asked, holding the empty container midair.

"We're on duty," Brooks said.

"Ah, silly me. Where are my manners?" Boris gushed. "Cops don't drink on the job, do they?" Brooks snickered, but the quick glance from Parker silenced him. Boris hesitated a moment in case they changed their minds, then fluttered across the room to the wet bar nestled in the corner among tall potted plants. "I'll just have a 'tish more, if you don't mind," he called over his shoulder.

Parker scanned the interior of the condominium. The living room stretched the left side of the expanse while a kitchen open to the living and dining areas occupied the right side. A wide, tiled foyer decked the entrance, and a narrow staircase to the upper level hugged the interior wall. The furnishings seemed expensive, a bit overdone for his taste. Thick oriental rugs covered most of the hardwood floors. Large wall murals trimmed in gilded frames depicting the old South, and a glass vase filled with orange blossoms placed on the table gave the room a bold citrus tang.

An array of camera equipment stacked in the corner in the foyer caught Parker's eye. Boris returned in a moment and took his seat. "Are you a photographer?" Parker asked, pointing to the gear.

"It's my vocation." Boris beamed, gathered his shoulder length hair and tossed it across his shoulders. "I have an eye for detail, or so I'm told," he chuckled as though he had just told a joke. "I can't complain. It's paid for this place," he said, sweeping his arm out across the room.

Parker glanced about the interior again. "You don't display your work?"

Boris caught his breath. "Lord, Heaven's no. I'm far too modest to flaunt my own wares. Besides, I'm afraid my art would make public servants like you two a bit uncomfortable."

"Try me," Parker challenged.

Boris accepted with glee. "I photograph men, detective, in the nude. Portfolios, calendars, periodicals, advertising stills, porn spreads, whatever. I work on consignment and have amassed a large client list over the years, not to mention a reputation. I have a studio in an old converted house on Cheshire Bridge Road, not far from here. I prefer to leave my work at the office."

Brooks cleared his throat and spoke up. "Was Jason one of your subjects?"

"They are called *models*," Boris smirked, a hint of disdain marking his face. "I discovered Jason," he snapped. "He's not one of those street hustlers you see hanging out over on Cypress or Ponce de Leon. The boy has real potential." He choked back tears again and caught his breath, patting his chest a few times. "I honestly can't believe someone would want to hurt that beautiful little lamb."

"You mentioned Jason didn't get along with his father." The cat had fled its owner and slunk across the floor to nudge at Parker's leg. "What else can you tell me about their relationship?"

"Are you kidding? Those two would kill each other if you locked them in a room together. Like I said, he's the one you should be having this chat with." Boris licked his lips and reached across the table between them for a pack of smokes. He lit a clove cigarette, exhaled a sweet aroma, and leaned back against the cushions of the sofa. "Jason despised his father. Always has from my understanding, and I sensed the feeling was mutual."

Parker scribbled in his notebook. "Did you ever meet the man?" he asked, studying the chameleonic expression of his host.

"No, and it's a good thing too." Boris sucked on his cigarette, releasing curls of smoke in their direction. "I'd have read him the riot act for being so hateful to that sweet boy."

"Did his father visit often?"

"Not much, as I recall," Boris said and gulped the remainder of his cocktail. "Jason's only lived across the hall less than a year." He rose to replenish his glass. "The man's visits were brief and often unpleasant. They were always fighting, Jason usually ordering his father to leave. Daddy North had a tough time with his only son being gay. He was always trying to lure the poor kid into counseling, to disavow his lifestyle and become a real man. You ask me, Jason was the sane one." He returned from the bar, striding across the floor. "Don't believe me? Just ask the other neighbors."

"We will," Parker said. The feline pressed its spiny paws into his thigh, picking at the fabric of his cotton pants. He fought the urge to kick the critter across the floor.

Brooks asked, "Does Jason have a lot of friends?"

"You're joking, right? What kind of lame question is that?" Boris caught himself. "The kid is very popular, if that's what you want to know. He has this way about him, you know, impossible to ignore. It's difficult to explain really. People want to know him, to be around him, even total strangers."

Brooks tried again. "Have you met any of his friends?"

"Some. They come and go. A boy named Johnny is his closest friend, BFFs they claimed. He's also a dancer at the Metroplex."

"BFFs?" Parker asked.

"'Best friends forever,'" Brooks replied, using air quotes. "Text talk."

Parker nodded. "Can you think of anyone who might want to harm Jason?"

Boris stabbed out his cigarette in a crystal dish. "I've pondered that very question since you mentioned finding Jason's Porsche." He stared across the table through red-rimmed eyes. "I honestly can't think of anyone who'd want to hurt that child. Everyone loved Jason."

"There's no proof anything has happened to Mr. North," Parker said, "but we would like to locate him as soon as possible." He and Brooks stood in unison. "Do you have the number to the president of the homeowner's association?" Boris nodded and padded over to a Queen Anne-style secretary. "We'd like to look inside Jason's unit."

Boris passed him the name and phone number. It took some time to convince the woman to meet them outside the unit. Parker pocketed his cell phone and offered his business card to Boris. "If you happen to hear from Jason or think of anything that might be important, please contact me."

"I will," Boris assured him with a wide smile as he ushered them to the door.

CHAPTER SEVENTEEN

An overweight woman in a lime-green jumpsuit and fingernails the color of cotton candy made a show of inspecting the detectives' credentials before opening the door. Keys jiggled on a large keychain as she slipped the correct one into the lock and turned. Cool air gusted out of the opening of Jason North's condo. Parker blocked the threshold and thanked her for giving them access. The men left her standing in the breezeway slack-jawed as Parker shut the door and turned the deadbolt. They both donned a pair of latex gloves, Parker flicked a switch on the wall, and the lights came on. The floor plan was identical to its counterpart across the hall, except in reverse and furnished sparingly. They stepped across the hardwoods of the foyer. The place was sleek and refined, a page out of an interior decorating magazine.

Dried eucalyptus and the acrid scent of leather permeated the air. The main floor held a long sofa, loveseat, a pair of identical upholstered chairs, and an assortment of accent tables. Glass sculptures of varying shapes accented the bold, contemporary décor. Several framed and signed prints hung on the walls.

"You ever heard of Patrick Nagel?" Parker asked, peering closer at the artwork hanging on the nearest wall. Brooks shook his head, and they moved farther into the living area.

"Shouldn't we get a warrant?" Brooks asked.

"It's okay, we have permission to enter," Parker said. "We're just looking around."

Everything on the main level seemed in order, so they took the stairs to the second level, which boasted three rooms connected by a narrow hallway lined with more framed art. The first room on the right held a desk and a huge computer monitor with keyboard, along with a backless stool on rollers, shelf-lined walls, and a giant lacquered entertainment center. The room across the hall appeared to be a guestroom with a private bathroom. At the far end of the hall was the master bedroom. They retraced their steps and entered the office for closer inspection.

Parker's soles sunk into the ivory carpeting as he moved to examine the bulletin board mounted above the desk. Photographs of the same young man posing with various others lined the corkboard. He examined the cabinet that extended most of an entire wall. A collection of alphabetically ordered CDs were stacked above the stereo, and a flat-screen TV was in the center. The shelf above it held several DVDs, all pornographic. Below was a shelf of textbooks and periodicals, stacked vertically, bindings facing outward. *What a neat freak*, Parker thought.

In the drawers of the desk, they found the usual items: bank statements, payroll stubs from the Metroplex, a telephone directory, a jar of coins, pens, paper, and a leather-bound, pocket bible inscribed, *To Jason with love, Mommy*. Inside, Parker found a snapshot of a boy about nine or ten posing beside a woman with the same color of hair. He flipped the photo over and read aloud. "Paradise Island, Bahamas." Near the last page of the book, he found clipped newspaper articles concerning an alleged mob-connected kingpin, Anthony Galloti.

"What do you think these mean?" asked Brooks, scanning the articles with the delight of a child.

"No clue." Parker shrugged. "Looks like North must have researched his employer at some point. For what reason, you'd have to ask him, and he's dead."

Returning the bible and its contents to its place, they moved farther down the hall to the master bedroom. A king-sized waterbed in a black lacquered frame flanked the far wall. Its hunter green, down comforter was drawn from the upper right-hand corner to bottom left, showcasing patterned sheets. Either side of the bed held identical glass-topped tables, each displaying crystal sculptures. A telephone with an answering machine sat atop the dresser near the door. Noting the blinking red light, Parker went to press the Play button.

Nine messages left since last Thursday evening corroborated the neighbor's story: four from Jason North's grandmother, three from friends, and one each from a warehouse wanting to deliver a piece of furniture and a hair salon calling about a missed appointment. None of the messages came from North's fellow employees, however. Boris claimed friends from the Metroplex had called out of concern for their friend, yet none had left messages on the machine. *Why wouldn't his employer have called looking for him?*

Parker continued his inspection of the uncluttered room and turned his attention to a black lacquered cabinet against the wall. Its façade, inlaid with beveled glass mirrors on each door, opened from the center. Inside were another flat screen television and more pornographic DVDs. On the left he found a series of drawers, to the right hanging clothes, arranged dark to light in color. He sifted through designer slacks, jeans, sport coats, and tailored shirts before moving to the drawers below.

In the top compartment, he found an assortment of socks, undershirts, jocks and briefs, but his next find wrapped him with an odd sensation. His eyes swept over a plethora of lubricants, prophylactics, handcuffs, chrome-plated and rubber cock-rings, leather studded wrists and collar bands, all lying among small amber vials of amyl nitrate labeled *Blast*.

The drawer held secrets far beyond what lay on the surface. Parker pegged Jason North as an escort who dabbled in the sexual pleasures of other men, men willing to pay him big bucks for their entertainment. *Who wouldn't*, he thought, as he recalled the striking young man in the photographs in the next room.

Brooks emerged from the bathroom as Parker closed the drawer. "Anything?" Parker asked. The rookie shook his head. They moved out into the hall. "Hang on a sec," Parker said. He returned to the office and removed a photograph from the wall of the missing homeowner before they left.

Parker's cell rang, and he answered Perelli's call. "Hey, partner, what's up?"

Perelli was excited and sounded winded. "You're not going to fucking believe this. The Porsche's driver may have been Jason North, but the vehicle is registered to Bradford Lyn North, the boy's father."

The muscles in the back of his neck contracted. "The real estate investor?"

"That's the one. I've dispatched a squad car to break the news about their missing son. Wanna swing by and pick me up?"

Parker made a wide U-turn. "Brooks is with me. Shoot me a text with the address. Can you hang out there and try to keep a lid on this? We don't have proof the vehicle belongs to the victim from the park, and I'd like to speak with the family before the media gets wind of a possible connection." He steered around a stalled vehicle and switched the phone to his opposite ear. "Have you informed the Lieutenant?"

"I was hoping you'd do that," Perelli chuckled.

"No thanks, be my guest." Parker stopped at a red light at the intersection of Peachtree Street. "I'll check in with you when we're headed back to the station." He disconnected the call and punched the accelerator after the light changed.

Not even three in the afternoon and Parker yearned for a drink. He turned onto West Paces Ferry Road, Buckhead, an affluent community northeast of the city is home to one-of-a-kind Georgian and neoclassical mansions. Manicured lawns the size of city blocks beyond iron-gated perimeters, many with private security guards and wide, circular driveways. A knot formed in his stomach as he turned into a tony neighborhood down the road from the Governor's mansion. He maneuvered through the dogwood-sheathed lane of Tuxedo Drive before stopping at the entrance of a colossal, nineteenth century English Tudor estate, obscured from the road by looming, wrought iron gates.

After inspecting his credentials, a guard allowed them to pass through the archway. The twin gates withdrew, peeling back on quiet hinges to either side of the stone driveway. Parker steered the vehicle up the winding pavement and killed the engine in front of the fortress. They stepped up to the grand portico as a tall, willowy butler greeted them in an English accent and ushered them inside.

A rotunda of pink marble took Parker's breath away. A free-standing, spiral staircase wrapped itself into the upper reaches of the home. Throughout the vaulted foyer were antiques and hulks of dark furniture, some brushed in gold leaf. A vase filled with fresh yellow roses sat atop a circular table in the center. The interior resembled that of an atrium in an exclusive European hotel more than a private residence.

"Please take a seat in the parlor, gentlemen," the butler said, sliding back a set of pocket doors on their left. "Madame North will join you in a moment." He excused himself and disappeared through a concealed door. Brooks shrugged his shoulders and led the way.

Parker fretted about taking a seat, fearful of the expensive fabrics the furniture was upholstered with. His experience with such wealth was minimal, though he knew the rich often forged ties with their local police precincts for mostly selfless reasons.

Parker and Brooks moved about the lavish interior of the room, inspecting everything with their hands shoved in their pockets. Across the room sat a collection of photographs in unique silver, crystal, and porcelain frames displayed atop a grand piano. A set of French doors opened onto a rose garden filled with buds simmering in the sun.

Parker examined the portraits. Most of the images were family members resembling one another, capturing an erudite expression difficult to conceal in such society. He wondered why he did not see a photo of Jason North among them.

"I have removed his photograph, if you must know," a voice said from close behind. They turned to see a slight, elderly woman with an ivory encrusted cane. "I find that I cannot lay my eyes on his face at this time, perhaps never will again. Such an innocent boy, naïve to the temptations awaiting men like him. It breaks my heart to think he could be gone."

Parker felt like his hand was caught in the cookie jar. "I'm sorry for intruding, ma'am. I didn't hear you come in." He reached out to accept her palm, dainty and warm, frail in his large hand. Her thin lips curled into a pleasant smile. "I hope we're not disturbing you."

"You are not." She responded her approval, and made her way across the room with an ivory-encrusted walking cane, though from Parker's observation, she appeared to use the stick as little as possible as if horrified by its necessity. "Please, do come and sit down with me, gentlemen. I will strain my neck staring up at you two."

The woman resembled the late Bette Davis in her formidable years: prominent chin, soaring cheekbones, and fiery eyes bursting with life. Judging from North's age, Parker figured the matriarch to be in her late sixties, though she didn't look a day over fifty. The woman's hair shone with a natural gray tint. The skin of her face and hands looked rosy pink, soft to the touch and lacking the blemishes so common in women her age. Diminutive in stature, Madam North carried herself with grace and elegance, a force of nature he felt no man had ever controlled.

They waited until she settled before sitting in the adjacent wingback chairs. "We appreciate your taking the time to see us," Brooks said.

Parker retrieved a small recorder from the pocket of his blazer. "Do you mind?" She nodded. "There are a few questions we'd like to ask, but some of them may be uncomfortable."

"Nonsense," Madame North said. "You have a job to do."

The woman made Parker nervous. He sensed that she could

send an approaching army hightailing like cowards with a mere stare. "Police impounded a vehicle this morning registered to your son within blocks of a crime scene. Receipts inside led us to your grandson. We stopped by his address, but a neighbor claimed he's not been home in several days." Madame North nodded, absorbing the information, never once averting her eyes from him. "Are your son and daughter-in-law home?"

The woman shifted in her seat, her back straight as she placed her hands atop knees. "My son is a widower, Detective, and no, he is not home. I wish he were." She stared off as a glimmer of sadness flickered in her eyes. "I have been trying to reach him since receiving the news from a police officer that my grandson may be…" She cleared her throat and stared into his eyes again. "Jason's father is in Asia conducting business."

Parker ignored the band of sweat breaking across his forehead as he spoke. "The body of a young man was discovered a couple of days ago in Piedmont Park. We suspect a victim of foul play. Early evidence suggests he could be your grandson." Cold, dark eyes stared forward challenging his. "We haven't been able to locate him." He swallowed the lump in his throat and glanced off, unable to continue their duel. "Our department needs a positive identification," he finally said, shifting his frame in a seat never intended for a man his size. "We'd prefer a family member."

"Yes, I understand." Madame North's lips narrowed. "Perhaps Maurice would be so kind…" Her voice broke as she gazed across the room.

The butler entered at the mention of his name, carrying a silver serving tray with hot tea. Parker sensed pride in the man's long strides, rigid posture, and expressionless face. "It would be better if…"

"Please," she said, touching the top of Parker's hand. Her eyes flashed like wildfire. "Maurice has been with the family for over thirty years. He has known Jason since infancy. Surely, your departmental standards can accommodate my wishes. He is most capable of identifying the remains in your morgue." She glanced at the butler, who nodded in obedience. "Would that be too much an imposition, Detective Parker?" she asked, returning her attention to him.

Parker glanced over at Brooks, then back to her. "Not at all. I'll have a patrolman drop by to escort him downtown." He wiped his clammy palms on his thighs and cleared his throat. "Can you tell us when you last heard from your grandson?" he asked.

Madame North sat rigid and unflinching. "Wednesday, last week." She touched the tip of her chin with a manicured nail layered with light pink polish. Her joints suggested a battle with arthritis. "Jason had joined me for lunch at Pricci's. We were to lunch again yesterday, but he never called to confirm our appointment. I assumed that he had made other plans."

Brooks spoke up. "You weren't concerned when you didn't hear from him?"

The matriarch's eyes fired like blazing cannons. "My grandson meant a great deal to me, Mr. Brooks. I do not appreciate your candor."

"I didn't mean…"

"Jason was an adult, albeit a rebellious soul," she said. "I did not chaperone his activities, nor did I condone his lack of common courtesy." She stirred, swiping an emaciated arm through the air as though clearing the space between them. "Of course, I was concerned when he never called to explain his absence. Any loving grandmother would have been."

The woman reached across the table between them and used tiny tongs to drop a lump of sugar in a cup before pouring a cup of tea. "Was I surprised? I must say no. Jason has never been one to keep all of his appointments. I became alarmed only after he failed to return my calls."

Parker leaned forward to accept the cup of tea from her. The tension in the air appeared to ease as she handed another to Brooks. He sipped, Madame North awaiting his approval before drinking her own.

"You are not without proper etiquette," she said, dabbing her lightly painted lips with a linen napkin. "I admire that in a man."

Heat rose in Parker's face. "Were you aware of your grandson's homosexuality?"

The woman looked over his shoulder. "Conversations between my grandson and I are confidential, but if you must know, he never discussed his choice with me." She shifted her eyes back to Parker. "I had suspected as much for some time now," she said, the corners of her mouth tugging downward. "The boy's mother nurtured him far too much when he was a child. Private tutors, selected playmates, chaperoned activities, her entire life revolved around him." She flung an arm through the air as though slapping the ghostly image of her daughter in-law. "That damn woman never let the child out of her sight. She suffocated him."

The bitterness rolled from her tongue easily before she caught herself and regained her composure. "Jason was an only child, you understand. That woman's insecurities stifled the boy from developing his instincts naturally, like any proper child." Her eyes pleaded for understanding. "Such an appealing boy, you see. Animated and full of life, forever teased by the other boys around. His mother doted on him so, sucked the independence right out of him. Jason could not escape her sheltering, up until the day she died." She glared at Parker. "The boy suffered as the result of his mother's selfishness."

"I heard Jason and his father didn't get along." Parker said, stirring the waters again. "Did Jason's sexuality cause conflict between the two?"

Daggers thrown from her eyes sliced through him as she stretched her neck an inch. "You question my son's actions? He acted appropriately towards my grandson's indiscretions. Any decent parent would have done the same." She turned away from them and stared off in silence for a moment. When she spoke again, her voice was brusque and controlled. "Bradford offered to seek professional counseling for Jason's abnormality numerous times." She brought her fist to her mouth, perhaps feeling the enormity of the news. "Jason refused to see a psychiatrist or seek help of any kind. So damn much like his mother, God rest her soul."

Madame North sat her cup down hard on the silver tray. "My grandson lived a frivolous life of his own choosing, detective. As you well know, men his age are prone to such vices. It is most unfortunate that his meandering cost him his life."

Parker dug his fingernails into his palms, squeezing his fists. He struggled to remain professional and deliberate, wanting to explode as he set down his cup. "You believe your grandson was a victim of his own sexuality? He was killed for being gay?"

"You condone such behavior?" Her chin tightened as she spoke and her brows arched in condemnation. "What kind of public servant are you?"

Parker stood, no longer wanting to be in the same room with this woman. A cop should always maintain his composure, but the way she spoke to him, and looked at him made his skin crawl. "Please have your son contact me when he gets into town," he said, placing his card on the table. "I can be reached at these numbers." Parker and Brooks stood.

Madame North must have detected his unease, and she softened. "Please understand, detective," she said, her frame like a matchstick next to Parker's bulk. "Jason's death is a tragic loss for us all, in spite of what you must think. Justice will be served."

"No doubt," Parker said. "You can bet I'll find out who killed your grandson, Mrs. North."

Parker moved to escape. The woman grabbed his arm, releasing her grip when he paused long enough to hear her out. "Of course, you will, young man. Of course, you will."

Outside the afternoon sun hung low in the western sky as a haze of humidity veiled the horizon in lazy slumber. Parker jumped into the driver's seat, smashing his knee against the dash as Brooks shut his door without a word. Parker cranked the vehicle and fastened his seatbelt. He glanced up at the mansion looming outside the windshield and wondered what kind of childhood Jason North must have had secured within those grand walls.

CHAPTER EIGHTEEN

Calvin Slade waited around Blake's Tavern until the bartender rumored to have served the park victim arrived for his shift. Slade learned from chatting up employees that the bartender's popularity had soared since word had spread. Ted would indeed be working on what was ordinarily his night off.

Grab his fifteen minutes of fame, Slade thought.

The bartender arrived a little after three, which worked out for Slade since the reporter planned to make one more stop before heading to the office. After speaking with Ted for about half an hour, he surmised the mystery tipster from last week must have stopped into the tavern after making the call.

"It's like I told that detective," Ted said, hands flailing to match the excitement in his eyes. "The dude was totally freaked, kept his eyes on the front door and out the window. He seemed to be looking out for someone."

Slade thanked the bartender, dropped a ten on the counter and exited the pub. Whatever the circumstances, the unidentified body had a connection to Mitchell Keyes, the City Council president, and he planned to exploit it on the front page once he checked a few things out. Slade had watched the man's career sink with each public transgression and embarrassment. The two

might have known each other, however remotely, and that association may have meant doom for the young man.

He grinned in spite of himself, walked across 10th street
toward the parking lot and tossed away his cigarette as he
hopped into his car. Merging into traffic, he headed to Mitchell
Keyes' office. He knew from experience the city official often
worked late in the day and he planned to confront the man,
hoping to catch him off guard. Slade needed more than a
reporter's intuition to link the two men before pitching this
latest spin involving the body in the park to his editor. His heart
ramped up double-time at landing another front-page byline in
as many days. He stopped at a red light and waited to turn left
onto Spring Street, ignoring the honks behind him the instant
the light changed to green.

Slade sensed his story had the makings of something larger
than he initially thought, perhaps the biggest of his career. *God,
I love my job.*

Slade waited over two hours outside Councilman Keyes office.
The Councilman's secretary approached him with a scowl across
her face. "I'm sorry, Mr. Slade." She stared at him down a
pencil-thin nose layered in foundation. "Councilman Keyes is a
very busy man. Without an appointment, I'm afraid you could
be waiting much longer. Perhaps you could return another
day," she said, offering a thin smile that turned down the
corners of her mouth. "I'd be happy to schedule an appointment for you."

Slade smiled and remained planted on the sofa. "I'll wait,"
he said. She rolled her eyes and stomped off, returning half an
hour later to once again prod him to leave. Slade had not
divulged the nature of his visit despite repeated requests, much
to the dismay of the receptionist.

After five-thirty, Slade spotted the councilman in the
hallway through the glass partition of the waiting area. Keyes
had taken a different route to leave the office than through the
lobby. Slade grabbed his computer bag and ran after the man,

stepping inside the elevator with Keyes before the brass doors closed. Both men faced forward in the confined space.

"I have been waiting to speak to you for hours, councilman." Slade turned toward the man. He towered over him by at least a foot. Keyes fumbled with the handle of his briefcase and refused to look at him. "My name is Calvin Slade. I'm a reporter with the *Journal-Constitution*. I wanted to clear up something about your arrest a few weeks back."

"I know who you are," Keyes huffed, turning and tilting his face upward. Slade noted the councilman's bald crown and flushing neck. "That's old news, pal. I was exonerated of all charges."

"You don't deny that cops found you sleeping at the wheel of your car at four in the morning?"

"I've admitted as much." Keyes stabbed the ground floor button several times with the stub of his forefinger. "Do your homework, son."

Slade forged ahead, noting several floors stood between them and the garage. "I'm curious, councilman," he said. "The night of your arrest, you attended a fundraiser at the Fox Theatre that ended before midnight." Keyes' jaw clenched and released. "I don't think you headed straight home from the event, did you, sir?"

Keyes scowled and turned toward him. "What's your point?"

"Where did you go between midnight and four a.m.?" Slade asked.

"How many times do I have to tell you people? All of you reporters cling to some crazy notion that I was up to no good. I am sorry to disappoint you. I have repeated many times since my arrest, I was tired and headed home that night. I'd been up before dawn that day, strategizing for a meeting with the city commissioners. On the drive home, I kept dozing off at the wheel, so I pulled off to the side of the road to rest. I didn't want to endanger anyone's life, including my own. Can't you just accept the truth?"

Slade glanced at the buttons on the elevator panel. *Two*

floors left. "Cops would have found your car sooner than they did if what you say were true." He leaned in closer to the man and caught the scent of his cheap cologne. "Where were you coming from, councilman?"

"What are you implying, son? I'm a family man with a wife whom I adore and three lovely kids. Your insinuation is absurd. Keep this up, and I'll have you arrested for slander."

The elevator jolted once it reached the ground floor. The door slowly opened to the parking garage odors of gasoline and engine exhaust. "I'm just trying to understand the facts, council-man. A little cooperation would help."

"Don't count on it," Keyes snapped, rushing out to escape the inquisition.

"Where *did* you go, councilman?" Slade called out. He watched as the councilman disappeared into the garage.

CHAPTER NINETEEN

Back to headquarters following the visit to the North family home, Parker clicked through messages from a slew of reporters and television producer's assistants left on his voicemail, all asking for his time. The case appeared to be acquiring a life of its own, fueled by a frenzied media motivated by headlines that boosted ratings and market share. The investigation had since gained the attention of prominent city leaders, including representatives from the mayor's office. Parker scanned several e-mail messages copied to him by business leaders written to the press promising the necessary resources to identify the person or persons responsible for the death of Bradford North's only child. North's wealth and notoriety afforded privileges beyond the average citizen, putting more pressure on Parker and his team.

He'd left the office earlier than usual, intending to catch some rest before stopping by Jason North's place of employment later that evening. He had left word for Brooks and Perelli to pick him up at eleven so they could ride to the Metroplex together. Tired, sweaty, and dragging from the day, he trudged upstairs to the second floor of the complex and shuffled along the walkway to his condominium. Built in the 1950s, the U-shaped, three-story brick structure opened to the street like a giant horseshoe. The center featured a courtyard bristling with crepe myrtle stalks and a rainbow of early spring flowers scattered about in raised beds, an oasis for residents or the occasional homeless bum who lounged on the teak benches placed about the expanse.

Parker's condo sat nestled at the far end of the west side, near the corners of 13th and Piedmont Avenue, about a block from the east entrance to Piedmont Park. French doors opened to a modest wrought-iron balcony overlooking a road often lined with parked cars. The complex, though clean and functional, was small and aged compared to others in the area, layered in dark green paint along the eaves and rusted railings. The units lacked more modern conveniences such as dishwashers and washer and dryer hook-ups, a given in newer construction. The structure had withstood the test of time and offered its residents character and charm, but more important to him, an affordable mortgage.

Inside the small foyer, he tossed a bundle of mail on the old secretary before shedding his blazer, tie, and shoulder holster. He hung them on the coat rack in the corner before moving to the elevated kitchen, which sat adjacent to the living room. Empty liquor bottles cluttered the sink and counter, signs of his recent attempts to suppress the pain churning inside him, a deep-seated gnawing he would have cut out with a hunting knife if it meant ridding himself of the emotional burden. He gathered up the bottles and filled the trash bin beneath the sink before retrieving a fresh bottle of Dewar's from the cupboard. Snatching a tumbler from the strainer in the sink, he poured the amber liquid over a couple ice cubes before bringing the glass to his lips.

He downed the first glassful, the cool liquid stimulating his senses and tearing his eyes. Soothing warmth flowed through him, beginning to release his tight muscles, easing the throbbing of his temples. He tossed slices of last night's takeout pizza into the toaster oven on the counter to warm. At the sound of the buzzer, he gathered up his dinner, cocktail glass and bottle of scotch and headed to the living room. He glanced at the French doors that led out to the balcony where he used to sit after spending hours on the job.

Watching passersby headed to the park for a jog or out for a stroll with a dog had once been his evening ritual, a way of relieving the day's stress--with the aid of an ice-cold beer or a tumbler of scotch or two--but no longer. Past summers he and Michael had grilled dinner outside, listening to Diana Krall's latest jazz tune. Since the accident, however, Parker had avoided the comfortable space even as the weather grew more inviting. Sitting out there alone was just another reminder of how his life had changed these past weeks.

With the touch of a finger, a flat-screen television sprang to life, and he surfed the channels before settling on baseball. The injury-plagued Braves were losing yet another game, the faces of the men in the dugout resembling how he felt after the day's assault. He sat on the edge of the leather sofa and devoured the pizza in large bites, washing his food down with scotch. After eating, he checked the messages on his answering machine: one peddled the latest credit card offer, and the other announced he'd won a free trip to Hawaii. Erasing both, Parker headed for the shower and emerged from the bathroom ten minutes later. He slipped on a pair of boxers and walked shirtless to the foyer where he grabbed his checkbook and a stack of mail from the secretary.

Wedging himself between the sofa and coffee table, he sat on the floor and extended his long legs. He touched the mute on the TV remote and hit the play button on a second remote for the CD player before refilling his glass. Diana Krall's soothing voice drifted through the room as he tore into the stack of envelopes, tossing the junk mail aside. He wrote checks and stuffed them in corresponding envelopes until only one bill remained. The plain white, legal-sized envelope arrived the same day every week, not once late in the last six weeks. Parker wished he could toss the invoice away and ignore the responsibility. Paying the amount didn't bother him nearly as much as the reminder that loneliness had invaded his world.

He could recite the return address of the unopened envelope

with his eyes closed and recall the amount of the remaining balance if asked. The debt would take a few years to settle since saving wasn't possible on a cop's salary, a reminder that his life survived from paycheck to paycheck. Death and the service commemorating it proved expensive to those ill prepared, he had discovered. The city could do whatever it damn well pleased with his corpse once his torch extinguished as far as he was concerned.

Parker scribbled out the last check, sealed the envelope, and set the pile on the secretary for mailing later. Crossing back to the sofa, he stretched out his large frame into a position more conducive of someone years his junior and continued to nurse his drink. Diana Krall gave way to Randi Crawford, her rambunctious vocals jolting the stillness of the room. His body finally relaxed, aided by the scotch flowing through his system.

Switching out the overhead lamp, he gazed at the ceiling. Brooding in the dark had become a welcome solace in the weeks since the accident. The darkness was comforting and serene, a chance to distance himself from the images of the crash embedded in his consciousness, no matter how hard he tried to erase them.

By ten o'clock, the moon's glow illuminated the room, casting its tendrils of light across a clear night sky. Florescent beams from the street snaked through the blinds as he huddled in the darkness among the stuffed pillows of the sofa, fighting to withstand the pain eating away at him.

Hopper had copped a paper, or about a fourth of a gram of methamphetamine, from a buddy of his and headed for an all-night diner. In a stall of the men's room at a Waffle House on Cheshire Bridge Road, he'd melted down the creamy-yellow rock in a used spoon and pumped the wonder drug into his veins. The free spikes given at the clinic, a needle exchange program listed in the package of materials given him at the hospital, aided in his ascent.

Wired and agitated by the time he trekked back to Cypress Street, he searched for a john to rob. He needed money, quick cash to buy more dope, the only *real* medicine for the battle waging inside his body. Guys on the street had warned him about injecting. Highly addictive they'd claimed, but he didn't care. *Who gives a shit?* He was dying for Chrissakes. Why not go out with a bang?

Bang! Bang! Bang!

He smacked his fist into the side of a parked BMW, denting the quarter panel of the car. *Fuck them,* he thought. Nobody cared about him anyway. Not his mom, his low life stepdad, baby brothers or sisters, not even the social worker who had visited his house once a month when he was little. Not his beloved grandparents whom he'd not seen in five years and certainly, *certainly* not that fucking asshole, Galloti. Him the most. Hopper blamed Galloti for his miserable life. *He* was the one who fucked over any chance he'd had of getting off the street, of having the life of a normal teenager.

Fuck Galloti.

Luck fell his way as a red sports car pulled up and offered him a ride. Hopper wiped the sweat from his face and jumped into the front seat, flashing his best smile at the man in the business suit and horn-rimmed glasses.

.

The deal went down at the lower end of Westminster, this side of Ansley Park, a posh Midtown neighborhood littered with million-dollar homes and yet so close to the recesses of lower life. For ten bucks, Hopper unzipped his pants and waited to make his move. As the pervert leaned over to go down on him, Hopper rammed an elbow into the man's face, shattering his glasses. Horrified, the john wailed like a baby as Hopper laid in a series of low-body blows and finished off with a fist into the face. The victim collapsed into the low-riding steering wheel sobbing and shielding his face with unsteady hands from further assault.

Hopper's heart raced, adrenaline pumping through his veins as he zipped up his pants. He snatched at the man's trousers, searching for a wallet, cash, anything of value. After ripping the watch from the guy's wrist, he slammed the jerk's forehead into the steering wheel before jumping from the vehicle. Racing up the dark end of the dead-end road, Hopper walked across Piedmont and ducked through Ansley Park, whooping and hollering as he ran. *Fucking easy target. What a dumb fuck. Got what he deserved.*

His anger shifted toward his former boss. He wanted Galloti next. Aiming his arm forward, he cocked his thumb and forefinger at a stray dog darting away from him.

Bang! Bang! Bang!

At midnight, Parker dressed in a pair of dark Levi's, pulled a light blue T-shirt over his broad chest and flat stomach, then laced his black Reeboks. He strapped his revolver and ankle holster against his shin, stuffed a few extra bullets in his pockets, and moved to the bathroom to splash water on his face. Perelli and Brooks had arrived and waited outside in the courtyard. He killed the lights, locked the door and wedged a sliver of paper between the door and the jamb, a habit he picked up years earlier patrolling the streets in uniform when disgruntled dopers dropped in unannounced.

The alcohol numbed his senses and depressed his emotions enough to realize how much of a dick he was earlier to Perelli. He needed to lighten up, accept the guy for his shortcomings, and let bygones be bygones and all that crap. *Does it even matter anymore?*

Perelli tamped out a cigarette in the grass as Parker approached, nodding to them as all they fell in stride down the narrow sidewalk. They piled into the unmarked vehicle and Perelli started the engine. Tension filled the car as they rode the few blocks to the Metroplex in silence. Perelli had said little to him since their blow-up and appeared as angry as he'd been earlier.

Just as well, Parker thought, as he clenched his fists and dug fingernails into the flesh of his palms to ward off his own ire. Staring out the window, Parker focused on the lights of the city, the darkness of the starless sky, on the promise he made to himself mere moments earlier, anything that did not require a glance toward his partner.

The three-story Metroplex, a palatial glass, steel, and concrete complex, stood on an entire city block off Northside Drive. The posh, all-male nude dance club and lounge offered access from the side streets flanking the complex and abutted by an alleyway. Parking seemed to be impossible, but after flashing their credentials, a young muscular security guard waved them forward to a spot reserved for special guests near the front. Perelli aimed the car into the space and cut the engine.

Giant white strobe lights aimed skyward and spun in unison as the men made their way past the life-size Grecian urns and statues of men from mythology that marked the entrance to the club. Perelli scowled and cleared his throat as they stepped up to the twin, smoky-glass doors that opened onto a large, black and white faux marble foyer. Washed in a lavender haze, Parker led his team past a line of mostly men waiting to pay the twenty-dollar cover. Parker stepped up to a granite counter and revealed his identification. They were shown in immediately as an employee rushed off to alert the boss.

A tall, dirty-blond, muscular tank introduced himself as Stewart Callahan, the manager of the establishment. He hustled Parker and his team through the expansive lounge of the main floor. Smoke, sweat, and cool air filled the space. Parker spotted multiple leather sofas with matching chairs scattered about the room, and mammoth artwork along the dark walls. Fresh, brightly-colored flowers placed around were likely intended to soften the dimness.

Callahan led them past the cozy anterooms flanking either side of a massive, glass-block circular bar. They continued to follow their host through a bevy of mostly male bodies: buff, shirtless waiters, drag queens, and transvestites. A door concealed in the wall on the right brought them into a small office. Parker strained to hear Callahan's words over the bass pulsating through the walls like a warrior's beat. Their host directed them to take seats in the sumptuous chairs in front of a rectangular desk, but Brooks chose to position himself standing near the exit.

"To what do I owe this honor, gents?" Callahan extracted a cigar from a rosewood box on the desk without offering them one.

Parker looked around the office, noting a rack of clothing holding various costumes and uniforms. "We're investigating the death of one of your employees, Jason North," he said, turning back to the man after studying some of photographs on the walls. If the news of the stripper's demise came as a shock, Callahan didn't show it. He sat stock-still and listened as Perelli whipped out a few black and whites of the crime scene and placed the photos of the victim atop the desk.

"ID'd him just this afternoon," Parker said, not explaining that confirmation was preliminary until dental records provided proof. "Can you tell us when you saw him last?"

Callahan stared at the glossies before leveling his eyes at Parker. "I guess it was about a week ago." The man's indifferent tone irritated Parker. "I remember because Jason should have been on stage last Thursday night, but he didn't show up."

"Did that concern you?" Parker didn't recognize Callahan's voice as the one left on North's answering machine.

Callahan's smirk spoke volumes. He puffed on the cigar and held the smoke in his lungs, appearing to savor its taste before releasing a bluish cloud off to the side. "Why would it? He didn't bother to let me know that he wouldn't be in, so why should I be concerned?" Callahan turned to Parker. "Dancers come and go around here, detective. You must know that. It's not uncommon for them to skip out, happens all the time."

"Sergeant," Perelli corrected, scooting forward in his chair as if ready to pounce. Callahan ignored the jab. "How was North's attitude lately? Any indication he felt his life might be in danger?"

"Not that I noticed. Jason wouldn't say if he were in any trouble. Wasn't the type and didn't need to be. The boy could take care of himself."

"Apparently not," Parker said, reaching out to take a cigar from the box on the desk. Callahan cut his eyes toward him, his lips curling in a slight grin before offering Parker a lighter. Parker sat back in his chair and puffed the smoke. "Who would want him dead?"

"Jason?" The manager stifled a laugh. "You kidding?" Parker noted the slight change in Callahan's demeanor; the man's shoulders twitched and his lips quivered. "Everybody liked the dude. He was fucking hot, man. Like, mighty popular with the customers." His attempt to suppress his emotions didn't escape Parker. Callahan appeared to be nervous. "He'll be sorely missed."

"Somebody wouldn't agree," Perelli stated. The men stood as if on cue.

Parker put the cigar in the ashtray on the desk. "You don't mind if we have a look around, do you? Nose around a bit, talk to the staff, that sort of thing."

The manager's face drained of color, but he managed to retain decorum. "I have no objections, of course." Parker shook the man's hand. "Drinks are on the house, gentleman. If I can be of any further help, please don't hesitate to ask."

"Count on it," Parker said. He held the man's palm a second longer than needed. "We'll have more questions later. An officer will drop by tomorrow for a list of your employees."

"Is that really necessary?" Callahan bristled. "I'm sure you can appreciate the privacy these men value."

"Yeah, it's necessary." The detectives exited the office and again threaded their way through the crowd. Brooks shouted something at them, but the dizzying beat carried his words away as he disappeared in the maze. Perelli peeled off and made a beeline for the bar. Parker moved around slow, figuring Callahan knew more than the manager had offered to them. He felt Callahan had lied about the last time he spoke with his employee North, which could explain this cool reaction upon seeing the grisly photos.

And hadn't Callahan dismissed North's death a bit too quick? Odd, considering he'd boasted about the dancer's popularity among the club's clientele moments earlier. *What are you hiding, Callahan?*

Parker made a mental note to check Callahan for any priors as he migrated his way through the crowded mezzanine. Men of varying ages shuffled through the club like cattle herding, pushing and shoving in a sea of sweaty, scantily clad bodies, most engaged in conversations in tight clusters throughout the room. Shirtless bartenders with bulging muscles served up cocktails and popped beer caps for guys five-deep in line around the bar. Dancers in G-strings connected to snatches of cloth danced on the elevated tabletops scattered around.

A room spilled out onto a large balcony with its own bar, framed by twin staircases on either side overlooking a dance floor the size of a basketball court. Smoke poured from the ceiling, obscuring Parker's view, as did colored lights that spun from multiple rising and falling chrome lattices suspended overhead. Music pulsated from speakers mounted throughout the space as more men jammed onto the dance floor, thrusting to Rihanna's latest mega-hit, bare chest to bare chest. The smell of musk and sweat permeated the room.

Parker descended the stairs and shoved past frenzied dancers along the wall toward a bar nestled in the corner, its steel counter illuminated by neon sculptures of the male torso. He ordered scotch on the rocks. At first glance, the bartender with the close-cropped peroxide-blond hair seemed to recognize him. The man stood rigid, arching his shoulders back and drying his hands with a bar cloth. He looked Parker up and down as he poured the scotch.

Turning toward the dancers, Parker watched in amazement as a thrust of dry ice fog began to engulf the floor. He spotted a few amber vials of liquid shoved up to some noses, heads thrown back with eyes closed. Men danced close together, bodies pressing tightly and moving in rhythm to the beat. A young, pierced, and tattooed couple clung to each other kissing, oblivious to the world surrounding them.

"The name's Jake." Parker heard over his shoulder. He took a plastic cup filled with scotch and ice from the bartender, who stared at him with ice blue eyes. "It's on me."

"Thanks," Parker said with a smile. "Did you know Jason North? He was a dancer here."

Jake hesitated before speaking, his eyes darting around the room before leaning in closer. "Who *didn't* know Jason?" he replied with a harsh tone. "The guy was a fucking jerk."

Not the sentiment Parker expected to hear. "You two didn't get along?"

The man scowled. "Jason was a prick, a snot-nosed rich kid who shouldn't have been dancing here in the first place. He didn't need the money, man, not like the rest of us. Most of these guys, the dancers here, couldn't take his attitude."

Parker sipped his cocktail as Jake filled requests yelled at him by a shirtless, muscled waiter who plopped a drink tray on the counter. When the waiter took off, Parker said, "I came away with the impression Jason was one of the most popular attractions."

Jake rolled his eyes. "The customers couldn't get enough of the guy. That's why the other dancers couldn't stand him. Most resented his talent, if that's what you'd call it. He crowded their space, man. If a pedestal some dude was dancing on had a larger crowd, Jason butted in. He landed the prime shifts, the best dancing spots and worked on his own terms. None of the other guys received the same treatment, that's for sure."

"You sound angry." Parker lit a cigarette and blew the smoke out the side of his mouth. "Holding a grudge?"

"Yeah, something like that." Jake glanced around the room. "Look man, Anthony takes care of his boys, all right? He doesn't give shit about the rest of us."

"You're saying the owner and Jason were sticking it to each other?"

Jake glanced up toward the main floor balcony. "I've said

enough. Fuck, I'll probably get fired for even talking to you."
He rushed off to attend to other customers.

Parker looked up in time to see a tall, sharply dressed figure
withdraw from the railing into the shadows of the crowd. From
photos he'd seen in the paper, he recognized the club owner,
Anthony Galloti, profligate nephew to one of the most lethal
crime families in Chicago. He also knew that Special Investigations had tried and failed to link Galloti to racketeering indict-
ments including prostitution, money laundering, police
corruption, loan sharking, and credit card fraud, to name
a few.

A meaty hand landed on Parker's shoulder.

"I've talked to a few of the bartenders," Perelli shouted,
leaning near his partner's ear. He stuck a thumb over his
shoulder as Parker turned. "None....good...say..."

Unable to understand, he motioned for them to move up
the stairs and out into the main room. "What were you saying?"
he asked, ignoring the ringing echo in his ears.

"No luck so far. I've talked to several employees, but nothing." Perelli tipped his cup on end, licking the remnants of
alcohol from the corners of his mouth. "I'm getting another.
Want one?"

"Take it easy on the alcohol, Perelli."

Perelli waved him off and shot across the carpeted floor,
returning moments later with a fresh drink. "Cops carry clout in
these places," he said. "No waiting in line either." The threat to
his masculinity had abated with a few drinks. So, it seemed, had
his cold shoulder to Parker. "Hell, this place ain't so bad," he
sneered. "Despite all the fucking fags."

Parker ignored his partner's comment, distracted by the
movement of a patron across the room. The young man was
edging toward the emergency exit and kept an eye peeled in
their direction.

"What's up, partner?"

"I'm not sure yet," said Parker. "You see the guy over there
in the red tank?" Perelli followed Parker's stare and nodded.
"Since we've been standing here, he's slipped through the crowd,

not a word to anyone, but kept watching us. Looks like he's headed for that exit."

"I'd say he's about to bolt." Perelli tossed his cup into a nearby trash bin and leaned in close to Parker's ear. "I'll head out front and swing around," he said. "He makes a run for it, I'll be there."

Parker studied the character over his partner's shoulder. "Keep it cool, Perelli," he said. "If the dude makes a break for it, detain him and that's all. It's probably nothing, but I want to be sure. And watch your back."

Perelli disappeared through the squash of bodies. Parker sipped his cocktail, peering over the rim of the plastic cup as he watched the man's eyes springboard around the room. Parker spotted Callahan and two goons moving in fast as the man rushed to make a break for it. A hand slapped onto Parker's arm about the time he started to advance. Calvin Slade.

"What the hell are you doing here?" Parker asked.

The reporter smirked. Parker turned back in time to see the red shirt had moved closer to the emergency exit. A cluster of chatty men blocked his view as Slade tugged his arm again.

"You're working the park homicide, aren't you? Why else would you be here?" Slade tried to follow Parker's line of sight across the room. "I know the victim worked here as a dancer, a mighty popular one, I might add."

"What's your point?" Parker turned away and craned his neck over the crowd in front of him. He spotted the tousled blond hair of the young man within inches of freedom. "Some other time," he said, shoving off in a hurry.

All eyes landed on Parker as he shoved and elbowed his way through the congestion, stepping on a few toes along the way. He heard some choice words and threats made in his wake. Patrons dashed out of the way to protect their drinks.

The guy threw open the door and set off the alarm. Someone nearby screamed and people scattered in the opposite direction. Callahan and his men retreated as Parker reached the exit, slammed through the door and leaped into the alleyway beside the club.

Pitch black. Retrieving his gun with his right hand, Parker clasped the butt of the weapon with his left and waited wide-eyed for his pupils to adjust. *Where was Perelli? Brooks?* The smell of sewage and stale beer hung in the night air. Behind him, the heavy metal door pulled closed.

An eerie silence invaded the area.

CHAPTER TWENTY

Parker stood in total darkness, his weapon aimed, and safety released. His heart pumped like a jackhammer as he scanned the area. He ventured forward, placing one foot carefully before the next in slow, measured steps. The grit on the asphalt crunched beneath his rubber soles and echoed in his ears.

The exit door had dumped him into the narrow alleyway accessed by main roads at either end of the Metroplex. A long, dark vehicle facing the opposite direction hugged the cinderblock wall of the building, exhaust from its tailpipe drifting skyward from an idling engine. The tinted windows were slick with raindrops, and the headlights off. Parker glanced to the left. A pile of empty liquor boxes seemed to be the only hiding place, because the guy didn't have enough time to get to Juniper Street.

Where the fuck's Perelli?

Seconds ticked away in the quiet alley. Parker edged forward to inspect the pile of rubbish, poking at the refuse with the barrel of his gun. Nothing. Moving around to the other side, he nudged at several lower boxes with his toe. No movement. His stomach constricted and his legs stiffened with anticipation. Perspiration slid down his temples, but he dared not wipe the sweat away. Two minutes had passed since his burst through the door and still nothing stirred.

Every cop dreaded such situations, slow dancing in the shadows alone with a robber, a thief…a *killer*. Fear had a way of clutching the heart and soul, controlling all logic. He knew from experience the anxiety coursing through his veins was enough to riddle a man's body stiff and lock his joints, even for tough cops like him. It had a mind of its own…fear, dominating the human psyche, causing one to act out of desperation, to strike when provoked. *Fear*.

Fear of the unknown or fear of *death?*

Parker backed away from the boxes, his eyes glued to the pile of cardboard, his breathing more rapid and his heartbeat echoing in his ears. *Easy,* he coaxed himself. *Wait him out.* He swung his arms slowly to the right, following the point just above the barrel of his weapon. *Steady…*

A cat screamed in the distance, sending chills up Parker's spine. He stepped into something cold and wet, the mess oozing into his shoe as a pungent odor hit his nose. A door in the wall next to the parked vehicle burst open and out stepped a short figure in a suit, bathed in the interior light when the car door opened. He heard a faint step, saw a flash of red clothing before something heavy struck against the back of his head.

Pain shot through his neck and shoulders. He stumbled forward off balance, and managed to fire a single shot into the brick wall before losing his grip on the gun. A broken bottle, lead pipe, splintered board—whatever the hell it was—held by a shadowed hand cracked hard across Parker's skull again. He tumbled to the wet pavement in time to see confusion flicker across the face of the suited man ducking into the backseat of the sedan. The vehicle's engine revved, and its tires squealed as it raced away. *Fuck!*

The attacker dropped its weapon and sprinted in the opposite direction. Parker got to his knees and fumbled around for his gun. He stood, staggered a second, and took off after the attacker in a running stumble. The pressure and pain at the base of his head pulsated as he ran. Warm blood flowed from above his right ear, filling his ear canal and running down his jaw and neck.

The suspect had darted around the building onto Juniper. Parker neared the corner wall and halted, putting his back against the brick wall to avoid another attack. He sucked in a deep breath and threw his entire weight around the corner with his pistol drawn. In the distance, two figures scuffled in the middle of the road, their struggle illuminated by a nearby street lamp.

"*Freeze!*" Parker chased after the man, spitting blood as he ran.

The suspect glanced up, panicked and clamped his teeth down hard on Perelli's arm before stabbing him with something. Perelli yelled, released his hold and fell to the asphalt clutching his neck. The perpetrator sprinted down the block and disappeared at the next side street.

Parker reached his partner in seconds. Perelli appeared dazed and confused as he crawled around on his hands and knees on the pavement. "Are you hurt?" Parker asked. Perelli gasped for air and shook his head in denial, his eyes wild with fear. Parker hefted him up and braced him against his left shoulder. They moved out of the street like a couple of drunks heading home for the night, a row of headlights guiding their trek to the sidewalk.

Perelli stopped, frozen in a coughing fit, but he managed to speak. "G-goddamn prick st-stabbed me," he wheezed, clutching the side of his neck. "I'm fuckin' bleeding!"

A few bystanders stood on the sidewalk, too afraid to approach them. A couple of uniformed cops appeared from out of nowhere with a pair of bulky bouncers. Parker tried to resist their offer of help, but the men hooked them both under the arms and rushed them forward. They reached the wall of the club and a hidden door opened. They were hustled inside and through the crowd.

Someone screamed, "Call 9-1-1!" Parker struggled to get a look at Perelli's injury as they moved along. He spotted Callahan's office ahead and tried to protest, but it was too late; they were placed at opposite ends of the room.

Hysteria raged among the men crowding into the tiny space. Parker strained to see over the large shoulders pressing him down in the chair.

"Stay back. Somebody get some wet towels and the first aid kit. Oh Christ, *he's bleeding!*"

"Move away. He needs room, air to breathe."

"Where's that fucking kit? Can I get some help over here?"

The room swam in Parker's brain. He squinted at the glaring lights overhead and struggled to get his bearings. Dizzy and sick to his stomach, he fought to see beyond the man wiping at the blood on his neck. Perelli mumbled in Italian in the distance.

"What happened to you two out there?" the cop asked in a voice too gentle for his size. He was crouched low on one knee, applying compression to Parker's scalp to stop the flow of blood. "You're bleeding from a gash in the back of your head. Stop fighting and sit still."

"I'll live." Parker scowled and snapped his head back, pain rumbling through his skull. He nudged the cop away and cradled his head, staring at the floor. "Who called you?"

"Nobody. I heard the commotion in the street and came out." The cop must have read Parker's expression because he followed with, "I'm assigned to the Fifth Precinct, moonlighting here to help pay the bills."

Parker understood all too well, recalling the days he worked security for clubs in Buckhead. "I chased a suspect through the emergency exit into the side alley. The guy attacked me from behind with something." He choked between breaths, trying to form the words. The room smelled of stale cigarettes as a feeling of dread began closing in on him.

"Hard to believe," the cop said, shaking his head. "A perp surprised you? You're a big motherfucker." He flashed a smile. "With the fight you put up getting you inside, it's a wonder the punk's not lying flat on his back."

Parker grimaced, wincing at the pain trailing down his spine. The overhead light glared down on him. "Can you get me some scotch to kill the pain?" he asked, attempting to get up from the chair. The pain in the back of his skull forced him back down. "How's my partner doing? How's Vince?"

"You need to stay put." The cop towered over him and placed both hands on his shoulders. "Your partner will be fine, just shaken up a bit is all. The perp took a plug out of his arm that'll take a couple stitches, but he'll be okay."

"Move aside." Brooks hustled his way forward and stood before Parker in a huff. "What happened, Sarge?"

"Where the hell were you? Parker demanded. "Did you see Perelli get attacked?" Parker caught his breath. "I-I went after a guy acting suspiciously who bolted out the emergency exit when he saw me advancing. He jumped me in the alley out back. Perelli caught him in the street, but the perp stabbed him and took off."

Brooks glanced across the room to the men kneeling in front of Perelli. "I'll check on him."

The off-duty cop moved forward. Parker sensed the man hadn't told him everything.

"Hey, what's going on over there?" Parker asked. "What's wrong with my partner? Why is he babbling like that?"

The cop glanced away but not before Parker caught his expression. "He was pricked, man. Right here." He pointed to the side of his neck. "We think it was a spike. A syringe was in the road where your partner went down."

The air in the room grew dense. Parker struggled to breathe with a ton of bricks sitting on his chest. "Wh-what? Don't just stand there, get him to a hospital." He tried to stand. "Perelli needs a doctor. "

The cop pinned Parker against the chair and scowled. "Hold up there, buddy. You ain't in no condition to go anywhere. EMT's are on the way," he said "Couple minutes out at most." His strength comforted Parker in an odd way.

The cop let go and returned in a flash. "Here," he said, holding a fresh cloth. "Keep this pressed against your wound. I'll be back in a few minutes, and don't move."

Feeling defeated, Parker fell back against the chair. The

thought of Perelli stuck with a dirty needle petrified him. Images from pamphlets and bulletins he'd seen during HIV and AIDS prevention seminars required at the precinct swarmed in his thoughts. One careless mistake could mean a lifetime of consequences. It happened more often than one might imagine.

"*Now* will you tell me what the hell is going on?" Calvin Slade stood before Parker with his hands on his hips and the expression of a parent about to scold a child. "The public has a right to know, sergeant."

"Fuck you, Slade." Parker spat on the floor and glanced up at the reporter. "Who the hell let you in here?"

Slade flashed his best *Who Wants to Be a Millionaire* grin. "I snuck in when no one was looking. I was concerned for your welfare," he said, with a sneer.

"Fuck off." Parker fumbled in his pocket for a cigarette. Slade struck a match and held the flame midair, still awaiting an explanation. "I have nothing to say to you."

Slade smirked and dropped the match. "You have a lead in the park murder, don't you? Who were you chasing? Before you lost him, I mean."

"You're wrong," Parker spat. He dabbed the side of his head with another towel handed to him by a staff member. After examining the small drop of blood on the fresh cloth, he tossed it aside. "You'll have to get your story from some other source."

"Why are you holding out on me?" Slade's tone was harsh and accusing. "I've been around long enough to sniff this one out, Parker, you know that." He leaned in closer and stared into Parker's eyes. "Don't forget who you're messing with. You can't keep me out this time." The reporter straightened up and turned to leave.

"You're not as persuasive as you think, Slade," Parker challenged with a grin. "You never were."

Turning back, Slade snapped. "Don't tempt me. Need I remind my readers of your negligence, Sergeant? How long has it been?" he prodded. "Six weeks since the accident that killed your friend?"

Parker glared at the man, knowing full well the sincerity of his warning. Fist balled tight, he shoved the reporter with all his strength. They landed in a fierce embrace on the floor and rolled about, arms and legs swinging, kicking the desk and the walls, and overturning chairs.

Parker landed two good punches to the Slade's face. Slade screamed as blood poured from his nose. He snarled, curled his torso and launched his legs forward, connecting with Parker's ribs and sending him flying backward. Instead of landing against the wall, he was caught by the cop who carried him in. He held Parker's shoulders with bone-crushing strength. Slade also found himself locked in a bouncer's arms.

The cop moved in front of Parker. "What the fuck are you doing?"

He hooked his arm under Parker's and escorted him out of from the room, through a stunned crowd and out the front door. "I thought I told you to stay put."

Parker noticed the squad car parked in front of the club just as EMTs removed a gurney from the back of their truck. "What's this shit?" He jerked his arm free. "You can't arrest me. I'm a fucking *cop*."

"The hell I can't." The officer placed his hand on Parker's scalp, forced him to duck his head, and shoved him into the backseat of the squad. "Just get in and shut up," the cop said. "I'm getting you out of here so you don't make things any worse for yourself. We're going to the hospital."

Sitting in the back of the car like a common criminal, the weight of Parker's actions hit him as the throbbing in his head beat in unison with the pain screaming in his ribs. The cop climbed in behind the wheel of the vehicle, slammed the door and punched the accelerator. Parker slumped in the backseat and realized the consequences coming to him once word reached the lieutenant.

CHAPTER TWENTY-ONE

"Michael."

The waves, rugged and stinging, lapped at Kendall's face. "Michael, can you hear me?" He spun around as he called out. "Where are you?" He pumped his legs in the water and paddled his arms as he searched through the wisps of fog layering the surface. "Michael, please! Answer me."

He heard nothing but leaves rustling from the trees that fronted the lake. The wind whipped across the surface as he ceased treading and strained to hear the cries of his buddy, injured and helpless out there somewhere in the water. The smell of charred wires and dead fish on the surface permeated the air, the mixture searing the membranes of his throat and nostrils. He fought to suppress the bile rising from his stomach. Where is he?

Like the center of a giant vortex, he spun in circular motions, desperate to locate Michael. Panic clutched at his throat as his arms and legs grew heavier with each stroke. Debris floated in the water all around: fiberglass, Styrofoam, and pieces of wood. Hail rained down on him, pelting his head and the top of his shoulders, driving him beneath the surface until the need for air exceeded the pain. He kicked off his waterlogged sneakers to gain some buoyancy. A large object bucking on the surface several feet ahead caught his attention.

The silhouette of a man's body appeared slumped over one end of the fiberglass.

Michael!

The storm pounded him, unleashing its fury in torrents of rain driven by the wind. The wreckage supporting Michael bobbed up and down in the water, threatening to capsize. He swam toward the jagged piece of fiberglass, fighting off the exhaustion in his legs as he pleaded for his friend to hang on.

His legs cramped against the current tugging in the opposite direction. Reaching Michael proved impossible as the wreckage drifted farther away with each stroke. Voices—some familiar, others strange—coached him onward, urged him to hurry. All that mattered was reaching Michael. His body grew weary, the pain in his legs numbing, but he kept trying. He began to lose consciousness, but somehow managed to get within a few feet of the refuse.

Michael did not respond to his pleas. A lull in the storm enabled him to get closer to the debris. He reached the mangled piece of fiberglass as the wind whipped again, but his arms proved too heavy to hold it steady. The makeshift raft bucked and tipped in the water. Michael's body broke free and slipped beneath the surface.

"Oh God, please. No!"

Kendall Parker woke from the nightmare with sunlight slashed across his face. A fine mist of sweat covered his bare skin. The air was uncomfortably warm, and seconds ticked by before he realized the cushions beneath him belonged to the sofa in his living room. He lifted his head, but a sharp pain over his right ear forced him back down. Pressing his hand against the bandage covering the stitches there and applying enough pressure to quell the pain, he worked his body up and legs over the edge before sitting upright.

The room began to spin and he snapped his eyes shut as tendrils of pain shot through every fiber of his body. His muscles screamed as though he had run the 10K Peachtree Road Race in record time. Alcohol didn't mix well with painkillers, resulting in a rumbling in his stomach threatening to unload. Parker sat a moment to steady himself and clear the fog from his head.

He didn't know how his partner was since they were taken to different hospitals. He had tried calling both Perelli and Brooks the entire time a nurse stitched his head wound, but neither had answered. After leaving the hospital, he learned from dispatch that Perelli had been treated and released. Full of pain meds. and too tired to drive over to Perelli's home, he had asked the cop who brought him in to shuttle him home.

Opening his eyes again, he noticed the empty bottle of scotch lying on its side on the coffee table. His stomach lurched, and he swore for the thousandth time in less than a year to lay off the booze. Foul liquid erupted like a volcano from his gut, filling mouth and nostrils as he bolted to the bathroom with his hand clamped on his lips. Stumbling through the hallway, he brushed a table next to the wall, which sent a lamp crashing.

He had left the toilet lid up as usual and reached it none too soon as he vomited. His gut emptied, he hovered over the sink and splashed cold water in his face before glancing up in the mirror. The image staring back saddened him. How did it come to this? he wondered. He stepped into the shower, careful to keep the bandage clear of water, letting the warmth soothe his aching muscles. Eyes shut and arms out splayed against the tiled walls, he stood beneath the steady stream and let the water cascade across his back.

Stepping from the shower, he toweled dry and went into his bedroom. The floor mirror in the bedroom showed the evidence of last night's assault. He twisted left and right, looking back over his shoulder to inspect the blue-black welts covering his entire left side. Abrasions crisscrossed his arms, chest and back from the scuffle with Slade. Broken skin scabbed over where the blood had congealed, his other wounds bandaged at the hospital earlier.

What now, he wondered?

CHAPTER TWENTY-TWO

Dark, ominous clouds rolled in from the west, turning the Wednesday morning sky gray and gloomy. A burst of rain brought cooler temperatures and relief from the spring heat by the time Parker reached the precinct on North Avenue. He entered through the lower level garage, showed identification and signed in with an attendant before heading into the locker room during shift change. The morning conference, or roll call, this morning in the unit dragged on forever and he found focusing on the number of announcements, reminders and assignment changes difficult.

Mention was made of the case Parker and Perelli fielded as well as Perelli's misfortune and a reminder to follow standard protocols while out there. The words "out there" conjured up memories of the old horror flicks Parker's mother used to make him watch as a child to keep her company. He stared at his feet, counting the laces of his shoes while feeling half the room's eyes on him. Those present heard commendations of heroism and valor performed by one of their own by the lieutenant. Formalities concluded, Parker poured a second cup of black coffee and headed down to his desk, scratching the skin around the bandage where it itched. Brooks looked up from a stack of paperwork and watched him as he sat down.

"What?" A copy of the *Journal Constitution* lay on Parker's desk; the large, front-page headline gawked at him like a movie marquee: ATLANTA HOMICIDE DETECTIVES STUNNED BY MIDTOWN MURDER. INVESTIGATORS REMAIN SILENT.

"What are you doing here? How's your head?" Brooks lost his smile. "You look terrible."

"My head is fine, thanks." Parker glanced about, looking for signs his partner had arrived. "Perelli in yet?"

"Nope," Brooks said. "I doubt he'll be in today considering what happened last night. I stayed with him until he was released and took him home. He's pretty shaken up, spent most of the night in the hospital."

"I tried to reach both of you several times. The pain meds made me woozy, so I had the officer from the club to take me home."

A detective appeared at their desks. "The lieutenant wants to see you in his office."

Parker glanced past his colleague and toward Hornsby's office. The polished oak door with frosted glass inlay awaited him. "How long has he been in there?"

"Couple of hours at most." The detective glanced at Brooks, shrugged and stalked off.

Parker sensed his comrade didn't want to be around for the fireworks. The detective cut across the room and stood outside his boss's door, feeling the tension in his face. Thick black letters, LT. J. L. Hornsby, stared at him like a dark omen. He swore the man existed on this earth to make his life miserable. Steeling himself, he knocked twice and entered.

"Sit down." The balding, portly man leaned back in his chair, springs and coils screaming in protest. "You want to explain to me what the hell happened last night?"

"Lieutenant, we were working the North case, see? We stopped by his place of employment to talk to some co-workers, his boss, the people he hung out with. I spotted some guy acting suspicious, looking like he was gonna duck out once he made us. He bolted out the emergency exit, and I pursued him while

Perelli went out the front to circle around and cut him off. I took a blow to the head by something hard and heavy before the perp took off. When I came out to the street, I saw Perelli attempting to apprehend the suspect when he was stabbed in the neck with a needle." He glanced over the man's shoulders at the wall of awards. "That's about it, sir."

Hornsby snorted. "No, that's not it. You didn't cuff the cocksucker, did you?"

Parker opened his mouth to speak but decided to keep quiet. Arguing with Hornsby was like pouring salt on an open wound. Parker wanted to escape the barrage of insults and put some distance between them before saying or doing something to make matters worse. The lieutenant's eyes bade him to remain seated.

"What's up Calvin Slade's ass?" Hornsby asked, evening his tone.

"He has a beef with cops, who the fuck knows?" Parker said. He explained how he and Perelli were moved inside the tavern following the attack and how Slade had provoked him. Hornsby absorbed his explanation, emitting grunts and snorts before unleashing his fury.

"Is that all you got, he provoked you?" Hornsby slammed his fist on the desk and glared at him. "You're a goddamn detective of this homicide unit, not some fucking beat cop straight out of the academy, Parker. You don't get provoked, understand?" He stood up and stabbed a finger at Parker.

"What I want to know is why you jeopardized the life of your partner—*a cop*—for a goddamn pervert?" Hornsby never hid his opinion of homos to the members of his command, labeling them sexual deviants akin to child molesters and rapists, the bottom of the barrel in his book. Hornsby opposed any rights afforded queers when away from the microphones of the press. Parker had heard rumors that Hornsby's brother-in-law was gay.

"Lieutenant, you weren't there." Parker shifted forward, perched on the edge of his seat. "That runner could be a suspect in the murder I'm investigating."

"Of a fucking faggot? Do you hear yourself?" Hornsby dropped into his seat, snorted and cleared his throat before spitting into the trash can. "It's a goddamned benefit to society if you ask me." He opened a drawer and dug around for a bottle of blue plastic liquid. "I'd pin a damn medal on the son-of-a-bitch if I could," he said, belching.

Parker shot back. "That point of view could get you transferred, if not fired." He regretted his words the moment they left his lips.

"Are you threatening me, detective?" Hornsby's eyes bulged, matching the size of the veins throbbing in his neck. Parker opened his mouth, but no speech escaped his lips. Hornsby took a deep breath, narrowing his eyes as he stared across the desk with the defiance of a bull.

"Get your priorities straight, detective. The park case isn't one of them." He dropped his eyes and began pushing stacks of paper around on his desk. "The next time you set out on a wild goose chase, I want to know about it," he said, without looking up. "Are we clear?"

"C'mon, lieutenant, I've got a homicide to solve." Parker stood in protest. "That man died as the result of a vicious crime, sir, one that deserves this department's attention, you can't argue that. We're obligated to…"

Hornsby's cheeks shot blood-red. He smacked his palms on the desk and propelled his large frame out of his chair. "Are you deaf? Have you not noticed your partner is out today?" Hornsby leaned in closer, the redness in his face putting off heat. "Because of your goddamn self-righteous attitude and sloppy investigating, detective, Perelli might have been infected with HIV."

A bolt of lightning ripped through Parker's chest and ripped the air out of his lungs. His ears burned as he stared at his commander in disbelief. "Wh-what? What are you talking about?"

"You haven't heard, have you?" Hornsby pulled back into a rigid stance and crossed his arms around his large belly.

"Haven't heard what?" Parker ventured a step back, feeling

dizzy and warm as the walls began closing in on him, the air becoming thick and harder to breathe. "What's going on, Lieutenant?"

"Perelli's wife called this morning. The spike used to stab Perelli was dirty, son. Tests at the hospital confirmed it." The lieutenant fell back in his chair and wiggled his bulk into a comfortable position. "Your hot-shot, *Hawaii Five-O* bullshit may well have jeopardized the life of your partner, sergeant. Doc gave him some shit that's supposed to minimize the risk of infection, but there are no guarantees."

Parker gripped the desk with both hands to refrain from slugging the lieutenant between the eyes. His legs wobbled and threatened to buckle. He needed to sit down at his own desk, where he could think. Not in Hornsby's office. Yet his feet refused to move. It had to be a big mistake. *It had to be!* Perelli would be fine, he was sure of it.

The lieutenant's expression spelled doom for Perelli, a man whose career spanned two decades longer than Parker had carried a shield. Perelli had brought down more criminals in his tenure with the APD than most new recruits would face in a lifetime. No Hollywood script could do him justice.

Parker unglued his feet and shuffled back to his desk in a daze. Glancing up, he spotted the last person he wanted to see. "Why the fuck are you here?" He knew he sounded annoyed but didn't care. Calvin Slade rose from the chair beside the desk. Parker collapsed in the chair behind his desk and loosened his tie, still numbed by the news about his partner.

"I'm giving you the chance to make a statement before the morning's edition," Slade said, rubbing his bruised and swollen nose.

"What about? Why I decked your ass in the first place? You know damn well why. You're a fucking nuisance, Slade, plain and simple. Now, get out of my face before I have you thrown out."

The reporter remained seated. "You have your side to the story."

"What's that supposed to mean?" Parker felt the heat rise

beneath his collar. "You provoked me, asshole." He fought the urge to pounce on the man again. "What difference does it make what I say? You'll write your point of view regardless, cops be damned. You always have."

Slade leaned in closer for a bit of privacy. "As hard as it might be for you to believe, I don't hold grudges. Unlike some people I know." He settled back in his seat with a smirk. "What happened last night is done, okay? Forgotten," he said. "Impartiality is an essential element of the trade."

Parker leaned across the desk. "Cut the bullshit. I want to know why you are here."

"The North murder, what else? Tell me what you're doing to solve the case. It's murder, right? Surely, you've at least established that fact?" Parker ignored the jab. "Have you any suspects?" he frowned. "The public has a right to know."

"If you think I'm enjoying this charade, Slade, well I'm not. You have something to say, say it. Otherwise, get the hell out of my face."

Slade blanched. "I should have known not to expect anything from you." His expression soured. "It's so like you to hold out on me, especially on this case. When are you ever going to learn?"

Parker remained stoic, staring back at the man as though looking at a stranger. Slade stood in a huff and stormed off, bumping shoulders with Brooks on the way out. Not twelve hours had passed and yet again Slade had managed to goad him. *Asshole knows just the right buttons to push.*

He rustled about his desk, shoving papers and slamming drawers. Who in the hell did Slade think he was, threatening him? *A goddamn ambulance-chasing reporter? Not a very good one at that.*

Slade incited anger in Parker like no other could, no one except the person buried six feet down in a cemetery a short drive northeast of Atlanta.

CHAPTER TWENTY-THREE

Parker glanced up into the face of Brooks hovering over his desk, a look mixing concern and reprieve on his face.

"You okay, Sarge?"

"I'm fine."

Brooks took the chair opposite. "You and that reporter don't seem to get along too well."

"Tell me something I don't know." Parker had trouble shaking off the edge to his voice. "He's a class-A jerk."

"In the academy, we were often encouraged to partner with members of the media and form good working relationships. We were told it helps with public relations."

Parker shot the rookie a flash of anger, then softened. "For the most part, that's true," he offered. "Not with Slade, though. The man's a menace to his profession."

"Mind if I ask what your beef with him is, sir?"

Parker leveled his eyes at the rookie, not wanting to get into this discussion at the moment. "Yeah, I do."

"Sorry, sergeant, I didn't mean to pry. I just thought that if I could…"

"Then don't, Brooks. Let it go."

"Yes, sir." Brooks shifted in his chair and tried to broach a new subject. "Hey, about last night…I'm real sorry for not being there when you needed me. I should have stuck with you two instead of going to take a leak. When I couldn't find you, I walked around and asked the staff about North. As soon as I heard the alarm, I came running."

"It happens," Parker muttered to himself, turning back to his paperwork. He found focusing on anything difficult since hearing the news about Perelli. Parker had sworn off pain meds in order to get some paperwork done, but now his head felt caught between the jaws of a vise grip. "Did you learn anything?"

"Huh?" Brooks seemed confused until a light went off somewhere in his brain. "Oh, about North? Yeah, I did. He landed the dancing gig about nine months ago. Showed up one day, and Galloti hired him on the spot."

"Doesn't seem unusual, considering the job." Parker glanced up, unfazed.

"The owner gave North the stage name, *Sterling*. Had to do something with his good looks and sparkling sexuality, or so I was told." Parker raised an eyebrow and Brooks cleared his throat. "A stripper's words, not mine."

"Just stick to the facts, Brooks."

"Yes, sir." Brooks glanced at his notes and flipped through the pages. "I got the impression none of the dancers appreciated the new arrival. Bartenders claimed a lot of bitching going around. One guy said—and I quote—'the kid had what all the others lacked: intelligence, incredible sex appeal, and a boyish sense of charm that drove men wild.'" Brooks flashed an uneasy smile. "Seems North was a natural on stage and customers couldn't get enough of him."

Touching his temples Parker leaned back in the chair, wincing from the throbbing pain in his head. "So, the owner finds a diamond in the rough that sparks petty jealously among the dancers. Could go to motive. Maybe North pissed off the wrong guy by moving in on their turf."

"Right." Brooks nodded. "Most whined that North was given the best shifts and the preferred dancing spots that attracted the high rollers. Those who complained to the owner saw fewer hours and made less money. Anyone who crowded Jason's space got the boot, no joke. One of the bartender's swore North received bonuses just by showing up, which of late amounted to just a few hours a night, three or four times a week.

Parker listened as Brooks described a well-to-do kid turned male stripper driven by some need for attention. "Most interesting," he said, eyes widening. "North had a brief relationship with Galloti that ended in a bad breakup. Some expressed surprise the kid remained employed after the nasty public fight they witnessed." Brooks glanced back at his notes. "Also, North's friend, a twenty-year old fellow dancer named Johnny Cage, aka *Scorpion,* hasn't shown up for work since North's disappearance." The skin between Brooks' eyebrows gnarled, giving him the appearance of a cartoon character.

"You think there's a connection?" Parker asked, leaning forward and doing his best to ignore the throbbing.

"I don't know. Guys I spoke to claim the two were tight, like brothers." Brooks' tone deepened to match the dive of his eyebrows. "From what I gathered, Cage didn't approve of his friend's involvement with Galloti. His dislike for the club owner was well known, to the point of antagonistic. Surprising that he kept dancing there."

"Not really. Guys like Galloti keep a tight rein on their boys, usually with drugs." Parker glanced at his watch. "We should pay Cage a visit. He may be involved or at least know who might have wanted his friend dead. Did you get an address?"

"He rents out a room in a house on Park Avenue, just a few blocks from Piedmont Park. The owner is a retired Fulton County schoolteacher who bought the place in 1977." Brooks grinned, pleased with his thoroughness. "North could have cut through the park, headed to his friend's place the night of his attack. I've left messages, but haven't connected with Cage yet." Brooks glanced at his cell phone.

"We can drop by his address after the autopsy," Parker said, noting the rookie's frown at mention of their afternoon appointment. "The procedure is scheduled for one o'clock, so we need to be there."

"Wait, I almost forgot," Brooks' said. His face brightened as he flipped through the pages of a pocket-sized notebook. He handed over a manila file folder. "After getting a warrant you recommended, I checked out North's bank accounts, credit cards, credit and criminal history, all the usual stuff. He has a couple thousand in checking and a little more in a savings account, but I didn't notice any irregularities. Zero activity with his accounts since Wednesday last week, the night he paid the tab at Blake's Tavern."

Parker examined the documents. "Odd..."

"Sir?" Brooks raised an eyebrow.

After closing the folder and placing it on his desk, Parker asked, "Any idea what North did with the money he earned dancing at the Metroplex? If he was all they claimed, I imagine a guy like that could pull down a thousand or more a night, double on the weekends. Deposits into his account don't bear that out."

Brooks snatched up the folder and began pouring over the contents. His face reddened when he finally glanced up. "I didn't catch that. Maybe he blew it on dope or booze, possibly both. We could be looking at a drug deal gone bad."

Parker glared at the young man. *There he goes again, reading far too many detective novels.* "Follow the evidence, Brooks, and assume nothing. Listen and learn. You got that? And don't believe everything you're told. People lie all the time, sometimes without even realizing."

"Yes, sir." Brooks shook his head in earnest.

Parker glanced up and noticed a sharply-dressed tall man with graying temples approaching them. He recognized Bradford North's striking features.

"Excuse me," the man said. "Would either of you be Sergeant Parker?" He offered a hand that engulfed Brooks' palm as the rookie stood to greet him.

"I'm Detective Brooks, and this is Detective Sergeant Parker."

Parker noted the fine manicure, the thick gold Rolex and polished shoes. He signaled for Brooks to give them some privacy.

"You're Bradford North," Parker said, standing to shake the man's hand. His grip was firm and unflinching, indicating a confident, strong alpha-male used to barking orders rather than following them.

"Bradley," he corrected, pleased with the recognition. "I stopped by the morgue to make arrangements..." He cleared his throat. "I was informed you have not yet released the body."

"An autopsy is scheduled for this afternoon. Once the results are available, the coroner will release the body to the family. It shouldn't take more than a day or two."

"Hum," Bradley said, appearing to ponder his statement. "Will you notify me?"

"Of course," Parker said, inviting the gentleman to take a seat opposite his desk. "I've seen photos of your son. The resemblance is striking." He waited for the elder North to settle himself before retaking his own seat. "I am very sorry for your loss, sir."

Bradley rebuffed with a slight of the hand. "It is done. I cannot change the fact, nor can you. I thank you for your concern, detective." He glanced around the room before pulling his eyes back to Parker. "Which makes my request all the more difficult to ask, I am afraid." He leaned in, the scent of his earthy cologne drifting across the desk. "I must ask you to close the investigation into my son's death and allow my family to put this tragedy behind us."

"Excuse me?" *Had he heard right?* "You want me to do what?"

Bradley removed his glasses from the bridge of his slender nose and placed them on the desk with both hands. His rehearsed, calculated movements reminded Parker of an actor. Fatigue showed in the man's bloodshot eyes. "I know this may come as a surprise to you, Mr. Parker, but please try to understand my position. Our family is shaken by the news of Jason's death. It will be quite some time before we can get past this."

He rubbed his eyes and steepled long fingers under his chin. "Dwelling on circumstances that cannot be altered is useless and a waste of your time. We want to put this horrible misfortune behind us as quickly as possible."

Parker felt his chin tugging toward the floor, his lips quivering. "You know I can't do what you ask," he said, glaring. "Your son didn't die in some freak accident, sir. His attack was vicious and brutal, one of the worst beatings I've seen. Preliminary forensics suggests blunt-force trauma, but we'll need autopsy results to confirm cause of death. The person or persons responsible will be held accountable, rest assured."

Bradley shifted his weight uncomfortably. His eyes narrowed in defiance. Replacing his glasses, he said, "I know what you must think, Sergeant, but focusing on my son's indiscretions is not going to bring him back. Nothing can at this point." Bradley glanced at his feet before raising his eyes again. "I appreciate your efforts, honestly, but I am asking that you spare the boy's dignity and our family the process. Can you do that for me?"

Dignity? Parker felt the bile roil in his gut. Instinct caused him to reach for a cigarette instead of the man's throat. Unable to light up inside the building, he resorted to fingering the tobacco instead. "Tell me you're not bowing to public opinion."

"Is that what you think?" Bradley's tone sounded less assured. He hesitated a moment. "Perhaps I am at that," he said, wringing his large hands together so tightly Parker saw the whites of his knuckles. "I have spent years building an empire, sergeant. I have made and lost fortunes many times over. Wealth built on the foundation of solid principles and an honest, good name." The corners of his mouth curved downward as he spoke. "I cannot allow something like this to threaten all I have worked so hard to accomplish."

The truth for his irrational behavior: money and greed, Parker thought. "Something like this? You speak of your son's death as if you had a bad day in the stock market. He was your *son*, your flesh and *blood*." Parker shoved back into the worn vinyl of his chair. "Doesn't *that* mean anything to you?"

Bradley withdrew a handkerchief from the lapel of his jacket and dabbed his upper lip. "It did once," he said with a heavy sigh. Stuffing the linen away, he fixed on a spot beyond Parker's shoulder. "When Jason was born, I realized for the first time in my life the opportunity to be the parent my father never was. I had the means to give the boy anything he should ever want."

His eyes returned to Parker. "I worshiped my son, sergeant. He was a remarkable child: smart, strong, and very capable. I saw myself in him as he grew into a young boy." He blinked away the mist in his eyes. "I vowed the day of his birth to always be there for him, through skinned knees and scraped elbows. I had planned to attend his Little League games, parent/teacher conferences, each important day in the child's life. I ensured he had the best that money could buy: tailored clothes, inordinate gifts, the finest tutoring in the country. Money was no object, you see."

North clenched and opened his fists as the corners of his mouth quivered. "But, my wife became ill with ovarian cancer and passed away before Jason's thirteenth birthday. The boy appeared to change overnight. I guess he never got over the death of his mother. None of us did." North glanced at Parker with wet eyes. "Everything became different, his ambition and mood, even his temper. He lost interest in his studies, his friends, even his own welfare. He withdrew from me and the family and grew increasingly rebellious, becoming unreasonable to manage, you must understand."

"You speak of your son like he was a commodity, something you could control," Parker said.

"Hear me out." North said, his nostrils flaring in anger. "I enrolled him in the most reputable private schools in the country, convinced he would adjust to the death of his mother under the guise of a firm hand. The boy required an atmosphere of discipline and accountability. Work kept me on the road most of the time and away from my family, so his rearing had been left to his mother."

North cleared his throat. "In the beginning, I thought Jason was experiencing a troublesome phase, like most boys of that age, augmented of course by the loss of his mother. He became more troublesome as time passed, throwing tantrums, ignoring curfew, lying to me, getting completely out of control. Every parochial school expelled him, citing delinquency. No one could handle his outbursts, episodes that bordered the psychotic. He refused to take medicine to manage his mood swings. I eventually ran out of options."

Parker sat unfazed, listening quietly as Bradley continued. "I bought him a condominium for his twenty-first birthday, a place of his own. I thought perhaps providing him with the freedom he demanded without intrusion might steer him in the right direction. He lacked proper discipline and direction in his life, I am afraid. He needed to mature, grow up on his own. I thought by experiencing firsthand how difficult it can be to survive in the world today, as I did at his age, things would get better."

"Is that about the time you learned your son was gay?" Parker asked. Undeterred by North's hard stare, he added, "Is that when you tried everything to change Jason's sexuality?"

North's lips quivered as though he was fighting long buried emotions. "I offered to seek help for the boy. My son's refusal to accept counseling further alienated him from the family and drove a wedge between us. What else could I do? In the end, he made his choice."

Parker had heard this song and dance before, too often from frustrated parents who saw only blame in their children and not in their own failures. "Did you take the time to listen to your son, sir? I mean, really pay attention to what he was trying to get across. Did you ever once consider that all he wanted from you was to be accepted by his family?"

"I could never have accepted my son's perverse way, sergeant, if that is what you are suggesting? The lifestyle…it is an abomination against God." Bradley's face grew hard. He stood without warning, his body going rigid. "Men should not lie down in the same bed together. It is immoral. I am surprised you would ask…"

"I was only suggesting a little compassion. He was your

son." Parker's raised voice drew a few stares from colleagues in the room.

Bradley failed to mask his humiliation. "For what it's worth, I lost my son the day he confessed his *lifestyle*." He turned to leave, pausing to impart a final appeal. "Drop this investigation, Sergeant Parker. The boy is dead. Jason chose his path in life and suffered the consequences. It's out of our hands now."

"Before you go," Parker interjected, grabbing the man's elbow as he began to walk away. "I need to know where you were Thursday night, the last time anyone saw Jason alive."

Bradley's expression shot daggers. "Your insinuation is absurd."

"Not if you have nothing to hide, sir."

North's face turned red. "You'll hear from my attorneys, detective," he snapped before rushing from the room. "Count on it."

CHAPTER TWENTY-FOUR

Outside the door of the freshly painted clapboard house, Parker sighed. He had not been by in a while and felt odd standing here now, as if he was stranger about to intrude on the old woman inside. The small abode sat tucked away in obscurity among the larger, newer homes in a revitalized section of town off Highland Avenue. A crude wooden sign tacked above the door welcomed those in need. Spiritual words of hope painted inside large hands in prayer taunted him, as if daring him to enter. Kendall Parker's faith had been tested and all but abandoned in the weeks since the accident.

Michael Abbott. Parker's thought of the man responsible for his pessimism of late, the deceased nephew of the resident within. Not a day had passed where Parker didn't wish the accident never happened, or he hadn't suggested the outing in the first place. Perhaps things would be different. Perhaps not.

Whom was he kidding? Michael was dead and he wasn't coming back. Isn't that what Bradford North had said of his own son?

Steeling himself, he rapped on the door. A distant, cheery voice beckoned him to come inside and he entered the foyer and looked into the small rectangular room off to his right. The area contained two rows of mismatched chairs, a couple of threadbare sofas along the far wall and a floor scattered with toys. A framed print of Jesus hung on one wall, opposite numerous placards and public notices from various government agencies.

Fleshy arms seized him. "Kendall," a robust, silver-haired woman shrieked his name with joy. "What a pleasant surprise. Why didn't you call ahead? I could have picked up the place a little."

"How are you, Hattie?" Parker felt the warmth of her heaving bosom as he held her close. "Is this a good time for you?" He again was stricken by the family resemblance to Michael. "I can stop by later if you'd like."

"No, no, this is fine. Never better, never better," she said. "Question is, how are *you* doing, my dear?" They walked arm in arm through the hallway and past an anteroom filled with brooding women sitting in a semi-circle. A few frightened stares locked onto Parker as they passed by and headed toward the tiny office at the back of the house. Hattie closed the door behind them and moved a wicker chair in front of her cluttered desk.

"Come now," she said, beaming as she patted the worn cushion. "Please, sit down and tell this old woman what you've been up to." She lowered herself into the chair behind her desk after Parker sat down. "I've not seen you in quite some time," she said, a hint of reproof in her words.

"Ah come now, don't exaggerate." Parker felt ashamed for having avoided her company for so long. Following Michael's death, visiting her proved too emotionally draining for him, and he often made excuses to avoid her company. "It has been a while, hasn't it?"

"Far too long." The smile across Hattie's lips narrowed. "You appear deeply concerned, my dear. Please, tell me what could be troubling that beautiful soul of yours?"

Parker knew Hattie Strauber had more to think about than wasting time on him, especially keeping the doors open to the women's day shelter, yet she always had room in her heart for another in need. Parker lost his smile. "I'm still having those nightmares," he confessed, glancing at his feet. "I'd hoped they'd be gone by now, or at least lessen in intensity."

"Oh, you poor thing." Hattie's brows furrowed as she leaned forward with a grimace. "Have you sought counseling? You know, you must get help sorting through all those emotions. A professional, who sorts the facts from fiction and helps you get rid of the demons that are haunting you." She brushed fallen strands of hair from her face with a tired hand. Arthritis riddled her joints, though she had never complained a day in her life. "You have to stop carrying all that weight around, honey. It's not healthy."

"If speaking to the department's psychologist qualifies, then yes, I have," he said. "The session couldn't have been worse, like I was talking to a brick wall with a pen." Parker crushed out a cigarette and then thought better of lighting up, avoiding her probing eyes. "The therapist sat there emitting these little grunting noises. The whole experience was humiliating. I left more frustrated and confused than before the session began."

"Perhaps you would be more comfortable with a private therapist? I could recommend some good ones." She rose and shuffled to the coffee maker atop a file cabinet shoved against the wall. "Would you care for some coffee? I brewed a fresh pot."

"I could use some, yes." Parker moved to assist her.

Hattie smiled, concern etching the corners of her mouth. "No offense dear," she said, touching his arm, "but you need to detach yourself from any bureaucratic influence where your emotions are concerned. The two simply do not mix. Trust me on that, I should know."

Parker frowned. "I know I can't be open with someone who represents the department, but I had no choice in the matter. Boss's orders."

Hattie had experience with bureaucracy, since she used to be a resident psychologist with the Department of Corrections, Juvenile Division, for Fulton County. She had met, married, and divorced her husband during the course of her thirty-five-year career. After being attacked by one of her patients and held at knifepoint for thirteen hours before rescued by S.W.A.T, she had retired and devoted her life to running a shelter for neglected and battered women.

"You're right, you know," Parker conceded after a few moments of silence, accepting the mug she handed him. He retook his seat and smelled the cinnamon spice aroma of the coffee. "I am able to talk about the accident and what happened afterward, but not about my...my relationship with Michael."

"I assumed as much," Hattie said in motherly tone. "It's never been an easy subject for you, has it? Michael told me some of the challenges you two faced getting to know one another." She grinned and stirred sugar cubes into her coffee before returning to the old desk constructed of milk crates and topped with a painted sheet of plywood. "Admitting part of the problem cannot cure the whole, my dear. You must get everything out, confess your true feelings and cleanse the soul, so to speak."

Hattie offered an engaging smile. "You know," she said, "Michael never shared with me what brought the two of you together. All he said was you were once a physical therapy patient of his."

Kendall smiled. Hattie exuded a genteel, southerly charm that enticed a person to bare their soul. "I assumed he told you all about it," he said, leaning back and feeling more relaxed in the chair. "Five years ago, I was still a beat cop. My partner at the time and I were tipped to a wanted drug dealer hiding out in an abandoned house on the backside of the Carver Homes project. We had obtained a no-knock warrant and coordinated a raid to commence at dawn one morning along with another team." Parker cleared his throat and tugged at his collar. "We were ambushed by a gang of Puerto Rican youths when we stormed the residence, outgunned and outmanned in every way. During the melee that ensued, I caught a six-inch blade in my right thigh." He rubbed the old wound absently, the intermittent ache—especially when it rains—a reminder of the night he went down. "The jagged edge shredded tendons down to the bone."

Hattie gasped and raised her hand to her throat. "Oh my, Kendall. Michael told me he met you after being injured on the job, but he never shared the details of your horrifying ordeal."

"I'm fine, except for occasional phantom pain shooting through my leg. Surgery repaired most of the damage, but doctors said it might take years for the nerves to regrow, if they do at all. Michael helped me to walk again without a limp. Intense physical therapy enabled me to regain full use of my leg again." Kendall stifled a laugh as he recalled the earlier sessions. "I wasn't a nice patient. I wanted everyone around me as miserable as I felt, to suffer the same pain and depression as I did. Michael understood me right off the bat, had sensed that my wounds ran deeper than my thigh. It took his incredible patience and unique sense of humor to counter the anger I had built up inside."

"And to find your heart as well, I suspect," Hattie said.

Parker's cheeks flushed. "Lucky for me, Michael felt the same way."

Hattie agreed. "He loved you very much, Ken."

Parker stared across the desk. "I miss him, Hattie," he declared, clutching the mug. "Every morning I wake wishing his death was just a terrible dream and that he'd be in the kitchen preparing breakfast, like always. Sometimes, I come home at night half expecting to find him in my bed, waiting for me to return from some late-night stakeout or midnight crime scene."

He saw nothing but compassion in her eyes as he continued. "I have his jacket, the black leather one I gave him for his twenty-eighth birthday. It smells like him, a hint of his cologne in the lining. I can close my eyes and imagine he's right there beside me, you know?" He blinked away the tears. "And at that moment, I don't ever want to open my eyes again."

Hattie leaned forward to take his hands into her own. "Oh, honey."

"Do you miss him?"

"You have no idea how much," she sighed, blinking away the moisture rimming her eyes. "But I refuse to let his unfortunate death consume my life." She let go of his hands. "For me," she said, placing a hand over her chest, "He is alive in here, where I can visit him whenever I want, no matter the day or time."

Hattie grasped his hands, offering reassurance as only she could. "I raised him, you know? His parents died in a small plane crash when he was five. I enjoyed watching the boy grow into a fine young man. Those years of wonderful memories are what comforts me now, and eases my burden. The happiness we had shared together." Her eyes beamed. "My pride is having known him at all."

"It hurts so much," Parker said, smacking his chest with a fist. "Like having a knife thrust in me and twisted." He sat down his coffee and leaned forward on his arms. "In my night-mares, I am treading water—in a lake, I think—kicking and stroking, desperate to reach a figure out in the distance that I believe to be Michael. As I grab hold of his arm, his body breaks free of the debris holding him and sinks below the surface. I try to hang on to him, but I'm too weak and he slips away." He dropped his face into his hands to hide the tears. "I wake up to the sound of someone screaming and realize it's me."

"You must stop blaming yourself for Michael's death." Hattie rose to comfort him. "It's time to get on with your life, Kendall Parker. Start anew."

He looked at her as though she spoke a foreign language.

"Harboring those painful emotions is not healthy," she said. "I'm no psychic, but I've witnessed enough to know that your nightmares will remain until you're ready to face your inner demons. Or you'll forever live with guilt."

Kendall knew she spoke the truth, but he seemed unable or unwilling to echo her sentiments. "I'm tired, Hattie," he said after a long silence. "Tired of the stress, the pressure I'm under, the secrecy that is my life—all of it including my job. It's over-whelming." He ignored her probing eyes, the same vibrant blue she shared with her nephew. "I wonder sometimes if I'm not chasing a dream that no longer exists for me. My life changed the day Michael died. I don't feel as confident and strong as I once did."

"Nonsense." Hattie smirked. She waved a hand through the air as if rebuking his confession. "Are you considering leaving your job?"

"Should I?" Parker searched her eyes for an answer, but Hattie offered him nothing.

"The choice is yours, my dear, not mine to make." Hattie returned to her seat. "Tell me, Kendall, what has brought this on? You have always been proud of the shield and your career accomplishments, Michael told me as much. You're an excellent detective, soon to be promoted, I expect. Have you really given this much thought?"

"It's *all* I've been thinking about, Hattie. That and my latest case. Maybe what I want more is freedom. I'm tired of using roommate or best friend as a euphemism for Michael. It's not fair to his memory. He deserves more than that."

"Your silence didn't seem to bother you before Michael's death. Why should it matter now?"

Parker stood and paced the room, feeling like one of her intakes. "Losing Michael has had an enormous impact on my life for reasons I don't yet comprehend. I'm feeling claustrophobic and trapped. I've been hiding behind this shadow of who I am *supposed* to be for so long that I'm no longer sure of who I *am*. Along the way, I lost my identity. Part of me wants to stop this ridiculous charade, step off the merry-go-round and quit maintaining a second bedroom for appearance's sake. I'm tired of worrying about what other people think."

"So, stop trying to live your life for other people," Hattie said with vigor. "Be true to yourself, Kendall. All else will fall into place, you'll see."

Parker sat across from her again, admiring the strength she possessed. "I'm not sure I could handle such a drastic change." He massaged his temples. "What if it's the wrong decision?"

"Wrong for whom? It's your life, my dear. God entrusted us with but one. Be honest with yourself." Hattie reached across and touched his knuckles with the tips of her fingers. "How can you expect others to accept who you are if you can't accept yourself?" She smiled radiantly, reminding him of Michael. "I've

been around long enough to know that life is a series of adjust-
ments. We endure the circumstances of our choices, good and
bad. The manner in which you choose to live is no one's business but your own."

Parker felt vulnerable but somewhat comforted. "Thank
you, Hattie," he said, smiling. "You can't know how much your
friendship means to me."

"Oh, but I do," she said, rising to walk along with him to
the front door. The dimples in her crimson cheeks made her
look years younger. "The eyes never lie, my dear," she whispered
as she pecked his check. "You remember that."

"Michael was lucky to have had you in his life," he said,
withdrawing from her embrace. He blurted out his words. "I
never knew my father. He was some trucker passing through
town, a one-night stand, fulfilling my mother's lust for bad men
and hard liquor. She was an alcoholic with an unwanted child,
but she loved me in her own way. I had to learn early on how to
take care of myself." He turned at the front door, took her hands
and smiled.

Hattie pulled him into her embrace again. She no doubt
had heard the same sad tale a thousand times from women who
passed through the shelter, many of them no more than children
themselves.

Parker pulled back. "My senior year in high school, my
mother died of liver cancer. After graduation, I enlisted in the
army and headed to the Gulf. I returned four years later without
a purpose to a homeland that didn't seem to care."

"You've had a rough time of it." Hattie squeezed his hands
and smiled back at him.

Parker nodded. "I married my high school sweetheart out of
fear someone would discover what I'd yet to accept myself. Thirteen months later, pregnant and not a dime to her name, my
wife up and left. She went to live with her mother out west.
Funny, aint it? I have a son I've never met, who doesn't even
know I exist. He'd be twelve about now."

Hattie seemed at a loss for words as she patted him on the

arm. "I know that he'd be very proud of you, Kendall, very proud indeed."

Parker feigned a smile, wishing like hell he felt as confident. Michael had understood him like no other, more than anyone had before or since. He couldn't explain it really. The man had released feelings in him that he'd suppressed for years, their time together thrilling and exceptional. He muttered with a sigh. "Michael was patient and caring. Something I've never been used to."

"He loved you very much," Hattie said, reaching up to touch his cheek. "Don't you ever forget that dear."

"Never," he said, tears pressing forward again. "Last year Michael suggested that I contact Sheryl, my ex-wife, and ask to see my boy. Her mother said Sheryl had remarried and moved to Montana. That cruel woman refused to tell me how to get in touch with them. How could I blame her? Sheryl had figured out my secret and was determined to shield her child from a queer father."

Hattie blinked back tears as he turned to leave. "All my life, I swore I'd not turn out like my father. Ironic that I've turned out just like him...a deserter. My son thinks I abandoned him, same as my father had abandoned me. I know I could find the kid, but I'm not sure I could survive the shame in his eyes."

Parker opened the door. The memories of Michael raged stronger than ever: the good and the bad, the laughter, and the tears. The love they had shared with one another and the unbearable heartache of his loss.

Nobody should know this kind of pain, he thought, before turning his collar up and walked away from the shelter.

CHAPTER TWENTY-FIVE

Parker returned to his desk as Detective Brooks jumped up from his seat and came over. "There you are. I tried your cell a few times, but kept getting voicemail."

"Yeah, I had an errand to run." Parker fished his phone from his jacket pocket before he took it off and hung it up. He spotted three missed calls, all from Brooks. "Sorry, about that. I must have silenced my phone by accident. What's up?"

Brooks handed an inch-thick folder to Parker. "We have a potential assailant in Perelli's attack," he said as Parker flipped through the pages. "Suspect's name is Dane Allan O'Connor, known on the street as 'Hopper', a real loser. Witness statements and confirmation from the Metroplex's manager led me to him." He pointed to a mug shot taken six months prior. "I pulled what I could without getting a court order. Kid's a juvie."

Parker glanced up. "Good work, Brooks," he said, skimming through the arrest reports detailing O'Connor's history with law enforcement.

"There's more," Brooks said, handing over a copy of a police report. "Seems O'Connor was busy last night. It appears he may have been responsible for robbing an Emory University oncology intern before giving you and Perelli the slip."

Parker's attention piqued. "Would explain the reason he was spooked when he made us."

"The wife brought her husband in to emergency complaining of chest pains. Turns out the doctor suffered a punctured lung and some cracked ribs. Claimed he was mugged at an automatic teller at the corner of Cheshire Bridge and Lindberg. Cops taking the report linked the description of the assailant to our suspect and alerted dispatch."

"Get that mug shot out," Parker said as he reached for his jacket.

"Already done," Brooks replied, grinning like a child far too happy for his own good.

"Good, because we're running late for an autopsy."

The prosector, the person performing the autopsy and preparing the written report, a tall thin man with long fingers and aged hands appeared perturbed by the time Parker and Brooks entered the medical examiner's room. Dr. J. Halverson had dressed head to toe in protective equipment: scrub suit, gown, double gloves, shoe covers, and a clear face mask. Tufts of wiry hair graying at the edges poked around the sides of the shield. He skipped formal pleasantries and instructed his pathology assistant, Jose, to remove the body from the cooler and place it on the autopsy table. Jose wheeled a sheeted cadaver over and single-handedly transferred the body from the gurney to the dissecting table with a combination of pulls and shoves. Halverson stripped away the linen and tossed it into a nearby hamper.

Brooks appeared anxious, staring down at the naked body of Jason North. Parker had wanted him to experience his first autopsy. Perelli usually stood at his side, making sick jokes with each slice of the scalpel. They watched as Jose measured the pale, bluish and bruised corpse from head to toe, calling out numbers to Halverson, who filled in the information on a document. Parker tried not to look at the disfigured face—which did not resemble a face at all—choosing instead to stare at the intricate detail of the scorpion tattoo riding the body's left shin.

The waist-high, stainless steel dissecting table was tilted slightly to allow easy access for the pathologist. It had raised edges and was loaded with faucets and spigots to wash away blood and other bodily fluids released during the procedure. Meat scales used to weigh the organs were in close proximity, as was a small, portable blackboard to mark down the weights of each dissected organ.

Brooks' eyes grew large as Jose placed a "body block" under the remains. The rubber brick-like appliance abruptly thrust the chest of the cadaver upward, giving maximum exposure to the trunk for the incisions. Halverson verified that the name on the toe-tag matched the autopsy permit and began describing abnormalities of the external body. He moved effortlessly around the table, a skilled surgeon lifting limbs and portions of the body for inspection. A voice-activated recorder chronicled his findings: scores of abrasions, contusions and blows to the chest, arms, shoulders, pelvis and face. No doubt the victim had suffered a violent attack.

Brooks turned powder-white the moment Halverson used a scalpel to carve a giant Y-shaped cut in the trunk of the body. Incision complete, he pulled skin, muscle, ligaments, tendons, and soft tissues off the chest wall. Jose pulled the chest flap upward and over the cadaver's face, revealing the front of the rib cage and the strap muscles in front of the neck. Parker had attended enough autopsies to see the damage done to the neck and chest. Halverson confirmed Parker's suspicions and pointed out the crushed larynx.

Parker drew in a deep breath and stared forward, but not seeing the autopsy before him. He imagined the horror of the malicious attack, what the victim felt the moment of imminent doom. He glanced over at Brooks, who seemed on the verge of vomiting, but Parker knew the guy wouldn't. All rookies needed to prove themselves one time or another and Brooks wasn't about to give his buddies the satisfaction of knowing he blew chunks at his first autopsy. The jibes and joking would continue for months to come. Brooks stood stoic and would swallow bile if he had to in order to save face with his comrades.

Halverson made a cut above the cadaver's crushed larynx, detaching it and the esophagus from the pharynx. The assistant pulled downward on the larynx and trachea and used the razor-sharp scalpel to free up the remainder of the chest organs from their attachment to the spine. After the diaphragm was sliced away from the body wall, the abdominal organs were pulled out and down. The organs remained attached to the body by the pelvic ligaments, bladder and rectum. With a swift slash, Jose removed the organ bloc and handed it to Halverson, who then placed the stomach-turning mass on the dissecting table for later inspection.

Poor guy reduced to this, Parker thought.

Jose removed the body block from under the cadaver's back and placed it beneath the rear of the head. For the next hour and a half, Parker and the rookie watched as the two men dissected the body with skilled precision, removing and studying the brain, and slicing up the organs for further examination before replacing the chest plate. They sewed the body up with baseball stitches so that the sealed incision would once again resemble a giant "Y".

Halverson's official report wouldn't be available for thirty days, but Parker had what he needed. He'd written down enough information called out by the pathologist throughout the procedure to know the victim had suffered broken ribs, foot, and pelvis, a fractured skull, crushed fingers and neck bones, and had deep cuts across the throat and jaw.

The damage to Jason North's liver was severe enough to cause internal hemorrhaging, which had filled the abdomen with as much as three hundred and ten cubic centimeters of blood, the equivalent of a twelve-ounce soda can. The most serious and lethal injury was the blow his body had suffered which resulted in his liver being cut in half.

CHAPTER TWENTY-SIX

Calvin Slade had wasted the day snagging new bits of information related to the Piedmont Park murder, and his efforts produced little more than filler for the newspaper's online website. At midday, he had filed an update that police were seeking a person of interest in the murder of Jason North, but he stopped short of calling the man a suspect. Slade followed up in the afternoon informing the public of the decision by the North family to hold a private memorial later in the week and asked everyone to respect their privacy during such a difficult time.

In order to pitch his managing editor to a possible Councilman Mitchell Keyes connection, Slade knew he needed more than a hunch or risk exposing the newspaper to pressure from the city, not to mention threats of a lawsuit. Without new information coming forth, the story faced death in a day, two at max. Did he really need to invest more of his time?

He had asked himself that question a lot in the last few hours, but something about the park killing kept nibbling at him, taunting his brain with thoughts just out of his reach. Slade contemplated the mystery caller from the other night, the sound of the young man's voice, the fear lacing his words.

"There's more to the story. He didn't leave the party alone."

Didn't leave the party alone. Slade tapped his pen against the keyboard of the laptop. No doubt the caller spoke of Mitchell Keyes, but he needed to link the anonymous caller to the victim in the park, get proof of an association between North and the council member, and then he would have one hell of a story.

If only it were that simple. Getting such proof would prove difficult since Councilman Keyes was very popular among his constituents. Any effort to tarnish the man's reputation would be met with fierce resistance. In Slade's view, Keyes had been arrested recently of suspected DUI, which could provide the window of opportunity the seasoned reporter could not ignore.

Parker and Brooks stood on a wide brick porch waiting for an answer at the front door. The 1930's style bungalow sat close to Park Drive, a street lined with poplars and oaks west of Monroe Drive in the Morningside community. The narrow lane, lined with cars on either side, ended at the southeastern entrance to Piedmont Park, an area frequented late at night by druggies and men looking for anonymous sex.

Minutes after their knock, the door creaked open. The action seemed to sap the tiny woman's strength. "Yes?" She stepped forward in a haze of bewilderment beneath a mess of gray hair, searching their faces for some familiarity.

"Excuse us, ma'am," Parker said, glancing at Brooks for assurance they had the right address. "Detectives Kendall Parker and Timothy Brooks, Atlanta Police, Homicide division. Do you have a tenant by the name of Johnny Cage living here?"

The woman stared at their identification and appeared dazed, as though rustled from a deep sleep. The name seemed to register, and she offered up a thin smile and her features relaxed. "Why yes, yes there is. Helps me around the house with the yard and other errands. He's a nice boy, you know?" Anxiety pressed forth and gripped the deep lines in her forehead. "Is he in some kind of trouble?"

"No ma'am," Brooks said. "We just want a word with him, if we may."

"Of course." The woman angled her small frame between the men and door and glanced back into her home before facing them with a smile. "He is not here right now, but I'll tell him you called." She moved to close the door. "Run along now, young men. Good day."

Parker stuck his foot inside the jamb to keep the door from closing. "Do you mind if we take a look at his room just to be sure?" He was inside before the woman could offer much protest. An expression flashed across her face that gave little doubt she'd refuse.

"Well, I-I guess so," she said, clasping the top button of her housecoat. "He stays in the basement apartment, pays his rent on time. He's no trouble at all, officers." Her tone turned sharp. "What's this all about?" She stepped aside to let them through.

Parker, followed by Brooks, rushed forward in the direction of her gaze toward a small wooden door at the end of the hall-way. A staircase descended to the basement below, and Parker hit the light switch on the wall. Both men ducked to avoid the water-stained, low-hanging ceiling as they entered Cage's quarters.

The basement door appeared locked, not dead bolted or chained. Parker surmised Cage used the door to come and go as he pleased. He and Brooks stepped through the door to an algae-covered brick patio furnished with a couple metal webbed chairs and oval wicker table with glass top, the type found at most box discount stores. An ashtray on the table swelled with cigarette butts and rainwater.

Brooks leaned over for a closer look at the ashtray. "The same brand of cigarette found in the deceased's coat pocket," he said.

"Maybe they were more than just friends." Parker looked around the area and saw fresh shoe marks embedded in the soft soil leading out from the patio. The tread appeared familiar, but he couldn't place it at the moment. "Put a car down the street. If Cage shows up, I want to know about it."

. . .

From a spot across the street and about a block away, the young man watched as the two men presented identification and entered the tiny house on Park Drive. The strangers emerged several minutes, the taller of the two walking out to speak to a female police officer who arrived moments earlier. The cop put her vehicle in reverse, backed into a spot down the road and killed the engine, no doubt to keep the house under surveillance, waiting for his return.

The home was no longer a safe haven; police had made a connection somehow, but he was not worried. His plan to put distance between himself and those looking for him was already in motion. Turning away he walked along the bulking sidewalk for a few blocks before the road dead-ended to Piedmont Park, passing the metallic pole preventing vehicles from crossing the narrow, ancient bridge overlooking the dog park to his right, and a wide, snaking, drainage basin on the left. Lighting a cigarette as he strode across the bridge, he cut left and headed into the belly of the green space.

He cut through the park in quickstep, then trudged up the slope of Oak Hill, before emerging onto 10th street where he walked along the sidewalk. Crossing the intersection at Piedmont Avenue, he hurried the couple of blocks to Midtown station. Using his *Breeze* card at the turnstiles, he descended an escalator to the landing and waited. Minutes later, a train pulled into the station with a rush of wind and screech of airbrakes. He hopped aboard and rode to the end of the line at Hartsfield-Jackson International Airport. Determined and growing more confident, he entered the airport terminal near baggage claim in the South Terminal, following the wide, hospital-slick corridor toward the security portals.

"ID, boarding pass?" the TSA agent asked. She sat perched on a stool, scowled and scanned his information. "Johnny Cage." Leaning forward, she dropped her chin and peered at him over her readers. "You look mighty different, son. You been buzzed?"

He flashed his best smile. "Yes, ma'am," he said in a fine southern drawl. "Enlisted in the army just last week. Headed to Texas for bootcamp, ma'am."

A big grin spread her pink lips that reached her eyes glowed. "Praise the Lord," she said, handing him his documents. "You a good boy, son. Ya'll be safe out there, hear? God be with ya, child."

Clearing the screening area without incident, he rode the steep steel-tooth escalators to the pedestrian corridor beneath the terminal and boarded a tram. He exited in the bowels of Concourse B, took yet another escalator up a forty-second ride to the terminal. Heading to his right, he strolled through the crowded passageway and passed a multitude of overpriced fast food restaurants and haberdashery shops, stopping a time or two to ensure no one was following him.

Midway into the concourse, he stepped into a small alcove crammed with double-stacked, built-in footlockers, and opened a top locker with his key. He rummaged through a black leather duffel bag filled with worn, crinkled fives, tens, and twenties—no greater denominations as larger bills might draw unwanted attention. The boy stuffed his pockets, then inserted payment to pay for another week's rent before shoving the bag back into the locker.

Retracing his steps, he hopped a tramcar in the opposite direction and rode back to the terminal. Taking the escalators to the main terminal, he skirted past car rental counters packed deep with impatient business types and confused tourists, and emerged once again near baggage claim. He headed in the opposite direction from which he came through a marble corridor before reaching the airline ticket counters. He purchased roundtrip tickets to New York, Chicago, Dallas, and San Francisco, each at different ticket counters, all in the name matching the identification he carried. He hoped the exhaustive exercise would slow down anyone still tracking him, throw them off long enough for him to complete his mission.

No one at the counters noticed the wads of cash stuffed in his faded jeans. None questioned why his hair appeared different than captured on the Georgia driver's license. No one seemed to care, and that suited him just fine.

CHAPTER TWENTY-SEVEN

Reporter Calvin Slade knew how to turn on the charm to suit a greater purpose when needed, especially in a room full of tightly clad, mostly young men milling throughout the lounge. He'd spent the last two hours perched on a stool fronting the main bar at Metroplex, engaged in clipped conversation with a few patrons and the bartender, occasionally scrutinizing the dancers. Each dancer stuck to his appointed spot for twenty minutes before changing location. In the expansive lounge area, he counted upwards of twenty go-go boys displaying their sculpted torsos atop raised mirrored cubes; others were surrounded by admirers in the anterooms flanking the circular walls. The oldest looked to be in well his late twenties, the youngest just about legal age. In his mid-thirties, Slade blended in with the clientele.

Slade caught the attention of one of the entertainers who slipped on a pair skintight Euro Briefs once he stepped off the stool. The youth sidled up to the bar, brushed up against Slade and suggested they retreat to a secluded spot for privacy. Slade paid the tab, slugged the last of his beer and followed the boy through a sea of bodies and up the grand stairs to the mezzanine level. Slade handed the valet twenty-five dollars cash for the use of one of the twelve private lounges, and shelled out another seventy-five bucks for a bottle of cheap champagne.

Once seated inside the dark, red velvet lined room with twin half-moon sofas, video monitor and circular glass-topped cocktail table, Chad the dancer said, "Sit back, relax and enjoy the show."

The young man placed himself mere inches from Slade, then began a series of slow erotic moves intended to entice the reporter into withdrawing more cash from his wallet. Circulating his smooth hips clockwise in time with the beat of the deafening beat, Chad never took his eyes off the reporter, Slade enjoyed the grandstanding, a perfectly choreographed dance right up until Chad removed his swimsuit to flaunt a bright green, impossibly thin thong.

Slade held up a folded, crisp fifty-dollar bill between two fingers. "How long have you been dancing here?" he asked.

Chad bent to accept the cash between crooked teeth, an amazingly flexible act in confined space. He pulled the bill from his mouth, ran the tip of his tongue across plump lips. "About eight months, give or take."

"Did you know Jason North?"

The boy flinched but regained his composure quickly. He palmed the money. "And if I did?" he asked, the easy tone matching the swaying of his body.

"You'd be able to help me out by answering a few questions." Slade offered a smile and reeled the twink in with even more cash. "That is, if you wouldn't mind."

The youth remained cool, withdrawing the bill slowly from Slade's fingers, the greenback disappearing as quickly as the first, Chad scrutinizing from arms-length before saying, "You wouldn't be a cop, would you?"

"Do I look like a cop?"

The boy frowned.

"No, I'm no cop," Slade said, "just a reporter looking into the young man's death. Maybe you could provide background information to help me out, you know, like who Jason hung out with, what kind of action he was into, that sort of thing." The reporter leaned forward with a grin sure to entice the young performer. "I could even mention your name in the newspaper if you'd like."

"I didn't know him that good," Chad purred, intrigue sparkling his liquid, brown eyes. "There are lots of dancers working here. It's hard to get to know everybody."

Slade studied the boy's ample crotch and glanced up at smiling eyes leering down at him. "What *can* you tell me about him then?"

Sensing renewed interest in what he no doubt was well-paid to offer, Chad inched closer, continuing to play the game. "Jason was real popular with the customers, but a jerk to the rest of us dancers. Health freak, too intense, worked out his body all the time. Uptight attitude, thought he was *it!* Claimed to be the *real deal*, man," Chad mocked. "Whatever."

"Did he have any friends here?" Slade let his eyes roam along the soft contours of the young man's hips.

"Just one that I know of, a dude named Johnny Cage. Come to think of it, I ain't seen him since I covered his shift last week."

"When was that?" Slade asked, taking in the taut body perched mere inches before him.

Chad cocked his head and stared up at the ceiling, as though searching for the answer in the dark tiles. "Thursday night, I think. Yeah, that's right, 'bout midnight or thereafter. Johnny said he got a call and needed to leave for an hour. My shift was over, so he asked me if I could cover for him until he got back. I hadn't lined up a date, if you know what I mean, and needed the cash," Chad said. "Like I said, he never came back to the bar, so I covered the rest of his shift."

Slade nodded and traced his index finger along the lines of the dancer's stomach. "Any idea what the call was about? Did Johnny mention who the call was from?"

"No, he didn't say anything other than it was urgent," Chad said, easing closer, encouraging the reporter to enjoy his body. "Wasn't my business to ask, so I forgot about it, you know? You learn to keep your mouth shut about what goes on around here."

"What else can you tell me about Jason North?" Slade produced another crisp bill for the taking.

Chad ran a forefinger along the seam of the tiny garment strapped well below his navel, a tease suggesting where he wanted the new bill deposited. "Everyone knew that Jason was Anthony's boy toy, that is, until a couple weeks ago. A bad falling out if you believe the whispers around this place. Word is some ugly shit went down. Didn't last long though. A dude named Matt took Jason's place in Anthony's bed. He dances here, too."

Slade slipped the cash into the pouch of the dancer's garment. "Was Jason in any danger? Do you know why someone would want to kill him?"

"How should I know?" Chad grunted, grinding his hips closer. "He probably fucked somebody over and paid the ultimate price, you know? Got what he deserved as far as I'm concerned."

"Is that how most feel around here?"

"You know how these queens are. Everyone's got his own fucking version of things, but nobody knows for sure. Most figure Jason was popped by a fucking john, man. Happens all the time in this line of work, you know," he said, indifferent. "He should have been more careful is all I can say."

Chad hiked a leg up on Slade's knee. It seemed unnatural how the boy managed to maintain perfect balance without even breaking a sweat. "Do you know about the guy who had caused the ruckus in here last night? Young and skinny, pretty blond boy."

"Hopper? Hell, everybody knows the dude. He's a real shit, and a thief, too. He worked here until last month. Bad news, man. Anthony fired his ass 'cause he's tainted."

"Tainted?"

"The *gift*, man. AIDS. Anthony tossed Hopper's ass out before it could run off any of the clientele. Should have done it sooner, if you asked me. Bad for business, you know?"

"Know where I might find this Hopper?"

"Ask the cops. I hear they're looking for him, too." Chad

relaxed his tough, street-wise stance. "Look man, I don't know. He hangs out on the street. Don't have a place to call home. Last I heard he was hustling up at the Male Room on Monroe. Try there. You just might get lucky."

"Yeah, I know the place." Slade smiled, producing a final twenty-dollar bill. He slipped the cash beneath the linen holding the boy's balls. "Thanks for the help, dude."

"Don't mention it," Chad said, surprise across his face when Slade rose and exited the room.

In a hidden room not much larger than a broom closet, recessed within the mahogany paneled walls of the owner's office, two men scrutinized images on the color monitor, listening carefully to the voices through headphones covering their ears. The screen embedded in the wall was linked to a dozen or so surveillance cameras throughout the Metroplex. The security was necessary to ensure profitability in a place where enough cash changed hands each week to finance a small army. The men watched as the reporter offered his final bill to the young dancer.

Anthony had had enough. He ripped the earphones off and threw them against the monitors. Leaning back in his rolling chair, the owner fired up a fat Cuban cigar and stared long and hard at the man he knew only by reputation. Anthony sneered at the reporter's gall and lack of respect. Calvin Slade needed to be warned of the consequences of meddling in other people's business.

Anthony and Stewart discussed exactly what form that warning might take for several minutes before Stewart charged from the room to inform the dancer his services were no longer needed.

CHAPTER TWENTY-EIGHT

Vincent Perelli returned to work Friday morning amid the fanfare usually reserved for the returning wounded. Trusted colleagues, career brethren, longtime friends, associates, and most of the office staff rallied around to welcome the veteran police detective back in the ranks as the Homicide Unit congregated for morning roll call. Investigators huddled among desks or straddled turned chairs and faced the lieutenant.

Deputy Chief William L. Hornsby ignored heckles and jabs as he chalked the morning's agenda on the blackboard. Flanking both sides of the chalkboard were corkboards jammed with departmental memos and communiqués, GBI and FBI wanted flyers, missing and exploited children photos, drug-screening schedules, and an occasional cartoon. The newest addition depicted a stressed out feline, back facing, hair standing on end with head swiveled around. Its caption read: *"I have PMS and a loaded handgun...Any questions?"*

The caricature echoed Kendall Parker's mood as he breezed through the room and took a seat directly behind his partner. He felt guilty not having visited Perelli over the last few days, regretful he'd not checked to see how he was getting along. Right now, he wished he had at least made the effort.

Hornsby briefed all in attendance on recent cases, reminded everyone to review the "Most Wanted" fugitives' board before hitting the streets and welcomed two new investigators to the squad. The desk sergeant closed with the usual housekeeping items, an abundance of mundane issues and a rousing welcome back to Detective Perelli. Formalities over, everyone scattered.

Parker followed Perelli to their desks. He wanted to say something encouraging, enlightening, inspiring even, *anything,* but he remained silent despite feeling such great need. Eventually, Parker chose to break the ice. *Nothing ventured, nothing gained.*

"So," Parker said, moving papers about his desk, "how are you feeling?"

Perelli glanced up and offered a half-hearted smile. "Never better, thanks for asking." He turned to his computer and typed with two forefingers.

Perelli seemed altered somehow, the graying of his temples far more pronounced, bushier than Parker remembered. The lines in the man's forehead creased deeper than before, criss-crossing aged, leathered skin. He appeared drawn and unyielding, his mouth a mask of scorn. Eyes once filled with energy, now appeared lifeless and distant. His thick body slumped in the chair and lacked his usual prideful Italian bearing.

"Glad to have you back," Parker said, turning to their latest case. "I have a file that will interest you." Perelli stared ahead as Parker tossed a thick manila folder across the desk, its bulk landing with a thud. Perelli picked it up and thumbed through it.

"The criminal who attacked you is suspected to be Dane O'Connor, a repeat offender and a menace to the system. No clue if he's connected to the North case, but thought we'd track him down all the same." He glanced over. "I figured you would want to anyway."

Perelli perked up. "Damn straight," he said. "A juvie? You gotta be kidding me? Who the hell let him in the club? Shouldn't we be boarding up the fuckin' place?"

"Not our concern," Parker said. "Let's not go off half-cocked and spook Galloti any more than we have. My gut tells me he knows more than he's letting on."

"The guilty always do," Perelli said, before tossing the file on the desk. His phone buzzed, and he yanked up the receiver. "Perelli!" His bark echoed through the office as he snatched a pencil from the caddy in front of him. "What? Where? And you're sure about that? Give me that address again. Myrtle Street, okay, got it. No, no, don't touch anything. CSU on the way? Okay, we're rolling."

Parker secured his gun and slipped it into his jacket by the time Perelli replaced the receiver.

"Let's go to work," Perelli said. "DB found in a house on Adair Avenue. Pansy-ass uniforms won't go inside 'cause it stinks worse than a septic tank. ME will meet us there."

"We'll call Brooks from the car to join us," Parker said, as they headed for the stairs.

The rotting, two-story house sat back from Adair Avenue approximately twenty-five feet, bordered by waist-high rusted fencing and giant hardwoods. Much of the lot had lost a battle with the encroachment of bottle-green ivy, which threatened the left side of the faded dwelling. A rainbow flag fluttered from one side of the porch.

Kendall Parker caught the reek of decaying flesh as he and Perelli passed through the rickety gate opening to the front walkway of the house. Parker noticed neighbors huddled on the sidewalk across the street, most covering their noses.

A team of three from the coroner's office hailed Parker from the front porch and complained about the delay the first responders had caused in refusing to remove personal items from the cadaver. Parker chastised the first officers on the scene for ignoring basic protocol just as Brooks came charging up.

Parker and Perelli entered the musty residence and brushed past the busted padlock on the front door. Brooks brought up the rear as the men mounted the stairs to the upper level. The reek from the bedroom near the back of the house proved worse than expected. They covered their noses and shuffled into the small room. At the foot of the undisturbed bed was a mound of naked flesh and bone.

The odor made Parker nauseous as he walked around the room, looking for anything to mark the death as suspicious. Brooks and Perelli stood off to the side, fighting to breathe in the acrid air. A team from the coroner's office dressed in white jumpsuits entered to begin their assessment, undaunted by the gore and stench of the remains.

"Who's gonna do us the honor?" asked a short, stocky female examiner, snapping on latex gloves and slipping a pair of protective glasses over her big brown eyes.

"I have my gloves, sergeant." Brooks stepped forward.

Parker grinned and raised his chin at Perelli. They stepped back to allow the rookie plenty of room. Snapping gloves over his large hands, Brooks crouched beside the corpse, which lay face down on the hardwood floor. The examiner lifted an emaciated wrist to allow Brooks to remove a watch from the cadaver. The metal left an imprint in the glob and shreds of tissue clung to the band. Brooks tossed the article into a plastic bag.

Brooks reached out to remove a gold chain from around the neck of the body. Releasing the clasp and peeling the jewelry away from the flesh. Parker noticed the rookie grow pale as he slipped one of two rings from the gaunt hand and tossed it into an evidence bag before struggling to free the remaining silver insignia. Brooks wrapped his fingers around the wrist of the deceased's arm, locked the tips of his fingers with the other hand on the ring and tugged.

To the rookie's astonishment, the ring, fleshy goo slipped off the middle finger to expose the white bone beneath. Brooks reeled backward, the glob sailing through the air. Everyone stepped clear to avoid contact with the flesh. Brooks scrambled to his feet and bolted from the room, where he vomited in the hallway.

Most everyone in the room burst into laughter with Perelli

latching onto Parker for support. Unfazed, the lead examiner sneered at the group, scooped up the soft tissue with a plastic putty knife and tossed it into the containment bag. The examining team regained their composure and huddled to probe, measure, mark, and label evidence, spraying a chalky white outline around the corpse.

"How long has the stiff been like this?" Parker looked into the hooded eyes of the team's senior member.

The burly man with hairy arms lined with tattoos fingered his thick mustache. "About a week I'd guess, a day or two more at the most."

"Cause of death?"

"No clue. It'll take us time to process the body." The man removed the rubber gloves and called over a homicide photographer. "One thing I do know is your DB must have a puncture or wound for the body to be in this condition."

"How do you mean?" Parker asked.

"Decomposition starts, right? The body emits gases that cause it to bloat and expand to the full stretch of the skin, sort of like an inflated balloon. Without a way to vent the expansion, such as through some break in the skin or tear of some kind, the mass would explode under the pressure in conditions like this. Not the case here, as you can see," he added.

"So, it's homicide," Parker declared.

"I didn't say that, detective," the examiner snapped. "That's a strong possibility, but that's all it is. I detect no evidence to support such a theory. I can't know more until we get the body back to the lab and autopsied."

Perelli came over to them. "Take a look at this," he said, flashing a laminated identification badge at them. "Found this on the dresser. Lamar M. Crater. Fuckin' stiff worked at City Hall."

"*Jesus.*" Parker winced as a shot of pain surged through his leg. He massaged the tightening muscles to relieve a cramp. *Damn injury.* "I'll alert the Lieutenant."

A gasp from the huddle working behind them drew their attention. They turned to see the body now flipped over on its back, covered in a mound of maggots. The victim's underwear had been stuffed in his mouth.

"Looks like a homicide to me." Parker slipped on his dark shades before walking out of the room to get better cell reception.

CHAPTER TWENTY-NINE

Friday afternoon under a clear blue sky, Calvin Slade watched a dozen demonstrators gather on the marble steps of City Hall. Some carried placards proclaiming *Gay & Lesbian Equality*, *Stop the Violence*, and *Hate=Death*, among many others. They came with yards of rainbow flags, demanding their voices be heard.

Two gay men found dead in one week had the demonstrators seeking answers. Slade sensed the energy around him and realized he could take his series of articles in another direction. He blended easily in the crowd wearing faded blue jeans, a T-shirt, and a well-worn Braves baseball cap frayed at the bill.

One by one, gay and lesbian advocates commanded the top step, wailing to the crowd through a bullhorn to demand equal protection under the law and freedom from injustices hurled their way. The activists called on prominent liberal and conservative city leaders to condemn the recent attacks on gays in Midtown. They challenged the radical right to cast aside its indignation and join them in support. The crowd cheered, jeered, sang, chanted, and cried. Raised their hands to proclaim solidarity and to rise above the bigotry and hate, and vowed to keep up the pressure and not back down.

Slade scanned the throng and moved to the periphery as a couple of competing news vans arrived and raised their anten-

nae. They aimed cameras toward the crowd, further fueling the
energy of those who spoke. The crowd soon doubled in size and
spilled into the street, stalling traffic in the narrow boulevard.
Horns blared and angry slurs competed with the cries from the
assembly. A battered pickup rolled by trailing twin Confederate
flags.

Mayor Ellis emerged with his entourage from the double
brass doors, flanked by uniformed guards. He greeted his
constituents with a wide smile on his round, cherubic face as he
attempted to quiet the mass. A microphone appeared, and
protestors quieted as the mayor stepped forward.

"Good afternoon." he said into the microphone. "Thank
you for this fine opportunity to once again extol my unbridled
commitment for both your safety and your importance to our
community." The crowd roared in unison. "I have on this day
directed Police Chief Turner to step up patrols in the areas of
gay and lesbian businesses," he proclaimed. "I met this morning
with senior advisors of the gay and lesbian communities, the
LGBT Liaison Unit to the police and bipartisan City Council
leaders representing areas of the most concern." Ellis paused and
pushed his glasses up on the bridge of his wide nose. "There will
be more police protection for gays and lesbians in our fine city."

Slade scribbled notes and recorded the shenanigans with his
cell for posting online. Cheers and praise rang out from the
mob. Slade noted many of the faces appeared weary of the
mayor's words even as they seemed caught up in the spectacle.
The mayor finished his address to resounding applause. Calls
rang out for solidarity among those gathered as they chanted.

The rallying cries triumphed. The assembly gained what
they came for: the lead-off story on the six o'clock news.

Perelli's voice snagged Parker's attention. They had been working
at their desks in silence since returning from the scene on
Myrtle Street, completing a mountain of reports on their latest
case, one of a dozen or so they currently had going. Both had
already changed into their street clothes upon arriving back to

the station to rid the odor of death that had clung to them like a disease.

Perelli hung up the phone. "May have something," he said. He closed the files on his desk and locked his computer.

"What?" Parker reached for his gun when he saw his partner grab his own revolver, apprehension clouding his face. Parker often wondered how his partner had kept the drive after all these years slogging through some of the worse crime in the country. Detective Vincent Perelli had devoted half his life chasing thugs, investigating everything from phony suicides and domestic disputers to shocking homicides. He'd seen it all in his tenure with the department. He still had a couple more years before retirement, but some calls still sparked the man to action like a rookie tracking his first case.

"A *Missing Person* report on Johnny Cage came in last Monday."

"Who filed?" Parker stood, locked his gun in the shoulder harness and slipped an arm into his blazer.

"The guy's sister."

The air-conditioning in the car sputtered once and died as Perelli turned off Boulevard into a neighborhood littered with autos up on blocks. Dogs barked all around, and a few of them even charged the car. The temperature outside had reached ninety degrees, and the humidity made the air thick and stifling. The smell of Perelli's musky perspiration didn't help the situation. Parker felt his skin swimming beneath his shirt as they rolled along in search of an address. Lowering the back windows did little to relieve Parker's anguish. Perelli seemed preoccupied and kept glancing Parker's way.

"You okay?"

"Yeah," Parker said, staring out at the neighborhood he had grown up in with the eyes of a boy having to fend for himself on the streets rather than those of a hardened cop. "This 'hood is close to the city and yet, seems worlds away from anything near normal. Still gives me the creeps to ride through this place."

Parker had been told the history of Cabbagetown by his
Gran, who loved to share stories of the abandoned, turn-of-the-
century mill before Alzheimer's sapped her memory. The village
sat at the eastern fringes of Atlanta where her parents and grandparents had once worked manufacturing cloth and paper bags
for flour, meal, and other agricultural products. Most of its
factory laborers were once farmers who had migrated from the
North Georgia Mountains in search of a better way of life. Parker's mother and her siblings grew up in one of the shotgun
houses erected on land adjacent to the mill for the workers and
their families. His mother never made it out of the neighborhood before she died, but she wasn't alone. Many of the ances-
tral families had remained.

Perelli steered left onto Savannah Street before Parker spoke.
"Do you know how this village earned its name?" Perelli shook
his head. "Back in the Fifties, a truckload of cabbage overturned
at that intersection we just passed. Times were tough then, so
residents just scooped up the spilled cabbage to take home for
cooking."

Perelli let out a deep-throated laugh, which lightened Parker's mood. Parker didn't know if the story was true or not, but
he loved to tell it.

They passed a narrow house with faded black numbers
poorly mounted atop a rotting front porch post. Perelli backed
up a few feet, then jerked the car against the curb, splashing
rain-swollen potholes before coming to a halt in front of a dilap-
idated structure.

The single-level wooden house was long and narrow. The
tiny yard in front of the porch ran rampant with weeds and
overgrown shrubs except for a small patch of garden off to the
side of the brick steps. A pair of worn gloves lay on the stoop.
Parker walked up the steps and tapped on the door. The shudder
sent paint flakes fluttering to his feet. The sound of a television
filtered through the thin walls. Perelli pounded harder.

Parker expected to find a frail old woman struggling to
answer the door, and not the attractive girl with the straight,
reddish-brown hair and shimmering green eyes who greeted

them. She couldn't be more than fourteen or fifteen, her doe eyes expressionless, and waiting for them to announce their business.

"Sergeant Kendall Parker with the Atlanta Police Department, ma'am. Homicide Division." Parker offered his badge for inspection and noted her stare. He stuck a thumb at Perelli. "This is my partner, Detective Vincent Perelli."

The girl shifted her weight, straining the tight Green Day T-shirt she wore. "It's 'bout my brother, ain't it?" Parker nodded and lowered his chin. "I'm Lisa," she said, losing the charming smile. She stepped back and ushered them inside the tiny home.

The place smelled of mothballs and fried food. Shades of brown and gold flickered from a flat-screen television screen set at an angle in the corner of the small living room. Various afghans were draped across the sofa and chairs. Stacks of gossip tabloids and magazines were stacked on the coffee table. A bottle of RC Cola with peanuts floating on top sat half-empty. The carpet had long since lost its luster and was worn by decades of feet resting in front of the furniture.

Parker and Perelli declined taking a seat. The girl disappeared down the hall flanking the east wall of the house. Moments later, she returned supporting an older woman with a shock of white hair. The older woman extended a frail hand with raised blue-veins out to Parker.

"This is Gran," the girl said, patting the woman's arm. "She'll wanna hear what you gotta say."

The wrinkled woman could barely keep her chin above her shoulders. She gazed into Parker's eyes as if searching deep within his soul. Her sullen eyes flashed concern. "Have you found my grandson?"

"Not yet, but Missing Persons is doing their best—"

The woman caught her breath and crossed an arm swiftly through the air, striking Parker's cheek, the contact knocking her off balance. Tears filled her hazel eyes and without another word, she turned away. Using the wall as her crutch, she shuffled back to the rear of the house. Johnny's sister pleaded for them to sit as her eyes brimmed with tears.

"I'm sorry." Lisa sniffled and sighed, as though she had the weight of the world perched on her delicate shoulders. "Gran's really close to Johnny, you know? She's afraid my brother got mixed up in something bad and ain't comin' back." Tears slid down her crimson cheeks. "Mama died five years ago, and Gran ain't never got over it. If something's happened to Johnny…"

Parker looked at the girl, knowing full well the sharp pain of losing someone close. "When did you see your brother last?"

Lisa's face dimmed, and her voice cracked as she spoke. Her behavior saddened Parker, who recalled his own feelings finding his mother dead on the floor of the kitchen all those years ago.

"Two weeks ago," Lisa said. "Johnny showed up all excited and full of his pipe dreams. Said he was going somewhere. Showed off these fancy pictures someone had taken of him." She cracked a smile, and a little light returned to her eyes. "It was hard not to believe him, you know? He said he was modeling and makin' real good money, that soon he'd have enough money to get us outta this place." She stood suddenly and beamed at them. "Wait right here and I'll show you."

Parker glanced over at Perelli. "Did she say *modeling*?"

CHAPTER THIRTY

Lisa rushed into the room holding a photo album open. "See," she gushed. "Johnny is *hot*. Everyone's always said he should model." She flipped through the glossies and stopped at a photo of her brother a wearing only shoulder pads and football pants, his lithe, muscular frame filling the page. "He gave me these. What do you think?"

Parker took the book from her delicate fingers and quickly flipped through the remaining photographs beneath protected plastic sleeves Most were eight by ten glossy prints of the young man in various stages of pose and undress. "He's photogenic," Parker offered, feeling the flush in his cheeks as he recalled seeing the same boyish face from the snapshot pinned to the bulletin board in North's condo.

"Folks say we look alike," she said, pointing to a photo of them together on the final page. "I added this one. Everyone says we should be on the big screen, you know? Gettin' all that money and fame. It's always been our dream to go to Hollywood, ever since we were little..."

The girl's voice trailed off and she turned away from them. "We talked about going away together soon," she said, sadness lacing her words as tears welled in her eyes again.

"You reported him missing," Parker prodded, sensing the

girl might lose it any moment, offering his best fatherly impression. "Can you tell us what prompted you?"

"Gran got a call over the weekend from someone claiming they found Johnny's wallet in some park. The asshole wanted a reward, can you believe it? I've tried to reach my brother for days, even left messages on his cell, but he ain't called me back. I reached out to his friends that I know and no one's heard from him." Lisa wiped her nose with the back of her hand, her black fingernails a shock against her alabaster skin. "When Johnny's landlady said she ain't seen him for a few days, I got worried and went to the police station."

"What park was that?" Perelli asked, clicking his pen to write in a small notebook. "Did you get this Good Samaritan's name and phone number?"

"Piedmont Park, I think it was. The man said he found Johnny's wallet by some trees and wanted to return it for cash. Gran wrote down the information beside the phone. I'll get it for you."

The girl rushed from the room and returned with a slip of paper, handing it to Parker. He studied her expression as she sat down on the edge of the sofa, unable to hide her apprehension. "Did Johnny mention going to visit friends out of town, heading off to find work somewhere else, perhaps?" Parker asked. "Did he have any reason to leave the city?"

Lisa's body slumped, and she fell back against the cushions. "Not really, why?" Doubt crept into her words and into the fine lines of her lips. "Is he in some kind of trouble? You have to tell me, I have a right to know," she said, covering her face and bursting into tears again.

"We're not sure," Parker offered, done with the fatherly charm. He glanced at Perelli, then back at the girl. "Lisa, listen to me. If you know any reason your brother might be missing, you need to tell us. Johnny hasn't been at his job in over a week. We've searched the room he rents out in town and spoken with the landlord. She's not heard from him either. A friend of your brother's was found dead in Piedmont Park last Thursday morning, a man by the name of Jason North." Lisa didn't seem to recognize the name or she was too shocked to respond. "Your brother may know something about North's death."

"Dead?" She coughed. She looked up, her appearance pale, confronting Parker's eyes. "Is Johnny all right? Please tell me the truth, I need to know."

"We don't know," Perelli offered. "Missing Persons has the case. Your brother's disappearance and the death of his friend may not be connected, but we have to look at everything. You'll be notified if we learn more, or when your brother is located."

Parker pointed to a photo from the album. "May we have this one?"

"Go ahead," she offered, lost in a reflective haze, tears streaming down her cheeks again. "I got plenty. No one ever said Johnny was camera shy." She chuckled at her attempt at humor before her smile faded to an awkward girlish grin. "He loved the attention, you know?" She glanced up at Parker. "Why would anyone want to hurt Johnny?"

A question Parker could not answer. He and Perelli moved slowly to the door as the girl followed them. "One last thing," Parker asked, stepping out onto the stoop in a blast of humid air. "Did your brother ever mention a guy who goes by the name Hopper or Dane O'Connor?"

Lisa thought for a moment then shrugged her thin shoulders. "Not that I remember."

Parker thanked her and slipped on his shades before walking away into dying sunlight.

Parker and Perelli returned to headquarters by early evening. Brooks appeared long enough to corroborate Bradford North's alibi. The rookie had verified with JAL and conferred with several of the man's associates in Hong Kong, all angry at being disturbed early in the morning. The men agreed to drop Bradford as a suspect for now.

They heard bits and pieces from fellow colleagues about the protest at City Hall and of the mayor addressing the crowd of mostly gays and lesbians. Perelli scoffed at providing special recognition to the group and excused himself for the evening. Parker remained at his desk a while longer returning calls and working on paperwork for other cases, along with notes of today's activities. He failed to reach the Good Samaritan of the lost wallet and left a message for a return call.

Johnny Cage's boyish image stayed in his brain like an ambiguous memory. The few facts of the case didn't seem to connect at all. His efforts to fill in the gaps had proven unsuccessful, frustrating him. A crucial piece of the puzzle that might connect Cage's disappearance with his friend's death eluded Parker. He doubted this morning's discovery of the city government employee had any connection to either the North murder or Cage's whereabouts, but he'd keep an open mind.

Jolted by a thought, Parker retrieved the manila envelope with the keys to Jason North's residence. Given this latest angle, he thought it would be a good idea to inspect the residence again, this time with a warrant. He needed solid evidence linking Johnny Cage to the death of his friend before going to Hornsby with his suspicions.

On Parker's initial visit to the man's condo, he hadn't known what to look for. This time around, he had a much better idea.

Entering Jason North's unit, Parker flicked on the overhead lights. He climbed the stairs by twos and entered the study to the right of the hallway. Hitting another switch, the room glowed brightly. He headed for proof that would blow the case open and ask more questions than he had answers, questions that would require the experience of a determined team of seasoned detectives and forensic experts to answer.

Among the multitude of photographs cluttering the bulletin board, one contained the boyish images of the two young men he knew to be Jason and Johnny, sitting among a group of people gathered on stools at an outdoor bar on a beach somewhere. Palms arched in the background and sugar-white sand contrasted with the boys' deeply bronzed torsos and legs. One of the young men sported a scorpion tattoo on his left calf, and it was not North.

Parker snatched the snapshot from the corkboard, shoved it in his pocket and killed the lights. Rushing down the stairs, his euphoria abated the instant he caught a whiff of jasmine. Slowing his descent, Parker instinctively shifted his right arm over his ribs and pulled his weapon from his holster. The lights had been dimmed since he'd entered. He swept the room with his arms extended. The sickly-sweet scent grew stronger, lingering in the cool air as he cleared the landing.

Parker had little time to react as a figure lurking in the shadows lunged at him, delivering a heavy blow to Parker's skull. He fell hard to the floor, smacking the side of his face and shoulder on the hardwood surface, knocking his weapon out of his hand. The attacker rushed to escape through the front door. Feeling blood on his upper lip and nose, Parker struggled to get back on his feet but grew dizzy from the pain exploding through his head. He twisted and fell back to the floor in fading darkness.

CHAPTER THIRTY-ONE

Parker regained consciousness. Feeling dazed, he drew himself into a crouch and summoned enough strength to stand. Massaging his skull, he felt a contusion then wiped the blood on his lip with his hand. The blow had aggravated the stitches behind his ear, but a quick check in the wall mirror showed little damage. He'd live. His lip on the other hand was about half the size of a golf ball. Unsure just how long he'd been out, Parker searched around for his gun, checked the chamber, and stumbled through the front door in an attempt to catch the perpetrator.

The air in the breezeway was thick with humidity. The smell of jasmine lingered in the narrow corridor. Following its path, Parker strode the platform to the neighboring door and knocked. No answer came. He pounded with both fists several times, even threatened to kick the door in if the resident didn't open the door. Distant, irritated voices rang out from other units below and across the parking lot demanding quiet. Someone shouted for him to take it inside.

Without a search warrant, Parker had few options. Undeterred, he bounded down the stairs and entered his truck. He moved to the end of the lot, parked out of sight, then sneaked back through the woodsy rear of the condominium complex.

He emerged at the base of Winecof's building, careful not to make any noise. He shimmied up the steps and propped himself against the stucco exterior. Hidden within the shadows, he was determined to wait it out until Boris emerged. He should have called for backup, but his instincts told him Winecof was harmless.

Shortly after midnight, the door opened, and Boris slipped out into the breezeway. Parker watched the big man stride toward him, waiting for the right moment. When Winecof passed within inches of his hiding place, Parker pounced with a vengeance. Boris's shrill cry pierced the night air. Binding the man's meaty right arm in a tight grip behind his back, Parker shoved Boris hard against the building. Two large binders fell on the ground, and one of them opened, exposing photographs of Jason North.

"You assaulted a cop, asshole. How did you get into Jason North's unit?" Parker demanded, tightening his grip and pressing Boris's face into the jagged wall. "You broke in to steal those, didn't you?"

"I did not," Boris pleaded. "Jason gave me a key." He stared down at the photos. "Those photographs are mine."

"Bullshit." Parker leaned in and put his mouth against the man's pierced ear. "Tell the truth. You were exploiting the boy and calling yourself a friend. You conned him into some kind of sick pornography scene, didn't you?" Parker improvised as he spoke, aiming to get a confession. "When Jason wouldn't go along with your scheme anymore, you killed him?"

"*What?*" Boris ceased struggling beneath the detective's weight. "I-I didn't kill anybody. I told you…those are my photographs. I wanted to get them back, honestly," he whined. "Don't you see? I couldn't have killed Jason," he sobbed. "I was in love with him…"

Parker turned the man about face and released his grip. "Why wait until now to go after the photos?" He stepped back and reached for a cigarette, wiping sweat from his forehead with his forearm. "You've had plenty of opportunities. Why take the chance now?"

Boris gazed at the smoke and lifted his chin. Shaking the pack twice, Parker offered a cigarette and lit it for Boris. "We should move inside," Boris said, reaching down to retrieve the binders.

Parker sensed there was more to the photos than the man's voyeuristic infatuation for his young neighbor. "Okay, but move slow and keep your hands visible."

Inside, Boris moved to the wet-bar nestled beneath a full stock of bottles lined up in front of the mirrored glass. Parker accepted the offer of a cocktail.

"I'm sorry I hit you," Boris admitted, handing the detective a tumbler of scotch and ice. "I panicked, I guess. Look at me. I'm not usually the brutal type." The large man fell into the leather wing chair across from the padded sofa where Parker sat. "You startled me something awful. I thought you might be Jason's *killer*." Boris fanned his face and wiped sweat from his brow. He took a deep breath and sighed. "My nerves are shot. I've not been myself since Jason's death, and now *this*. You'll have to excuse my boorish manners."

"That stunt you pulled just promoted you to the top of the suspect list," Parker chided, savoring the cool, crisp taste of fine scotch. "Why shouldn't I haul your ass in right now?"

"Okay, okay. Fair enough. Give me a minute, will you?" Boris nursed his drink a moment before settling in and cracking a scurrilous grin. "A few months ago," he started, encircling the top of his glass with a perfectly manicured finger, "Jason wanted me to shoot him—um, *photograph* him, I mean." He took another sip. "The boy knew of my vocation, and asked me to capture his fine physique. I didn't mind, of course. I ending up spending numerous hours, multiple sessions trying to capture that perfect angle, the precise lighting needed to highlight such beauty. The ideal shot, you know?"

Boris's face flushed, and he fanned himself mightily. "A lot of good it did me, but I simply could not turn down the time to be with him." He paused, perhaps absorbing the significance of his obsession, and glanced at Parker, steeling his eyes as if wagering a challenge. "You wouldn't understand, would you? Longing for another man, I mean."

Parker remained silent. "Of course not," Boris snapped, then slurped the remnants of his cocktail before setting the glass on the table between them. He stabbed out his cigarette in the ashtray.

"Jason was a real charmer," he continued. "The boy could make you give him anything, anything in the world that he desired. And you'd want to, really want to." Boris glanced off, as if in another world. "Jason had the most angelic smile, soft and gentle, his eyes warm and inviting." Boris chuckled. "Sure, I knew his flattery was artificial, any fool would have known, but I couldn't help myself. The boy's beauty was toxic, what can I say? Can you understand that? Being near him was the next best thing to having him, I guess. He was such a pretty boy." He sighed, a long baleful moan. "Pretty boy dead, now, I guess." He burst into tears.

The man's moment of reflection brought forth images of Parker's own lost love. The detective pushed his aching memories aside and reached across the table, flipping the pages of the photo album. "You're not telling me everything," he urged. "If you wanted these just for sentimental reasons, why burglarize to get them?"

Boris rose to refresh their cocktails. "You don't miss much, do you Mr. Parker?" Boris said with renewed defiance. "After a few sessions, Jason encouraged some of his friends to sit for me, some even younger than Jason." He returned and plopped down on the sofa. "I protested at first, of course. I wanted no part of such nonsense, but Jason insisted. No one would ever find out, he assured me." He slurped his drink. I believed him."

Boris leaned forward and plucked a cigarette from the pack on the table. "Don't you see? Those pictures are most incriminating now that he's dead. I had to get them back." He exhaled a cloud of bluish smoke in the air. "Go ahead, see for yourself," he challenged. "Open the other book."

Parker flipped the folio's cover on its metal coils. The nude figures of Jason North and Johnny Cage were locked in a seductive encounter, seemingly oblivious to the camera lens and lost in a world of their own making.

Boris poked the cigarette in his mouth, sucked hard on the filter. He leered at Parker. Clearing his throat, he said, "I know Cage is missing. After learning about Jason, I went to the Metroplex looking for Johnny. I thought the boy might tell me who Jason had hooked up with the night he disappeared." Boris drew a deep breath and narrowed his eyes. "What I learned scared the hell out of me." He took another long drag on the cigarette and blew smoke out the side of his mouth. "Johnny hadn't shown up for work since the night Jason had died." He choked back the tears. "I know it was wrong, but I just had to get rid of those pictures."

Parker flipped through the photos. "You claim Jason put you up to this?" Boris nodded. "What did he want with these?"

The photographer stood abruptly, sloshing his drink as he sauntered across the room flailing his cigarette in the air. "He never told me, at least not in so many words. Didn't matter. I believed whatever the hell the boy wanted me to believe, simple as that." He picked up a glass bowl and returned to his seat, offering chocolate. Parker declined. Boris palmed a handful of M&Ms and continued. "Jason was involved in prostitution for, shall we say, the privileged class. Young studs for hire to those willing to pay big bucks for discretion. These photographs cataloged their enterprise."

"*Their*?" Parker questioned. "Who else was involved?"

"Figure of speech, detective, I assure you. One would assume such a venture had to require more than one person to carry it off undetected. Jason never told me the details. I just took the photographs."

"This could be motive for Jason's death," Parker stated. In truth, he wasn't sure. The investigation had stalled, becoming more complex as he and his team peeled away the layers. "Jason's family is from money. His father is a wealthy real estate developer. Why would he turn to prostitution?"

"I have no idea. Jason kept me in the dark about most of his affairs. When I'd question him and press the issue, he'd say something silly or irrelevant, bat those beautiful long lashes and have me forgetting I'd ever asked."

Parker gulped the last of his drink and tried steering the conversation in a different direction. "Where were you headed tonight, just now when I caught you in the breezeway?"

The question caught the plump man by surprise, and his expression hardened. "I was going to Metroplex. I was intent on confronting that bastard, Anthony Galloti. His showplace is nothing but a front for illegal drugs and rent boys. That's who you should be questioning about Jason's death. If the boy somehow became mixed up in something dangerous enough to get him killed, I'd blame Anthony and his goons."

"What's your association with Galloti?" Parker asked.

"Not much. I've done some promo shoots for him, but that's all."

"What makes you think Galloti had something to do with North's death?"

Boris caught himself and glanced away from Parker. "I don't know. Suspicion, I guess. It's no secret Anthony is well associated, detective," he offered, glaring back. "I also heard he's related to a famous crime family from Chicago. The man gets what he wants." He cried out suddenly. "Don't you get it? I have to do something. I just can't sit back and watch Jason's killer go free." He fell back into the wing chair, the soft leather crushed beneath his weight.

"That's not going to happen," Parker found himself saying. "You can't take the law into your own hands, Boris. Stay out of this, or you're liable to get hurt."

The man's shoulders slumped. "You know," Boris said, "in spite of the obvious, I think Jason actually cared for me a little. He was such a puerile young man, anxious when expressing his emotions, his innermost thoughts and feelings. It's a shame, really," he said, tears flowing freely now. "Jason was such an energetic and carefree young man, so full of life and yet dreadfully naïve to the world around him. I always feared something like this might happen."

Parker explored the creases of his host's face, the suffering

Boris must be going through eerily similar to his own, if some-what displaced. Boris was struggling with the finality of death as much as Parker, the torment of never again seeing a friend's gracious smiles...or feeling a lover's touch. In truth, Parker felt compassion for Boris, understanding the man's feelings more than he even realized.

"Jason was a user, never a giver," Boris confessed, his tone bitter as his eyes narrowed. "The boy's personality was noxious, implicitly addictive. Jason knew this all too well, of course. He was a spoiled child, detective, who sought the arms of older men for personal gain. Is that so hard to believe? If there was some-thing to be had, Jason wanted it, and he wouldn't let up until it was his for the taking."

"I think Jason was afraid of giving his love to anyone, honestly. He was terrified of commitment," Boris continued, staring down at the floor. "I questioned him once and he told me that everything he ever cared about, had ever loved had been taken from him. His beloved dog drowned in a creek when Jason was five years old. When he was nine, a childhood friend who had been hit by a car died in his arms. A few years later, his mother died of cancer." He looked up, bloodshot eyes conveying his misery. "Jason had this twisted concept that by not committing himself, by not giving into his deepest emotions, he could somehow spare himself the pain of life's unpleasant uncertainties."

Parker wanted to believe the tormented man. Boris didn't seem like a killer, but his association with the victim and Jason's missing friend could not be discounted. Passionate feelings often resulted in lethal actions. "I'm sorry for your loss," Parker said. He stood and reached out to the man, placing his hand on Boris' shoulder. "You may not believe me at this moment, but time will heal your pain."

Parker didn't know if he had recited Hattie's comforting words more to reassure Boris or himself. He reached down and retrieved the photo albums from the table. "I'll need these for evidence, you understand?"

"Sure, take them." Boris sighed and rose from his chair. He followed Parker to the door. "Thank you, Sergeant Parker."

"For what?"

"Not arresting me."

"Promise me you'll stay put. Leave the detective work to the professionals." Boris nodded. Parker paused before he left. "There is one more thing." Boris looked skeptical, his eyebrows knitting. "Did Jason have a scorpion inked on his calf like his friend, Johnny Cage?"

"Not that I know of, why?"

"Not important." Parker stepped into the breezeway. "If you think of anything that might help our investigation, you know how to reach me. Call me anytime. I mean that."

Boris returned Parker's smile. "I will, detective," he said before closing the door.

CHAPTER THIRTY-TWO

Anthony Galotti glanced around the room at the group gathered in the wee hours of the morning. The associates staring at him had all insisted on secrecy and discretion since their activities meant jail time if they were discovered.

The club owner was poised to ask for more cash from the members. He sensed their anxiety and waited until everyone had settled. "As you all know," he said, "Councilman Mitchell Keyes introduced legislation six weeks ago to stamp out nude dancing clubs in the city." Galloti paused until the chorus of angry slurs died down. "His actions threaten *us*, our livelihoods." Shouts and obscenities were hurled. "Keyes' act is a deliberate attempt to win favor among conservatives to assure his re-election to the board this fall."

Anthony made eye contact with each person. "Atlanta has been known for decades to conventioneers and tourists alike as the 'Naked City.' We have a wealth of 'gentlemen's clubs,' among the best in the nation." Hails and cheers rang out. "More than fifty clubs stretch from the city center out to the suburbs." He paused to ensure all eyes remained on his. "Forty percent of the city's convention trade, which brings in tens of millions of dollars each year, would be lost if our clubs were run out of business."

"Doesn't deter that right-wing nut one bit," Levi Daughtry snapped. The larger than life, farm-raised owner of the *Pussycat's Tail* stared hard at Galloti. "I've deposited my money into this cash-cow fund for five years now without a single word of protest, but I'm not convinced our efforts are actually paying off."

Manuel Greene, co-owner of *The Fox Trot*, complained out loud. "The Religious Right is relentless in their attacks on our constitutional right to own and run our clubs. This shit has got to stop."

Anthony knew the seven gathered here represented the best of the best, handpicked for their single-minded determination and brilliant business acumen, incessant in their lust for power and wealth. They were proprietors of the most well-established and prosperous of clubs, each bloodthirsty masters of the trade, who would stop at nothing to protect their millions.

Anthony agreed. "The Right continues their undue influence to force the more conservative counties in this state to pass ordinances restricting alcohol sales in our clubs. It's only a matter of time before they'll start squeezing their liberal cousins bordering the city." He wiped his lip bottom lip on a starched handkerchief. "I don't need to tell you we can't make it without selling alcohol."

Those gathered hooted and hollered, and Anthony smiled. He was a master of vision and had realized long ago the growing trend of Georgia conservatives to stamp out nude dancing clubs entirely. Eloquent and polished, influential with those who mattered most and vigilant when required, Anthony had learned to be a smooth moderator. It helped that his club featured male dancers who stripped for a mostly gay clientele, viewed as non-threatening by the others in the consortium. It had its advantages too, for it was indisputable from the start that the mobster would act as ringleader of the bunch, with the dubious role of manipulating a pile of their money to finance their operations. The secret fund had amassed millions. Unknown to the contributors, much of the stash consisted of profits Anthony had skimmed off many of his enterprises.

The orator continued in a confident tone. "We've spent our money wisely, most used to finance our political interests with private yacht parties, gambling junkets, college tuitions, and a host of extravagant gifts from six-figure automobiles, furs, and precious jewelry to all expense-paid vacations for the entire family. We've bribed, bartered, influenced, compensated, extorted, and otherwise swindled key city leaders, politicians, lobbyist, solicitors and, authorities, just about anyone to protect our profits."

"We know all that, Galloti," Levi said. "Get on with it. Tell us why you've dragged our asses here in the wee hours of the morning."

"All right then." Anthony stood and placed his palms on the table. "I've called you in to ask that you make a deposit of a quarter million dollars to the fund." He waited for the news to set in. "City Council is poised to begin debating legislation introduced a few weeks ago by Mitchell Keyes in the next session. We're running out of time."

"Two hundred and fifty thousand dollars. Are you fucking out of your mind?"

Buddy "Bud" Nelson, proprietor of *The Lion's Den,* ex-cop, ex-convict, ex-drug addict, ex-husband, ex-just about everything else in his life smacked the table. "What the hell for, more bribes? Look around, boys. Half the city's on the take as it is, and it's not bettered us. I'll be damned if I'm throwing more good money after bad. It's downright ludicrous."

"You fucking whacked," shouted Manuel Greene. He chewed voraciously on an unlit cigar, moving it from side to side in his large mouth. "Why so much fuckin' cash?"

"It's necessary," Anthony said, impassively. "The stakes are higher than ever before. We need more money in the reserves."

"Says who?" Myrna Lynch, the only female of the bunch, challenged Galloti.

Galloti narrowed his eyes at the rotunda of womanhood determined to intimidate anyone in her path. "I do." Galloti shouted, again gaining control. "You think you can do better, step forward." He raked his eyes through the audience. "Any of you fuckwads."

Myrna glared at Galloti, Galloti at Levi, Levi at Bud, Bud back at Myrna. Let just *one* step forward, and all hell would break loose.

Wayne Abernathy, the stoic entrepreneur of the high-end *Platinum Club* sat quietly, bemused at such behavior. He was a third-generation adult businessman who grew up helping his grandparents and parents run their bookstores in Los Angeles and San Francisco. The other as yet silent attendee, Kenny Dalton, the youngest and most handsome of the bunch, stared blindly across the table at nothing in particular. A former Chippendale's dancer with slicked-back dark hair, sky-blue eyes, and an easy smile, he sat directly opposite Myrna Lynch.

"Do we have Keyes in our pocket?" Wayne Abernathy interjected his question loud enough to boom over the chaotic chatter. He intended to move the meeting along; wasted time meant lost dollars to him. "Right where we want his ass?"

Anthony seized the opportunity. "He will be soon. Copies of the damaging photos we have in our possession were delivered just this week to the iniquitous councilman. He'll be eating out of our hands before the end of the week, I bet." The man sat again. "If that doesn't convince the errant politician, then murder will."

"Murder?" Myrna shoved her hefty frame away from the table, distancing herself from the jolly ole men's club. "Who the fuck ever said anything about killing somebody? I for one want no part of it."

All eyes fixed on Anthony, who appeared like a cobra ready to strike. "You've heard by now that the body of a dancer from my club was discovered in Piedmont Park only a few days ago," he said with ease, rubbing his big hands together to distract his audience from noticing the sweat lining his upper lip. "Police now suspect homicide, and rightly so." His smirk slid into a knowing smile. "The whore we paid to pose with the councilman, and the dancer found in the park are one in the same."

Bud Nelson grinned greedily, leaning back in his chair and sucking in a deep, satisfied inhale.

"Jesus *fucking* Christ!" Manuel Greene ripped his glasses from his face and began to clean the lenses, ignoring the wide-eyed expressions of others in the room.

Those present suddenly found their voices, blurting out at once.

"*Fuckin' A.*"

"Can you believe this shit?"

"Why weren't we consulted 'forehand?"

"Who authorized the hit is what I want to know?"

"Do you have any idea what you've done?" Myrna shouted above the others. "You fucking *idiot*. Now you've aimed suspicion directly at us."

Anthony Galloti shot up from his seat, appearing stern, locking eyes with each member. "*All* of you agreed to the risks when you signed up. Think what you will, but I'm not the responsible party. The kid had plenty of enemies. Any one of them could have taken him out. The authorities will connect him to Keyes soon enough."

Bud Nelson snorted. "I'm no longer comfortable that you get to keep all our cash stashed away in the safe in your office. I don't trust it's security."

"What would you have me do, make a deposit?" Anthony gripped the edge of the table, locked in a stare with the only one in the bunch who had the balls to question him, the dyke at the opposite end of the table. Myrna didn't flinch. "For all we know, the horny councilman killed the dude himself," he said. "Think of this as a favor. It's made our job much easier." He relaxed his posture, eased the tension in the room. "We proceed as planned, nothing's changed."

At the same time Anthony Galloti met with his cronies early Saturday morning, a dark early model Honda Accord cruised down an empty Cheshire Bridge Road. The two tough, street-wise occupants huddled forward near the cracked dashboard, scanning the area for any sign of alarm, police cruiser, or nosy citizen who might witness the crime they intended to commit. They drove past the target a few times before parking the ratted-out vehicle in an abandoned parking lot across the street from the photography studio. After waiting another twenty minutes to be sure no cars drew near, they made their move.

The Honda eased from the parking lot and moved across the street. A Molotov cocktail was lighted and with precision, the flaming bottle sailed through the plate-glass window of the print shop adjoining the studio. The structure exploded in flames.

The young criminals laughed as they sped away and headed for an all-night bar a few miles away on Buford Highway, intent on blowing the cash earned for doing the easy deed.

CHAPTER THIRTY-THREE

"Mi-chael…"

Kendall called through the wind that had descended upon the boat without warning. His pleas of anguish died in the violent air currents.

"Michael, hurry up and secure the skis and lifejackets in the sideboards before they're tossed overboard.

"We need to get the cruiser in and tied down before the storm gets any worse.

"Michael, did you hear me?"

Kendall clutched the slick wooden steering wheel of the cruiser as a wall of water hurled toward them. "Michael, hold on to something!"

Michael was stowing the ski rope beneath the rear seat, and hadn't heard the warning. He worked feverishly, struggling to maintain balance in the turbulence. A ski broke free and crashed to the rear of the craft. The cruiser dipped forward, sending the ski soaring. The metal rudder beneath the fiberglass plane grazed Michael's head before it careened overboard. Blood poured into his eyes and down his face as he attempted to regain balance. A swirling wall of water clipped starboard and hurled the men into the water.

"Michael!" Kendall cried out, his voice barely audible as the rough water lapped at his face. "Michael, where are you?" He

pumped his legs steadily in the cool water. Fog descended and obscured his sight. "Michael, answer me, please."

Kendall removed the sneakers from his feet and swam forward, dodging debris and calling out. Seconds felt like minutes and minutes like hours as he trudged through the unforgiving current toward an object drifting a short distance away. Michael's limp body was draped over a piece of wreckage.

Kendall's legs cramped, and his arms weighed him down. He struggled against the rough current, fighting for control. The wreckage drifted farther away with each stroke. Finally, he got within arm's reach of the floating refuse. Michael appeared unconscious. Kendall grasped the piece of fiberglass, maneuvering to reach his injured companion. He stretched out his arm to grab Michael by the wrist when the wreckage rocked violently, threatening to toss the man overboard. Kendall fought hard to keep his lover from slipping away into the water, but he soon grew weak in the swift undercurrent. He managed to grasp a finger, which ripped from Michael's hand.

Kendall screamed…

Parker woke with a jolt from his nightmare. Sweat ran from his forehead, the salty residue stinging his eyes. Dazed, he lifted himself off the sofa and noticed it was a quarter after three in the morning. Bleary-eyed, he padded to the bathroom to piss before crossing to the guestroom where he fell, naked across the small bed.

Low-hanging vapors hugged the city by early light, the tops of skyscrapers swallowed by dark, ominous plumes. The thunderclouds opened up and sent a crashing assault of rain against the windshield of Parker's truck as he headed to Headquarters. Traffic stalled and pedestrians on the sidewalks scurried for cover.

Brooks shadowed Parker the minute the detective entered the break room to get coffee. "GBI Forensics' report on the suspected murder weapon in the North case is in," Brooks said as they arrived back at their desks. "Lab techs lifted a couple of

prints from the bat and are running them through AFIS."
Brooks' cheery disposition made Parker's stomach turn so early
in the morning, heightened by his lack of sleep.

"Nothing we don't already know," Brooks said. "The bat was
the weapon used to inflict damage to Jason North."

"Morning, Perelli—I could've told you that," Parker said as
he rounded his desk and set a cup of coffee down. He removed
his raincoat, gave it a couple of shakes, and hung it out of the
way. "Anything on the glove found with the body?"

"Guys in the lab are confident the glove didn't belong to the
victim due to its size—or at least the size the glove was before
water damage. Could belong to the killer, but they're not sure.
They couldn't lift any prints from inside the lining due to conta-
mination. It's too common of a brand to trace, but I could give
it a shot if you want?"

"Probably a waste of time." Parker held out his hand. "Let's
have the report."

The sergeant sat down, skimmed the twelve-page document.
When finished, he reached over and rifled through the wire
basket on his desk, searching for a file. The folder containing
Jason North's autopsy results included several eight-by-tens of
the victim. Parker spread the glossy images across his desk, took
out the photograph he'd taken from North's bulletin board and
studied the two tattoos with a magnifying glass. No doubt
about it, they were a match.

"I'll be damned."

"What's up?" Perelli glanced up from his computer screen.

"We've been duped, old partner." Parker handed over the
magnifying glass. "We've been headed down the wrong path.
The body from the park isn't Jason North at all. More likely, it's
his missing friend, Johnny Cage."

"That would explain Cage's disappearance." Brooks leaned
back in his chair to prop his feet on his desk. Perelli shot him a
look of disdain, and the rookie dropped his legs to the floor
without protest.

"There's more," Parker said. "I went back to North's residence last night to retrieve this photo. As I was leaving, the

neighbor from across the hall jumped me. He'd broken into the condo to steal these." Parker laid two open photo albums across the desk. "The neighbor is a photographer by trade with an interesting connection to the dancers from the Metroplex."

"Sex for hire," Brooks said, flipping through the binders. "Galloti has long been suspected of prostituting his dancers within Metroplex, some have claimed for an exclusive clientele of rich, closeted men. Grand jury indicted Galloti five years ago, along with several of his associates, for money laundering, extortion and racketeering that included, among other things, male prostitution. As the federal case wound through the courts, the lead federal prosecutor fell ill and couldn't continue. Galloti and his thugs were later accused of jury tampering and obstructing justice. The indictment eventually was thrown out for lack of evidence. There's never been enough substantiation to get another grand jury interested." He glanced up. "Link him to this murder, and it might be enough to take the man down for good."

"Where the hell did you get all that stuff?" Perelli appeared more annoyed than impressed.

Brooks cracked a wry smile. "I researched at the library and federal courthouse, reviewing newspaper archives, court records, transcripts, and old press footage following his indictment. I trolled the web for hours. I wanted to learn as much as possible about the man we're dealing with. Rumor is that Galloti has plenty of mob protection."

Perelli rolled his eyes and moaned.

"Not so fast, we still have to prove connection." Parker reminded them as he glanced at Perelli. "Winecof claimed North involved him. He denies knowing what the photos were intended for, but I'm not convinced he was telling the truth."

Perelli appeared ready to move. "Let's get a warrant, search Galloti's fag bar and tear his fucking home apart if we have to. Get a grand jury to indict."

Parker sighed. "You heard Brooks, easier said than done. We don't have enough to convince the lieutenant to authorize a warrant, much less get a DA brash enough to present it to a judge. No, I think we should sit tight for now with what we have and keep connecting the dots."

Perelli frowned. "If what you say is true and the body is actually Cage, then we have a bigger mystery to solve. Possibly two murders," he said with a sneer.

"True." Parker concurred. "Let's review what we have so far."

"We've established Jason North was in Blake's tavern late last Thursday night. We have a witness who can identify him at the bar, along with a couple of charge receipts from the place. The contractor for the city towed North's car less than a block away. A report indicates the engine of the vehicle had been tampered with. What I'd like to know is, if North was the intended target, how did his best friend end up in the ditch in the park instead? And, where the fuck *is* Jason North?"

They did not have a clue, nor did they know at the moment how to tie any of the links back to Anthony Galloti, assuming a connection existed. The scumbag had long covered his trail by now. Still, Parker wondered why the North's family butler had identified the body in the morgue if he knew otherwise. There could be any number of reasons for misidentification.

Dental records had been requested for analysis to confirm a match, but Parker didn't need more to convince him. He sighed. More questions than answers and clues without truths had the team in serious need of a break in the case. They needed to define a clear motive for the crime, one to steer the investigation toward a killer or killers. Perhaps they had stumbled upon it.

Brooks appeared to be tossing the facts of the case around in his head before charging over to his desk. He retrieved an inch-thick computer printout and hauled the stack over to Parker's desk, spreading pages out across the surface. "I haven't finished examining all the records of the pay phone from the bar used by North to determine who he called the night of his attack." Parker snatched up sheets and began scanning through the printouts, searching through the calls logged last Thursday night between eleven p.m. and one a.m.

"Hold on," Perelli said, searching through his own notes. He glanced at Parker. "Didn't you mention the bartender at Blake's said North had left the bar that night only to return minutes later asking for change to use in the pay phone?"

"That's right," Parker said, scanning the lines of data for calls made about the time North would have used the phone. "He claimed the kid appeared restless, nervous about something."

"North may have known he was being followed." Perelli offered a rundown. "When his car didn't start, he panicked and returned to the bar to call a friend for help."

"Johnny Cage." Parker said.

Brooks interjected. "I flagged several calls here starting at a quarter of twelve to the same number, the final call in sequence lasting a little over two minutes." He recited the ten-digit number as Perelli punched in the exchange into the phone on his desk. The line connected to voicemail.

"Callahan's direct line at the Metroplex," Perelli said. He replaced the receiver without leaving a message.

Parker asked for the copy. "All right, this proves North called his employer the night of his attack, but for what reason? Why not call a tow truck or a friend to come get him?"

"More important, why did Callahan lie to us?" Perelli asked.

"My thoughts exactly," Parker said.

Brooks reminded them of their previous theory. "We still don't know how Cage wound up in that ditch instead of his pal, North."

Perelli spoke up. "Isn't it obvious? The bartender claimed North wore a trench coat when he returned, but evidence suggests Cage is lying in the morgue instead." Brooks nodded. "The body in the ditch wore a trench coat, so it stands to reason Cage switched places with North, perhaps allowing his friend to leave the bar unnoticed?"

"A little far-fetched, don't you think?" Brooks hugged his chest.

Parker held out his palms in open handed prayer, his eyes bursting with excitement. "Suppose North spoke to Callahan and the manager sent Cage to help out his top performer." The sergeant's suggestion prompted curious stares. "Cage would go, right, since North was his friend?

"I'll buy that," said Perelli.

"The guy's in real trouble." Parker continued. "Cage goes along with whatever North asks of him. But somewhere along the way, their plan goes awry, and Cage takes a hit instead."

"Making Callahan an accessory." Brooks brightened like a child who understood got the joke.

"Or co-conspirator," Perelli said, scrunching his eyebrows and staring across the desk at Parker. "What happens if the killer realizes he's made a mistake?"

"He—or she—won't, not if we keep it to ourselves and out of the press." Parker tucked the photo albums into his desk drawer. "By some miracle, Jason North may still be alive, and he's in serious danger. My gut tells me he's still in the city and hiding out."

Blake said, "His picture has been splashed enough across the tube he may be waiting for things to die down a little before trying to make a run for it."

"Which is why we need to find him before the killer figures out he took out the wrong target," Parker said, nodding. "Let's start with the butler, then confront Callahan with evidence of the call North made to his office the night of his demise."

"My thoughts exactly," Perelli said. The men looked up at the sound of their boss's voice.

"Parker! Perelli!" Lieutenant Hornsby leaned his ample frame outside his office door. "Get your asses in here."

Perelli glanced at Parker, who shrugged. The detectives bolted from their seats and moved briskly to the lieutenant's office. Hornsby closed the door after them and lumbered around his large wooden desk. "What's this bullshit?" His expression displayed his anger as he tossed the newspaper across the desk.

The headline plastered across the front page read: SECOND VICTIM FOUND DEAD IN MIDTOWN; COPS BAFFLED.

"That son of a bitch!" Parker grabbed the paper and scanned the article before glaring back at Hornsby. "Slade is barking up the wrong fucking tree."

"What's with you and that reporter anyway?" Hornsby cut Parker off with a wave as he started to answer. "Whatever the hell it is, I want you to straighten it out. Do you hear me? Stop that motherfucking, leftwing zealot from targeting my goddamned department."

"Lieutenant..." Parker said, stepping forward to protest. "You need to talk to public relations. PR has to demand all journalists—Slade included—stop publishing rumors and pushing innuendo concerning the investigation. For all we know, the media's tainting witnesses as we speak and hindering our ability to get to the truth, the real facts. How the hell do we conduct an effective search with everyone and their dog out playing private dick?" Parker tossed the newspaper into the trashcan. "I'm sorry, but I won't play into that jerk's hands."

"Why not?" Hornsby snatched a plastic blue bottle of antacid from the desk drawer and chugged from it. "You don't have much, so what's there to lose?" He tightened the cap and put the bottle away. "Every goddamn faggot group in the city has been calling the mayor's office demanding action, worse since yesterday's discovery of another dead homo. The mayor and the chief both have been forced to meet with members of the Gay and Lesbian Task Force. They agreed only because some faggot group calling themselves QUEER DAY is threatening to disrupt Monday's session at City Hall."

Hornsby rocked back on the heels of his feet, his eyes boring into Parker. "Did you hear what I said? I will *not* tolerate another media circus in my department, detective. Not again. Now, give that damn reporter what he wants and get him the hell off my ass."

Hornsby's reference to the tumultuous days following the boating accident and subsequent internal investigation aggravated Parker more than he'd expected. He was transported back to within hours of the mishap, when the media had reported an Atlanta homicide detective's alleged consumption of alcohol before getting behind the wheel of the craft. The week's long coverage became yet another controversy for the department, plagued for years by allegations of corruption, racial profiling, and excessive use of force.

The media assault had been vicious, no doubt fueled by the detective's record of successful convictions and rumored alcohol troubles. Though a thorough investigation eventually cleared Parker of any criminal responsibility, the media, embodied by Calvin Slade himself, had forever labeled Homicide Sergeant Kendall Parker *negligent*.

Parker rushed from Hornsby's office and bounded through the sea of cluttered desks and shuffling personnel. He had no intention of sharing undisclosed details of the investigation with Slade, or anyone else outside the department for that matter. They would threaten discipline or worse, but he would be damned if he'd relent.

Perelli caught up with him midway through the room. "Why didn't you tell Hornsby about the identity of the body in the park? It might ease the pressure knowing the victim wasn't from that prominent family in Buckhead." He sneered. "The press will eventually move on."

"We don't have positive ID, Perelli. Not yet anyway." Parker halted and stared hard at his partner, disdain washing over his face. "Tell me you aren't suggesting we be less concerned because the victim wasn't the son of a wealthy businessman?" Perelli glared at him. "That's bullshit, Perelli, and you know it." Parker walked off, not caring to continue this conversation, not here, not now. His felt his anger surfacing when he passed midway through the room with his partner hot on his heels.

"Pissing off the lieutenant ain't gonna help matters," Perelli said. "What is it with you anyway, Ken? Do you like goading the Lieutenant? 'Cause if you do, I'd just as soon sit this one out."

Parker retrieved his revolver from the desk drawer and pushed his thick arms into his blazer. He clutched his raincoat in one hand, shaking it toward Perelli. "Hornsby doesn't give a rat's ass about this case. You know what I say to that? Fuck him. Fuck him and the whole goddamn department. He's so concerned about his reputation and political ambitions that he chooses to blame me for the division's shortcomings. He won't hear us out without more proof, Perelli. So that's what we're going to give him, indisputable proof."

Parker had made up his mind, and that was that. It always was in these situations, whenever and wherever it came to enforcing authority, and enforcing the law.

One of the main reasons Parker enjoyed so few friends in the department.

"What did you have in mind?" Perelli asked.

"We pay the good butler a visit."

CHAPTER THIRTY-FOUR

Detective Javier Torrez had been an investigator assigned to Vice in the Atlanta Police Department for a little more than six years, having transferred up from Gulfport, Mississippi after the devastation wrought by Hurricane Katrina in 2005. His large family of five children, a wife, and mother-in-law lost everything during the storm. Crooked insurance adjusters along with the rip-off construction trade made it impractical, if not impossible, to rebuild life in the coastal town. Torrez settled on relocating his family to Atlanta because other fleeing residents had boasted of the affordable housing and a friendly, diverse make-up of the people.

In a town saddled with its share of corrupt politicians and dishonest lawmen, Torrez had learned quickly the benefits afforded those who maintained a sharp eye and a careful ear, who listened for the unexpected or caught the occasional bit of information or significant fact. A devoted Catholic, Torrez kept to himself for the most part, ignored by white cops and shunned by the blacks. The opportunity for advancement in Atlanta became a joke in the cruelest sense. Yet the resolute policeman remained dedicated to enforcing the law, becoming a devoted partner and a determined member of the staff, dead set on providing a decent life for his family and protecting the citizens.

Javier Torrez's mind proved razor-sharp and deliberate, making him a master of assimilating information, able to sort and file away the significant as well as recall vital facts upon command. He was a virtual walking database far underutilized by the department. So, when Torrez overheard three homicide detectives near his desk discussing the Piedmont Park homicide and the discovery that the victim was not who he was first reported to be, he reasoned the information was valuable enough to chance a call that could very well jeopardize his career.

The short, stout Latino son of immigrant parents took a scheduled break just before noon and exited City Hall East. He stood steady on the front stoop, facing north across Ponce de Leon Avenue, lighting a cigarette and gazing across to a new strip mall that seemed to have sprung up overnight. Its brightly colored banners promised the lowest prices in town, as though the city needed yet another reason to cull thrifty shoppers in an economy so weak. Torrez exhaled a large huff of bluish smoke and watched as cars and trucks of all sizes sped past in both directions, most exceeding the speed limit, indifferent to the authority looming about. People these days seemed eternally hurried, never slowing to take in the sights and sounds of their daily existence, always in a rush. Such a shame, he thought. Life is simply too precious to waste.

Torrez stubbed out his cigarette in the ashtray atop a trash-can, descended the steps and walked up Ponce de Leon Avenue, passing the looming Old Ford Factory building with its refurbished three-hundred-thousand-dollar loft condominiums. Making his way through the southern end of the Kroger parking lot, he entered the crowded grocery store, cruised several aisles without actually shopping, then headed for the pay phone tucked in a corner at the front of the store. He dialed a ten-digit number he'd called only once before.

Though familiar with the man's voice, the deep-throated reply sent chills up the detective's spine and caused him to scan the interior of the grocery once more. Patience was not one of Anthony Galloti's virtues, so Torrez quickly spilled the information he had obtained.

Galloti slammed down the receiver so hard, his right arm tingled. He jumped up from his comfortable chair and strode across the room to the bar nestled between twin mahogany bookshelves filled with famous twentieth century literature he never read and poured a double bourbon, neat. Downing the smooth contents from the cut-crystal glass, he opened his dark eyes and stared at the ceiling, his expression a deadly scowl. *How could this have happened? How did that punk, Jason, avoid the wrath of a trained assassin?* It seemed impossible, far less believable had he not heard with his own ears. If the detectives investigating the North's case were correct...

Anthony recalled a comment his business associate and manager, Stewart Callahan, had made the morning the body was discovered in the drainage basin at the south end of Piedmont Park. "One of the dancers hasn't shown up for work in the past few days. In fact, not since the night Jason was killed."

The revelation complicated matters twice over. The notion Jason lived was incomprehensible, grave enough to bring forth a massive migraine which threatened to cloud his judgment. He poured another bourbon neat and paced the room, contemplating his next move, daring as it may need to be. He gulped his drink and cursed himself for ever having fallen for the sexy young man.

Where was Jason now? The dancer must have learned he had become a target, but how? Who had betrayed him? What other explanation was there for Jason to have avoided work, to remain hidden from public view? Even as local news sources plastered the city with his angelic face No one had heard from Jason in days: not the police, not his family, and certainly not his employer. Anthony Galloti knew there was a good reason behind the young man's disappearance, but he had a hard time bringing himself to believe it. Such an admission simply scared the hell out of him.

He walked over and picked up the phone, speed-dialing Callahan's office. "You still have Hopper secured and out of sight?"

"Yeah, he won't be going nowhere soon, if that's what you mean. Keeping him pumped full of heroin, some mighty fine stuff if I might add, not like that shit we used to OD'd Crater. The kid is stashed in a fleabag motel off I-20 in Douglasville. He'll be there when we need him."

Galloti informed Stewart of the disturbing news about Jason and proceeded to ramble off a string of orders. A diversion was in order, tossing police a bone while providing Anthony the necessary time to rid his house of evidence linking him to any crime and to finish once and for all what he'd set out to accomplish. They were simply too close to successfully extorting Councilman Keyes from putting forward legislation targeting the multi-billion-dollar nude dancing business in the Atlanta metropolitan area, and Anthony refused to allow his meticulously planned scheme to be compromised because of some rotten homicide detectives and a pain-in-the ass investigative reporter.

"I am afraid the family is not available at the moment," the dutiful butler informed Parker and Perelli with inherent arrogance. "They have left for the weekend. I will inform them of your visit upon their return. Now, if you will excuse me…"

Cut the crap, Parker wanted to shout with one hand clasped against the gentleman's neck. Instead, he stared into the man's defiant eyes.

"We're not here to speak with the family." Parker growled his words. "We want to talk to you."

The butler glanced at Perelli, then back to Parker before stepping out onto the portico. A few white wisps left from earlier clouds streaked the horizon. The air hung thick with humidity. "How may I be of assistance?"

"You lied when identifying Jason North's body at the morgue," Parker said, his eyes fixed on the butler. "I suspect you've known all along the body wasn't that of your employer's son. You mind telling us how you knew?"

Maurice smiled with assurance, relaxing his stiff posture. He took a deep breath and exhaled slowly, as though ejecting some of the guilt he held. "I thought it was him at first," he offered, shutting his eyes momentarily. "Not until much later when I recalled the gruesome images in my mind's eye, the lifeless body lying there on the cold table, did I appreciate it could not be him. Mind you, the body was strikingly similar to Master North, no doubt about that. Enough to fool anyone, I suppose. He would never have disfigured his body in such manner."

"You're referring to the tattoo," Parker said. The butler nodded with indifference. "Yet you didn't come forward to correct your mistake. Why not contact us with your suspicions?" asked Parker.

"He hasn't admitted he made a mistake," Perelli said. "Perhaps he knows more about the killing?"

The butler lost his rigid posture and grimaced. "That is preposterous. I know nothing of that young man's death. Your accusation is insulting, detective."

"But you do know who does?" Parker said. "Mind telling us where we can find Jason North, Mr. Williams?"

CHAPTER THIRTY-FIVE

Monday morning, Calvin Slade entered the foyer of the brick ranch that housed the offices of WGNX news. He stated his business to the receptionist behind the chest-high paneled counter, signed the visitor's log, then clipped the "VISITOR" badge on his wrinkled shirt before following a hallway to the end to a flight of stairs. At the bottom of the landing, he changed direction and moved along an identical hallway filled with several glass-enclosed editing and viewing rooms. He located an attendant and produced a slip of paper with the information he needed to locate newsreel tapes covering the recent Democratic Fundraiser at the Fox Theatre. Through sources, Slade learned WGNX had filmed the entire event, the only local television station to do so. The college-aged attendant returned within minutes carrying a set of four large cassette tapes.

Slade followed the man to a dimly lit room slightly larger than a utility closet, crammed with a multitude of technical equipment: viewing monitors, projectors, video tape players, mixers, and splicing machines, all trailing cords and wires along the walls and floor. The lone window had been painted over to prevent light from sneaking in. Slade sat down on a hard stool in front of a monitor atop an elaborate VCR with lots of buttons and knobs. Tom, the attendant, inserted one of the cassettes and within seconds, numbers in coded sequence appeared against a dark background. Next, a crudely type-written title identified the film footage on the reel and the date shot. Slade stared intently at the screen as the ornate façade of the Fox Theatre came into view, fronted by a stylish reporter speaking into a microphone branded with the call letters of the news station.

"Don't let the switches and dials intimidate you," Tom said. "Turning this green dial to the right will advance the tape, back to the left for reverse. The white button here will freeze the frame, the yellow button zooms in and out, and the red switch over there shuts off the power." Tom pointed to the equipment on the metal stand beneath the monitor. "Here's three more tapes when you're finished with that one. If you need a copy of any portion of the footage, just jot down the sequence of numbers located at the bottom of the frame from start to finish. It'll take at least a day to splice them together and be ready for pickup." He turned to leave. "If you need anything, I'll be in the room across the hall."

"Thanks," Slade said. He glanced at his wristwatch. The time was 10:15 a.m. when he turned back to the screen.

He settled in and moved the video along slowly, searching for any image that captured the less than imposing Mitchell Keyes. The first tape consisted of arriving attendees, each oblivious to the recording lens, but conscious of their appearance as they entered the wide lobby. Several black Lincolns and a stretch limo here and there delivered Atlanta's fashionably dressed and politically appointed. There were wide smiles, delicate air-pecks, phony hugs and waves cast about as though the evening was Atlanta's own version of the Oscars rather than a boring political fundraiser.

At 10:45 a.m., Slade inserted the second tape. This camera, positioned in the receiving hall of the grandiose Egyptian Ball-room captured Keyes pressing forward, taking the hands of friends and supporters, surrounded by political aides. He was dressed in the same suit he'd worn to the office earlier in the day, his jacket unbuttoned showing a white shirt crinkled at the waist from the day's assault, and a tie slightly askew. Several frames later, Keyes appeared disinterested and withdrawn from the events as he moved in and out of camera range, giving rehearsed greetings to his constituency.

By 11:30 a.m. and midway through the third tape, Slade found it increasingly difficult to spot each frame capturing the councilman. He'd counted upward of thirty or more shots, none with any clues of Keyes' intentions upon departure. For the better part of the evening, the councilman moved around alone, save for the occasional aide, constituent, or roaming waiter offering champagne. Near the end of the tape, however, some-thing odd caught Slade's attention. He sat up straight, punched the white button to freeze the frame and carefully examined the images on the screen.

In the foreground, the democratic incumbent to the State Senate, Margie Simmons, danced the two-step with her tubby husband, but that wasn't what Slade was interested in. Instead, he studied the shadowy figures in the rear of the dancehall, huddled just inside the narrow opening between the platform and the heavy red velvet draperies flanking the darkened stage.

Slade enlarged the background, distorting the foreground dancers. Councilman Keyes appeared to be chatting with one of the many servers roaming through the crowd with glittering silver trays of champagne filled flutes and tiny food. A closer examination of the young attendant's movements provided the connection the reporter was searching for. Slade rubbed his sweaty palms against his thighs, then advanced the green knob slowly to the right, creeping the video feed forward. He watched the men through several more frames until assured the two were indeed embarked in private conversation.

A few frames later, the purpose of the encounter began to materialize, at least to Slade's eyes. The vibrant server appeared to be soliciting the haughty councilman, who did not seem affronted in the least. In fact, Keyes' languid stance confirmed as much. He openly brushed against the attendant at least twice during their lively conversation before the councilman reached out to accept a small object offered him. In the frames following, Keyes finished his drink, placed his glass on the server's tray and strode out of view. Slade continued the feed to follow the movements of the handsome server, who emerged from behind the heavy draperies before skirting the dance floor toward the NewsCam.

Slade punched the machine's white button the moment the blond youth passed before the camera lens. There could be no mistake. The sharp, angular face and striking features of the young server caused a shot of adrenaline when he recognized the attendant as the Piedmont Park victim, Jason North.

Rewinding to the beginning of the tape, Slade searched for more images of the good-looking server. He spotted the suave server meandering through the crowd multiple times, dispensing fluted champagne to the honorees and guests. But the next scene capturing the affable man had Slade nearly pissing his pants. He punched the white button again to freeze the frame and then zoomed in on the image of the server speaking with a taller, slightly built male figure. From photos recently published online, and appearing on the city councilman's website, the reporter recognized the mystery man as the one found dead in his home by police yesterday.

Slade rushed across the hall and burst into the filing room as Tom appeared poised to take a hefty bite out of a sandwich. "Is it possible to magnify the hands of someone in the background of the video feed?" He tugged the man's arm to follow him across the hall. "I need a close-up of Councilman Keyes' hands." Slade led Tom back to the monitoring room.

"Hum, yeah, it's possible. Piece of cake. All you need to do is…"

"Don't bother explaining," Slade said, pushing Tom down on the stool in front of the monitor. "Just do it."

Slade showed him the frame of the exchange in question. Tom spent the several minutes working his magic before claiming victory. When finished, he cut across the room to another piece of equipment and retrieved a black and white copy of the councilman's hands receiving a key. The diamond-shaped, dark green, embossed keychain of *Holiday Inn Express* leapt from the page. Slade instructed the technician to reverse the feed to the image of the dead City Hall employee speaking with the same server, then repeated his request.

Task complete, Slade thanked the attendant for his amazing assistance, grabbed the prints and rushed from the room.

CHAPTER THIRTY-SIX

"I need to see you." Slade had whispered loud enough so his editor could hear. Slade stopped short of entering the room.

"Not now, Calvin," Marsh snapped, gesturing with irritation at the others at the meeting table. "Can't you see I'm in a meeting?"

Slade disregarded the group and rushed to the editor's side. He leaned down close and whispered a few words into the man's ear. The two men engaged in whispered conversation and ignored the aggravated stares of the other executives.

Marsh had heard enough. "Who covered the Crater case?" Marsh blurted out to the men seated around the table. "The death of Councilman Keyes' aide?"

"Greenfield," said the Metro editor from the end of the table.

"Get him. Adams." Marsh barked orders. The city deputy editor snapped his head up from doodling on the pad. "I need two of your best junior field reporters, a couple of top-notch research assistants and throw in a few green clerks. We have a hell of a lead to authenticate before word leaks to the other media. Have everybody meet in the war room in fifteen." Marsh capped his Waterman pen, picked up the papers on the table before him and shoved back from the table, signaling the end to the meeting.

The war room was a large conference room on the same floor as most of the staff clerks and journalists. Used for departmental meetings and occasionally reserved by print staff thrown into crisis where timing proved critical, it was a think tank for senior field reporters, editors, copy writers, researchers and common clerks working together at breakneck speed to draft a blistering front-page story, a scoop that required swift action and exceptional writing skills. An eight-foot table with folding metal chairs, topped with dual triangle-shaped speaker-phones for conference calls, filled the center of the room. Flat screen monitors tuned to local and national news programming were hung on the walls.

Everyone gathered as requested, poised for instruction and ready to roll up their sleeves. Young clerks were brought in to run errands for the troupe during what might become a multi-hour marathon of making photocopies, getting coffee, fresh donuts, fetching take-out, distributing afternoon snacks, everything to keep the group focused and on track.

Slade perched at one end of the table and outlined the events responsible for bringing them together. Reading from typed pages with scribbled highlights, he brought the assembled staff members up to speed on the story. Based on the facts presented, those gathered believed the victims indeed knew one another, and the video from the fundraiser proved they both had connections to the councilman. Their job now was to confirm and source all the facts, authenticate the details, and fill the gaps for tomorrow's front page.

Slade organized his pages of notes under the managing editor's direction, who doled out the assignments to each participant. Everyone relished the adrenaline rush associated with what might well be the hottest story of the year. Covering the city councilman had proved mundane of late, but connecting two dead bodies to the man would fire his unpopularity factor into the ozone.

By 9:00 p.m., Marsh approved the third draft and gave Slade the okay to contact Councilman Keyes at his home in Buckhead for a comment. The top brass listened in on extensions as Slade dialed the number. A recorder engaged before the first ring and Keyes answered.

"Councilman Keyes, this is Calvin Slade with the *Journal*. Can I have a moment of your time?"

"I told you before I have nothing more to say, Mr. Slade. How did you get this number? You know what this is? It's harassment. I'll have you thrown in jail if you don't stop pestering me."

"I am required to inform you, councilman, this call is being recorded. I think you'll want to listen to what I have to say."

"Are you serious?"

"We're running a story in the morning detailing a connection in the murders of Jason North and your office aide, Lamar Crater. We'll be including a photo of you taken at the Fox Theatre fundraiser speaking to the Piedmont Park victim. We'll also be running down the young man's affiliation with the male strip club, Metroplex. It's our assertion you have knowledge of their deaths, enabling you to be blackmailed to kill your proposed legislation banning alcohol sales in nude dancing clubs in the city."

Silence. Slade heard a few heavy intakes of breath as what sounded like a drawer opened and closed before he spoke when it became clear that Keyes still remained stunned.

"Councilman Keyes, with all due respect, you must know I am calling you out of professional courtesy. I want to give you an opportunity to share your comments with the public who elected you. We will be going to press soon—"

Keyes's words exploded through the receiver. "Your assertion is preposterous! Who put you up to smearing my name with the primary coming up? What gives you the right to call my home with such an asinine claim?"

Slade steadied himself and repeated his offer. "Councilman Keyes, with all due respect, I am calling you out of courtesy. I want to grant you an opportunity to share your comments with our readers. We will be going to press soon…"

"You can go straight to hell, Mr. Slade."

Slade's face burned. "We're going to press soon, sir. Just give us your side of the story and I'll personally guarantee—"

"You'll hear from my lawyers."

CHAPTER THIRTY-SEVEN

Kendall Parker finally made it home late Monday evening. He had spent several hours at the precinct with Perelli questioning Maurice Williams, the North's family butler, at length and alluding to the Englishman's obstruction of the investigation should he not come clean and offer up Jason North's whereabouts. Perelli became so dismayed with the man's refusal to cooperate that at one point he'd offered to punch the man's lights out right there in the interrogation room. He probably would have had Parker not intervened. Mere moments later, Lieutenant Hornsby burst through the door and stepped aside as Bradford North and his attorney entered the room. Parker figured the enigmatic family knew more than they had professed. He became more determined than ever to uncover just what they might be hiding.

After a long, warm shower to loosen the thickness in his muscles, Parker toweled dry. He ran his thick fingers through his damp hair before entering his bedroom where he slipped on a pair of cotton boxers. He trekked into the kitchen to pour a hefty dose of scotch over ice before crossing into the living room. Picking up the remote to the stereo, he collapsed on the sofa. The wound behind his ear throbbed with pain, and his body felt tired and worn down. He massaged his temples, applying force in gentle strokes to ease the pressure between his eyes. Soft jazz billowed from floor speakers camouflaged behind wilting potted plants that had been Michael's idea. His dead lover was the one with the green thumb, not Kendall. A variety of pots were scattered throughout the house, on the balcony and out along the front walk and in various stages of decay. Like most things these days, Parker had neglected caring for them.

An evening jazz program on WJZZ cranked into its second hour. Sunk deep into the polyester fibers of the overstuffed sofa, his body began to relax after several hearty scotches. He dozed off and on as his mind mulled over the case that had all but consumed him the past week. He also reflected on his ordinary career of late, the mundane trials and tribulations of a dream headed south, then on to more haunting images of the fatal accident that took Michael from him forever before he finally passed out.

The shrill ring of the telephone woke him with a start. Kendall reached across the sofa and slapped around the marble surface of the table with his eyes closed until he found the cordless receiver. He punched a button and pulled the receiver to his ear. "Parker."

The caller's hysterics jolted him upright.

"Hey...hold on a sec." Parker switched on a lamp and pulled himself to the edge of the sofa, cradling his head. "I can't understand a word you're saying." The clock on the mantle showed 11:40 p.m. "Brooks...is that you? Calm down. What's going on?" Parker searched the coffee table for cigarettes and a lighter.

The rookie sounded more excited than Parker had ever heard him before.

"I think you need to come in, Sarge," Brooks said. "There are people in the lobby shouting and uniforms are trying to get them under control. The press wants to speak to the lieutenant. I think someone has called the chief to come down."

"What's this about?" Parker lit a cigarette and searched the floor for his shoes.

"Perelli made an arrest about an hour ago, a suspect in the park murder. Somebody leaked the information to the press, and now there are people here demanding answers."

"*What?* What suspect? *Why* didn't he call me first?" Parker shook the fog from his head as he fought to get his wobbly feet into his shoes. "Who's in custody, Brooks?

"It's O'Connor, sir. The suspect arrested is Dane O'Connor."

"Are you shitting me?" Parker dropped his cigarette, feeling the sting of a burn, but quickly retrieved it before it left a mark. "I'm headed in. Don't say anything." Parker tossed the cigarette in the glass of watered scotch on the coffee table. "Try to get the press to wait until I get there," Parker yelled through the cordless receiver stuck between shoulder and chin as he stumbled into the bedroom searching for the clothes he had discarded earlier. "Where's Hornsby?"

"The night clerk can't reach him."

"What about Perelli?"

"He's still in interrogation."

"What the fuck, *shit.*" Parker struggled to get into his pants, forgetting about the shoes. "Listen to me, Brooks. Get in that room right now and stop Perelli from going any farther." He stepped out of his shoes. "Does the kid have a PD?"

"PD was summoned a while ago, but I think she's coming from night court and hasn't arrived yet." Brooks cupped the mouthpiece as he shouted something to someone. "I need to hang up now, Sarge. I can't hear a word you're saying…"

Short of fifteen, Parker squealed his truck into the parking garage of the sixth precinct at City Hall East. A few reporters, bright lights on tripods with crew in tow, charged him. Parker exited his vehicle and rushed to the employee's entrance. An angry group of people swarmed between him and the press. Reaching the door, a water-filled balloon burst across his right shoulder. Parker turned sharply. Members of the recently formed activist group, QUEER DAY chanted, "Homophobia kills. Homophobia *kills*."

Inside the lobby, hysteria flourished. The desk officer spotted Parker as he met up with Brooks and had a patrolman assist them getting beyond the crowd. Parker ordered Brooks to find Perelli and bring him to Lieutenant Hornsby's office.

An eternity passed before the annoyed detective presented his sweat-covered face in the doorway. Brooks volunteered to wait outside and closed the door on the two men.

Perelli's features appeared taut and strained beneath the harsh fluorescent light. Parker noticed the dark circles below his eyes. When offered, Perelli declined to take a seat.

"Why didn't you contact me before you charged off to make an arrest?" Parker demanded. "We're supposed to be a team, Perelli. What the hell happened? You should have called me."

Perelli had been perspiring, the front of his shirt soaked. He wiped at the sweat across his forehead, his wild eyes dancing around the room, searching for words in the air. "I didn't want to disturb you," he said. "I thought you needed the rest, so I took the call alone."

"It's protocol." Parker slammed his fist on the desk. "Dammit, Perelli, this was our collar, *our collar*, you and me, together. How could you do it without *me*?" Parker stuck a cigarette in his mouth, but thought better of lighting up, shaking the lighter at Perelli instead. "You should have called me."

"Ken, I get that," Perelli pleaded in a more controlled tone. "I didn't think it was necessary, all right? I made a mistake, okay? What's the big deal, anyway? We have O'Connor now, so relax. I'm sorry I didn't bring you in on this."

Parker peeled away from his partner's sullen stare and noticed several of his comrades watching them through the office windows.

Perelli raised his voice a notch. "Didn't I warn you about getting too close? Look at what this case has done to you, Ken.

You're a fucking mess." Parker turned back. "You smell like the bottom of the bottle you've been drowning in."

The sergeant practically crawled across the desk to get at his partner, stabbing the unlit cigarette within inches from Perelli's face. "Who's accusing who, Perelli? Cut the bullshit. You've had every intention of collaring O'Connor given the chance, and you took it." He edged closer to Perelli, enough for his wide-eyed partner to feel spittle. "What, did you think I might interfere with your plans? Did it occur to you that I just might prevent you from carrying out your own personal vendetta?"

"You have it all wrong." Perelli objected to Parker's verdict. "O'Connor's a suspect in a murder investigation, ain't he? It's what you told the Lieutenant." Perelli's hands flapped at his side. "It was *you* who suggested I beef up efforts to find the perp, remember? It's a good thing too. The punk had a bus ticket in the motel room where I found him. If I'd waited on you, he'd be halfway to D.C. by now."

Parker simmered. He wanted to accept his partner's explanation, but something didn't seem right to him. "Give it up, Perelli," he said.

"What are you talking about?

"Who tipped you?"

"No one, I tracked him down on my own."

"Bullshit. Who told you where to find O'Connor, dammit?"

Perelli leaned his large butt against the desk and crossed his arms, obviously irritated. "An anonymous caller, all right? Why the third degree?" He grunted. "Look Ken, the call came in, and I took it. What's the harm in that? Give an old man a break, will ya?" Perelli fell heavily into one of the chairs fronting the lieutenant's desk. He appeared drained, no longer up for the fight. "Besides," he said, "you'd been drinking. It wouldn't have been smart with you on the job."

A moment of silence hung in the air before Perelli spoke in a subdued, almost soothing tone. "O'Connor went to confront Anthony Galloti the night we spotted him snaking through the bar, the night he popped you in the head and stuck the dirty needle in my neck. The punk claimed he was upset at the owner for firing him and was there to get his job back."

"Dane told you this?" Parker glanced sharply at his partner. Perelli nodded. Parker's heart sank at knowing the conversation the two must have had. "Tell me you didn't say anything about Cage."

"Of course not." Perelli sounded irritated. "O'Connor denied any involvement in the park murder, regardless of who got whacked." Perelli looked down at his shoes, rubbed a scuff mark with his heel. "I had a couple cops search the kid's room at a boarding house on Euclid Avenue after finding a receipt in his coat pocket," he said, clearing his throat. "Turned up with nothing."

"You searched a suspect's room without a warrant?" Parker's anger surfaced again. "Are you kidding me? What else have you done that I should know?" Parker had a sudden thought. "Where is O'Connor now?" he asked.

Perelli's expression went blank. "He's in isolation. There's nothing more we can get from him right now. I was with him for over an hour. Give it a rest, will ya? You can talk to the kid tomorrow."

Parker sensed something was awry. Department procedure dictated anyone arrested and suspected of having HIV/AIDS had to receive medical attention at Grady Memorial, the city's largest indigent hospital. After examination, they were to be housed in secure medical units after receiving proper medical care. Suspects were never held in maximum security unless they had declined treatment or were labeled mentally unstable. Parker doubted either was the case.

Parker called out for Brooks. "Put O'Connor in an interrogation room," he said. "I'll be down in a minute." He turned back to Perelli. "Is there anything else I should know?"

The detective lowered his head and stared at his hands, balled his fists and released them.

Parker moved to the door. "Fine, I'll deal with you later." He turned and exited the office.

CHAPTER THIRTY-EIGHT

Parker trudged down the narrow hallway leading to the holding cells that lined both sides of the cinderblock walls. Muffled voices, hard stares, a few obscenities and catcalls followed him as he rushed past crowded cells with mostly blacks and Latinos. Brooks came charging up the corridor with panic in his eyes.

"What's wrong?"

"O'Connor's down on the floor," Brooks said, terrified. "I tried to move him, but he's unresponsive. I'm not sure he's even breathing."

Parker bolted to the end of the holding area, shoulder to shoulder with Brooks. They pushed through a three-inch thick steel door and two barred gates before reaching the isolation cell. O'Connor's body was crumpled on the cement floor in the corner of the shadowy room like a broken-winged bird.

"*Jesus...*" Parker rushed to the young man and dropped to his knees.

O'Connor lay handcuffed and shackled, his face hidden beneath matted blond hair. A torn shirt covered the boy's back, his jeans soiled with dirt and grime. His shoes were untied, the right one halfway off his bare foot. A pool of liquid surrounded his body. The odor of urine pierced the air as Parker knelt to check for a pulse or breathing.

Parker lifted the youth's smudged face and removed the surgical mask from his mouth. The kid burned with fever. Dark purple encircled O'Connor's right eye which was swollen shut, and his nose was bleeding.

"Remove the restraints." Parker swept wet strands of hair out of the young man's eyes. Brooks removed the metal binding Dane's ankles. Parker spotted a series of small bruises spotting the boy's inner arms. "Why the mask?" he asked.

Brooks stammered. "He threatened to bite and spit on the cops processing him," he said, slipping the suspect's hands free of the cuffs. "He has HIV, and the officers didn't want to take any chances." He shrugged. "Look at what's happened to Perelli," he added.

Parker glared at Brooks. "He's not a fucking animal."

Brooks lowered his head. Parker knew the rookie wouldn't rat on his comrades, a time-honored code of silence that would prove impossible to break. It wasn't worth pursuing. He scowled and turned back to O'Connor.

"He's having trouble breathing," Parker said, searching the small body for broken bones. "Call for paramedics and have the bus meet us around back. No lights and sirens, okay? Now g*o.*"

Brooks rushed from the room.

"Dane?" Parker whispered in the boy's face and searched his glassy, bottomless eyes. "Can you hear me? Tell me where you're hurting."

The insensible youth lolled his head on thin shoulders. A face devoid of expression stared back at Parker, beyond him, seemingly through him, then back again. O'Connor's eyes rolled to the back of his head, and he uttered two simple words that sent cold chills up Parker's spine.

"Help… me."

Brooks returned with some water. "They're on the way," he said. Kneeling down, he offered the kid a drink and gently wiped at the dried blood on the boy's cheek with a wet cloth.

Staring into O'Connor's red, puffy eyes, Parker didn't see the malicious kid of their first meeting, the streetwise youth full of hatred. He did not see the violent stalker that cracked a board across his skull or the wild maniac that stabbed his partner. The boy was vulnerable, reduced to a frightened creature devoid of hope and destined to become another insignificant statistic to a virulent disease that held no boundaries.

"He doesn't look good," Parker said, breaking his silence. "He needs a doctor." Parker motioned for Brooks to go to the back door. "Wait for the paramedics and tell them we'll be right there. I'll try to get him there without drawing too much attention."

Calling for an ambulance proved risky enough should reporters spot it, but following through with Parker's intentions might get them suspended, if not booted out of the department.

"Dane," Parker said, scooping the youth up into his powerful arms. "Hang in there, kid. We're taking you to the hospital."

Brooks returned carrying a patrolman's jacket and cap. "Too late, some reporters have managed to get past the lobby. Here, put these on him. I'm not sure how far we'll get before being noticed. With any luck, we can sneak down the left corridor and out the back with him propped between us."

Together they hoisted the frail young man to his feet, cradling him under the arms, his head recoiling back and forth like a drunkard. Brooks draped the oversized leather jacket across the boy's hunched shoulders and secured the cap over his tousled hair. O'Connor groaned as they made their way through the doorway and into the corridor. Upon verifying the coast was clear, they slipped around a corner and shuffled awkwardly down the hallway without coming across anyone.

O'Connor grew heavier as the detectives stepped out the back door of the building and into the arms of the waiting paramedics.

"Get him into on a gurney." Parker transferred the weight of the boy to the paramedics. "He blacked out."

Dane O'Connor was hoisted into the ambulance and laid out on a gurney. One of the EMTs began an IV of saline as the other placed an oxygen mask over the boy's face. Once the boy was stabilized, the shorter of the two medics jumped out, closed and secured each door with Parker and the other paramedic inside with O'Connor.

The Rescue Unit rolled to the end of the parking garage, turned right on to North Avenue, hit the lights, and engaged its siren.

At 2:20 a.m., Parker glanced at the old Hamilton clock hanging on a bright yellow wall. He sat in one of the crowded waiting rooms of Grady's Emergency Ward. On his left, a foul smelling old man waited to have a laceration on his forehead stitched, the red stain seeping through gauze. Adjacent to him, a Jewish father and his brood hovered together like frightened little sheep while their mother—in surgery to remove a gang member's stray bullet—clung to life beyond the white double doors. To Parker's right sat a gaunt, ghostly pale adolescent teen dressed in black; shoes, black jeans, black halter-top, black leather jacket and black silver-studded belt. She had explained earlier how her boyfriend was stabbed in a fight outside a Little Five Points pub. She spouted broken English, yet struggled in earnest to explain the circumstances of the incident to those present, whether they displayed interest or not. Parker listened politely until someone tapped his shoulder lightly.

"Ain't no use waiting no more, detective," a large black nurse reeking of garlic and lilac perfume whispered close in his ear. "You can't talk at the boy tonight." Parker stretched his long legs, stood and towered over her stubby frame. "He's been moved to ICU."

"Can I have a word with the attending physician?" Parker asked.

The nurse motioned him to follow her beyond the automatic aluminum doors to a large nurse's station. "Wait here," she said. "I'll get 'im." She waddled down one of the polished corridors, the polyester covering her plump legs rubbing together as she trailed. The nurse returned some thirty minutes later with the doctor in tow.

"I'm Dr. Patel." The short physician introduced himself,

accepting Parker's hand with a powerful handshake. The doctor appeared too young for an attending physician. Likely one of the multitudes fulfilling their residency requirements in the city's indigent ER. "Sorry I couldn't meet with you sooner. I've been attending to a stabbing victim."

"Yes, I heard," Parker said, avoiding the spattered blood on his tunic. "The girlfriend's in there." He turned and motioned behind himself. "She told me the story."

Parker's comment brought a puzzled expression from the doctor. "Girlfriend?" Parker nodded. Patel addressed the nurse standing beside them. "Inform the young lady in the waiting room her friend has died."

Patel touched Parker's arm and led him along the wide east wing corridor of the Emergency Unit, away from peering eyes at the nurse's station. "We can talk down here," he said, voiced strained by fatigue.

An unexpected weakness invaded Parker's body, threatening to buckle his knees. The mention of death conjured up repressed memories of the doctors' tenacious efforts to revive Michael following the accident, their teamwork failing before it even gained momentum. The station nurse on duty that night appeared in Parker's mind, her soft ivory skin accentuating the highlights of her shoulder-length auburn hair. She shuffled toward him as she had that fateful night, even in memory her pristine face an etched plane of affirmation.

Parker had guessed her mission. The news was embedded in her expression, in the tiny wrinkles in the corners of her small mouth, in the arch of her thinly penciled brow had devastated him. She needn't have uttered a single word. Michael was *dead*.

Parker wanted to hear her say it. He had wanted to hear her recite those few words of regret in order to try and accept the nightmare for its reality.

He never had the chance. The woman halted a few feet shy of his quivering body, and he realized she didn't intend to speak at all. The expression stamped across her scarlet face had been that of a well-trained professional, experienced in handling such life-altering news. Yet for reasons he had never known, the nurse had felt it best to remain silent, allowing her moist eyes to convey the dreadful message.

The eyes never lie.

"Are you all right?" Patel had stopped and looked up at Parker. "You appear ill."

"Huh? Oh…yes, I'm fine." Parker shook off the reverie and caught up with the physician. "Working too much, I guess." They walked past an elderly gentleman wheeling an IV bottle down the corridor like a child sneaking away from its mother. How's O'Connor doing?"

The doctor glanced away, exhaled and stuffed his fists into the pocks of his lab coat before continuing his stride. Parker followed alongside. "He's been worked over pretty good," Patel said.

Lost for words, Parker felt ashamed for events he had no part in and yet blamed himself for not preventing. "I'll take care of it," he said, reassuring the man.

Patel hung his head. "Ahem…" He began by mumbling his words as his tired eyes conveyed more than the message he intended to impart. "He may not make it through the night, sergeant. The patient has advanced AIDS and a T-cell count well below thirty. Compounded with these new injuries, I'm not sure…" His voice trailed off as he spotted a gurney rushing past.

"We'll have to wait and see," Patel said. He began walking again as Parker followed. "He is stable for now. The next twelve hours will be the most critical."

For the first time since seeing O'Connor curled on the floor, Parker realized the seriousness of the young man's injuries. He clutched the doctor's slender arm to halt their stroll. "You're saying he could die?"

"You look surprised, detective." Patel frowned. "You shouldn't be."

"The suspect resisted arrest, doctor. Sure, he got a few bruises in the scuffle, not uncommon under the circumstances, but not enough to put his life in danger. I don't understand."

The doctor pulled free of Parker's clutch. "My *patient* suffered trauma to his skull in three distinct areas. His kidneys are badly bruised, his spleen has been ruptured, and he sustained several cracked ribs, among other smaller injuries. I don't think I need to explain to you how this happened."

"You think cops did this intentionally, don't you?" Parker stared at the doctor, his anger more at his partner than Patel's raised eyebrow.

"I can only comment based on what I have examined first-hand." Patel walked away but paused long enough to impart one final thought. "You should know also that your *suspect* was in handcuffs when he 'resisted arrest', as you claim. Injuries sustained support my findings."

Parker thrust his business card at the doctor. "Please call me if there's any change. You understand I'll have to post an officer in the corridor?" Patel's icy stare cut through him. Parker added one final request. "I'd appreciate your handling this discreetly."

The physician bowed his head in agreement and scuttled down the hall.

CHAPTER THIRTY-NINE

The media gathered on the front steps of Police Headquarters and milled about the wide concrete courtyard early Tuesday as reporters from local TV stations and cable news awaited a news conference with the chief of the APD. Parker walked parallel to the crowd and headed toward the side entrance marked for employees. Someone recognized him and the cameras swung around, microphones were thrust forward and the crowd headed for him like a swarm of bees. Cameras clicked rapid-fire as the reporters surrounded him.

"Sergeant Parker, Sergeant Parker!" A lean, antagonistic young woman screamed at the top of her lungs and shoved her angular frame forward. "Is it true you have apprehended a suspect in connection with the murder in Midtown's Piedmont Park?"

"We've detained a young man for questioning," Parker said, nudging through the cluster. "The suspect's not been charged with any crime."

Questions rained from every direction. "Have you linked the suspect to Councilman Mitchell Keyes? Jason North's murder?" Another reporter blurted out, "What about a connection to the death of Keyes' aide?"

Parker paused, glaring at the reporter. "I cannot comment on the specifics of an ongoing investigation."

"Sergeant, you've had the suspect in custody since last night. Why hasn't he been charged?"

"Investigating homicide is a laborious process," Parker said, adding, "Our responsibility to the citizens of this jurisdiction is to be accurate and thorough, nothing less. That's exactly what we're trying to do. Now, if you'll excuse me—"

"Yet the suspect you have in custody sustained serious injury during his capture, Sergeant."

The mass quieted, and all eyes gazed at the newsman who had yelled the statement. Parker scowled at Calvin Slade. The insolent man basked in the glow of his big scoop alleging a connection between City Councilman Mitchell Keyes and the recent murders of two young men, one in the councilman's employ. Parker had received a call from the lieutenant before sunrise and ordered to get to Headquarters. Slade's byline had prompted swift action from the top brass. The suspect Perelli hauled in last night already had city leaders demanding answers.

Slade thrust his dumpy frame forward. "Would you care to confirm or deny such accusations, Sergeant?"

Parker glared at the reporter. "The suspect refused a request to come downtown for questioning," he said, edging toward the entrance. "It's yet to be determined how he sustained injury."

Everyone began tossing questions at once.

"Why haven't you released the suspect's name, Sergeant?" a voice cried out from within the cluster of restless journalists. "Exactly *how* bad are his injuries?" another reporter asked.

The atmosphere turned chaotic. Parker scanned his employee ID card through the reader on the wall, and fled through the steel door just as another reporter shouted, "When will we get an official statement from the department?"

Rushing along the side corridor, Parker hurried through the main floor of Headquarters, descending to the lower level. Anger had swelled within him, but he managed to steel his fury as he bounded into the hole. He saw Perelli with his back turned at his desk.

Parker ignored Detective White's pleasantries and confronted Perelli. "What the hell happened last night?"

"Wha—?" Perelli's shot up as Parker rounded the desk. "What the hell are you talking about?"

"This is me you're talking to, dammit! Stop the bullshit. You roughed up that kid, didn't you? I want to know why? Why didn't you say anything before I went to question O'Connor and discover for myself? What were you afraid of?" Perelli scowled back at him. "That I'd bust your ass for laying a hand on a detainee?" Parker paused a moment to catch his breath. "Well, I would have," he finally said.

Parker lowered his voice. "Look, I partnered with you five years ago because no one else would after what happened to your former partner. I've respected you, Perelli, your sharp eye, your experience on the job. This isn't like you."

Perelli's expression remained stoic. The lines in his forehead narrowed as his jaw twitched. "The guy resisted arrest, Ken, what would you have me do?" Perelli cleared his throat. "Besides, O'Connor would have split by the time you sobered up."

Parker ignored the jibe. "You busted his ribs, *Vince*. O'Connor's just a kid, not some hell-bent banger loose on the streets. You handcuffed that boy and beat the crap out of him." Perelli lowered his head. "Why, Vince? I want to hear it. Tell me why you thought it entirely acceptable to rough up a suspect in custody."

His partner stared hard at the floor without uttering a word, his face flushing red and stern.

"What did you hope to achieve, Perelli? Did beating the crap out of that boy make you feel like a big man? Some sick justification for what happened to you?"

Parker noticed as a couple of detectives in the squad watching them. Perelli still remained silent. Parker leaned down and got within inches of his partner's face, wanting… *needing* to be heard. "O'Connor didn't deserve the beating you gave him."

Parker stood back and threw up his hands. He turned away from his partner and stared at the cinderblock wall behind his desk, lined with approbations of valor. Years illustrating Parker's sworn allegiance to enforcing the law, motivations perhaps, driven by the fear of having to face the toughest part of his existence; a life outside the precinct alone. A testament to a closeted homicide detective haunted by the death of a loved companion, intimacy he could share with no one in the department. Forever faced with the threat of discovery and what it would mean for his career.

And for what, some sense of pride? At the moment he didn't really know how he felt, but he was sure that doubting Perelli made him sick to his stomach. Nothing had prepared him for such a life-altering consequence. He had accused his partner, his trusted friend and colleague, a man with whom he'd lay down his own life, of using unnecessary force, of intentionally and willfully causing harm to an unarmed suspect in custody.

"Perelli, we've been partners for over five years," Parker said, feeling the heat beneath his collar. "The one thing you've always stressed, pounded into my fucking head every chance you got, was to never, *ever* let your emotions compromise doing the job." Parker turned and gripped the edge of the desk, the whites of his knuckles pressing through his thick skin. "You went too far, Vince," he said. "The boy could die."

Perelli's fists slamming on the surface of his desk launched the detective to his feet. "What the hell did you expect, Ken?" He spit his words. The muscles in his jaws contracted as the veins of his neck bulged. "I was a little rough, so what? Do you *know* what that little shit did when I arrested him? *Do you?*"

Parker stared in disbelief.

"He fucking laughed at me, Ken. That's right, he laughed," Perelli sneered. "The son of a bitch mocked me!"

Their exchange had drawn the attention of others in the room. Hoping to avoid a scene, Parker laid an arm across his partner's shoulders. "Look, I know it's been hard on you lately," he said, lowering his pitch. "No one knows more than I do. Regardless, you shouldn't have taken it out on the kid."

Perelli rolled his chair away from Parker and bolted to his feet. "You can't possibly know how rough it's been for me, Ken. You have no idea what it's like to be treated like a leper by your colleagues. To have friends avoid shaking your hand. Having others look at you like some freak."

Perelli blocked Parker's attempts to reach out to him. "Don't touch me," Perelli said, tears brimming from eyes red with fatigue. "I'll tell you what it's like," he shrieked. "It's fucking miserable."

White and Mendenhall approached. Parker waved them off and attempted to get Perelli to retake his chair. The elder man pushed him away and continued ranting.

"It's like you don't even exist. Everyone's afraid to touch you or come near you. My friends hardly speak to me anymore, Ken. Do you know what that's like?" Perelli caught his breath, choked on his spittle. "It's a nightmare." He whined through tear-soaked eyes. "Worse than you can possible imagine."

The detective glared at his colleagues milling about. Most had gathered at the sound of raised voices, the chance to witness yet another explosion between comrades.

"You don't think I notice," said Perelli. "I pass through these halls every day with you leering at me, talking behind my back, *all of you*. Whispering 'there he is,' or 'oh, his poor wife.'"

Perelli wiped the drool from his mouth with the back of his hand. "Yeah right, my poor fucking wife." He covered his face with his hands and paced in circles. "I don't even know Jane anymore. Lying next to her is like cuddling up to a block of coal."

"I'm sorry," Parker said, wishing on some level it had been *he* who had felt the needle that night. "It happened, all right? Sucks I know, but there's nothing we can about it now except follow your doctor's orders and take precautions." He drew in a deep breath to steady his nerves. "It still doesn't justify what you did, Vince. You really *hurt* that boy."

Perelli shot him a look of disdain. "You expect me to feel *sorry* for what I did? Well, I don't, Ken. The guy ruined my life!"

"Vince, it's out of our hands. Let the courts decide justice to be served." Parker reached out, but Perelli deflected his arm.

"You defending the fucking queer now?" Incredulity laced Perelli's words as he scanned the room for support. "Any one of these guys would have reacted the same," he said, ignoring the downcast eyes of those nearest. He turned and addressed Parker again. "I expected more from you, Ken. You're my *partner!*"

Perelli began to walk away but turned back suddenly. Betrayal etched his features. "You son of a bitch!" He glowered at Parker. "All this time I thought I knew you. Knew you like my own son." Perelli's eyes grew narrow as a wicked grin brushed his quivering lips. He stepped forward in challenge. "But I don't *know* you at all, do I, Ken? How could I have been so fucking naive?"

Parker felt knees his go weak and his cheeks flush. It struck him suddenly that Perelli might actually be about to disclose his secret; emotions so private Parker himself harbored deep within, and away from those who cared for him the most. He had tucked that skeleton safely away from public scrutiny, from condemnation long ago. Perhaps even on some level, from himself, the most critical of them all.

Kendall wanted to flee, but something deep within held him firm, a consciousness which matured in the several weeks since Michael's death. Accepting his sexuality—what he stood for had left him exhausted, and mentally drained since the rollercoaster of emotions following the accident. He had grown weary of the lies and deceit, tired of hiding who he was, and disenchanted with the easy excuses at the ready when someone ventured too close to the truth.

And, Kendall David Parker no longer wanted to hide.

CHAPTER FORTY

Parker stared at his partner and pleaded with him, all but ignoring those looking on. "Vince, please. Give me a chance to explain, but not here. Not now."

"I've been fucking blind!" Perelli wiped the sweat from his forehead. "Michael… Michael wasn't just your best friend, was he ole' buddy?" He spoke with contempt. "That's it. That's why you've been so damned consumed with North's case." His partner's face flushed. "Jesus, Ken, you must take me for a fucking idiot."

"Vince, listen to me. You don't know what you're about to do. Say we get outta here, go sit down and discuss this over a cup of coffee, huh?"

His partner wanted none of it. "We've been best buddies for years, you and I," Perelli wailed, anger straining his features. "We've collared thugs and celebrated together, gotten drunk and fought together, hell… we've even bawled together, you and me."

"Vince, don't do this here."

"Goddammit, Ken, I trusted you." Perelli slammed his fist on the desk, knocking the telephone receiver from its cradle.

"You still can, Vince. Nothing's changed, buddy." Parker felt helpless and vulnerable among his colleagues, a scrawny kid changing into gym clothes among older boys in the locker room. "Would you just hear me out?"

"You're one of them, aren't you?" Perelli glanced up, wiped at his running nose. He looked lost, bewildered. "Five years, Ken. Five fucking years, all of it one big fucking lie." He stood suddenly. "I won't listen to your lies."

"Fine!" Parker shot up from his chair. "While you're at it, why don't you blame me for your incompetence, too?" Perelli drew back. "Where were you, Vince, that night when I chased our suspect into the alley behind the bar?" Parker had hit a nerve, and he aimed to squeeze even harder. "Why were you not there to back me up?"

Perelli glared at Parker, confounded.

"*You* were supposed to have my back, buddy," Parker said. "I could've been *killed!*"

"I was coming around as fast as I could," Perelli said, noticeably irritated at the accusation. "I didn't have time to get there before you were attacked."

"You were too slow, ole' buddy," Parker said, gaining the upper hand. "You fucked up. You didn't have my back." The next words leaving Parker's lips made him regret them even before he finished speaking. "Just like you weren't there that night for your former partner, Pete. The man never had a chance."

The pain in the detective's eyes reined unforgiving. "*Fuck you!*"

Perelli swung a hard left at Parker's gut and missed. Parker caught his partner's thick arm and attempted to subdue him. Their scuffle attracted a greater audience and a few catcalls.

"Get your pervert hands off me." Perelli struggled to wrestle free. "Get away from me, you faggot."

Lieutenant Hornsby stepped between them with a snarl. "What the hell's going on?"

"It's okay, lieutenant." Parker attempted to explain, drawing back to catch his breath. "A slight misunderstanding, that's all."

Perelli began to speak but was silenced by Hornsby. "The two of you get in my office now."

Hornsby slammed the office door shut after the detectives entered. The man was so enraged, he misjudged the chair behind his desk as he reached out and set it spinning. He kicked the chair away, choosing instead to remain standing. "You assholes have really done it." He snorted, nostrils flaring. "My wakeup call this morning was the Captain. I've had to put off the mayor's office, and the goddamn ACLU is threatening a lawsuit."

Parker opened his mouth to speak, but Hornsby silenced him with a wave of his hand. "And *you*, Perelli." Hornsby glared at the detective. "I should kick your fat ass down Peachtree for your actions."

The lieutenant rounded the corner of the desk and leaned within inches of Perelli's reddening face. "What you did was stupid, plain and simple. It'll cost this department a great deal of embarrassment and headache, which I don't need right now." Stepping back, he wiped sweat from his brow with a creased handkerchief. "Why is it always hot in this damn place?"

"Lieutenant…" Parker tried again.

"I'm not finished," Hornsby glared at them from behind his mammoth desk. "The situation has gotten worse," he said, glancing away. "IA wants to speak to you both as soon as possible. O'Connor, your suspect, died an hour ago."

Parker punched at Perelli's arm and missed. "You son-of-a-bitch!"

"Sit your asses down." Hornsby gripped the edge of the desk and peered down his nose at them. "The kid was a goner anyway. A matter of time, I'm told. You may have saved him from a lot of painful suffering."

Parker recoiled at his commander's words, his narrow mindedness. He wanted to reach across the desk and pound some sense into the old man.

Parkers penchant for violence of late as the first resort frightened him.

"What's important is that we're on the same page and get the facts straight in the report. We have to substantiate the boy's incarceration," Hornsby said, cupping his round chin with his hand. "I'll release a statement that the department intended to charge O'Connor with three counts of aggravated assault, two against APD officers, the other against an Emory surgeon, before the boy succumbed to a preexisting condition while in our custody."

The pounding in Parker's ears matched the rate of his heart. Perelli sat silent, shell-shocked by the news. Hornsby added, "We've got to explain how the hell O'Connor died in our detention." He pushed himself away from his desk. "O'Connor was a suspect in one, perhaps two deaths," Hornsby said. "We had every right to detain him, no question. IA will put us through shit, no doubt about it, but we know what happened," he said, locking eyes with Parker. "Until then, this department did nothing wrong."

"What?" Parker sensed a cover-up. "I saw the kid's injuries. O'Connor was handcuffed and shackled, face down in his own urine." He caught his breath. "The *suspect* needed medical attention, lieutenant. No way he could have resisted arrest, much less defend himself as my partner claims."

"I wouldn't repeat those words," Hornsby said. "None of this is for you to decide." He shot a look of disdain at Perelli, then looked back to Parker. "Is what Perelli said out there true?"

A hand seemed to reach through Parker's chest and clutch his heart. His throat thickened, became dry. He felt suffocated standing in a room full of hot air. "My life outside these doors is none of your business."

"I've heard enough." Hornsby flicked his hand, his eyes narrowing. "You've left me no choice. I'm reassigning the case."

Parker shot up in protest. "C'mon, lieutenant! There are gay cops in the department!

The lieutenant bristled. "And none of them have ever or will ever made detective."

Parker fumed. "You can't take the case from us, sir. We've done all the legwork. We're really close to capping this one. Please?" He brought his hands together. "We've worked hard to get what we have obtained so far."

Hornsby's glare bored into Parker. "Forget it. You're on a desk until further notice."

"Why? I'm not the one who beat the crap out of O'Connor, my distinguished partner did."

Perelli stood suddenly. "That's right, blame me for what's wrong with your fucked-up life."

"Quiet, the both of you." Hornsby held out his hand to Perelli. "Give me your badge, detective. You're suspended pending a full investigation."

"What? But I thought…" Perelli brandished his gold shield, rubbing the engraved surface before relinquishing the badge. "I've put my life on the line in the streets for over twenty years, longer than you've been a cop, Lieutenant. This is the thanks I get?"

"It's not my decision." Hornsby said. "Word came from upstairs." The lieutenant lowered his eyes on the detective. "The press has stirred this town up, Perelli. People are demanding justice, and they've put pressure on the right people. You know the routine." He grimaced, putting Perelli's shield away in the top drawer of his desk. "Citizens have demanded action and they're getting it, which means you two must step aside. It's out of my hands now."

Hornsby stood and squeezed into his blazer, straightened his patterned tie. "Now, if you'll excuse me, I need to go out there and tell the crowd camped outside that our suspect has died."

"What about me?" Parker demanded answers. "Whose decision was it to stick me at a fucking desk?"

"Mine." Hornsby glared at Parker. "You're tired, detective. You look like hell. Go home, get some rest. I'd be lying if I said you've been yourself these past few weeks. Your work is sloppy and unfocused, and your cases are backlogged. I'm getting complaints from the files department." The lieutenant moved from behind his desk. "Your head is not in the job, Parker. You're a danger to yourself and anyone around you. I've got plenty to worry about around here without having to cover for your poor judgment."

Hornsby softened his tone and moved toward the door.

"Look, your pals won't tell you this, but it's my job to do so. You returned to work too soon after your accident." He reached for the doorknob then turned back. "You've been through a lot, Parker. You should consider a leave of absence. Take the rest of the afternoon to think about it." Hornsby opened the door. "Check in with me later, by the end of the day."

"How much leave?"

"As long as you like. Take a month, maybe two. At least until this shit blows over and you get your wits about you again. It'll get fucking ugly around here before it gets better, no thanks to you two." Hornsby cleared his thick throat and eyed Parker cautiously. "The press is merciless. You of all people should know. Best for you and the department if you disappeared awhile."

"The truth." Parker demanded more, anger cutting his words. Hornsby's sudden interest in his welfare made Parker suspicious. "You don't want me near the press, do you, lieutenant? Afraid I might say something to embarrass the department, or some hotshot reporter might learn you have a faggot detective among the ranks?"

"Don't test me, Parker," Hornsby said, visibly irritated. "You know how the system works. I'm following protocol, that's all." He stepped closer to Parker. "It's not always about you, Ken. Talk to your union rep if you have a problem."

"You don't know *what* to do with me," Parker fired back as Hornsby turned to flee. "We're not done here."

Hornsby rushed from the basement with Perelli not far behind. Angry and needing to get the hell out of there before he exploded, Parker rushed to his desk, collected the North and Crater case files, along with his notebooks and a couple of flash drives. He snatched his blazer from the rack, retraced his steps and tossed the material onto Hornsby's desk before leaving the building for what he sensed could be the last time.

The temperature outside had risen, the humidity thick and stifling, a typical sultry morning in the South. Bloated clouds drifted across a pale blue sky, partially shielding the sun's rays. Parker wiped the sweat from his forehead and slipped on his shades. He watched from the far corner of the brick building as a ring of reporters stood before Lieutenant Hornsby, television and still cameras recording the impromptu news conference at Police Headquarters.

"...*An internal investigation will determine what happened, where the department missed an opportunity, and what can be done to prevent this kind of thing from ever happening again.*" Parker listened as the stoic man answered questions. Asked if results would be made public, Hornsby said, "*I can assure you the findings of this investigation will be made public, however any resulting disciplinary actions are confidential and will be treated as an internal matter.*"

Frenzy erupted from the crowd, reporters demanding answers, shouting speculation, or resorting to blame as the lieutenant made a quick retreat after the press conference and disappeared inside the precinct.

No one asked for Parker's side of the story. Nobody cared how he felt betrayed and abandoned by the union he'd grown to love over the years, a pseudo-adoptive family of men and women in uniform he had accepted as his own.

Once again, Parker felt completely alone. He turned and slipped away unnoticed.

CHAPTER FORTY-ONE

Kendall Parker roiled with anger as he sped along Peachtree Street, pissed off at Perelli, but more fired up about losing his case. He crisscrossed through downtown streets trying to cool his head, perhaps even to ease his conscience. Had he done the right thing? Not denying his partner's claim could mean no turning back. Could he really do this?

What about reassigning the case? Was the lieutenant's reason due to the department's damage control or Hornsby's homophobia? Parker didn't know; still, he felt vindicated as he passed through the southern tip of the city, beyond the Fulton County Courthouse. Rounding the southeast corner of Mitchell Street at Central Avenue, he caught a light and glanced over to stare at the historic eleven-story Neo-Gothic City Hall building with its unimpressive cream-colored terra cotta veneer. A couple of city clerks with badges hanging from their necks chatted and speed-raced through cigarettes outside the large double brass doors.

Parker ate lunch at the Colonnade restaurant on Cheshire Bridge road. He always ate at the bar, preferring conversation with the timeless bartender called "J" over the elder, blue-haired ladies serving the tables and the customers alike. He liked the place because no one bothered him about his job working for the city. Afterward, he picked up a bottle of cheap scotch in an

Ansley Square liquor store before heading home. At one-thirty in the afternoon, he mounted the steps to the upper floor to his unit, still pissed at the world because all its miserable problems rested comfortably on his shoulders.

Parker saw a man in a suit perched on the balcony railing outside his front door, waiting for him. "I called your office and was told you were out. I took a chance you might come home for lunch."

"I've had lunch," Parker said. He paused outside the door to his apartment and considered Councilman Mitchell Keyes a moment: gray-flecked hair slicked back from a glistening forehead, bright red cheeks and sunken gray eyes. The man wore an olive green suit a size too small for his squat frame, offset with a fat orange tie and crinkled white shirt.

Scraggly beard visible in the sunlight, Keyes glanced up at Parker, his polished wing-tips scuffing the cement walkway. He stood with both hands in his pockets, fidgeting like a child caught in a lie. "I need your help."

Parker had met the councilman once before at the groundbreaking ceremony celebrating the approved joint police and fire headquarters eighteen months earlier. The department had moved into to the ancient, rotting Sears building while the new, modern complex was to be constructed adjacent to the city jail downtown. Credited for securing the public and private funding for the ninety-million-dollar project, Keyes's popularity with the citizens of Atlanta rang right up there with the Pope.

"You shouldn't be here," Parker said, opening his door as flashbacks from that night in the alley behind the Metroplex— the big black car and a glimpse of the face of a man ducking inside—Keyes' face—flooded his thoughts. "Homicide detectives will want to talk to you." Parker shed his blazer and hung it on the rack in the foyer.

Keyes kept his jacket buttoned.

"How'd you find me?" Parker asked.

"That's not important." The councilman bounded across the threshold without invitation, and Parker closed the door as the elected official threw himself on the sofa.

Keyes wrung his meaty hands together. "I have a big problem."

"You don't say." Parker feigned disinterest, but actually wanted to hear what the man knew about his case, if anything. "I heard on the news this morning."

Keyes jumped to his feet, shoved his hands deep in his pockets and charged about the room like a wild boar. "I could be accused of *murder*," he said, a coward in his own skin.

"Do you want a drink?" Parker asked, unfazed by the man's declaration as he moved to the kitchen and called across his shoulder. "I'm having a scotch."

"Isn't it early in the day?" Keyes called out. "Oh, what the hell. Same as you, I guess."

Parker poured two drinks and returned with glass tumblers. "It was you ducking out the back door of the Metroplex last week." He offered his guest the drink. "Wasn't it?"

Keyes flinched. Perhaps he had realized the inevitable as he relaxed and sunk into the sofa cushions. "You saw me?"

"Yeah I did, about the time I got whacked on the head by the guy I had been chasing." Parker said, taking a seat in the chair opposite Keyes. "I don't recall you coming to my aid."

"Yes, well, I'm sorry about that. Had I known it was you, I would have..." Keyes let his words trail off as he lapped at his drink. "I went there to confront the owner, Anthony Galloti."

"What business do you have with Galloti?"

"He's trying to blackmail me with compromising photos, but I informed him I wouldn't do what he asked."

"I figured as much," Parker said, reaching for a cigarette.

"You knew?" Mitchell flushed. "How could you possibly—"

"About you and North?" Parker shook his head. "I didn't for sure until now. I'd suspected the kid was prostituting, but it didn't add up. He's from a wealthy Buckhead family, so why would he need to—"

Parker cut himself off and glanced over at Keyes. "The picture of you two on the front page this morning gave me a pretty good idea."

"I didn't murder him." Keyes affirmed his admission with

more valor than he seemed capable. He slugged the remaining alcohol in his glass, pulled forward on the sofa with his knees wide apart and held out the empty tumbler. "Could I have another, please?"

Returning with both their glasses full, Parker said, "I know you didn't kill North. He's not dead by the way, least not that we can determine. The body found in the park last week is a boy named Johnny Cage, a friend of North's." Parker paused to give his guest a moment to digest the news. "It's possible Jason is still in the area, in hiding since he's not come forth to dispel reports of his demise."

Keyes appeared speechless. He stared at Parker as though the man had two heads.

"You can relax," Parker said, returning to his seat. "Besides, what interest would Galloti have blackmailing you? No offense, but threatening a politician these days with exposure can't be worth that much."

"Are you kidding?" Keyes shrieked. "We live in the Bible-belt, if you haven't noticed." He frowned and knotted his eyebrows. "I'm not gay, so get that out of your head."

"Right," Parker said, not masking his scorn. "What do you have that Galloti wants?"

"That scalawag has been trying to force me to withdraw a nude dancing ordinance I drafted a few months ago before the legislation comes before committee," Keyes said, exhaling loudly. "Passage of such regulation would cost the industry millions in lost revenues."

Parker nodded, beginning to see the motive. "Something to do with limiting or denying liquor licenses to nude dancing clubs, as I recall."

"My proposed directive is rooted in reducing major crimes, thereby protecting property values. That's all." Keyes offered his best politician's smile. "There is a little known and rarely used state constitutional amendment which allows cities and counties to ban the sale of alcohol in nude dance clubs."

"Such an ordinance would mean doom to hundreds of bars reliant on the two vices," said Parker.

Keyes laughed. "And win me the election in November."

"Is that what all this is about? Your re-election?" Parker grunted. "How did you get mixed up with Galloti in the first place?"

Keyes stared at the floor before speaking. "A homosexual aide in my camp, Lamar Crater, discovered my fondness for young men a few months back."

"He's dead. Did you kill him, too?"

"No!" Keyes flushed. "Look, I'm not proud of my condition, all right? I'm not a saint, but I did not kill anyone." He sat up straight. "Please, I have a wife and kids at home, and I'd like to keep it that way."

Parker fought the urge to slap the man. "Tell me more about your connection to Galloti."

"I am a public figure, detective, hounded by reporters who follow me everywhere, day and night. I have so little privacy, you know? I was forced to take special precautions to address my needs." He flashed a sickening grin. "Lamar Crater said he could introduce me to a man in town who could provide discretion for men and would keep quiet should the opportunity ever arise." Keyes cleared his throat. "Anthony Galloti sent Jason to meet with me at the fundraiser. I didn't recall meeting that young man until seeing my picture with him in the paper this morning."

"You're not making sense, councilman," Parker said. "I need to know everything. Don't lie to me."

Keyes sounded irritated. "Detective, I followed Jason to a motel across the street from the Fox that night. During my time with him, I was drugged without my knowledge."

Parker raised an eyebrow and his glass. "North slipped you something?"

"I don't know if it was him, but somebody did. I am sure because my lawyer obtained a sample of the blood taken from me the night of my DUI arrest. The lab we hired found traces of gamma hydroxyl butyrate in my system."

"GHB," Parker said, "the date rape drug. When ingested, it can render a person unconscious. The subject usually suffers memory loss of the events that occurred while comatose, hence the date-rape signature. Too much of the stuff can kill you. Why would North—or anyone else for that matter—want to slip you GHB?" Parker asked.

Keyes licked the liquor from his lips. "You don't understand," he said, splaying his hands out as if asking for forgiveness. "A man in my position must be discerning. Public image means everything in my line of work." Keyes frowned. "I must admit the indulgence can be expensive, but what choice do I have? I can't very well hang out in the bars, now can I?" He smirked. "I used Anthony's service only a few times. The last was with Jason North. One time too many, I suppose."

Parker pressed for more. "Mitchell, you mentioned blackmail."

The councilman stood and paced the hardwood floor on thick, short legs. "A package arrived at my office last week by personal courier." He jiggled the ice in his glass, signaling he was ready for another. "Inside was a photograph of North and me. We were naked." Keyes swallowed hard and extracted an envelope from his coat pocket.

Keyes handed the print to Parker. "No note. The photograph spoke volumes, however. Two days later, I got an anonymous call threatening to release the picture to the press if I didn't withdraw the nude dancing bill."

Parker took the man's empty glass and headed to the kitchen where he poured them both a full glass of scotch. He returned to the living room. "Go on."

"I refused, of course," Keyes said, wiping his eyes. "Then, this morning my photo is on the front page with that North boy." Keyes looked at Parker through red-rimmed eyes. "Legislation was supposed to be put forth to committee tomorrow morning."

"You're pulling the bill?" Parker asked, actually surprised.

"What choice do I have? North may still be dead. Crater is dead and Galloti doesn't accept refusal." Keyes worked the muscles in his jaws. "He won't let this go."

Parker frowned at the councilman's lack of nerve. "You could still call Galloti's bluff."

"Are you serious? Not a chance. I have a family to consider. I want to spare them the embarrassment of a public spectacle. The scandal would be worse than resigning the job I love most." Keyes covered his face with his hands. "I have to move on, salvage my career as best I can. I'm no match for Galloti." He dropped his hands and perched on the edge of the sofa. "Will you help me?"

"You should be talking to your lawyer, not me."

Keyes rejected at the idea. "It's your investigation, right? You could divert attention toward that scumbag, Galloti... scare up a few leads and connect the dots. Renounce my involvement as happenstance. The press will have to move on. My career will be tarnished, but not unsalvageable."

"There's something you should know," Parker said, sipping his drink. "Lieutenant Hornsby reassigned the case after what happened at headquarters last night."

"The alleged beating of that suspect in custody?"

Parker nodded and reached for a cigarette. "Hornsby's not interested in the facts of the case," he said, lighting up. "His only concern is protecting the department's reputation. Internal Affairs is involved now. The case will be shrouded in a hail of bureaucratic nonsense, then buried as quickly."

It was Keyes' turn to brood. "That's tough talk coming from a sworn enforcer of the law."

"Yeah, well, I've got my own problems." Parker glanced at the clock and stood. "I'm sorry, but I can't help you."

Keyes jumped to his feet. "Surely you want justice as much as I do, detective." He pleaded. "You're just going to let Galloti get away with this?"

"Of course, I want justice, but there's not much I can do, except perhaps..." Parker went silent, contemplating a dangerous idea, but one that could work.

"What?" Mitchell pressed, primed for another cocktail.

"I know someone who could help."

CHAPTER FORTY-TWO

At first, Parker ignored what sounded like a pattering on his front door, choosing instead to roll over and cover his head with a pillow. The insistent pounding intensified, compelling him to open his eyes. He glanced at the clock beside the bed.

11:30p.m. What the hell?

Throwing off the sheet covering his naked body, he swung his feet off the bed. Groggy and sluggish from too much alcohol, he got to his feet and pulled on a pair of gym shorts. The battering against his door echoed in his head like a mallet striking a drum. He grabbed his gun from the side table before padding down the hallway and through the living room, holding his head. He jerked open the front door, lost his grip, and sent it crashing against the wall.

"Brooks! What the *fuck?*"

The rookie's eyes were giant as saucers and restless. "You're needed at the hospital," Brooks stammered, stepping inside. "You need to get dressed,"

"What's wrong?" Parker asked. His knees threatened to buckle. Hospitals scared the hell out of him.

"Perelli's been shot. He's been taken to Grady. Trauma Center."

Ice water could not have sobered Parker faster. "Wait here. I'll be right back."

In his bedroom, Parker pulled on a pair of jeans and a shirt, strapping on his shoulder holster. He checked the safety and secured his weapon before hurrying to join Brooks in the foyer.

"Let's go."

On the ride to the hospital, Parker's mind raced with mixed emotion, replaying all sorts of scenarios. Did Vince accidentally fire his gun while cleaning it? Had his wife mistaken him got a burglar? Whatever, it didn't matter. His thoughts returned to the argument he had with Perelli earlier, and felt guilt gnawing at his insides. He sat silent as Brooks raced the Ford Taurus south on Peachtree Street. The thought of his partner taking a bullet or two made his stomach lurch.

He finally asked Brooks what happened when rain began smacking the windshield in torrents as they sped down Peachtree.

"Couple Unis who came by the house said Perelli caught a couple of bullets at a convenience store. An apparent robbery." The rookie smacked his fist hard against the steering wheel. "Vince never had a chance, Sarge. Fucker shot him point blank in the chest, in cold blood."

Brooks pulled up to the emergency entrance at Grady. Parker bolted from his seat and was out the door before the vehicle came to a complete stop. Hurrying through the sliding-glass door, he rushed up to the reception desk to ask about his partner.

Several agonizing minutes later while glaring at the flustered woman hissing at her computer, Parker spotted Detective Mendenhall on a cell phone exiting the elevator on his left.

"Where's Perelli?" Parker asked the detective.

"He's still in surgery on the second floor."

"Thanks." Parker stabbed the "up" button for the elevator multiple times.

A group of uniformed officers and plain-clothes detectives held vigil in the upstairs hallway, spilling from the waiting room. A quick conference with Lieutenant Hornsby informed

Parker that Perelli had taken two rounds to the abdomen and one to the shoulder. Parker listened to a discouraging prognosis, glancing about as though in a dream, staring but not really seeing anyone, praying somebody would wake him any moment. He glanced over and spotted Jane, Perelli's wife, leaning against the wall opposite the crowded waiting area. Folks hovered around the terrified woman like vultures.

Parker's heart sank when their eyes met. Mrs. Perelli moved effortlessly to join him. He wrapped his arms around her in a cocoon of warmth, wishing he could ease her agony.

"Thank you for coming, Ken." Jane whispered her voice hoarse from crying. "He would want you here."

"What happened?" Parker asked, as gingerly as he could manage.

Jane steeled herself. "I'm not sure, really. I sent Vincent out to pick up some milk." The woman buried her face in Parker's shoulder and sobbed. "I'm to blame, Ken," she cried. "If I hadn't asked…"

"Now, stop that." Parker held her tight. "It's not your fault," he said. "Don't blame yourself. You could not have known what would happen." Parker pointed to a couple of vinyl chairs up the hall, away from the group. "How long will he be in surgery?"

Jane sat down and dabbed her eyes with a knotted tissue. "A few hours, maybe longer." She burst into tears. "I don't know anymore."

"Jane," Parker said with tenderness. "Where are the kids?"

"Mark's skiing with friends in Colorado, and Caroline should be home from work any minute now." She waved her arm in the air. "I should call Mrs. Gamble to bring Caroline here. She's our neighbor and someone Caroline has known for years."

Parker placed his cell phone into her trembling palm. "I'll just be a moment," she said, kissing his cheek before stepping away.

Hours after getting an update on Perelli that was not encouraging, a nurse came and got Jane, Caroline and Parker.

They all passed through large automatic doors into the intensive care wing of the hospital. The stark-white area contained at least a dozen rooms, each encased in glass. A circular nurse's station cluttered with electronic monitoring equipment stood at the center. The air was crisp, even chilly, as they shuffled to Perelli's side.

Hissing from a respirator caught Parker's attention. He followed the trail of a small tube from the machine attached to a pulley mounted in the wall that connected to a mask over Perelli's nose and mouth. A similar tube disappeared below his neck and beneath the blanket tucked around him. Flowing from atop his partner's wrist was a tube that extended from a bag of clear liquid attached to a metal rod on wheels.

Parker slipped his hand into his partner's. Perelli stirred and opened swollen, dark eyes.

"Don't talk. Just relax, take it easy," Parker said. "We're here with you."

Perelli squeezed Parker's hand, urged him closer. "I—I'm sorry, Ken…"

"Shhh…" Parker leaned near the mask and laid his hand on Perelli's head, struggling to withhold tears. "Everything's going to be all right. You hear me? Save your strength."

Perelli pulled the mask off. "Please, Ken. I-I'm s…sorry."

Fear flooded Perelli's eyes, and his face went white. The shrill of the alarm from a machine off to the side sent shock waves through everyone. Hands grabbed Parker's shoulders and yanked him aside. Medical personnel swooped in to stabilize their patient. Jane and Caroline stood transfixed, mother and daughter clutching each other.

A clinician snatched off the blanket covering Perelli's body and pulled the hospital gown to expose the man's pale torso. A doctor smeared jelly onto twin pads that looked like funky earphones and placed them on Perelli's chest.

"Clear!"

Electric current arched Perelli's body skyward. A flat, white line split the screen on the machine sounding the alarm. The doctor made eye contact with the nurse assisting him and applied the paddles again. Perelli's heart refused to respond. A nurse broke in to pound on the man's chest, another began CPR as yet another injected a clear liquid in an IV leading to Perelli's arm. Someone called out, "Code blue!"

For the third and final time, the doctor yelled, "*Clear!*"

An eerie silence fell over the room. Parker stood motionless, staring at Perelli's lifeless frame. After eighteen minutes, the doctor interrupted the quiet by calling for the time.

Parker moved to Perelli's side and laid his head against his partner's shoulder. A rush of anger and guilt filled him as he held onto his fallen friend. *Why?*

"I wanted to apologize," Parker said to no one, to everyone. "I wanted to tell him that I didn't mean what I said." He sobbed. "I wanted to tell him…"

Jane put her hand on Parker's shoulder. He saw her wet face staring into his as she urged him to step away from her husband's body.

Dazed and distraught, Parker emerged from the ICU clutching the two women. "He didn't make it," Parker said to the frightened faces that greeted them.

Tears and shouts of frustration filled the area. Angry expressions swept through the brethren lining the hospital corridor, all vowing to avenge the slain officer's death.

"Kendall, my goodness. Have you any idea what time it is?"

Hattie held open the door and ushered Parker inside the shelter. She had come from the rear of the house, breathing heavily as she shut the door. No doubt she had mistaken his pounding on the door for that of another battered victim seeking help. "It's the middle of the night, is something the matter?"

Parker stepped inside the harsh lighting in the foyer, fidgeting and distraught. He burst into tears when Hattie reached out to hug him.

"Kendall, honey, what's wrong?" She held him tightly. "Are you still having those nasty nightmares, dear?"

"Perelli was shot," Parker said, the words sounding numb to his ears. He pulled back and gazed deep into her warm hazel eyes. "He... he didn't make it."

"Oh my, Lord!" Hattie placed a hand over her heart and ushered him to take a seat in the main room. They sat together on the worn sofa. "Please, dear, tell me what happened."

"I don't know all the details. I'm told Perelli may have walked in on a robbery at a convenience store. He was shot twice in the abdomen." Parker gasped for air as if hearing these words for the very first time. "Something happened, and he went into cardiac arrest just after surgery." He burst forth, covering his nose and mouth in his hands.

"Go ahead, dear. Let it all out," she said, squeezing his hand and hugging his shoulder. "I am here for you, honey."

Collapsing into the arms of this warm, giving angel, Parker cried. He cried for Perelli, he cried for Johnny Cage, and cried for Lamar Crater. He wept even harder for his lost love, Michael, never to hold in his arms again. So much death, so much loss and sadness to bear.

Parker slipped from Hattie's embrace. She stood and offered to prepare a pot of tea. A short time later, she returned carrying an indigo tray with two mugs, packets of sweetener, and slices of lemon.

"Thank you." Parker offered a smile as she set a cup before him. "Once again, you're here when I need you the most."

"I will always be here for you, Ken. Wait here, I have something to show you. I'll only be a moment."

Leaning back against the cushions in a more comfortable spot in the sofa, Parker rubbed his tired, aching eyes. He was exhausted, completely spent. Hattie returned with a manila envelope and removed its contents before rejoining him on the sofa.

"I realize this may not be the best time to bring this out, but I've been thinking a lot of what you said the other day about your dreams of the accident and your desperate struggle to keep Michael from slipping beneath the surface of water."

Parker sipped herbal tea and eyed her carefully.

"I know you have been blaming yourself for Michael's death, Kendall. Anyone could see that. Subconsciously or otherwise, it explains the nightmares you have been having."

Setting his mug down on the coffee table before them and not wanting to have this conversation, not wanting to go *there,* Parker said, "It's late, Hattie. I should be going."

"Please, Kendall, hear me out." She pleaded with him, her eyes blazing beneath a forehead of deep lines. "I can help you, dear."

"No, you can't," Parker snapped, a little too harshly. "You don't get it, Hattie." He jumped to his feet and began pacing the floor. "Don't you see? I couldn't hold onto him. Michael's body was weighed down, too heavy to lift on my own. The more I tried, the farther he sank beneath the surface. I just couldn't hang on any longer." He looked directly at her. "I didn't have the strength to hold onto him. It's my fault Michael drowned that day."

"Nonsense! You are not responsible, Ken." Hattie's voice grew harsh and urgent. "No one was more upset about Michael's death than me," she said, holding papers in her hand up to him. She sniffled. "It had never occurred to me to read my nephew's autopsy report. It didn't seem important at the time. My nephew was dead, and that's all that mattered to me then." She handed the document to him. "You should have a look at this."

"I don't see how a few pieces of paper can possibly—"

"Ken, please. Look at the report."

Parker scanned the pages to the middle of the second page, section two, line twenty-three. The words typed across the pre-printed form rang clear to him.

"Michael broke his neck," he read. "He died on impact, before he ever hit the water." Parker felt his shoulders relax, the burden of guilt that had weighed him down for weeks slipping away like the receding tide. This new revelation was a welcome consolation, albeit bittersweet since Michael was still gone. *It wasn't my fault.*

Tears slid down Parker's cheeks. "It wasn't my fault."

"No, it wasn't, dear." Hattie hugged him tight. "You've been torturing yourself needlessly all this time."

After crying a few more tears, Parker pulled back and gripped her shoulders. "I was still in shock in the days and weeks following the accident. I never thought to ask for a copy of the autopsy. I had assumed he'd drowned, like everyone said at the time."

He hugged her again and breathed in the familiar scent of her jasmine perfume. Moments of silence passed between the two before Parker spoke again. "Thank you, Hattie. I can't imagine what losing Michael has meant for you these past few months." He smiled and squeezed her hands before leaving.

Hattie called from across her shoulder. "Kendall, time will soothe your burdened heart, dear. Holding on to the past can only delay your healing. Michael will always be with you. Don't forget that. *He* is your guardian angel now."

Parker blew her a kiss and walked out the door.

The air felt dry and light. The humidity was low, the heavens were clear. City lights brightened the dark canvas and the moon was high against its backdrop. A single light shot across the bespangled sky as tingles slid up Parker's spine. Somewhere, he knew Michael was watching, smiling down on him with that incredible smile. He grinned back and swallowed the lump in his throat down before stepping from the porch.

CHAPTER FORTY-THREE

"Good morning, *Atlanta Journal-Constitution*. How may I direct your call?"

"Newsroom, please." Parker was placed on hold. He cleared his throat, tapping the pen in his hand on the kitchen counter while waiting. A pang gnawed his stomach as he considered the consequences of his plan.

A grim voice came on the line. "Newsroom."

"Is Calvin Slade available?" Parker had the urge to hang up, but held firm.

"Hold the line, please."

Again, he held, listening to oldies between static. He became distracted by a news bulletin on the television screen. A red-haired black woman dressed in a lime green blazer and white silk blouse spoke in a monotone, her face expressionless. In the foreground, upper right-hand corner flashed a photo of Vincent Perelli in uniform. The caption below read: *Policeman Slain.*

The anchorwoman called Detective Perelli a hero for his attempt to foil an apparent robbery of a convenience store while off duty. A suspect had since been apprehended and was being held at the Fulton County Pretrial Detention Center pending arraignment. Bail had been understandably denied. The department had released a statement commending Vincent Perelli's service of twenty-five years. Brief mention was made of the internal investigation surrounding the death of Dane O'Connor and Perelli's alleged involvement.

A spokesperson for the department said O'Connor remained the primary suspect in the murder of Jason North, son of noted Buckhead businessman, Bradford North. The anchor-woman concluded by providing details of the funeral services for the slain officer. A feminine hygiene commercial filled the screen.

"I'll connect you now," the flat voice said before completing the transfer.

Parker licked his lips and waited. A bold, dispassionate voice answered. "Slade."

"It's Kendall Parker," he said. "We need to talk."

"It's about time." The reporter's tone sounded churlish. "Have a change of heart, have we?"

"Don't push it," Parker said. "Can you be at my place in an hour?"

"Not sure I can get away, but let me check…" The sound of a keyboard clicking echoed through the connection. "…I'll see what I can do."

"You do that. It'll be worth your while."

Parker hung up and went to the kitchen to start a pot of coffee brewing. He showered, dressed in a pair of worn jeans and dark t-shirt before returning to the living room. After clearing glasses, pizza boxes, and ashtrays and straightening cushions on the sofa, he went to the desk and retrieved a framed photograph of Michael from the drawer. He placed it on the mantle above the fireplace and smiled.

Around nine-thirty, the doorbell sounded. Parker looked through the peep hole and opened the door to greet the reporter.

"I brought doughnuts," Slade said, shoving a white bag forward. "An apology for the way I've acted of late. I admit I may have been a little roused."

"That's an understatement." Parker shut the door after ushering the man inside. "Have a seat. I'll get you some coffee."

"Make it black." Slade shuffled past him and headed for the sofa.

Parker returned from the kitchen and set coasters and two mugs of coffee on the table between them. He took a seat and eyed the man cautiously, wondering if he could trust him.

"Thanks for coming on such short notice," Parker said, reaching for a jelly doughnut.

Slade sipped his coffee and peered across the rim of the mug. He appeared expectant, barely able to mask his curiosity. "Don't mention it." He put down his coffee and reached for a powdered doughnut. "I'm real sorry to hear about your partner. You guys were together for a while. If you need someone to talk—"

"I'm fine," Parker said.

Slade grimaced, took a bite of his pastry. "We were close friends once, Ken," he said, chewing with his mouth open. "I still care about you."

"That was a long time ago."

Parker glanced away. They'd met when Parker was a beat cop assigned to a housing project on the south side of the city. Slade had been roaming the area one night gathering material for an expose he had planned to write about subsidized housing and corruption in the local housing authority. He'd become trapped in the crossfire of rival gangs and Parker had been the cop to save his ass. They had formed a deep friendship thereafter, a rarity among cops and reporters. It wasn't until Parker had met and fallen for Michael that Slade had confessed his own sexuality.

Parker glanced over at the reporter. Their friendship had ended in a raw breakup he didn't care to consider at the moment. He had more important things to discuss.

"I didn't ask you here to talk about the past," Parker said. "I called because I need your help."

Slade chewed his donut and wiped powder from his lips. "I'm listening."

Abandoning his half-eaten doughnut, no longer finding the pastry appetizing, Parker sipped coffee. "I've been reluctant to discuss the details of the Jason North murder case," he started. Slade nodded agreement. "I felt releasing too much detailed information too soon would jeopardize the investigation and, frankly, we didn't have much to share."

"What has changed now?" Slade crammed the rest of his doughnut into his large mouth, chewing enthusiastically.

"Certain information has been withheld from the public," Parker said, as he stood and walked across the room to the large window overlooking the breezeway and courtyard of his condominium complex. Groundskeepers scurried about, mowing grass and clipping hedges in ripped jeans and soiled T-shirts. "I'm no longer in control of the case, so I don't trust that the information I've gathered will get much attention."

He turned back to Slade, sincerity in his tone. "Everything has gotten out of hand, Calvin. I'm afraid if I don't make a move soon, O'Connor will be branded a killer and North's case will be closed without further investigation."

Slade leaned back against the sofa cushions, nursing his coffee. "What about Lamar Crater?"

"I no longer believe the man was murdered," Parker said. "It's more likely he overdosed on some drug. Toxicology results should bear that out."

"Great." Slade sat down his mug, retrieved a small pad and pen from his coat pocket, and began taking notes. "So much for my repeat killer theory," he said, disappointment clouding his face.

"You were way off base there, buddy. Hell, we all were." Parker chuckled, then turned serious. "But there's more. North wasn't the dead man discovered in Piedmont Park last week. The killer may have planned the attack to look like a crime motivated by hate, but he attacked the wrong guy."

Slade sat slack-jawed. "What? So, where is North?"

"Who knows? He could be in hiding or dead for all I know. What I *do* know is Jason North was a prostitute who had planned to blackmail one of his clients with photographs of their exploits, which could explain why he's not come forward. Turns out said client was Councilman Mitchell Keyes."

Slade scrawled across a thin sheet of paper at lightning speed. "This *is* interesting." He mumbled something before glancing up. "I don't buy your theory though."

"Why not?"

"I have reason to believe North was the source behind the headline that ran in this morning's paper. He contacted me late last week." Parker raised his eyebrows. "At least, I think it was him." Slade set down his pen. "I received a tip that day before deadline from an anonymous caller. A guy claimed Councilmen Keyes had not been alone the night he left a fundraiser at the Fox, prior to his DUI arrest. I had traced the call to a pay phone located on the corner of 10th and Piedmont, down the block from Piedmont Park."

"So that's how you were able to put Keyes and North together," Parker said, tapping the side of his head.

Slade frowned and cocked his head. "You said North planned to blackmail Keyes? For what, money? I thought the man's family was loaded."

"Its true North was a spoiled rich kid with a taste for finer things in life, used to getting his own way. But his relationship with his father was strained. Apparently, he had tightened the purse strings when his son refused counseling for his *lifestyle*."

"I'm beginning to understand why the kid was working as a go-go boy," Slade said, frowning. "It was his way of lashing out at his bigoted father, embarrassing him." He crinkled his eyebrows. "If he was indeed planning to extort Mitchell Keyes, why are you telling me?"

"Because I need your help," Parker said, sighing. "I'm convinced Jason had a partner, someone with enough savvy and connections to have set up such a scheme to target the councilman. Keyes showed me the photos. They were slick and professional, not taken by some amateur wielding a camera phone."

"Do you think this person is responsible for all this?"

"I'm not sure." Parker steepled his fingers beneath his chin.

"How familiar are you with the nude dancing legislation Keyes was about to introduce?"

The reporter picked up his pen. "I wrote a Sunday edition exposé several weeks back outlining the councilman's push to stamp out nude dancing clubs within city limits. He claimed his reason was to save the city's youth from the associated drugs and violence often associated with such businesses. I think it was to cement his reelection." Slade laughed. "Weak, I know, but in a state where right-winged conservatism has enjoyed a resurgence because of the advancement of the far-right agenda, no red-light enterprise is immune."

Slade paused a moment, then his eyes widened. "Wait a minute," he said. "Are you suggesting some kind of conspiracy aimed at getting Keyes to back off his proposal?"

"You guessed correct," Parker said. "It doesn't seem coincidence to me that North's employer is Anthony Galloti, owner of the most popular nude male dance club, Metroplex."

"Galloti would have reason to kill Keyes' proposed statute, but take it as far as murder? I don't know?"

"It's possible to think North was silenced because of some disagreement with his partner, money, or to cut the trail back to Galloti. It's only a matter of time before those photographs are traced to their original source."

"Hence the motive," Slade said, squinting. "What do you need me for?"

"To get the story out. You print this, and the police can flush out Galloti, connect the dots and get an indictment."

Slade's brows arched and his lips twisted as he contemplated the detective's proposal. "You want me to tell everything?"

"I can do little more to help at this point. Lieutenant Hornsby removed me from the case today."

Slade stared straight ahead, appearing unsure. "Why me?" he asked.

"Because you're thorough, Slade." Parker extracted a cigarette from the pack on the table between them. "You've always had a greedy personality. Given the opportunity, you'd bleed the life out of this story if it meant another byline, a shot at a Pulitzer."

Slade grimaced.

"Enough is never enough for you." Parker sharpened his tone. "Don't forget, I've witnessed your wrath first-hand."

The reporter ignored the reference to articles he'd penned in the aftermath of Michael's death. "If I go along with your plan, what's in it for me?"

"An exclusive, details of a police cover-up, a recorded statement, whatever it takes."

"What cover-up?" Slade's interest peaked. "What haven't you told me? You said you were removed from the case. Why?"

"Look," Parker said, "you've maintained from the start the department was ignoring this case because of homosexual prejudices." Slade nodded in agreement. "That's partly true. You don't know the half of it." Parker shifted in his seat. "Dane O'Connor died as a result of injuries he received the night of his arrest. An act of vengeance carried out by my partner for having been pricked with a tainted syringe. The truth is being concealed to thwart a public cry for action."

Slade squirmed, unable to contain his excitement as Parker continued. "If this gets out, the department faces grave embarrassment and lawsuits. Look what happened in Los Angeles after the Rodney King beating. Higher ups want this case closed and allegations of misconduct put behind them, the quicker the better."

Sighing, Parker said, "That won't be hard to accomplish since both involved are now dead. The internal investigation will likely be abandoned and O'Connor blamed for North's murder based on circumstantial evidence."

"What, a cover-up to thwart public outrage?" Slade asked.

Parker stabbed out his cigarette, extracted another. "Precisely."

"But you hold the trump card. Who else knows of North's attempt to screw Keyes?"

"Besides you and Keyes?" Slade nodded, pen poised at the ready. "My guess would be the murderer or perhaps the person who hired the killer. I'd like to keep it that way, too." Parker struck a match, puffed hard on his cigarette and exhaled bluish smoke above his head. "You should mention the pictures in your story, that I have a lead on who took them."

Slade cupped his chin. "You'll be setting yourself up to take a fall from the department or worse."

"It's my intention."

Slade sat his mug on the table and scowled. "It's too dangerous, Ken. The killer's liable to come after you."

"That's what I'm counting on."

CHAPTER FORTY-FOUR

Slade extracted a small digital recorder from his lapel pocket and placed it on the coffee table. He glanced over at Parker, eyebrows arched with worry. "Your career as a detective will be ruined," he said.

"Doesn't matter anymore. The lieutenant knows I'm gay. I'll be forced out of the department regardless, so best to do it on my own terms."

The reporter did not appear shocked by Parker's pronouncement. If anything, the man appeared to understand the detective's motives, even if Parker doubted himself.

Slade asked again. "You sure you want to do this?"

"Positive," Parker said, glancing over at the picture of Michael atop the mantle. "But you can't leave out the fact that I'm gay, either. It's time I stood up to be counted."

"I'm sorry I blamed you for Michael's death," Slade said in almost a whisper. He stood and walked up to Michael's photograph, calling across his shoulder. "I guess it was a lame attempt to force my guilt on to you."

Parker stared at the floor. "It's forgotten, Calvin. Now, let's get started."

"No, Kendall, please hear me out." Slade turned around.

"What happened between Michael and me should never have happened, but it did. I can't change that fact."

"I don't want to hear this." Parker clenched and unclenched his fists, feeling a knife piercing in his gut.

"He showed up at my door that night crying. You two had been arguing again about his desire to be more open, participate in the gay community. I intended to comfort him, that's all. I was shocked he'd even come to me, but he did. I couldn't just turn him away. I don't know how or why, but it happened, okay? I've regretted it each day since." Slade walked over to Parker, tears trailing his red cheeks. "It hurt when you cut me out of your life, Ken. Eight years tossed aside without warning, without giving me a chance to explain, to apologize for my behavior."

Slade began to pace the room and flail his arms about. "You were being stubborn as always. You wouldn't listen to me, no matter how much I tried." He choked on his tears, caught his breath and stopped, cutting his eyes toward Parker.

"I was angry with you, Ken, angry with Michael and myself. Then, the accident happened and I used the newspaper to get back at you for cutting me off." Slade knelt before Parker, taking the man's trembling hands into his own. "What I did was self-ish, I know, but I was hurting, too. I had lost two friends that day on the lake and had no one to comfort me."

The room fell silent. Several minutes passed before Parker spoke up. "Michael and I had been arguing about his plans to volunteer time at the Gay Center. He'd wanted to counsel trou-bled teens, help them to understand their sexuality, how to get along in life with a bigoted society. He thought his medical training and experience as a physical therapist afforded him a chance to help, and he wanted to give back."

Parker withdrew his hands and slid back on the sofa. He did not wipe away the tears trailing down his cheeks. "I was selfish," he said. "Afraid what the exposure meant for us, to me, really. What a connection to such a visible organization could do to our careers, our lives once people heard. I was afraid our being lovers would become public knowledge..."

"As long as I can remember," Parker said, wiping his nose with the back of his hand. "I have lived in fear my sexuality would be discovered. Afraid of being who I was, being exposed a fag." He grimaced. "It probably explains my aggressive nature, who knows? The point is, I had managed to keep my relationship with Michael hidden to all but a select few, you being one of them."

Slade smiled back at him, tapped his chest above his heart twice.

"Michael's dream threatened to change everything for us, how we lived our lives, what guys at the station would think, what they would say. No matter how much I tried to share in Michael's enthusiasm, I couldn't escape my true feelings." Parker wrung his hands together, the whites of his knuckles stark against his skin.

"I never blamed Michael for being angry with me." Parker couldn't mask the guilt he felt. "What choice had I given him? Michael had talked about moving out. I guess I underestimated how much giving back meant to him."

"You don't have to explain to me, Ken." Slade sobbed, wiping away the tears on his sleeve. "I don't need to know the details."

"I want you to know," Parker said. "The thought of losing Michael had been too great, so I'd decided to give in. Ironic, isn't it? The reason we went to the lake that weekend was because I planned to surprise him with the news." Parker dropped his head and stared at the hardwoods. "I never had the chance to spring my surprise, to tell him how much I loved him."

Slade pulled Parker into his arms. They held tight to each other and cried hard for their own loss, suffering, and insecurities. They cried for Michael. With this finally out in the open, each could now concentrate on rebuilding the fragile friendship that had once meant a great deal to them both.

Parker withdrew from the embrace, smiling. "C'mon, we have work to do."

. . .

After Slade left to write his story, Parker headed to headquarters to fulfill his duty of sitting at his desk for the day. He parked in the employees' lot, tossed his cigarette butt, and headed inside, nodding to a few colleagues along the way. He spent most of the day catching up on paperwork long overdue.

Arriving home later in the day, Parker noticed the late edition of the *Journal* outside his door. He removed the rubber band securing the roll and looked at the front page headline: MURDER SUSPECT DIES IN CUSTODY AMID POSSIBLE COVER-UP; CONNECTED TO ATTEMPTED BLACKMAIL OF POPULAR CITY COUNCILMAN. Photographs of Parker, North, O'Connor, Keyes, Hornsby, and Perelli were scattered on the front page, the feature continuing inside Local news.

The telephone was ringing as Parker entered his place. He closed the door, stripped out of his shoulder holster and hung it and his revolver on the coat rack before walking over to the answer machine. Most calls were from radio and television reporters requesting interviews, and a few were from guys at the precinct offering support. A couple messages came from anonymous callers threatening him. The final message came from Mitchell Keyes, who congratulated him on his courage and wished them both luck.

Popping a frozen dinner in the toaster oven, he poured a glass of scotch and contemplated the case. Though Hornsby had reassigned the investigation to another team, the habit of turning off his thoughts, running through facts of the case and pondering theories wasn't easy to break. He knew North had had a partner in setting up the blackmail scheme. The kid couldn't have pulled off such a scheme on his own.

Boris Winecof wielding the camera screamed accessory, still Parker knew a judge wouldn't issue a warrant for the photographer based on speculation. He had to come up with a better lead. He didn't believe it was as simple as a jilted lover driven to kill and responsible for disrupting so many lives. Was Boris capable of murder?

Of course, he thought. Driven far enough, anyone was capable, not uncommon in the throes of heated passion. Calculated or not, evidence had suggested a killer of superior strength, one mean enough to brutalize before striking the fatal blow. Though shorter and heavier than Johnny Cage, Boris didn't fit the profile in the least.

Contemplating possible scenarios and feeling warm, Parker opened a section of the window overlooking the breezeway. He opened another on the other side, letting the cooler evening air circulate. He thought he'd take a shower.

Walking naked into the bedroom after toweling off, Parker slipped on a pair of boxers and padded through the hall to the living room. Whether it was instinct, paranoia, or both, something commanded him to freeze. He cocked his head left to right, listening again for that odd noise he thought he'd heard. His shallow breaths reached his ears in the quiet.

Slowly, Parker crept forward, placing one foot in front of the other, his ears pitched for sound. He peered into the living room where all appeared normal. He eased forward, each step widening his visual range. Pausing at the mouth of the hallway, he scanned the area. A quick glance into the foyer exposed his revolver still secure in its holster, hung on the coat rack to the right of the front door. A second glance confirmed the dead-bolt secured.

Then he noticed the front window was closed.

CHAPTER FORTY-FIVE

Parker's heart jackhammered in his chest as adrenaline kicked in. The hair on the back of his neck stood on end. He realized he had to risk going for his gun, but the second he chose to make a dash for his Glock, the telephone rang. Startled, he stood motionless. It rang a second and third time before engaging the pre-recorded message. Parker listed as his voice filled the room. At the beep, Brooks' words screamed out the tiny speaker.

"Sergeant Parker, pick up if you're there. Lot's happened since you left work, but I thought you'd want to know that State Patrol stopped a suspect—ugh, Clark D-u-c-a-n an hour ago for speeding. Search of his car uncovered a handgun missing its serial numbers. He was arrested and transported to Fulton County Detention. An interrogation uncovered he was the shooter responsible for Perelli's death. He claimed he was hired to make the hit on Perelli."

Brooks took a deep breath and continued rambling. "Ballistics just confirmed the weapon confiscated from Duncan's car was the same gun that shot Perelli. The suspect begged for a deal. The assistant DA agreed to take the death penalty off the table if Duncan fingered who hired him. The guy named Anthony Galloti and Stewart Callahan. A squad's been dispatched to pick them up. I'm on my way to get you. I thought you'd want to be included."

The machine halted at the sound of the dial tone, clicked a couple times and rewound the tape before shutting off. The message light started flashing red.

Parker had no choice but to go for his weapon. If someone had entered his condo, they heard the message with him. Parker glanced at the closed window then back to his pistol before making the split decision to dashed across the room for his weapon. A figure darted out from behind a wall and tackled him from behind. Parker twisted, kicked and elbowed his attacker in the groin.

A piercing pain exploded through Parker's body, paralyzing him. *Stun gun.* He fell to the floor like a stiff doll. Flight was out of the question. Parker struggled to regain his limbs enough to fight. His muscles refused to function. He managed to prop himself up on one elbow, and tried pull his right arm still pinned behind his back forward.

The attacker towered over Parker, straddling his legs. Parker could see his pistol visible on the coat rack beyond the intruder's hip.

Parker recognized the Metroplex manager. "Callahan?" Parker slurred his speech. "Why the fuck are you here?"

Stewart Callahan snarled like a Pitbull. He brandished the stun gun again and prodded Parker's leg. A blistering charge surged through his body. He doubled over in pain, splayed across the floor like a piece of deadwood.

"Stop, please! I-I can't take it anymore," Parker wheezed, eyes locked on the weapon. Flashes of a terrified Jason North facing his attacker occupied his mind. "Wh-what do y-you want?"

"I have what I came for, detective." He laughed. "A shame too," he said, looking back down at Parker. "I was beginning to like you."

Stewart stepped over Parker's legs and circled the room. "A rather unique situation has developed," he said. "Until now, we've been sweating it out, hoping you and your dumbass partner didn't get any closer to solving North's murder. Hell, we actually thought we had the police baffled." He stopped, eyes turning cold. "Then we read that damn article in the paper today."

Walking over, Stewart kicked Parker's legs, taunting him. "Your partner is dead, detective. Johnny Cage is dead. Lamar Crater is dead. O'Connor is dead." His eyes widened, exposing pinpoint pupils set within glassy eyes. "They're all dead. Which leaves just you and that nosy reporter as the last loose end."

"You're wasting your time. I'm off the case," Parker wheezed, calculating the distance between his gun and Callahan. "Consider me out of the picture."

"We can't afford to take that chance." Stewart slipped on a pair of black leather gloves. "You must be dealt with now before you can cause any more trouble."

Attempting to keep the man talking, Parker changed direction. "Who's the other half of 'we'?"

"That's not important!" Anger spiked Callahan's words. "It'll all be over soon. Trust me, you're not going to feel a thing."

"Was it Galloti? Did he order you to kill those men?"

"What? No, I didn't kill anybody," Callahan taunted, reveling in his genius. "Galloti is as naive as Cage ever was. As your partner even, same as you. He had no idea what we had planned once he hatched the scheme to blackmail Councilman Keyes."

"What are you planning?" Parker challenged, regaining some of the strength in his arms. "Who are you working with? North? He's the only one missing in this scenario. It's no secret Boris Winecof snapped the incriminating photographs."

Callahan scowled.

"What, did I hit a nerve? The way I figure, North had met Lamar Crater early on, more than likely while he danced at Metroplex. He learned Crater worked in Councilman Keyes' office. Jason told his boss, no doubt. They were bedmates after all, and that's when Anthony came up with the idea to drug the councilman, obtain the photos of Keyes with North and coerce public official into aborting plans to introduce the nude dancing ordinance. Keyes would do almost anything to keep his fondness for young men a secret, right? Am I getting warm?"

"Shut up!" Callahan shoved his weapon forward, threatening to jolt Parker again.

"Galloti knew Keyes wouldn't contact the police, so it seemed the perfect scam. Once your boss received the blackmail photos, all he needed was to cover his tracks and that meant those involved had to die."

Stewart flinched. "You don't know what you're talking about. None of this would've happened if Anthony hadn't put out the hit on Jason. Nobody had to die."

Parker cocked his head and offered up a wide grin. "I bet you are fucking North, huh?"

"That's none of your damn business." Callahan glowered at Parker.

"It doesn't matter anymore, Stewart. You're going to kill me anyway, so why not tell the truth at this point? What I can't figure is why. What was your motivation? Galloti clearly had motive to blackmail Keyes against introducing legislation that would kill his business. Along the way, he must have decided to rid himself of all the players. More insurance for him." Parker jutted out his chin. "What was your motive? Why get involved? Was it because of your love for North? He and Galloti had called it quits, so you had no trouble moving right in." Parker stole a glance toward his gun. "Or was it good old-fashioned greed? The promise of lots of money?"

"It's always about money," Callahan said, crossing to the foyer.

"I imagine skimming off the profits of the lucrative dance club could be mighty rewarding."

"Not as profitable as the millions Galloti has stashed away from an underground group of nude dance club owners intent on securing their mega profits."

"And they let Galloti hold on to the money? Very trusting of them. Foolish, but trusting."

"Of course, they couldn't very well deposit all that cash in the bank, now could they?" Callahan hesitated, his nostrils flaring. "Anthony hatched the idea to blackmail Keyes, get him to back off. It made sense for them to pool their money together to keep that rightwing ignorant from stamping down their businesses."

"So what went wrong? Why target North, which resulted in the attack that killed Cage?"

"That didn't need to happen." Callahan's lips curled in defiance. "Galloti had changed his mind before reaching out to the councilman. He didn't want to chance any players involved would come forward and confess their involvement if Keyes went to police."

"So you warned North to keep him from harm, but you needed to devise a way to get Galloti to back off and get North off the hook. That's where Johnny Cage, North's friend, comes in. He was set up to make it appear the hit was successful against North. Whether Cage agreed to take North's place or not is anyone's guess. Am I right?"

"You're good." Stewart hissed. "You think you've got it all figured out." He delivered a hard kick into the side of Parker's gut. "More reason you can't be allowed to remain alive."

Parker struggled to move his legs. "Killing me would be a mistake," he said through gritted teeth. "Cops know you were involved in my partner's ambush. You heard the call. It's a matter of time before police apprehend you and Galloti."

"They'll be busy," Stewart said, his eyes growing cold. "It'll take them awhile to figure out what happened here. See, you've been depressed, losing your partner and all, even the case. You couldn't handle all the pressure, the stress."

Callahan snatched the pistol from its holster, released the safety and retraced his steps. He placed the cold barrel against Parker's temple. "You're going to commit suicide," he said, forcing Parker's right hand around the butt of the revolver, directing his finger on the trigger. "No one will suspect anything amiss."

Parker stared at the man from the corner of his eye, the compact simplicity of the Smith & Wesson more frightening than ever. He squeezed his eyes shut and whispered a silent prayer as a deafening crash broke through the tension. Callahan looked up as a clay-potted plant skittered across the hardwood floor amid a flurry of broken glass. Parker spun around and blasted an uppercut into Callahan's gut and thrust his legs up in the air, striking the man's ribs. Callahan growled and charged forward. The sound of fracturing bones was nothing compared to the sound of the gun as Parker unloaded the chamber into his attacker's body, bullets penetrating Callahan's muscular torso. The man's face flashed confusion and fear as he went down with a thud.

Parker got to his feet as the door burst open and Brooks stepped in, his gun drawn. Stewart's body lay at Parker's feet, quivering in spilled blood.

"You saved my life," Parker said. He could hear sirens approaching.

Brooks whistled. "I'm glad I arrived when I did." He checked Callahan's body for a pulse. "I got here as soon as I could. Are you all right?"

"Yeah, I'm fine." Parker sat down on the sofa. "How did you know to come here?"

Brooks holstered his pistol and moved across the room. "I heard on the box Cobb PD fished Galloti's body from the Chattahoochee near I-285. Stranded motorist alerted authorities he'd seen something large tossed over the bridge into the river. I figured since everyone else connected to this case was dead or missing, you'd be in danger."

Both men turned toward the thundering footsteps rushing down the walkway. A rowdy pair of patrolman entered with guns drawn. Upon recognizing Parker and Brooks, they holstered their weapons.

Within minutes, more cops came barreling up the corridor. Detectives converged on the scene and a team from GBI began collecting evidence as Parker recited what happened. A crime scene photographer shot the bloody scene while Parker surrendered for routine questioning before joining the detectives at APD headquarters. Less than two hours later, he was allowed to leave after having proven self-defense.

With Brooks' assistance, Parker ducked out the rear of the precinct, bypassing reporters and news cameras holding vigil on the front steps of the building. They piled into Brooks' sporty ride. The rookie steered out of the parking garage, turning opposite the crowd standing in front of the precinct.

Several minutes passed before Brooks said, "Tough news about Perelli. I never would have guessed Galloti was responsible for ordering the hit on him."

"Yeah, Vince could be a pain in the ass at times, but I miss the old kook. It's never going to be the same around the precinct with him gone."

"Has anyone told his wife?"

Parker glanced over and frowned. "Lieutenant went to see her before word got out in the press. I'll stop by tomorrow after she's had enough time to process the news."

"It won't be easy on her knowing the truth," Brooks said.

"No, it won't."

They feel silent until arriving at Parker home. Parker thanked Brooks for the ride and begged off company for the night.

CHAPTER FORTY-SIX

Jason North adjusted the baseball cap covering his shaved head, pulled the bill down lower over his eyes and shoved his hands into his pockets. He walked in casually through the smoked glass doors of the Metroplex, and flashed his ID before thrusting a twenty across the stone counter. The attendant didn't even look up as he snatched the money. North continued onward around the partition and into the bar.

The change in his appearance since the last time he was here proved good enough cover that he moved through the sparse crowd unrecognized. He headed straight for the door concealed in the laminated wall to the left of the coat-check. Standing outside the office with his back to the door North glanced around a few minutes before leaning backward on the walled panel. The door was locked as usual. From his pocket, he withdrew a gold key Callahan had given him weeks earlier, unlocked the door, and slipped into Anthony Galloti's office.

The room was in total darkness, except for a multitude of tiny green and red LED lights from the electronics along the right wall. North extracted a small flashlight from his back pocket and moved toward a giant 1958 movie poster of *Attack of the 50 Ft. Woman,* which concealed a large wall safe. Clasping the rubber sheathed flashlight between his teeth, North swung

the framed poster open and grabbed the black combination dial
of the wall safe hidden behind. He worked the combination,
yanked downward on the thick black handle and opened the
safe door.

The lights flicked on. North froze mid-step and turned to
find someone sitting in the chair behind the large desk. After a
moment of blindness, he recalled the detective from images
posted in the newspaper and broadcasted across news channels.

North caught his breath. "How did you know I'd
come here?"

"Not hard to figure once Galloti's body floated down the
river and Stewart Callahan died trying to take me out," Parker
said in a matter-of-fact tone. "You're the last player with
anything to gain. The one person connected to this twisted mess
we hadn't caught. Didn't take long for me to realize you had to
be the accomplice Callahan sang about once he told me he'd
ignored Galloti's order to get rid of you. Considering all the
background and research information on Galloti found in your
condo, I figure you had planned all along to infiltrate Galloti's
inner circle for your own personal gain."

Parker stood and reached behind his back for a pair of cuffs.
"What I haven't guessed is why, Jason? Why go to all that
trouble cozying up to a known criminal for such little money?"

The former dancer refused to speak. Parker leveled his eyes
at the young man and waited another minute before continuing. "Look, this will go far better for you in the long run to
come clean now and not drag it out. It won't bode well for you
to waste more of my time than you have already. I promise I'll
ensure you get segregated from the more dangerous criminals in
city lockup."

His offer received only stone-faced silence. Parker shrugged
his shoulders and pinched the bridge of his nose with both forefingers. "All right," he said. "We'll play it your way. How about I
tell you what I already know and you fill in the blanks? Will
that work for you? When Stewart confessed what was going
down, that Galloti had ordered your death, you set up your best
friend to take a hit meant for you."

North wrung his hands. "That's a lie! I loved Johnny like a brother. I never did anything to hurt him."

"So you say," Parker said, laying the trap. "According to the law, you're just as guilty of murder as if you had swung the bat that bashed in your friend's face."

North winced, as if visualizing the nasty image, perhaps realizing for the first time how close he actually came to being murdered. "Johnny's death wasn't my fault," he said with conviction. "I didn't set him up, as you say. I needed his help. My car wouldn't start, and I sensed someone following me. I ducked into a bar called Blake's on 10th for protection and I called him." North held out his hands, palms up, and narrowed his eyes. "*He* insisted that he could divert whoever was after me by cutting through the park that night. The plan was for me to sneak out the back while he went out the front door wearing my trench coat."

North ventured a step forward, putting Parker on his guard. "Believe me, detective. None of it was my idea. Johnny traveled through the park all the time heading home from his shift at Metroplex. If anyone could lose a tail, he could, so I let him talk me into it." North dropped his arms in frustration. "When I didn't hear from him the next day, or several days after, I knew what had happened."

"You could have gone to the police."

"And say what? I thought somebody planned to kill me, and I let my best friend impersonate me leaving a bar to cut through Piedmont Park? What does that say about me?" North opened his arms. "Nobody would have believed me if I tried."

"What about Lamar Crater?" Parker asked. "Did you have a hand in his death?"

"What? No!" North seemed shocked at the implication. His body went rigid. "Stewart had warned me Anthony wanted me and the councilman's aide dead. I went to Lamar's house last week to warn him to get out of town, but when I arrived at his place, I found him on the floor of his bedroom convulsing and foaming at the mouth. I feared he would bite off his tongue, so I grabbed the nearest piece of cloth and stuffed it into his mouth to keep him from injuring himself. Unfortunately, he stopped breathing before I could do anything to help him."

"You could have called an ambulance."

North's shoulders slumped forward as a defeated expression crept across his pretty features. "Lamar was about dead when I showed up, so there was nothing I could do. Calling 911 would have put blame on me for the guy's death."

Parker raised an eyebrow, not yet convinced anything North said rang true. "Suppose you chose not to call because you didn't want to interrupt your long awaited chance to steal Galloti's money."

"Anthony's money?" North huffed. "Tell that to his underground goons, the band of greedy club owners who skimmed profits from their businesses for the purpose of bribing and extorting police and city officials to get what they wanted." North scratched the back of his head and frowned. "I learned about the clandestine group after I began dating Anthony. It didn't take long to learn how much of a scum that man was, I might add. Taking from him would be like robbing from a terrorist, nobody would care. Besides, it's not like Anthony would have gone to the police to fess up now, is it?"

"You tell me," Parker said. His challenge met a smirk. "Is that why you killed him, to get at embezzled money?"

North let out a shallow, discomforting chuckle that made Parker's skin crawl. "I didn't have to," he said, placing his hands on his hips and cocking his head. "Once word leaked that Anthony had absconded with cash the group had amassed, his hours were numbered. They never trusted him anyway. One wrong move sealed his fate."

Parker held out his hand. "Hold out your arms," he said, brandishing the cuffs.

"What I've told you is the truth, detective." North complied. "You have to *believe* me!"

Ignoring the pleas, Parker clamped the metal shackles around North's wrists. "I might have believed everything you said son, had you not left out one very incriminating fact."

Fear clouded North's eyes. "I-I don't understand."

"You made one very crucial mistake that convinced me that you had orchestrated most, if not all of this. Hell, you probably sent Callahan after me, sealing his fate."

"That's a lie!"

"The big mistake you made?" Parker teased. "Stealing your friend's driver's license and flashing the ID to rent hotel rooms on the south side, purchasing airline tickets you had no intention of using in order to confuse Galloti's men."

North appeared confused. "That's right," Parker said, "one of my guys kept tabs all along with detectives searching for Cage. See, the boy's grandmother and sister filed a Missing Persons report when he didn't show up for a scheduled dinner, and they couldn't reach him. Cage was discovered missing his wallet, but a Good Samaritan happened upon it near where the attack had taken place. We recovered it a couple days ago, minus the driver's license of course. What do you suppose we'll find when we empty your pockets down in booking?"

The door of the office opened and Brooks entered the room as if on cue with a patrol officer in tow. North slumped but didn't struggle when he was led outside the room as Parker read him his Miranda rights.

Once they reached the waiting cruiser, Jason North turned to Parker. "My father," North said.

"What about your father?"

"You asked me why I got mixed up with Anthony in the first place." Parker raised his chin. "It's because of that jerk I took the job dancing at Metroplex in the first place. He cut me out of my inheritance because I've refused to abandon my sinful ways and let his religious zealots cure me of being gay." The kid laughed out loud. "My father takes great pride in his neurotic, conservative austerity. Having a homosexual son was bad enough, but hearing that his own flesh and blood stripped bare night after night for old and fat, groping men drove him crazy."

Brooks put the arrestee in the back of the police car, guiding North's head through the door to avoid bumping the roof. Parker never took his eyes off him, wondering what would eventually become of the pretty boy, Jason North.

EPILOGUE

APD Homicide experienced major changes in the wake of the O'Connor cover-up scandal. As Parker anticipated, Calvin Slade led the efforts to force the removal of Homicide Lieutenant Hornsby, and earned a promise of policy changes from Chief of Police. Bowing to intense public scrutiny and political pressure, Hornsby was forced to transfer to a post in Kennesaw, several miles northwest of the city proper, a mostly segregated farming town spotlighted in the national news for a local ordinance requiring resident gun possession.

Jason North moved through his arraignment at lightning speed, yet denied bail and remanded awaiting trial. Boris Winecof managed to avoid any jail, courtesy of a high-profile attorney who argued his client possessed no prior knowledge of a conspiracy to commit murder, or of his involvement in any blackmail or extortion schemes.

Within the week Johnny Cage was buried, the funeral reserved for family and close friends. For reasons unknown to Parker—perhaps guilt more than kindheartedness—Bradford North covered all costs and provided a decent burial for the young man. Most attendees were from the local gay community. Kendall Parker, Timothy Brooks and Hattie Strauber also paid

their respects. Though offered an invitation to the service he
funded, the elder North never showed his face.

Having faced his own mortality twice in as many weeks,
Parker took Hattie's advice to let go of the past, and vowed to
get on with his life. He listed his condo for sale with the same
real estate agent he entrusted to find a suitable home farther
away from the craziness of the inner city. Forced to deal with
Michael's possessions, he donated most to his partner's beloved
charities. Within two months, Parker accepted an offer on his
condo, signed a contract to close in thirty days to purchase a
tiny three-bedroom brick bungalow in the transitional area east
of Atlanta called Reynoldstown, and pledged a new beginning.

Setting the final box outside on the walkway of his former
home, Parker surveyed the main room one last time. Now
empty, the rooms had none of the warmth and happiness of the
past few years he'd lived with Michael. Only blank walls and
scuffed hardwood floors reminded him of days gone by and
dreams lost forever. A dark stain remained on the wood floor
where Stewart's body had fallen not long ago. The new owner's
planned to install wall-to-wall carpeting over the hardwoods.

A strong hand landed on Parker's shoulder and squeezed
gently. "Ready?" Brooks grinned wide as he retrieved the last
container. Parker nodded. "I'll pull the truck around and wait
on the street for you," Brooks said and headed for the stairs.

Parker pulled the door closed a final time, locked the dead-
bolt and shuffled along the corridor. Brooks had pulled the U-
Haul ahead of Parker's truck and waited for him to follow.

"I'll meet you at the new place," Parker had to shout above
the sputtering engine of the old truck before waving Brooks off.
He hopped in his truck and cranked the engine, glancing up for
the last time to the place he'd once called home. Shifting into
gear, he maneuvered out of the parking spot, turned the corner
and traveled up 14th Street headed for the interstate.

Twenty minutes later, Parker coasted through his new neighborhood, consisting of older, smaller homes than those being
built today. A few of his friends were busy unloading more
fragile items from backseats of their cars when he arrived and

parked on the street. Hattie stepped out of the house to call everyone over to the front porch for sandwiches and refreshments.

"Kendall, honey…" She called across the sliver of lawn. "It's absolutely beautiful out here. I can't believe it's so close to the city."

"I think I'll like it," Parker said, walking up and taking the tray from her hands. "The slower pace will provide some much needed respite."

"I'll second that," Brooks said, snatching a handful of sandwiches from the tray. "A little rest, and you'll be back at headquarters in no time."

"We'll see about that." Parker guzzled a cold glass of fresh lemonade. "My stint as homicide cop may be over."

"Speaking of which," Calvin Slade said, moving from behind and snatching up a sandwich. "I heard rumors you might be thinking about moving to private investigations."

Parker shot a look toward Hattie, who raised her arms in mock surrender, smiling. "Nothing's decided yet." He grabbed a peanut butter and jelly sandwich of his own. "For now, I'm going to take more time off to relax in my new home before getting started on fixing this place up some, maybe even refinishing the hardwood floors."

The men moved off to chat with others as Hattie and Kendall found a couple of lawn chairs vacant. Parker reached into his pocket, then held out his hand to Michael's aunt. He placed the chip into her palm.

"What's this, dear?"

"Thirty days sober today," Parker said, grinning wide. "All thanks to you."

Hattie glowed; her hazel eyes misted. "Oh, honey, I am so proud of you." She leaned over and offered him a big hug. "Very proud indeed!"

THE END

Jon Michaelsen is an author of multiple short-stories, and a Lambda Literary Award Finalist in Mystery for the debut novel in the Kendall Parker Mystery series; *Pretty Boy Dead*. He is currently working on the next Kendall Parker mystery; The Deadwood Murders. He lives in Atlanta, Georgia with his husband of 32 years and their two monstrous terriers.

TRADEMARKS ACKNOWLEDGMENT

The author acknowledges the trademark status and trademark owners of the following places and items mentioned in this work of fiction:

Porsche/Porsche Boxster: Dr. Ing. h.c. F. Porsche Aktiengesellschaft

Atlanta Journal-Constitution: Cox Enterprises, Inc.

Delta Air Lines: Delta Air Lines, Inc.

Rolex: Rolex Watch, U.S.A., Inc.

Glock: Glock, Inc.

Mercedes: Daimler AG Corporation

CNN: Cable News Network, Inc.

Fox News: Twentieth Century Film Corporation, Inc.

Dewar's: Bacardi & Company, LLC

BMW: Bayerische Motoren Werke Aktiengesellschaft

RC Cola: Royal Crown Cola, Inc.

M&M: Mars, Incorporated

Chippendale's: Chippendales USA, LLC

Honda Accord: Honda Motor Co., LLC

Ford: Ford Motor Company

Kroger: The Kroger CO of Michigan

Fox Theatre: Atlanta Landmarks, Inc.

ACLU: American Civil Liberties Union Not-For-Profit Corporation

U-Haul: U-Haul International, Inc.

Made in the USA
Monee, IL
07 April 2021

65043691R00204